Bloodbound

Book Two: The Binding Tenets Trilogy

G.J. Terral

All characters and events in this book are fiction, and any relation to a real person, place, or event is purely coincidental.

G.J. TERRAL WRITES

Contents

Dedication

For those we've lost, and all those we've yet to lose.

Acknowledgements

Bloodwoven had many iterations— but once the final draft was done I knew the eventual ending of Lin's story. I couldn't have done this without the support of my loving wife, Megan, and my family and friends. The year I wrote this wasn't the best for me or my family, from scares to losses, and everything in between. I couldn't have done it alone, so thanks to everyone who helped make it possible to tell the story that mattered to me.

I want to express my deepest thanks to Cristiana "Cru" Leone for once again bringing my vision to life on the cover. I must again thank Jack, for designing the map used both in Bloodwoven and, now, in Bloodbound.

A huge shout-out to the Secret Scribes; A collective of wildly different authors who've banded together to make the experience that much more bearable. (They're listed at the back!)

L a
Calm's Peak
Lyre
Fallc
Duchy of
ERROND
Drekinsburg
Wakewatch Lake
Elswood
Duchy of
ELMORE
Wakewatch
Fentis
The Duchies of
DANICA

drica
forest pass
Creekside
Hol's Land
Duchy of
HOLLANDER
Riversbend
Wellgrove
Duchy of
WELLGROVE
Townsbridge
The
Ferrucium

The Fall

A signed accounting from Scholar Initiate Denro, formerly a Ferrucium Evaluator.

I pen this knowing I haven't received a full accounting of events, but doing my best to piece them together. Please bear in mind that while I was present in Danica, I'd been in the southern sections nearer to the coast evaluating children than in the northern reaches where much of this transpired. I write an unbiased account as best I can, for posterity. History is often written by the victor, but who has won or lost this long war is yet to be decided and I can't imagine a man better suited to the task than myself.

Lindel, Escorter of the Ferrucium, was assigned to escort Margaret and Aemun from northern Danica to the Ferrucium so that they might raise their child as befitting Aemun's noble stock. Through Lindel's recollection of events, things went bad nearly right away. Aemun, near enough a monster, murdered his partner Margaret. The why of it was hidden until the Fall but speculation on Lin's part says she would have ruined Aemun's careful planning. It seems his plans were ruined well enough, as by the time of the Fall, he was a corpse added to the many pyres.

I will leave out Lin's recounting of Fallo, penning only that the place was massacred in a grisly manner and Lin himself nearly lost his life. I try to avoid hyperbole where possible, so understand when I say this was where things worsened beyond belief. But you must believe me.

Lin was now with the priestess Tylle, who was also present at Margaret's death, and while she undoubtedly saved his life, the how or why is lost on me. My feelings on it are mixed and while I'm thankful Lin lives, I doubt he is the same man I once knew.

Together Lin and Tylle made their way to Wellgrove, meeting with a man Lin only ever called Grovetender. It should be noted, by this point in his retelling, that he could tell my feelings for him and his part in the Fall had soured. Wellgrove was set upon by members of the King's Noose, brought there by Aemun somehow, and Tylle, Lin, and Aemun fled.

Lin had a habit of mentioning Aemun's child often in his retelling, and I think he has grown to care for her as if she were truly his. For this, I don't blame him. She is a sweet child, prone to smiles and giggles. I've left her out so far as she was a babe and offered little in the way of causing the flow of things to change, but as I pen this she stares up at me, a lone beacon of joy compared to my own sour disposition.

A brief encounter in the woods between Wellgrove and the Ferrucium with the Nooseman saw Tylle gravely wounded, and Lin returned the favor. Another name, Pael, was mentioned, but Lin went into no great detail about this man.

Lin grew quiet, telling me little of the meeting with Grovetender's people and the Fall itself, but from what I've pieced together, Lin was abandoned by who he thought allies and he snuck into the Ferrucium under the guise of a Nooseman. Earlier

I avoided details of Fallo out of respect for the people. Here I will do the opposite, telling you that the Ferrucium was assaulted from within by someone who had sworn oaths to serve. It was a massacre and the cause just or not, our brothers and sisters in red deserved better. A true Nooseman also attacked and between the blood Lin spilled, the Nooseman spilled, and the assault led by Grovetender's people, we lost too many good brothers and sisters to count. Two Weavers were slain, Aemun lost his life, and chaos ruled for a time. But the Dukes had been moving and alongside Weaver Azhura, a semblance of peace was restored.

What I can say now, I saw with my own eyes. A fortification meant to protect the people, filled with the corpses of people I've known my whole life. I couldn't stay. Not knowing that my failure in shaping Lin may have resulted in this outcome. I saw Lin, nearly unrecognizable, covered in blood, viscera, and Stitches.

So let this be a record, poor as it might be as I sit beside the man who I struggle to look upon, of the Fall of the Ferrucium. Many arguments could be had that the Danican Accords are to blame and that better teaching, better structure, and better knowledge of why we are meant to be controlled and corraled as we are should be necessary. But things are the way they are and few people have the power to change them.

Perhaps I will throw this away and re-pen it. Perhaps I will keep all these words locked within, as the Six know I have little to say to Lin now. Which hurts me as much as it does him, of this I'm sure. Perhaps in time, all of this will be but a notch on a whorled branch of a tree that the Grand Tapestry hangs from. But for now even as

I set out to be unbiased, I can tell my feelings have soured even this simple account.

Chains of Hope

"While it is unclear at the time of penning exactly what happened to cause Vellia and her subsequent ilk to discover their Danican blood fueled their magic, it is clear that the explosive growth of Wieving from that point on couldn't be stemmed, much like a wound to the artery running along the neck. It was in the best interests of all sane individuals of the free world to then begin the preliminary stages of drafting the Danican Accords." Excerpt from the Histories of Southern Danica removed and redacted due to the Danican Accords.

Lin slammed the tome shut. The book— *Histories of Southern Danica*— was relatively slim compared to the number of monstrous reads he'd gone through over the last three or so months. Denro didn't so much as glance up from his own reading at the noise. The man, one he'd once considered a mentor and friend, had barely spoken to him since their arrival at Fentis. Of course, there'd been polite conversation and meals spent discussing small matters. But they hadn't even run a finger along the surface of what happened at the Ferrucium, an event the Scholars had dubbed the Fall. Not to mention the lack of progress related to Lin's current predicament-- removal of his Inlays.

Lin watched Denro thumb to the next page, the older man lazily crossing one leg over the other. Bringing up the removal would be like asking for a tour of Fentis. Pointless.

Their shared space, a sparsely used archive room repurposed into a polite holding cell, had numerous oaken desks, several wood chairs, enough space for two sleeping cots and a crib, and a window that showed the expanse of the bay. Really, the view was a reminder of how they were caged. A fall or jump would be lethal, and in the months of seclusion, Lin hadn't suddenly grown wings.

Lin rose and grabbed the book, tapped the spine several times, then set it back down. He stalked to where Mellyr slept, glowering at Denro as he passed. But Gods, even looking at Mellyr calmed his ire. One of the Fentian scholars had knitted her a stuffed rabbit, and her tiny hands had already torn the fabric near the neck. However the various scholars felt about Lin and Denro, there was no denying they doted on Mellyr the way they cared for her. And Lin couldn't blame them.

Even asleep, she bore an uncanny resemblance to Aemun. The man had been fair of face and Mellyr was an adorable extension of that.

A rap on the door preceded the sound of rattling keys, pulling Lin's attention from the sleeping child. He ran a hand along the polished wood of the crib's rail and sidled half a step toward the door. He glanced out the large bay window. It wasn't quite late enough in the day for lunch. A terribly bland meal, all things considered. Being housed by the scholars meant he was forced into their diet. Salted squash and a type of paste that they swore was derived from fish. Denro often ate alone, and Lin suspected the man received better food than he did.

Lin lost himself over the waves, mind drifting like one of the myriad fishing vessels dotting the expanse. The Pellic Sea stretched far into the horizon. The view over the docks lapped his attention as workers came and went, much like ants crawling on a splintered branch waiting to float away.

If Lin had learned a single distilled thing the past few months, it was that Danica, the Ferrucium, and especially himself were all so much smaller than he'd ever imagined. Of course, he'd known there were other nations, kingdoms, masses of land. But he hadn't known Danicans were intentionally kept as isolated as they were. Trading galleys were only allowed at Fentis and the Ferrucium. Other than that? Illegal by the Danican Accords. If Lin wanted to leave the country, cross into the Northern Kingdom of Ladrica? Illegal. Build a ship and sail away? If he were ever found out, he'd be put to death. The world had come together several hundred years ago and decided that his people, the Danican people, needed to be secluded. Isolated. Imprisoned.

"Can you truly not hear the scholar?" Denro's deep voice pulled Lin from himself.

Lin blinked and turned back from the window. He'd gotten lost in the waves, then lost in himself. Something he'd done more and more over the last month. "I'm sorry," he said. "Please, say it once more."

Gronccio, one of the regular scholars who attended to them, smiled politely. His hands were clasped behind his back, silken sleeves trailing down covering his forearms.

When Lin first met the man, he assumed he was Inlayed, but the lines along his flesh didn't glow, hum, or feel like magic at all. Ink, they called it. And despite all the talk of flesh, none would tell him how to remove his Stitches.

Gronccio cleared his throat softly, waiting for Lin's eyes to rest on his. "As I was saying. You have a visitor, Lindel. We have prepared an adjacent chamber. If you would follow me."

Denro didn't move from the chair he lounged in. Draped in his cream-white scholar's robe with plush pillows at his sides and back, his old mentor had never looked more comfortable.

"Go. I doubt I or Mellyr will be going anywhere," Denro said without looking up.

"Who is it?" Lin hadn't heard from anyone, not even Tylle. Not that she owed him that, but he'd expected something after everything they'd been through. He had briefly considered penning letters himself, but Denro had dissuaded him. No good if you don't have a bird to send them.

Gronccio was a master of two things: ignoring Lin's questions and moving silently. The man's flowing robes skirted through the open door, urging Lin to follow or be left behind.

"Has there been a consensus?" Lin asked.

The man never sighed, but he did slow his pace. "There has been headway. There was a clause in the original drafting of the Accords."

"Regarding what?"

"The well-being of your people. If the Ladrican system in place can be shown to have failed in the safekeeping of your people and their resources, then it is possible that... Ahhh. Here we are. Find me later, and I would be happy to tell you more."

Lin sucked his teeth. It seemed later was always where answers would be found. "Later never seems to come," he leaned in and whispered.

And there it was. The apologetic smile was never far from the man's full lips. "I have learned much in my time here, but that is an eternal truth from your lips to the Gods' many ears." Gronccio waved toward the door, knocked on it three times, and slipped away. His slippered feet made little sound on the stone floor.

Lin ran his hands down the front of his tunic, plain white clothes, same as Denro's, gifted to him by the scholars. A shade off from the alabaster stone that made up the imposing Fentis towers. The door opened, and Lin took a half step forward, then caught himself. Of all the people who might've been waiting in the room, he somehow hadn't expected to see Pael lounging with his dirt-stained bare feet resting on the table, toes reflected on the polished wood. A tea tray with two poured cups steamed beside his left foot, and the balcony doors were open behind him, allowing the breeze to blow the curtains in easy, lapping ripples.

Pael smiled, his wide-brimmed hat hanging from the back of his seat and fluttering every so often. "Worried they'd killed you already, slow as they were bringing you to me."

"I came as soon as they told me I had a visitor."

"Doubt they told you I've been here the better part of a week."

Lin cursed and took a seat, grabbing and tilting the nearest teacup to get a whiff of the curling steam. Ginger and honey pleasantly teased him. "They hadn't."

"Erias assumed as much. Figured the letters weren't getting through. None of it. That's alright. I'm here now."

Lin smiled. Letters. "And now you're stuck with me." Lin snorted. Not that he'd tried to leave. If anything, he'd been thankful to have the respite, days spent reading and with Mellyr. She'd grown more aware, and it was a marvel watching her personality grow.

Pael leveled a stare at him, and his hands collapsed across his belly, fingers interlaced. "I'm no more enchained by teacups and fluffed rugs than iron bars and prison cells." To accent his point, he spat to the side, a glob of dark fluid staining the material.

"I remember some of your claims," Lin said, a smile coming at the memory. Gods, he hadn't smiled this hard in weeks.

"Bah. Claims. I mean it. If they hadn't brought you to me today, I'd made it very clear that I'd be visiting you tomorrow. But here we are." Pael shifted and pulled his feet from the table. He gave the slightest shake of his head.

"Here we are." Lin took a sip from his cup and then pushed it away. "How is Tylle?"

"Well enough. The little one?"

"Same. Cared for better with this group than I might've expected alone."

Pael scrunched his nose. "Well, I've brought news. A letter to Scholar Pontis, already delivered personally. And... have you seen this view?" Pael turned in his chair, nodding out the open window.

"Our chamber, the one Denro and I share, has a view of the sea."

"Sure, but look at the cliffsides from this angle." Pael rose and jerked his chin.

The balcony had its own small, circular table with a slight overhang meant to catch only the lightest of rains. As warm as it felt, it was hard to imagine that the northern border would be dealing with everything that the end of winter entailed.

Pael leaned against the thin metal rail and stared down over the edge.

Lin hesitated at the table, then followed and did the same.

With a glance around, Pael leaned nearer to Lin and whispered, "Grovetender thinks the Scholars have made a decision already and have been simply waiting for the thaw to announce it."

Lin nodded. "They likely have. I've been treated well, but more like a captive than anything else. Denro has had several meetings, and the scholars I've spoken to are hesitant to relay any news to me."

Pael rocked against the rail. "Not much in the way of news. Azhura and Erias have reformed the Ferrucium in small, manageable ways. Carine has helped on that front as well. Dukes Wellgrove and Hollander have been able to persuade Elmore to join his militia with theirs. All good things. Though Duke Errond, closest to the northern border, has remained silent."

"And I've been sitting here useless," Lin muttered.

Pael shrugged and squinted into the distance. "Any luck removing the Stitches?"

Lin shook his head. "None of the scholars I've discussed it with seem to know the method. Though, it's clear it is possible and has been done. There's been more than one thick tome that mentions the removal. But... none on the process of it. But the person didn't die. So...." Lin let his hand fall over the rail as if spilling all his hopes from his palm and scattering it out into the wind.

"The last thing I need to tell you is something little Tylle requested. There has been a reported rise in untethered attacks on villages. Outposts going silent. Duke's people going missing."

"Really?"

"Unfortunately." Pael sighed out the word and rubbed the bridge of his nose.

So, either the Ferrucium under the Weavers had kept the untethered plague in check or the uptick that they'd noticed back at Lyre had continued. Lin closed his eyes against the sun and exhaled a long, slow breath. When he opened his eyes, Pael had turned to face indoors, back against the rail. "I'm sorry, kid."

"It's alright." Lin stared down at his hands, tracing the lines of magic on his left hand with the fingers of his right. "Aemun played us all. Maybe me most of all. I convinced myself... pushed myself into doing Inlays in the hopes that I might keep up with the shadows haunting me. Unaware the shadows were caused by my own closeness to the light."

Pael nodded. "You," he patted Lin on the shoulder, "Have had your nose in too many books talking like that."

A knock sounded from the main room's door, and without pause, the door opened to four scholars. Three of them wore the same pale cloth that Lin and Denro sported, but one wore the deep, dark azure of a higher scholar. Lin hadn't puzzled out exactly how Fentis structured their hierarchy, but it was clear that the closest to white one of the scholars wore, the lower their position was.

"Lindel, you've been summoned to the Hall of Scholars. Please." Denro was barely visible in the hall behind them, standing impatiently.

"Pael," Lin whispered. "I'll be seeing you?"

"Odds are I'll see you first," Pael whispered back. He tapped a finger to his nose and gave a reassuring smile.

Lin followed the scholars down the hall, falling in line beside Denro. They walked in silence down several flights of stairs that would have made Lin's legs ache before he'd worked the Inlays into them. "Any idea what this is about?" Lin asked once they moved from the stairs to a plain hall lined with tapestries of varying length and design. Each one seemed sourced from a different locale, the weaves different, the style unique.

Denro glanced at him. His oiled back hair had grown in the last few months and curled up at the ends just above his shoulders. He'd let his beard grow, too, but kept it trimmed neatly. Any remnants of peppered streaks in it had gone, leaving it as bland white as the tower's stone and clothes he wore. "No."

"Who is watching Mellyr?"

Denro sighed and slowed a half step, so he was in line with Lin. "Scholar Gronccio kindly volunteered to watch the child as she naps. Hopefully, this marks the end of our captivity, as pleasant as it's been."

That almost made Lin trip. So, the Fentian Scholars had come to a decision. Or they'd finally decided to share what decision they'd made, however long ago they'd made it. Good news with any luck.

The Hall of Scholars opened into an amphitheater-styled room with a crystalline skylight in lieu of open air. Less a hall, really, as Lin studied it. It was where they'd first been presented to the High Scholars. And it was where the High Scholars— a committee of ten scholars, all wearing robes as dark as the night sky on a moonless night— now sat. The room was meant to house as many scholars as the Tower itself held, but only the ten High Scholars and the four who had escorted Lin and Denro were gathered. It made for a long, solemn walk to stand in the center before them.

"Months ago, you came to us bearing several things," the High Scholar said. She looked barely older than Lin, and her head was entirely shaved. She must've been the designated speaker, seeing as she was also who had spoken to them when they first arrived. "Now we are the ones who bear several things. While the Tower is often silent, it isn't idle. While the Scholars are learned, we are not all knowing. Are there any final thoughts on the inclusion or abstinence of Fentis from the coming war?"

Lin held his breath. He wasn't sure if the question was meant for he and Denro, or the other High Scholars. The whole thing made him shudder, the way it ungently reminded him of the Chamber of Judgment. But the differences were enough to calm his nerves. The High Scholars were earned leaders, and they worked through a democracy. No single scholar carried weight the way the Weavers did. No executions were dispensed for breaking laws made to shackle the people they should've protected.

"While I'm a new initiate, I doubt my voice carries loud enough to affect change. Yet. I would be remiss if I didn't say my peace." Denro's deep voice resounded from the empty stone seats, and Lin turned to stare at the man. He knew exactly what stance Denro held. One of passivity. Let the new Ferrucium rot in the grave it had dug.

"Please speak, Initiate Denro," The Speaker said.

"I served the Ferrucium most of my life. My whole life, in fact. I've watched small changes take place over long periods of time, not all for the best. I've seen countless brothers, sisters, and friends die at the hands of untethered. But I've also seen good people wrongfully persecuted. I've had time to read, reflect, rationalize. This war, if allowed to progress, will likely break old oaths. Old Accords meant to keep the peace. So, I beg of you, all of you, more learned than I might ever achieve. Please abstain from joining this pointless conflict. Let Ladrica and King Lodram find a resolution without outside aid. His failure shouldn't result in our inclusion."

"Very well spoken, Initiate Denro. Lindel?"

Lin frowned at that. "I also have thoughts, if I may."

"You may," the Speaker said.

Lin stared at the faces gathered. There was no single common factor between them save the color of their clothes. Some were old, ancient even, others clearly not Danican from their hair and complexions.

"I've also had the time to read, though I've got to admit the selection felt… limited. But that's neither here nor there. What I mean to say is that I was asked to come here and speak with you. Was kept mostly locked in a room for the better part of a season, was stripped of clothes and weapons, and didn't have a single question I asked answered fully."

"Lindel," Denro practically growled his name.

"And I'm fine having all this done if it would mean something. If it meant anything. Please, you scholars aren't so different from Binders, Wievers, or whatever you want to call us. I have the Sight. I see some of you bearing Inlays such as mine. Stitches marking your skin. How long did you stand by and let Danica, a land you roost in but claim no part of, be subjugated? Tome after tome on the Accords say centuries, if not longer. Now is the chance to take a stand for yourselves and your neighbors. If you let Lodram push down and place his boot on Danica's neck, you will be next. You'd have to be next, for the greed of Ladrica knows no ends. Stand with the Dukes, as they've requested. Stand with the Ferrucium and stop being complicit!" By the end, Lin's voice was hoarse, and he blinked tears from his eyes. His fingers hurt from clenching his fists so tight. And his heart throbbed in his ears against the silence of the room.

"An impassioned speech. Not something we see often here, where logic and reason are touted above all else. Thank you, Lindel."

Lin hung his head and waited. Denro put a hand on his shoulder, and though it was the nearest thing to comfort the man had shown him since arriving, Lin shrugged it off. He wanted to scream louder. Take a Weft and cut through all the bullshit with it.

If they deliberated, they somehow did so silently. It felt like it lasted ages, but when Lin looked up, the sun still shone from the same spot through the skylight.

"Thank you both. It is with a heavy heart that we've made this decision, and it is not one we came to lightly. As Lindel stated, war is something that will reach us eventually. We do share many similarities with the Ferrucium Binders, once known as Wievers before the Accords. So, it is painfully clear we must continue to differentiate ourselves. War will come, and we will have our place in it." The Speaker's face was impassive as she spoke. She waved a hand, dark sleeve rolling down to reveal several bands of dark tattoos along her wrists and forearms.

Lin's breath caught in his chest. They meant to aid Danica, after all.

Rough hands grabbed Lin by the shoulders, and before he could react, he'd been pressed to his knees, a slippered foot pressing into the backs of his knees. Gods, they were strong.

"What?" Lin couldn't turn to see behind him, but Denro hadn't been forced to the ground. He'd been so lax, thinking himself safe here. Lin started to form a Weft, but as he reached for his spul, he felt nothing. An emptiness he hadn't noticed for lack of needing to draw on it.

"Fentis will go to war, and as an emissary for the traitorous Dukes, you will be held as a prisoner of war." Weaves as strong as steel banded his arms, biting into his soft cloth sleeves. "Denro, you arrived here with Lindel but have taken the first step of many in shedding your old role and becoming a Scholar. You will be bound alongside him for a short time. But it is only temporary. Please, prostate yourself."

Lin watched as Denro kneeled voluntarily and allowed golden Weaves to bind his arms to his side.

"Take them to the prisons," the Speaker said, waving her hand once more.

Chains of Bone

"There are several known magics throughout the free world, but none so terrifying as the Danicans' Wieving. Blades in the dark are often referred to as a feared thing for the common man. If you aren't born with the Sight, everything Wieving creates, you are blind to. In the dark about. Blades. Wievings. If Danicans decide to go to war, they will have a distinct advantage over the more common man and his more common magic." Argument presented by Lord Pollan Strat, a representative of the Ladrican Kingdom, given at a conference to discuss the burgeoning conflict at the southern border of Ladrica.

They'd gone from a prison cell of tomes and open windows to a damp place more akin to the chambers Erias had put Lin in back at Wellgrove. Being lost in pages for months, it truly seemed like a lifetime ago. Lin's wrists and ankles ached, each chained to the wall by a heavy shackle. The shackles made him sick and stung where they touched him. Bound Metal. He was sick of the One-loved metal.

"Why do you think I wasn't able to Bind?" Lin asked.

"Maybe your heart wasn't in it," Denro said. Though he shared the same cell, he was seated on a cushioned chair. No chain in sight.

"Fuck off."

Denro looked at Lin through a circle he'd formed of his thumb and ring finger, the tell-tale golden glow of a Binding winking into existence. "Maybe something to do with the crystalline skylight?"

"Metals. Crystals. Lies. What's next to chain our people?" Lin asked, wrists chafing as the chains pulled taut.

Denro tsked. "Calm yourself before they decide to gag you as well."

Lin rattled his chains as he leaned back and let his head rest against the cold stone. "You act like you knew this was coming." Odds were Pael had also been captured, but the cells, the few that there were, were silent.

Denro let his hand drop, the magic fading from it. "I had suspicions."

"Is that how far we've separated? You couldn't even share a suspicion with me? Now I'll be imprisoned, likely turned over to the King, made into a martyr if he decides to kill me as a message."

The chair creaked underneath Denro as he folded one leg overtop the other. "I doubt the Scholars will turn you over. A prisoner of war is one thing, a peace offering wholly another."

"How could you not warn me about this?" Lin hissed. He blinked back tears. "You've been like a father to me. I cared for you and thought of you every day we were separated. And Denro, the fear... the fear I had in my heart that when you'd first see me, you'd recoil. But you hugged me. You held me and pressed your brow to mine, and you made me think things would be alright. Then, you built a wall of silence between us that I couldn't scale. Dammit, man, I've shared a room with you these long months, and yet I still miss you." The last bit came out pleadingly, painfully. It hurt to say it. There wasn't enough flesh on his body he could Stitch that might dull the pain of rejection.

Denro sighed, and he steepled his hands across his lap. "And you were like a son to me, in some ways. In many. You and Fren, Gron, Bent, Tumos, Jenn. And countless others killed when the dukes made their move. You might think I am glad that one of mine survived, but as much as my silence hurts you, what you helped happen inflicts worse on me."

Lin railed against the chains, lunging toward Denro. The man didn't flinch. "I didn't touch them!" But Lin couldn't be sure that was true. And it made the words brittle. He'd killed his fair share of Ferrucium soldiers that night. But only ones he'd thought allied with Aemun. "I… I chose the lesser of two evils."

"A path Wicked Tel'Myr will always want one to take," Denro said softly.

"You've read the books here as well. We were shackled. Boots to the neck of our people."

"There were Accords put in place because Danicans can do things no others can do."

"And that means we should be corralled like animals?" Lin snarled.

"It means that certain safety precautions should be maintained. Untethered are a real threat. Was the Ferrucium's system the best? No. But it was something that could be fixed. War isn't fixable. Not when Danica is a land-locked nation that has subsided on the governance of the Kingdom the dukes now plan to war against. And not one of the other free nations out there will side with Danica as things stand."

"Because of the Accords," Lin spat.

"You're not at fault, but you must see this is a lost battle before it has even begun. You've traded the bully for the brigand, so to speak."

Lin sat there in silence. He avoided the stale bread and thin soup brought down to him and only drank the offered water once he was sure there wasn't any noticeable poison or drug within. Eventually, Denro was brought a book and a candle and started reading right away.

"What's that?" Lin tried to get comfortable, shifting his weight from one hip to the other.

"A book."

"About?"

Denro placed a finger in the center of his pages and closed the tome. "The studies done on Bound Metal. I'd thought it odd that Aemun had placed the stuff into his flesh. Sent me down a rabbit hole, so to speak. It is a very unusual, unsafe practice. Hence why his flesh became infected almost right away. But I gave his arm to the scholars to examine, and they've graciously given me initiate tomes related to the subject."

Lin blinked. "You gave them his arm?"

Denro frowned. "What was left of it, I mean. I thought you knew. I had it in my satchel the whole time. Cloves and wildflowers only helped the smell so much."

"Gods," Lin whispered.

The side of Denro's mouth twitched up. "You used to only ever say 'Six,' but now it's 'Gods,' eh?"

Lin stared at the ceiling, rolling the back of his head on the ridge of cold stone. "It's just easier. If there are any Gods out there, they'll know who I'm talking to when I say it. Six. Velkath. Maybe any of the others from the Free Nations."

"See, that's how I've always looked at it, but I know who blesses my dice when I need to roll them."

Lin did a double-take at the speaker. Pael stood just outside the cell, looking like someone had lost part of their shadow. His hat was slung across his back, but he gripped the same dusty, worn satchel he'd carried since Wellgrove.

Denro stayed seated, eyes shifting from Lin to Pael. "Friend of yours?"

"Friend of any in need, most days. We don't have long. They do any testing on you?"

It was Lin's turn to frown. "Testing?"

"They only allowed me in a week or so ago. Before being let in, I let myself in, and they seemed none the wiser. I was doing some... investigating down here. Nobody is dying, as far as I can tell. But they'll take Danican blood any chance they get." He rifled through the satchel, pulling out a chunk of wanderer's ore, staining the dark cell with overly blue light. It sent shadows dancing and gave Pael's teeth a sickly blue hue as he smiled. He set the ore down on a crossbar and pulled a ring of keys from the third pocket he checked. "Come on."

The barred door opened with a rusted groan.

Lin raised his chained hands and eyebrows at the same time.

"Never easy with you," Pael groused. He stepped into the cell, stepping wide around Denro and angling so that his back wasn't to the seated man.

"You can say that again." Denro chuckled. He seemed to ease into his seat and blew out the lone candle he'd been reading with. "But Lin, think about what you're doing. Really consider it. What good will leaving with this man do?"

Lin rolled his left wrist, the cuff dropping as Pael moved to work on his right. "What good will staying do? They mean to go to war alongside Ladrica."

"Have you not been listening?" Denro leaned forward and rested his elbows on his knees. "It isn't us versus the north and now the Scholars of Fentis. It is Danica against everyone else."

Pael whistled low as he finished unlocking all the shackles. "Always has been. Difference is we've given people a reason to finally move. Grovetender's lot gave them a reason to remember why they're afraid. Now, are you planning to join us?"

"Absolutely not," Denro said. He exhaled and reclined back in his chair, shaking his head. "In fact, I've half a mind to—" He couldn't finish his sentence. Not as quick as Pael had a dagger to the underside of his nose.

"You'll have half a nose if you want to test me. Ain't that right, Lin?"

"Let him go, Pael. It's alright."

"Fuck it is. He screams and we're caught, it'll be more than blood they drain from you. I knew something was off when they made me wait. I knew something was *off* when the letters weren't getting to you. Bet he had a part in all of it."

Lin stared at Denro's face, the man's wrinkles starker under the light of the wanderer's ore. "No. He wouldn't do that."

Denro licked his lips, but no words came from him.

Steps, slippered and near silent, came from down the hall. Lin might not have even heard them if he hadn't been focused on listening to whatever words Denro might've uttered.

Pael pulled away from Denro, swiftly pocketed his ore, and pushed the cell door mostly shut before he melted into a corner of the cell.

"Denro. Please. Come with us. This isn't your place anymore than it would've been mine. And think of Mellyr. She loves you. And I'm not leaving her."

"The war isn't yours any more than it's mine." He threw Lin's words back at him.

"Please," Lin whispered. Denro's face wasn't visible, and the bobbing light from whoever approached grew brighter and brighter. "I know I'm not half the man you are, and I can't raise Mellyr without your help. Not if I expect her to turn out any good."

Denro's chuckle flooded Lin with memories of better times. Times spent recounting tales of the road, stories of people and their peculiar traits, rumors of untethered back before they'd become a very real threat. "I don't know that I'd do a good job, seeing how you turned out."

Lin had expected it, and it still hurt. He stiffened and shifted the chains to look like they still held him. They'd waited too long to run and now had to hope the guards continued past. They approached, lantern light revealing a gaunt man and bone-thin woman, each wearing the bone-white garb of initiates. These two didn't bear any markings on their flesh, and both had dark circles under their eyes. Something Lin thought he hadn't seen much of since coming to Fentis. The people here, even the ones originally from the Ferrucium, didn't show most of the common traits of Binders. No cracked, brittle nails. No stringy straw-like hair. And certainly, no ashen complexions. But Fentian Scholars did Bind. He'd seen it himself.

The pair continued through the hall, slippers barely tapping out a rhythm as they went. The lantern they held didn't house a candle or oil. It was wanderer's ore resting within stained glass that obfuscated the light, turning the harsh, overbearing blue glow into something closer to the warm glow of a fire. Then they stopped, and the circle of light came back until the cell was painted in the false light. Lin knew better than to glance into the corner Pael rested in.

"Marron," the gaunt man started. He spoke slowly as if forcing the words out was a chore he only half-committed to.

"Mm?" The partner, Marron, sounded.

"Him. In the chains. Take him."

Lin fought down the fear. Take him. He wouldn't have thought much about it before Pael's ominous musings, but now? On the cusp of freedom, he'd be selected for some sort of test. Fuck.

"Might I ask what you plan to take him for?" Denro asked.

"Testings requested by the High Scholars. An initiate *prospect* shouldn't ask questions," Marron said. She didn't speak cruelly or even haughtily, but she clearly spoke with finality in mind. She opened the cell door and stepped in.

"But we should seek answers," Denro countered.

"We should," the gaunt man admitted. He raised the lantern a bit higher and squinted past his partner. "Marron."

"Mm?"

"Go ring—" his words died in his throat. The dagger Pael had thrown tapped against the nearest bar as it twinged in the man's neck. Blood leaked and stained the front of the gasping man's white tunic.

The lantern crashed as the man clutched his wound. The glass shattered, turning the faux warm light into the eye-stinging blue of natural ore.

Marron moved at once, and Lin lunged up. He tried a Weave—but his spul still didn't answer his call. Denro didn't shift from his chair, and Pael, well, the man moved like the bars had never been there and caught Marron around the neck. She was on the floor in moments, struggling in vain as the man's arm constricted around her throat. He wrapped his feet around her waist and squeezed.

A sharp pop sounded. Followed by several more sparking shards. Lin froze, feet from the initiate's puddle of blood and the wanderer's ore it pooled around. Another pop from the ore burned into Lin's vision. Wanderer's ore wasn't meant to be wet. It was part of what made it so unsafe, aside from the irritation to one's eyes.

The chunk that had been safe in the lantern was now sizzling and popping and shooting off sparks that even charred the stone of the tower. Burning and eating the material as if it were dry grass.

Denro moved first, taking his chair and using the back of it to push the sizzling ore away from the blood. It continued to pop and hiss and spark, but once it was away from the puddle, it slowed its intense reaction. "For fucks sake, was any of that necessary?"

"Maybe not. Not if you wanted Lin here to be taken and tested on. These two ghouls," Pael untangled himself from Marron's limp body and kicked her in the temple, "Are the main two I spotted lurking about and taking blood from people."

"And you don't think, if you planned to sneak away, that you might've been able to grab him without the violence?"

Pael took in a deep breath and looked from Denro to Lin and back to Denro. "War gets messy. Locking yourself here in these pristine towers and ignoring what happens in their shadows makes me wonder how Lin learned anything from you!"

"If he learned anything from me—"

"Enough. Both of you," Lin snapped. Whatever Denro was about to say, Lin was sure he'd heard it before. Heard it moments ago, even. He didn't need to hear again how he'd failed Denro's expectations. "We need to go before this becomes a problem." Lin dragged the dead man into the corner of the cell, and Pael did the same to Marron, who was maybe dying, but not dead by the slow rise and fall of her chest.

"And you'll leave me here to explain the two bodies? They'll think I didn't try to stop you." Denro's face was cast in dancing, dying shadows from the sparking ore.

"You can try," Pael whispered, venom in his voice. "Or we can make it look like you did."

"Denro, this place isn't what I thought it was. And everything I knew about it came from you. Which means this can't possibly be what you imagined, can it?" Lin took a half step toward the man, palms out and low.

Denro seemed to mull on Lin's words, head hanging lower and lower until he whispered. "Let's go. You aren't entirely wrong." He looked pained saying it, and that pained Lin.

Pael was already moving, slinking into the hall and scooping up the calmed wanderer's ore. Lin followed, and Denro, after a long pause, did the same. Tome in hand.

Lin slowed so Denro could get in front of him, and Pael stopped at an unadorned doorway. "We move quick and quiet, and we can be out to the horses in a blink. Already got them settled for us near the north side of town beside the willow on the hill."

"And Mellyr?" Lin asked.

Pael sucked his teeth and shook his head. "Running away with a child isn't—"

"Aemun managed it. I'm not leaving her here with them," Lin snapped.

"She'd be safer," Denro said.

"We don't know that. For all we know, they'd use her against us. Against Danica somehow. She's the daughter of the man who started this all and the woman who might've stopped him. They'll use her as a tool. And I refuse to let that happen. I'll go get her."

"She isn't in the rooms." Pael and Denro spoke at nearly the same time, and each looked at the other.

"Why do you know that?" Pael snapped.

"How do you know that?" Lin corrected. It made sense that Pael might've checked the rooms, but he and Denro hadn't gone back.

Denro shook his head and took a deep breath. "They've been testing her. With us both locked away, I'm sure they've got her now."

"Testing? She's barely even a child!" Lin snagged the front of Denro's tunic and pressed him to the wall. He could tell his limbs weren't being bolstered by the Inlays glowing along them, but Denro didn't resist, and his back thudded against the stone. Gods. The times he'd let a wet nurse or initiate take her under the guise of propriety or fawning. He'd been a whole fool.

"They wouldn't hurt her," Denro said shakily.

"If they have, there isn't a tower you could hide in that might save you from me. Not a memory we might share that would keep me from doubling whatever pain she felt onto you!"

"Calm down before you get us spotted. I can go check the—" Pael cut off at the glare Lin shot his way.

"No. Me. I will go and get her." Lin didn't say what he was thinking. As much as he wanted to, he didn't trust either of these men. Not here and not now. "Where would they have her?" Lin released Denro.

"They keep a library down here, even amongst the dungeons. Archives really. That is where I've watched them work," Pael said. "Several rooms though, easy to get lost."

Lin nodded as Pael gave the best directions he could manage. "Clear the way out for me and Mellyr, and I will join the both of you shortly. If I don't make it out, don't come back for me. Get to Grovetender and tell him about this update. Tell him they seem to have found more ways than just pieces of Bound Metal to quell our magic."

"Lin," Denro said.

"What?" Lin swallowed past the tightness in his throat.

"If you happen to see a book bearing Velkath's Sigil on the cover, do your best to get it. Please. I've heard mention of it, and it might be the key to unlocking much of the mysteries behind Bound Metal and our magic as a whole."

Lin glared at Denro, closed his eyes, and nodded. No words of remorse or plead for Lin to be safe. The man wanted a book. Lin would break his nose with it if he found it. Make him look like Lyre's Alderman if he could. "If I see it."

Chains of Hate

"It was odd realizing I was born with what is commonly known as the Sight while having no ability or aptitude to wield or conjure the magic I could see. So I've taken to studying it, as any inquisitive mind might. The threads of magic are vivid, often singular in color, but not always. And while it can be mesmerizing to behold, I can't help but notice the strands of madness that seep into those who wield the power. It is an insidious thing, slinking firstly into their mannerisms. Seemingly eating away at their health. Frail teeth, nails, and hair. A graying of flesh, no matter the person's original tone. Especially as they work more and more magic. It was a great surprise, first seeing someone with the threads of magic embedded into their flesh. Stitched, as some call it. And not being able to operate around those "stitches", as if the magic had become wholly tangible once joining flesh." Records from the personal diary of Physiker Sichael.

Lin kept to the rightmost wall, hand running along the smooth-cut stones. He'd refused the spare ore at first, not wanting to risk using it to aid his vision when he could simply form a Weave to light the area. But when the magic still wouldn't blink into existence for him, he took the chunk with a frown. So, with the ore held gingerly in one hand, he'd left Denro and Pael behind.

Pael's instructions led him through the cell-lined corridor until he hit an intersection that mirrored the one he'd left them at, and he took a right. The floor seemed to slope up, but as he took a left-hand turn into a narrower hall, the steps descended.

The Archives, as Pael had named the place, wasn't far. Each scrape of foot on stone and other subtler sounds that Lin didn't see a source for unnerved him. Groans from far off seemed carried on the wind. The hall he walked through matched what he was told to look for. Doors were spaced every ten or twelve steps, and intermittent sconces of opaque glass were mounted to the wall, holding a chunk of Wanderer's Ore each. Lin had half a mind to toss his ore away as the passage lightened, as putting it into his pocket made him fear it might catch fire if he got damp. He shuddered, imagining the thin white cloth consumed along with him in the flames. All from sweat. At least the air was cool down here, if not a bit damp. All the more reason not to hold the ore too tight in his hand. Gods, he wished he'd just been able to Bind. Lin settled with leaving the ore against a door.

What only took a handful of minutes felt like far longer, and by the time he stood near a wide-cut entrance, he was positive Pael and Denro would leave him behind. But Pael had only come for him. Lin chewed the inside of his lip. Had the man had some other motive? He'd said he'd been here an entire week skulking about.

Lin blinked as he realized voices carried from the open room ahead and Lin peeled himself from the doorway. He needed to cross through the room. Shelves lined horizontally across the room, with books and scrolls filling the bottom to top. Desks, with open tomes and pushed-in chairs, were scattered throughout wherever they might fit, and ladders leaned against the tallest of shelves. This area, as damp as the air felt and dim as the light was, was exactly what he'd always pictured when hearing tales of the

Fentian Scholars. Studious. Wise. Powerful. Not the passive and downright plain individuals who'd watched over him the last few months. He leaned against a shelf, trying to hear the voices, but they spoke in barely carried whispers.

Two individuals sat at one table centered between the lines of shelves, books, and papers sprawled in front of them. Gray robes, not Initiates, then.

Lin scanned the nearest shelf, and a pit of dismay settled into his stomach. The chances of him finding the book Denro had requested were slim. Another failure to be added to the long list. But Lin could see the door Mellyr should be behind if she'd been brought down here.

Whoever the two men were, they hadn't moved. Lin slunk to the far side of the shelf, trying his best to emulate the silent stepping Denny from Carine's group. In all honesty, he hadn't much thought about them. While he'd come to give Carine and Erias's request to the Scholars, that had been secondary to requesting the process for removing Stitches. Part of him had never expected to see any of them again. And the scholars hadn't given him even a hint at removing the Stitches.

Lin silently stalked from shelf to shelf, thankful that the only source of light came from the occasional ore lamp glowing on every other desk. He held his breath as one of the men yawned. Lin fought the tingling, itching urge to do the same. It passed as Lin sucked in a breath through the crease of his elbow and made his way behind the men.

The handle was cold to the touch and, more importantly, unlocked. Lin tightened his grip and went to pull the door when the loudest alarm he'd ever heard resounded from all corners of the expansive room. He released it and pulled back into the nearest shadow, knowing that if either man looked his way and had the Sight, he was spotted.

"A test?" Of the two men, only one had stood, and he rested his hands on the desk. His back was to Lin, and he looked around, not seeming to notice him there in the shadows.

"Not sure," the other man replied, closing the book and rising alongside his companion. "Best to report to the hall."

"Wait," the taller of the two said.

The pair froze and whispered something. They stood there silent for a long moment then Lin risked leaning to look their way. Gods, the two were kissing. Relief washed over Lin, followed by a pang of jealousy. Not that he'd had anyone to kiss, let alone hold in the quiet moments of his life. Tylle had been the closest thing, and she'd practically told him she wasn't interested.

"If we don't report in, we'll get another reprimanding from High Scholar Anya."

"If it is a test, it will be a tongue lashing at worst," the tall one leaned in again, stealing another kiss.

They held each other in an embrace as the alarm continued, finally releasing their romantic hold as the shorter, bald one pushed the other away. "Bookmark this." They said more, but the husky whispers weren't audible, and Lin was thankful. He hadn't snuck down here to be a voyeur. They shifted the book and pages into a neat stack, walking closer to each other than propriety might encourage, and left toward the hall Lin had come from.

About time some of Pael's luck shines on me. Taking a deep breath, Lin opened the door. He expected tables and test tubes and Mellyr. He found what looked to be an office more than a physiker's room. A desk, dark in the dim light of a small encased portion of wanderer's ore, sat in the center. Its surface was clear of clutter, and a comfortable-looking chair was neatly tucked under it. The walls were much like the outer area, shelf upon shelf laden with book upon book. Scroll caps were visible through a polished sheet of glass, and on the highest tier of the shelves, flowers, bones, and ore looked to be decoratively spaced.

He might have misheard Pael's instructions, but this was where he'd described seeing people brought in for testing. Even if it didn't look like it. Lin considered Erias's shadowed door and wondered if perhaps one of the many shelves hid a passage to the *actual* room.

Lin sucked his teeth and wiped beads of sweat from his brow. He needed to move quicker, but he couldn't—Mellyr couldn't afford for him to get lost in thought as he had so many times over the last few months. Suspicion boiled up within him at the thought. If the scholars had always planned to side against Danica, they might be responsible.

Despite circling the room several times, running hands along the shelves, and testing the joints where the wood met, he didn't find a door.

If Mellyr wasn't here, perhaps she'd been taken back to the room. Lin cursed. He'd been blinded by the pleasantries of the tower and hadn't thought he needed to be on guard anymore. The Scholars of Fentis were supposed to be reasonable, logical individuals— A click sounded from one of the drawers he'd been busying his hands with. It slid out easily as if on greased, silent tracks.

The book was thin. Possibly one of the thinnest Lin had seen. The cover was aged leather and dark. It looked like gold and blood were used to make the embossed design on the cover. Scarlet needlework stitching a representation of an outstretched body. The legs and arms spread wide. Overlaying the positioned body was Velkath's Sigil, done with a golden inlay. Like Bindings. Wievings. He hadn't decided what to call them now that he'd learned how right Tylle had been. Bindings still *felt* right. But the connotation left a sour taste any time he considered it. Though, most things these days from his old life seemed to.

Gods. The book was as light as a scroll, and when Lin ran his hand over the cover he knew it must be the thing Denro was asking after. He opened it, thumbing gently through the first few pages, but other than various diagrams, he didn't have time to read it. And even the diagrams made no sense without context. He took it, sliding it into his waistband and shutting the drawer. It clicked into place, and Lin scanned the room one last time. He swallowed. This had been his chance to get Mellyr back, and like with Margaret back in Lyre, he'd failed. Tears stung his eyes. Why was he always failing?

Lin exhaled and tried to calm down. Mellyr was a child. Worst case, she'd be used as a pawn by the warring factions. Best case, the scholars had truly taken a liking to her, and she'd be raised as one of them. Tested on, but kept safe. Lin frowned. Wasn't that the life all Danicans had before Aemun's intervention? His excuse for inciting a war had been to make a better life for his daughter. Lin shook his head. Aemun was a piece of shit, and it didn't matter what his intentions were. He'd murdered his bound partner and brought the wrath of Ladrica to bear against the dukes. Lin wore doubt like a cloak as he walked to the door, then froze as the handle jiggled.

Chains of Blood

"Elodis, while a small part of the Free Nations, has forever changed the outcome of these Accords. Without the Elodian Empire's intervention, the Danicans would not be allowed to police themselves. They suggested, to an overwhelming agreement, that select ruling members be petitioned and allowed to choose: Submit to Ladrican rule under Just King Gunthyr or be broken like a ship by shallow tides. Ladrican rule is not absolute, but given proximity and relation, it is all that stands between Danica and being crushed by the Free Nations. Ladrica seems poised to benefit nothing, save dominion over powerful magics only to control those self-same people." Excerpt from the Histories of Southern Danica, removed and redacted due to the Danican Accords.

Lin stood in the darkest corner, tucking his arms behind his back and hoping with held breath that whoever came in didn't have the Sight in case any stray Stitch was visible.

A scholar, robed in a color closer to a moonless night sky than blue or black alone, stepped in and observed the room. She was short, with a shaved head and deep bronze skin. Her brown eyes scanned the room, never settling on one place for long. In the dim light, her eyes were similar to the depthless brown of Tylle's. The alarm continued, muffled once the door shut. It was as if pipes ran through the walls, allowing the sound to reach even the depths of the tower.

Lin squinted. He was sure he'd seen her before. One of the High Scholars. *Anya?* Lin clenched his fist. Of course. She was *the* speaker. The one who'd condemned him. *Leagues away from the Chamber of Judgment, and I've finally been sentenced.*

Anya moved to her desk and sat, grousing as she did. Complaints about the alarm. Curses that Lin and Denro had escaped. She moved at her desk, unrolling a blank parchment. Where Lin stood, he could just barely make out what she'd begun penning.

Escaped. Be mindful—

Her quill scratched quickly, fervently as if she felt like she needed to finish before the alarm quit its task.

Lin leaned forward, mindful to do so silently, hoping to see whom the letter might be addressed to.

"I'll give you a headstart. I don't mind as much. But I must call the guard. Surely you understand."

Lin checked the other corners. There wasn't anyone else. She had to mean him. He stepped forward silently, and she turned, deep brown eyes locking onto his. If he was capable of pulling from his spul, her blood might've stained the letter instead of ink, but he wasn't, and try as he might, his gaze alone wasn't sharp enough to cut her.

"I am sympathetic, I swear. But times are what they are." Her voice was smooth but firm. Worst of all, it sounded genuine.

"Mellyr," Lin growled.

Anya looked down as if gathering her spilled thoughts from her feet. "The child, you mean? By now, likely gone from Fentis entirely."

Lin lurched forward and grabbed Anya by the hem of her dark robes. Gods, he wasn't sure he'd ever felt material so soft as if spun from clouds. His hands trembled, and she didn't resist.

"You came to us to remove those, did you not?" Her gaze lingered on his left hand and slowly roved up his arm.

"No." Lin snapped. "I mean, I did. But no. You don't get to change the subject. Why is Mellyr gone? Where is she being taken?"

"A Ladrican emissary bearing a writ from King Lodram requesting the child arrived days ago. They've taken her, as is their right as custodians of Danica per the—"

"Right. The *fucking* Accords. Why let me see those books but not the ones that might help me rid the Inlays from my flesh?"

"Oh, so you can change the subject, but I can't?" Anya rolled her eyes, shrugged, and softly said, "I can't speak to that. Though I'm the speaker, I'm not the decision-maker. Certain things are limited."

"By the Accords?"

Anya nodded. Her skin, though it didn't glow, had faint lines like scars along her flesh where Inlays might've been once. That and the tattoos along her raised forearms made her appear like a poor imitation of an Inlayed individual.

"You've removed your own. No?"

She didn't say anything.

"How?" Lin asked.

Anya cleared her throat. "If you think you could rescue that precious child, taking the time here to interrogate me would only prevent that from happening. You *might* still be able to get to her if they haven't left the docks yet. Ship that size takes time."

"Answer me, and I will take my leave." Mellyr was important. Of course, she was. But these were answers he'd been waiting for since Tylle first saved him in Fallo. And there wasn't a single person alive that might keep him from getting that child back.

She looked pointedly at Lin's left hand. "May I?"

Lin released her robe and let her take his hand. She pulled his thumb back with a jerk and swept up from the chair. It wasn't enough pressure to snap the digit, but it made Lin buckle and crumple to one knee. A scream played at the back of his throat, and he forced it down.

"Danicans have unique physiological... structures." She released a slight amount of pressure and ran her other hand over his Bludwieve. "There is something about your flesh and blood that makes Inlays bond to you in a way that they simply *don't* for others."

"Bullshit." Lin snarled, yanking his arm free.

"You ask for answers, then balk when they're given. Do you know that of all the disparate people of this wide world yours are the only ones capable of calling on the magics from *within*?"

"Scholars wield Wievings. You can't deny that." Lin rose and clutched his hand, the magic lacing his flesh thrumming as he touched it.

"We do. Some of us are Danican. Most aren't. The ones who aren't don't conjure it from within, though we've tried." The alarm continued, and she eyed the door. "It has something to do with your blood, or rather what makes up your blood. It's why, try as you might, you've been unable to Bind this entire time."

"W-what?"

"Trace metals, we think. Iron and others. You're people draw it from your blood somehow. Other people simply can't, even if they have the Sight. Even if they have the determination. And that, aside from the madness that takes hold of your people, is enough reason for Danicans to be viewed as threats to *most* people."

"So you've poisoned me this whole time?"

"Nothing nearly so morbid. Diet restrictions. Foods with little to no iron on a small scale. An extension of older tests, to be sure."

Lin struggled to take his eyes off hers. "Why take Danican blood?"

Anya smiled ruefully. She pulled a vial attached to a leather cord from under her dark tunic and raised it so the dim wanderer's ore lit it from behind. Dried blood crusted the interior like brown wax. She clutched the vial tight, knuckles paling from the force.

Between them, suspended in the air as if held with invisible threads, a Weave floated. It looked like a folded sheet of paper. "This is why. With the right intention and Danican blood, magic *is* possible for anyone. It levels the battlefield, at least for a time. But this was the first method. The safest. The weakest."

Lin's stomach twisted. The image wasn't as horrible as Fallo, with all those stitched limbs hanging from roofs, but the implication was far worse. How many of his people... how many had been tested and used? Fed and cared for like livestock in the name of study. Lin blinked and pushed it down. The Ferrucium. Fentis.

The whole world, monsters, all of them. "Monsters," he whispered.

"Monsters." She nodded. With steady hands, she tucked the vial back under her tunic and smoothed the front of the fabric. "All of this really to say, removing the Inlay from your flesh would be a painful endeavor. It is as much a part of you now as your lungs are. You don't see them working within you, but they are."

Lin fought back the tears. "When I get Mellyr back, I'll come for you, and you will remove these markings from my flesh."

"They aren't *markings.* But do be careful what you wish for. I said I'm sympathetic to your cause, not because of you or that child, but because what Ladrica and the Free Nations have done by sequestering Danica has limited our understanding and evolution of magic as a whole."

Lin shifted and stood at his full height. He took a step toward the door, and she placed a single hand out as if the motion itself might halt him. He was halfway to the exit before she said, "Wait."

Waiting was a luxury he couldn't afford. He'd spent months waiting only to be betrayed at the very end of it. Lin shook his head. No, he knew the betrayal had come as soon as he arrived here. He looked at her out of the side of his eye.

"Leave the book. Please."

"Why should I?"

"The answers you might find in it aren't worth the questions you'll have to ask to get them."

Lin ignored her and stepped through the door. He'd expected her to try to stop him, but instead, as he warily glanced back, she sat down and finished the letter she was penning. She looked up at him, face lit from underneath by the ore and casting a large shadow on the back wall of the room. Lin shuddered.

If the two initiates still lingered anywhere in the Archives, Lin didn't see or hear them. Worse, he didn't see or hear anyone. No prisoners in the cells, though it wasn't as if he'd seen any others to begin with. And no Initiates searching the halls. He found the wanderer's ore he'd set aside unbothered and used it to light the twisting halls ahead. The cell Pael had killed the stringy-haired man sat empty, a dark stain the only evidence violence had occurred at all. Lin lingered for a moment and did his best to still his heavy beating heart. Perhaps he *had* wasted too much time talking to High Scholar Anya. All his bravado about rescuing Mellyr would amount to nothing if she was taken on a boat. He punched the stone wall, knuckles immediately throbbing at the contact. "Fuck," he exhaled the word but held back the tears that promised at the edges of his eyes.

When he arrived at where he'd split from Pael and Denro, he expected to see a trail of bodies. Pael seemed to be built for subterfuge, the way he skulked about, but that didn't mean he wouldn't kill once push came to shove.

The halls widened once he made it up a set of stairs, and the floors sloped up. Lin recognized the path as the one they'd been led down originally once he did multiple double-backs up a tall flight of stairs. Once again, sconced ore lit the surroundings in a false firelight that managed to put him on edge just as much as the painfully bright blue of unfiltered wanderer's ore might have.

Then, a set of thin windows, barely the breadth of his hand each, showcased ribbons of the early morning sky. Mist hung in the air. If he turned up the flight behind him, he'd continue into the tower proper. How foolish he'd been to think that the beautiful branches of this building might reach the heavens without having roots dipping down to the hells.

Lin steadied himself and continued through the door. It groaned like a dying man and then he was running across a field. He expected arrows to take his back. Or magic. Or... anything. But instead, he made it to the shade of a rocky outcrop fifteen strides away without another alarm.

Lin swallowed and caught his breath. Over the last few months, he hadn't needed to Bind. But he had found time to train his body. He'd originally thought he had become used to the Inlays with time and training, but as he stood beside the rock, back flat against it, a fear crept on him like the shade of a cloud overhead. How long ago had they begun altering his food, limiting his... what had she said? *Iron intake?* Lin scowled. It wasn't like he was chewing on bars of metal before coming to the tower, but certain foods did replenish a Binder's— Wiever's— spul.

The back of the base of the tower, the part accessible from the surface anyway, was near the edge of the short drop the Scholar's towers were built on. It was called the Tower of Fentis, but really, there were two or three structures comprising the singularly named compound. Below, Fentis, the actual town, was coming alive. Lin squinted toward the docks. Not like he could even see that far. Pael probably had some tool or gadget that would allow him to. Keeping wide of the towers, wary of any windows or balconies, Lin wrapped to the north.

Underneath a willow that looked as old as the Fentian Towers itself, two horses stood. *Nebra*. Gods, he'd missed her. There had been a lone, short visit when he'd been escorted through the town proper. But he hadn't had a chance to ride or care for her. It was a small miracle they hadn't sent her away if they planned to lock him up.

Pael stepped out from behind the tree first, a bolt-shooter lowering as he saw Lin. "No child?"

Lin shook his head and moved to climb atop Nebra. "I need to get to the docks. A Ladrican emissary took her. I didn't see any Initiates on the lower levels. Or out here." Lin let the accusation sit unspoken.

"We didn't encounter anyone," Denro said.

Pael shifted his weapon and put a hand on Lin's reins. "If she's at the dock, it's too late. Better that we go than risk getting caught. And it's entirely possible that the studious fucks found their noses stained with more than black ink." He grinned, then let it slide away when Lin didn't return one. "Likely, they found the body of High Scholar Dellis a more urgent affair. One death over many."

Lin didn't know any of the High Scholars personally, but Denro cursed.

"Dellis was the most likely to press for *peace*," Denro growled as he wheeled on Pael, then slowed as the shorter man's bolt-shooter rose.

“Peace in *passivity*. Peace to Dellis and his camp meant a new collar placed around *our* people’s throats.”

“Better a collar than a noose!” Denro’s face had gone red, and the veins at his temples raised.

“There is no difference once they’re tight enough!”

“Fuck both of you. From the bottom of the One’s black *fucking* heart, fuck you both.” Lin whispered. “I’m going to the docks and getting Mellyr back. And I swear to all the known Gods if you’ve kept me from getting to her...” Lin choked back the frustration and exhaled. He yanked the reins and turned Nebra, not bothering to check behind him to see if the two men joined him. He slid a hand into one of Nebra’s saddle bags hoping to find nuts, seed, or dried meat. Empty.

Crushed Hope

"I watched, nervous at first. I assumed mercury, a magical-seeming metal by all accounts, would be the penultimate source of magic in Danicans. Never had I seen a liquid metal before, and never again after the tests. I blame the lack of preparedness from the scholars primarily overseeing the testing, but, truth be told, some fault also lies within the test subjects. They were eager to expand their powers. And with such fruition from other trace metals, none of us could guess the terrible results that awaited. It is safe to say that once ingested at high volumes, the subjects were no longer themselves. The following is a comprehensive list of symptoms."
Records from the personal diary of Physiker Sichael.

Lin slowed Nebra so as not to cause a scene as he approached the shoreline and docks. Fentis proper was a fishing town more than anything else and far more industrious than any village or locale in Danica, even Wellgrove. Before understanding the Accords, Lin thought the town was one of learning. Now he knew better. It was a place not so different from the Ferrucium had been, keeping Danicans in the dark and secluded. And now, alone and without escort through the city, it was more clear than ever. Fentis might reside on Danican shores, but it wasn't home to any aside from those who'd taken up roles within the tower.

A press of citizens clogged the main thoroughfares, congesting so much so Lin took the side roads, eventually leaving Nebra near a kind-looking older woman and rushing on foot. If he had the Ferrucium to thank for anything, it was how well-trained she was.

Salt hung in the air, making each breath heavy with the taste, and the sound of the sea seemed to compete with workers at the docks as they yelled words that meant nothing to Lin. Most of the boats were small, meant mostly for offshore fishing from the times Lin had stared out the tower window.

One ship dwarfed the rest, looming like some great wooden beast. *The Pollsh Dreamer.*

Lin elbowed past a man rooted in place and finally broke through the crowd. The waves lapped in a steady, slapping rhythm, and Lin was taken back to the moment at the Ferrucium where he and Tylle had rested on the much smaller, much older dock. Mellyr hadn't even had her name yet, instead bearing the foreign-sounding name Aemun had placed on her. But she'd been so warm on his chest—

Hands were on his shoulders and shaking him. The man, red-faced with a sneer that might curdle milk, yelled. Apparently, Lin had elbowed him *too* hard.

Lin pulled away, breaking the man's grip with ease and leaving it at that, turning to face the boat again. He squinted, took another step forward, and nearly tripped as the man shoved him from behind.

"Cutting in line! Bastard."

True enough, now that Lin thought to look for it, there was a line. The milling people had been... waiting to board? That didn't seem right.

Lin raised his hands, palms out to show the man he meant no offense, and noticed Pael and Denro breaking through the crowd not far from where he'd come through. There were too many people. And he wasn't even sure the Pollsh Dreamer was the correct ship. What if the boat had already left? He could barely see anyone on the deck from the slope of the docks.

A commotion, even more disruptive than the one Lin seemed to be a part of, came from the back of the main press of people. It sounded like the clanging of pans. Then, men and women moved aside, and those who didn't move in time were pushed. The sneering man turned as if to give this new disturbance a piece of his mind, not that he had much to give based on the dullness of his eyes. But he became one of the latter, bullied from his position by two gray-steel armored soldiers. Plates of armor layered across each other rattled with each step.

Lin swallowed and moved to the side before he was moved. The whole outfit reminded him of the Ferrucium Enforcer who'd nearly crushed him in the woods. Worst of all, it resembled well-pressed Ferrucium steel. The main reason Ferrucium soldiers wore leathers or cloth gambesons was because the steel was supposedly too scarce to forge armor out of it. And if a soldier was skilled enough with Wefts and Weaves, the armor wouldn't be needed against untethered. But... Lin's heart dropped. What if the Ferrucium was only *told* Ferrucium steel was scarce? Ladrica could have untold amounts. Lin was sure these were armored Ladrican soldiers based on the coiled serpent crests pressed into the chest. If the Ferrucium's sigil was a two-headed bird, Ladrica's was the snake that would coil around both necks and strangle them.

How he hadn't seen the procession as he rushed from the north was lost on Lin. Different paths perhaps but still, it didn't sit well with him. What if Anya had sent him out early? What if she wanted him to stop them? But that didn't make sense given that the scholars had already sided with Ladrica.

Five soldiers walked in formation, a single person in dark garb between them. Like shifting sand, the crowd filled the gap behind them. Most groused or cursed, but none made moves against them.

Lin craned his neck. The person in the middle was undoubtedly Ladrican, with her flash of curly copper hair tied tight into a bun. She carried a bundle. Lin's chest tightened. She held *Mellyr.* He hadn't been too late.

A single soldier at the rear of the procession turned and faced what quickly seemed to be developing into a mob. "Order." His deep voice carried, booming. He stomped a foot. "There seems to be confusion. We aren't a delivery vessel. There will be no goods unloaded." His thick accent, syllables stretched and cramped in all the wrong places, made the words grate.

And the crowd erupted. Lin moved away, angling, working toward the ramp where the other four soldiers and the emissary walked.

"Halt!" The same soldier bellowed as Lin approached, the hissing of his blade being drawn like a serpent's warning.

A scream, high and full of fear cut the air, and then a surge of bodies pressed Lin nearer to the ramp. Shouts rang out and the overwhelming odor of the docks mixed with a tang of sweat from the crowd.

Lin stared after Mellyr, just past the point of the blade leveled at him. He tugged at his spul, but no Weft formed in kind.

More screams and more pushing. With Lin's luck, he'd be pressed onto the sword tip.

"Untethered!"

Lin froze. It was the last thing a crowd like this needed. And one by one the various screams were silenced, Wefts cleaving through the crowd. Of all things, an untethered here? Lin considered lunging past the soldier, desperate to reach Mellyr. But when he looked back at the crowd he saw the terrified faces. Every single person fearful for their lives. What had started as a mob for supplies had turned into a deadly crush of bodies pressing to flee the slicing magic the untethered unleashed.

Lin saw Pael. The man lay prone atop an adjacent vendor's stall. Bolt-shooter out in front of him. A bolt whistled through the air. Lin could barely track it. But it wasn't heading into the crowd where the untethered wrought death. The emissary then. He'd surely shot at... Inches from the bundle that Lin was sure was Mellyr, the bolt broke with a flash of light and the sound of a thin tree branch cracking. A Weft had sliced it and shattered on impact.

The speaking soldier spun, then righted himself, leveling his sword at the terrified crowd. Most of them stopped, the ones in front at least, but those behind continued forward and pushed more than one person onto the end of the soldier's sword before he gave up ground. Wails continued to rip from the throats of those stuck between a monster and an uncaring soldier.

If all they were here for was Mellyr, surely they could spare a man or two to combat the untethered.

The soldiers around the emissary moved in unison, creeping tighter, armor grinding, until they were fully on the ship and gone beyond view.

"Back!" The lone soldier growled from half up the plank, face hidden behind his helm. People pressed toward him, still mostly against their own volition, and corpses fell beside him.

"Do something about the untethered!" Lin screamed. He took a step, then stopped as he stared down at the face of a wheezing woman. Blood trickled from the edge of her mouth and her breaths were raspy and pained. A stab through her lungs by the look of it. A slow, painful death.

Whatever orders the soldier had been given, he sure as fuck wasn't moving or allowing any of the citizens a path to flee the death in the crowd. Sailors were visible on the ship preparing it to sail. Men and women danced from rope to rope, untying things and unfurling sails. But he'd been so close. He wouldn't leave Mellyr. *Couldn't.*

"Lindel." Denro's voice. Something that should have been a balm but stung as it brought the world back into focus.

It was then that Lin realized he was sobbing. He'd bent over, and he could tell he'd been trying to form Wefts, but nothing had come. The lone soldier had managed up the ramp, and the incensed crowd had stopped pushing after him once two other armored soldiers had come back onto the deck with bows pointed at the crowd.

"We need to move, boy."

"I can't leave her." Lin's voice cracked.

"Regroup is all we can do. But in case you've forgotten, we've escaped from the towers just over there, a mob has formed here, there is an untethered causing havoc, and the ship is leaving!"

Lin clutched at Denro's arm, squeezing as tight as he could. "I failed her. Like I failed her mother. Like I failed Tylle when I couldn't kill Aemun in the woods. Like I failed *you*."

Denro slapped Lin. Not hard, but enough to bring Lin's arm up defensively. "We don't have time for this."

And like that, he was following his old mentor, pulled along by the current of his will. The crowd was chaos manifest, some people trampled, and others crumpled and bleeding out. Lin slowed. There it was. Pale and scrawny. Barely even a true untethered compared to some of the monsters he'd seen. A woman clad in average clothes for the area. A woman who must've only recently untethered. And she looked as desperate as the citizens had been to get to the ship.

Lin screamed. Never again would he be useless. Never. He rushed the monster, nearly slipping on the bloodied, cobbled stones that lined the roadway. His momentum carried his shoulder into the untethered as it tried to rip through a father protecting his daughter amid the sweaty, slamming bodies.

Weakened as he was for having his body deprived for months of certain things, rage fueled him. No Wefts. No magic. Just his hands slamming the monster's head over and over into the stone ground. He lost count of the times, didn't care that the untethered had stopped scraping his arms and face. Didn't care that a Weft had formed at his throat countless times only to be broken—presumably by Denro.

It was Denro who pulled him up, the monster's head a bloody pulp leaking from between his fingers.

Thick, rust-hued blood coated Lin's hands and when he looked at the faces of those he'd saved— father and daughter, countless others, they all looked as if the monster was still among them.

Denro pulled him away. Silent as the crowd closed in on itself, tending to the wounded, giving space to the dead.

Pael was walking with all three horses away from the woman they'd left them with, a dour expression on his pinched face. When he looked at Lin he slowed and shook his head. "Seems the Pollsh Free Navy is aiding Ladrica. Not that Grovetender didn't expect it." His tone matched his expression and the man stuffed his head into the wide-brimmed hat he so often wore.

Lin stared at him, hands trembling. "You almost killed Mellyr."

The short man shrugged. "Would've been a shame," he mumbled.

"Say that again," Lin raised his voice. More than one bystander turned and watched him. More people he'd saved, considering him a blood-soaked monster. Lin didn't care. It didn't matter what the Fentians thought of him anymore. They'd decided how they felt about him when they locked him in a cell. It didn't matter what *anyone* thought of him.

Pael stopped what he was doing and took two steps forward, looking up at Lin.

"We need to go," Denro said.

"You *tried* to kill her," Lin said. He stepped forward. The only thing keeping him from taking the diminutive man by the throat was the space and history between them. But neither would save the man if Lin just took one single step forward.

"And I stopped the bolt from finding purchase. No one wanted that child stolen away. But taking the life wasn't the answer and fighting each other isn't either." Denro spoke in that irritatingly calm way of his. "We need to go before they come looking for the man that killed the untethered. It is easy to forget that many people only saw you murder a deranged woman in broad daylight, not someone who has untethered."

"If she'd have died, you'd have followed shortly after." Lin's voice shook. It was all too much. He'd failed Margaret. Failed Mellyr time and time again. And he'd *froze*. It seemed the moments where he lost himself to thought had worsened over the last few months. Rage boiled in him. It *had* to be related to whatever the High Scholars had done to him and his food. In the little moments inside their room, losing himself seemed less of an issue. He'd drift in thought for a short period, then snap back and see Mellyr still sleeping, Denro still reading, the world *unmoving*. But now? He couldn't afford to let his attention drift. Lin clenched his fist. It was like using a bowl to take water from the river, knowing the bowl had holes and wouldn't stay full, but forgetting to block the holes when he went to sip from it.

Pael seemed to notice a shift in Lin and sniffed the air. "Is that so?" Pael pressed even closer, dark eyes barely visible under the brim of his hat. "Can't magic, can you?"

"Doesn't matter," Lin said. "Just killed an untethered. Don't push me."

"We need to continue—" Denro stepped between them and Lin shifted to move from behind him. "And without your magic, you're *barely* a soldier, green as the grass underfoot." Pael spat at the ground. "I like you, kid. I do. But if you can't understand why I'd take that shot, next time I'll take an extra."

Lin pushed past Denro and punched Pael across the chin. He put his weight behind it and they tumbled and rolled but Pael was to his feet in an instant. A blade flashed into his hand quicker than a blink and he shook his head. His hat had fallen off and the edge of it threatened to be stolen by the coastal winds. Lin climbed up a moment later, trying and failing to form a Weft.

"Fuck you," Lin spat.

"First hit is free 'cause I can tell you aren't thinking straight. Anything after that comes at a *heavy* cost." Pael sucked on his bottom lip where it had split.

"Lindel. You're being irrational. We know it's a Pollsh trading galley, which might mean deep waters, but a Ladrican emissary tells us everything else we need to know. Danica only has two official ports, save for those which might be run by pirates and the like," he looked at Pael as he spoke, "and that means they aren't likely to land anywhere anytime soon."

"How does that help—"

"Let me finish. The nearest Ladrican port is Fort Talmsdale, just on the other side of Vellia's Fingers, or Talms's peak, as it's known by the Ferrucium. They're likely headed there. And if they're traveling the coast, if we begin to move *now*, we may be able to beat them there."

Lin listened and hated how rational Denro was being, how *calm*. But he nodded, slowing his breaths.

"Now I know for a fact that you've been attracting all the wrong attention since leaving the tower. We need to move now or we'll have a more pressing issue to deal with."

"More pressing than getting back Mellyr?" Lin couldn't help but snap at the implication in Denro's words.

"Listen. If they took her," he measured the pace of his words as if talking to a toddler, "they don't plan to hurt her. Tests? They were already doing those here, so they won't do anything worse."

Lin bit back the anger at remembering Denro had *let* her be taken for tests. He calmed in small waves, the anger fleeing from him and leaving his limbs heavy and aching. Adjusting his shirt, he made sure the book was still safely tucked into his waistband. He'd actually planned to hand it over to the man, but the sad truth came to him as if filling in where his anger had left a void.

Lin didn't trust Denro. Even though the man had saved Mellyr. He couldn't trust him.

They rode in silence. Lin atop Nebra, Pael and Denro sharing a horse. The Tower of Fentis stabbed into the sky and dominated the horizon until night fell and only the vaguest shape of the tip of the tallest tower was visible. Silence consumed them, worse than the few times Lin had argued with Tylle on the road. Gods, he missed her. Tylle wasn't the sort to let someone she cared about be taken without penalty. And Lin? He'd always thought himself a hero of sorts. Nothing like in the old tales, but the kind that did the right thing no matter what the cost. But what hero lets a child be tested on, let alone stolen? Aemun's last moments echoed in his mind. The lying snake was many things, but Lin struggled to imagine a version of events where Mellyr was stolen away if he still lived.

"You look like you're chewing on something with more bones than meat," Denro sidled his horse alongside Nebra.

Lin cleared his throat. It was like his failure insisted on choking him from within. "I'm wondering if I've done the right thing."

"Now? This is what makes you wonder if aiding a coup and Stitching yourself may have been a bad decision?"

"No," Lin snapped. Part of him didn't even want to talk to his aging mentor. But when he looked at his expression, he saw flashes of the man who used to truly care. "If Aemun's death and the resulting chaos were worth it. Despite how you may feel about everything around the Fall, I still wish to remove my Inlays. But I do think it's odd not a single scroll or book in that whole place seemed to mention the Six in any foundational way."

Denro frowned. "I... I don't know what to believe sometimes. But I do think..." he sighed exasperatedly. "I think that the risk of madness isn't worth the "benefits" the magics grant. Especially seeing how you've been the last few months. Like you aren't there sometimes." He tapped the side of his head.

"And how would you know? You've barely spoken with me and on the few occasions you have, enthusiastic wouldn't describe the quality of conversation."

"I'm far from perfect. There have been moments crystallized in my heart and mind that replay time and time again. My first love, lost. A child I'll never meet. Oaths I've made and... what I mean to say is I could've done better at expressing how I've felt about this whole thing. I resigned myself to the life of an Initiate, to be digested piece by piece in the bowels of that tower."

"And what now?" Lin asked.

"You want me to be honest?"

Lin stared at the crease in Denro's brow. He'd seen it on rare occasion between missions, but now? Now it was a fixture the man never seemed to leave far from his face. "I've never asked you not to be."

"Now I feel, if I don't travel with you and watch after you, you might somehow manage to make matters worse for Danica. If you'd asked me ten years ago if I thought one man was capable of changing the fate of a nation like ours, I would've said you're a fool. Now I'm not so sure. When I look in your eyes I see a man who feels like he's already lost anything that might matter to him."

Lin pulled his eyes from Denro and glanced at Pael. The change had felt gradual to him like he'd been perched atop a cliff that was losing stone and earth bit by bit, not from the top but from below.

And he slid down away from what he once believed, unaware of how far he was moving from who he'd once been. But he'd *always* been like this. Always cared about those he cared about and *wished* for freedom. Gods, he thought he'd had freedom back then. An occasional escort and only returning to the Ferrucium a handful of times. Riding with Nebra. He'd been free until he saw that the fields of freedom were fragile painted fakes. The sky the same. What was freedom when it was merely spoon-fed lies?

Fuck. Lin blinked, pulling his thoughts free from the muck he seemed stuck in. More and more he found himself lost. "No more."

"No more what?" Denro asked.

"I still have things left to lose, myself most of all. And I'll die before that happens." It was clear from the worry creasing his brow, Denro could tell Lin wasn't wholly himself.

If Lin was truly slipping into madness, riding this crashing cliff down to the depths of the sea, he'd fight his way back up. Bloody nails and all.

Crushed Bone

"Verbanth and Velkath have the most story, as far as Danican heroes of old go. It should be clarified that the distinction between God and Hero, especially in the ancient Danican spoken form, was a stressor over the middle of the word. Gudin. Goodyn. Either way, despite the overarching goal of Ladrica to replace the pantheon, to rewrite the histories so that Danican people refrain from abusing their innate magical proficiencies, it is clear that Verbanth and his kin were already too established to be erased entirely, and as such were made into martyrs." Excerpt from A Study of Religion, author unsigned.

The crackling logs spat embers up the hearth as wood shifted, their steady pops a sporadic cadence of calm. By the time winter's cold winds reached this far south, warming along the way, it felt like fall typically did in northern Danica. A crisp coldness that reminded Lin of his time on the road with Tylle. He picked at the eggs on his plate, staring into the flames.

Pael and Denro sat at the table on either side of him, but no one spoke. Everyone was upset at the other, and no one wanted to be the first to break the obstinate silence. They'd arrived at the town, Ellsbrook, early enough to get fed breakfast at the inn and see their horses cared for. No comments came from the proprietor, though the man did stare hard at Pael's dirty bare feet.

They cleaned themselves and changed into clothes Pael returned with. Most of which didn't fit quite right, likely stolen.

And now they ate in silence.

Pael scratched the end of his nose and stared up at the ceiling where the sound of steps rattled loose dust from the floorboards above. "I've had plenty of time to think," he said slowly. "And I don't regret taking that shot."

Lin nodded and stabbed the yolk of his egg, golden innards leaking out much the way the untethered's skull had oozed. He'd played the scene over in his head several times. And despite his rage, he'd have done it all again. Someone had to stop the creature.

"But," Pael said. "I'm not you, or him, or anyone else. I'm a Dukesman and always have been. The concern with them taking that child is severalfold. And I've already sent a bird to Grovetender."

"They'll use her as leverage," Lin said.

"Maybe," Denro brought himself into the conversation, sliding his empty plate away. "If this turns into a war of attrition, they might try to raise her to take the Ferrucium one day. Say what you will about Weaver Azhura and Aemun, but that bloodline is old."

"Then they've shot themselves in the foot with their own bolt," Pael chuckled. "A concern, to be sure, but the people of Danica don't *know* any authority other than the Dukes. Sure, some are aware of the king and that Ladrica exists and the Dukes answer to it, but they don't know any more about the inner workings of the Ferrucium than they do about the Free Nations." Pael took a long gulp from the foamy drink he held and wiped his mouth with the back of his arm. "Correct me if I'm wrong."

"You're right," Lin said. Or at least Pael was right if the common person knew as much as Lin had when all this started. He took the mug in front of him and swirled the dark ale within. It smelled rich and earthy. "But then what are the several concerns."

Pael raised all five fingers on his right hand. "Leverage and potential replacement, to be sure." He lowered two fingers and waggled the other three. "Leverage makes the most sense, grabbing Azhura by the metaphorical balls. Grovetender doesn't trust her still, but she seems to be working in tandem with the Dukes on our side and reforming the Ferrucium from within."

Reform. Lin glanced around the room. Even if being stuck inside with the scholars had been restricting and they had treated him more or less like a pampered prisoner, he'd grown used to not having to look over his shoulder. Ever since Fallo, he'd been running from something, toward something, maybe.

Denro frowned and shifted in his seat. "Bait?" He asked after a long moment.

Pael's third finger fell as he nodded. "It's not as if the events before the freeze weren't relayed to them. The lengths Lin and Tylle went to for revenge. They want Lin, or someone, to attack them. It would show justification to the Free Nations and world at large that their continued control of our people is valid and vital."

"In speaking with several of the scholars, it's clear they were surprised by my... demeanor. Most think we are barely better than animals, meant to be kept in cages. Others were Danican themselves and often taken in at such a young age they didn't know better. And the worst is they do so unmaliciously. They truly view

Danica as a place of violence, considering the reports and accounts of untethered attacks."

"And the coup now," Lin added.

"And the Fall, as they've named it," Denro nodded.

The ale stung a bit as Lin downed half his mug. Strong stuff there, but it eased him and helped him keep focus on the conversation at hand. Perhaps he'd had too much free time over the last four months, and that played some small role in the unfocused wanderings of his mind. Lin sniffed and took another sip before he could spiral into his thoughts. "And the last two?"

"Revenge. Weakest of the lot, but possible."

"Send her to us one day as a Nooseman?" Lin asked.

"Or worse, if that's possible." Denro mused. "But that is only four possibilities."

Worse than a Nooseman. Now that was a chilling thought. Those bastards had all been strong and capable. Dennick especially— only losing to the sheer number of Carine's people.

Pael nodded as if he had expected that. The one finger he hadn't laid down was his ring finger. He pointed at the base of it. "The last is the unknown. Impossible to say and harder to guess what those Ladrican fucks might be capable of."

Lin licked his lips and stared back into the flames. It went without saying, but he didn't want any of that for Mellyr. Guilt twisted his stomach, and he pushed his plate to the side. Only three bites of seasoned potatoes, soaked in the runny egg yolk, remained anyway. "Do you really think they're taking her to that fort?"

Denro tapped his fingers on the tabletop and eyed the proprietor's back. "I do. It could also be part of the bait theory. Not everyone on that ship would be Ladrican, seeing as it was marked as a Pollsh trading galley. Having sailors from Polin who could witness what destruction you're capable of might be part of the plan."

Pael rubbed his chin and pushed his chair out. "Way I see it. Now that the child has been taken, leaving her in the hands of the north isn't an option. Even if we disagreed on the best way to keep her from being taken. I'm going to bed. I'll ride with you as far as Townsbridge if you'll have me. But then I'll break off, meet with Grovetender's people."

Once Pael left, Denro pulled Lin's plate over and picked at the potatoes. "Much like him, I've had time to think. Did you find the book, by any chance?"

Lin looked up slowly, meeting the man's eyes. "No. Why that book?"

There were small moments over the last few months when Lin saw Denro look *hungry*. Not for food, but knowledge. Most of the books he seemed to read were ruminations on the Accords. Or journals from people involved. He'd shared those, but there had been times when he secreted what he was reading and that was when he appeared the hungriest.

"I was hoping it might hold the secrets of the untethered. What makes them tick? What drives them mad? How to prevent it."

If prevention was known, so was causation. The scholars hadn't been testing for no reason. Ladrica hadn't been testing for *no rea-*

son. Thinking about tests sent Lin's mind spiraling to Mellyr. Not to mention the scholars had a way of preventing Danican magics.

"You saved her when I couldn't," Lin whispered as he sloshed the ale in his mug, rocking the pewter back and forth. "You were able to Wieve. The scholars didn't think they needed to change your diet."

"They did," Denro corrected. "But I built trust over the last few months. Squandered now, maybe, but I did."

Lin reached for his spul and like the sun climbing the horizon after endless nights, a Weave sparked into existence. Gods, it was threadbare. Thin and weak. But it had formed and Lin carefully grasped it, until it fell apart in his hand.

"You'll likely have it back in a day or so. The good news is if eating this small meal replenished you so much, I doubt you were poisoned."

A snort escaped Lin. "Silver linings and all that."

"Precisely. But the thinking I mentioned I did during that over-abundance of silence. Lin... I've known you long enough to know you won't reconsider this path you're about to go down. Even if you look less like the man I thought I helped raise, even if you find yourself cloaked in Verbanth's wrath and Tel'Myr's wickedness, I know you want to do the right thing."

Lin stared at Denro. Did he look so much unlike himself that his old mentor had to rub it in his face? "I do." Lin pulled his plate back and took the last bite before Denro could. "No matter the cost."

"Right." Denro wiped his hands and wrinkled his nose. "But do you truly think *that* man is the one who should be deciding what the right or wrong thing is? Not just here about Mellyr, but about Danica as a whole."

Lin took another sip of his ale, staring at Denro over the lip of the mug. "If we want to name the Gods, let me be as honest as truthful Vellyr," Lin stressed the pronunciation to leave no room for misunderstanding where Mellyr garnered her namesake. "I don't trust either of you. And I don't expect either of you to aid me in rescuing her. If we took Pael, he'd be as likely to kill her as save her. He's been the way he is as long as I've known him, which fair, isn't long. But the worst part is he only acts like this when he's certain he's right.

Denro opened his mouth but Lin set his mug down hard.

"And I wouldn't want you coming because you had no qualms letting her be tested on. No qualms about letting them hold us for months, knowing they were doing Gods know what to her. Testing her blood? Is that what *good* people do?"

"Right and wrong from where we sit can only ever be so narrow. Think on a larger scale. If our people are a threat, which we know they can be, what if there was a way to keep people from ever becoming untethered? The scholars aren't out there abducting Danicans. Volunteers come. I gave consent for Mellyr."

"You had no right," Lin said.

"I had as much right as you did, ripping her from her father."

Lin rubbed the bridge of his nose and blinked away the frustration welling up within him. It was a moot point. "Perhaps...

perhaps I've tried to open your eyes with a dagger's edge, where flower petals might have sufficed."

Denro sighed and leaned forward. "There are petals whose edges are sharper than razors. There are dull, blunt daggers."

"Can I get you two anything else?" the owner of the inn asked.

Lin nodded up at the broad-shouldered, stocky man. His nose was bulbous and round, really the opposite of Lyre's Alderman, when Lin considered it. "Top off, please."

The man grunted, wiped his hand on the clean apron folded around his waist, and took the mug. "You?" he asked Denro.

When Denro shook his head the man moved off. They weren't alone in the small, warm room, but the only other figure at the table rested with their head buried in their arms and a plate of half-touched food beside them.

"You evaluated me," Lin said after the mug had been returned to him, full to the brim with dark, swirling ale.

"I did."

"And when I was taken in, not long after, you became an Educator and taught me."

"I did," Denro said softer.

"What were my parents like?" Lin asked.

A line formed across Denro's brow and he rested his left hand over his mouth. "I don't recall."

The drink burned a bit going down, but Lin took another, longer pull. "Did I cry when I was taken?" He thought of Roge and his sister as he asked the question. He wondered how they were now. Wondered if Ladrica did push in, how soon they might get to those shitty little homes. Danica's spread-out villages might survive a war between dukes and the Ferrucium. But how were they meant to fare against an army that considered all of them as tainted blood monsters not worth saving?

"Most do."

"But did I?" Lin asked, leaning forward.

"What do you want me to say?" Denro snapped.

"Say that you love me. Care for me. Say that together, if we try, we can work past this!"

A chair skirted from behind them and the person who'd been slouched across their table was up and alert, staring at them in confusion.

Denro waved politely, and the man slowly slunk back into his seat.

Lin frowned. It was far from okay. When Aemun had fled at Fallo, he and Tylle hadn't had a moment to rest, to truly talk. But now look at him, sitting here after enjoying a bath and change of clothes, warm food, and lukewarm ale. All while Mellyr was being spirited away to a kingdom that treated Danicans like cattle.

"I... Your father was a kind man. Heart bigger than his head, no insult intended." Denro reached across and put a gentle hand on Lin's and squeezed. "Your mother was an amazing woman. And despite the harsher things we've said over the last few days... and the silence the months before... I think they'd both be proud of the man you've become."

It was like he'd been struck square in the chest. Breath wouldn't come to Lin. "You knew them?" His voice cracked. Then he forced a deep breath and pushed it down. Further and further down, the pain of this joined the piling loss of failure.

Denro patted Lin's hand and nodded. "Not as well as some. But..." He looked around the room and then stared up at the slatted-wood ceiling. "They were Ferrucium soldiers. And they ran from the life. Hid out in the northern woods, past Lyre. Not quite to Talm's Peak, but northward."

"And you found them?" Lin whispered the implication. The accusation.

"Gods, no. We were friends and they told me they were leaving. Told me where I might find them one day. Asked if I would leave with them."

Tears glistened in Denro's eyes and he looked as if he was staring at a scene unfolding. Shadows danced across his face from the flames beside them and the only sounds in the room were the occasional cracking of embers and the snores coming from the man behind them.

"I take it they died?"

"I... I found you there, hidden under a pile of blankets three times your size. It looked like an untethered attack. You were barely old enough to walk on your own, but I could tell you at least had the Sight. And the way you clung to me." Denro squeezed Lin's hand again and pulled away, letting out a breath that sounded like it had been held his whole life. "Back then, I'd have done just about anything for you. I hunted for the untethered responsible but lost track of them in the deep forest. And when you got sick...

I thought I'd failed the memory of your parents. But I gave up the vengeance and looked to truly care for you instead."

He'd lived an entire life clueless. Born to runaway soldiers, saved by Denro. He'd been like a father figure, certainly a mentor, but he'd never once shed a hint of this. But then, it seemed Denro was a more capable liar than Lin would've guessed based on Mellyr and the Bound Metal research.

"Are... are you lying?" Lin regretted his words as soon as he spoke them.

Denro's lips pressed thin and he shut his eyes for a brief moment as if pulling himself together. "What I mean to say by all of this... is that I've broken the Tenets too. I've done things that betray the Ferrucium but always for what I thought was the best. So yes, I hope we can move past this, *all* of this, but I need time to process it. And I need you to know that when it comes to this war, violence might win us the battle, but not the favor of the wide world. Sometimes setting aside vengeance is the best act of revenge. Please, don't stay awake worrying about what-ifs."

His fingers tapped a rhythm on the table and his chair dragged across the floor, loud only because of the silence that otherwise surrounded them.

"Why didn't you tell me sooner?" Lin looked up at him, at the wrinkles. At all the signs of an unforgiving life marked across his features.

"Knowing wouldn't change anything and if it had, I doubt it would've been for the better."

With that Denro walked from the room, his steps soft in the stillness. Lin licked his lips and finished his mug off, the ale smoother now that he'd had enough of it. He stared into the fire until the light from the windows seemed brighter, then stared out the dirty glass for a time.

"Need anything?" The bulbous-nosed innkeeper asked.

"Name?" Lin croaked.

"Mine?"

Lin nodded, looking the man in his eyes. Hidden under a broad brow and eyebrows that could have been shorn from a farm animal. Lin stopped himself. He'd wanted the man's name, not to pick apart more peculiar traits. Those times when he and Denro might trade interesting details belonged to the past and the fun of it with it.

"Most call me Trunk," Trunk said, flashing a wary smile.

There were a hundred reasons a man might earn a name like that and Lin wasn't sure he wanted to think about any of them. He hoped it was due to the man's nose. Which implied he'd taken the thing that made him different and made it his own. "Thank you for the food and drink, Trunk."

"Did you need anythin', though?"

Lin looked into the empty mug before pushing it away. "One more plate of eggs and if you've any meat."

"Pork. Grilled and spiced same as the potatoes."

"Perfect."

While Lin waited, he ran his hand over the dull Stitches along his knuckles. They hummed, the energy calming. More and more the Inlays along his limbs came alive. They hadn't been taken from him, but somehow restricting his ability to Wieve had separated the sensation from him. Even more disturbing was that it had taken this conflict for him to realize what was being kept from him. Now, sitting here eating and drinking he felt more alert, more like he'd been before arriving at the Tower. If the Fentian Scholars insisted on siding with King Lodram, then they were truly surrounded by enemies with no allies to call on. *Except*. It had always seemed odd that a manned ship had been waiting for Aemun. Somewhere out there, someone was willing to aid Danica, if not solely Aemun. Lin chewed at his lip and smiled when the steaming meat was placed in front of him. He'd eat. Briefly sleep. Then chase that damned ship.

Juice exploded into his mouth with the first bite, pepper crunching between his teeth. He wiped the corner of his mouth, stared out the window again, and contemplated leaving Denro and Pael altogether. No. Not yet, not now. But, soon possibly. If they slowed him down too much.

Crushed Hate

"I've come to know how ignorant I was. Stitched, as it were, is a derogative term used to insult those who have practiced the art of Inlaying. Before the "Gods" gave the "gift" of Wieving, people still Inlayed their flesh as a religious practice. Though it was done with bone and dye, tapped hard to pierce the flesh. It marked prowess at one thing or another, notably skills that our ancestors valued as integral. Some might call it primitive, but I'd say all cultures were such at one point. Moving forward, I will only refer to the people talented enough to Inlay themselves, even those driven mad by the magic, as Inlayed." Records from the personal diary of Physiker Sichael.

"And sleep, or lack thereof, hasn't convinced you to come with me to meet Grovetender, has it?" Pael asked. He spoke the words slow and a bit throaty as if he was the one who hadn't slept hardly a wink.

Lin grumbled and rubbed his eyes. They'd left the town, traveling along the main road heading north. It felt odd not feeling like he had to look over his shoulder as often as he had with Tylle. Even when they'd passed a Ferrucium outpost earlier, the sense of dread he expected when he saw it looming proved unfruited. Sure, there'd been a look or two from one of the soldiers, likely because of Lin's Inlays, but since Erias and Azhura had been reforming the Ferrucium, Inlays didn't immediately equal untethered.

"No. We should be pressing north as hard as possible. Not turning south." Lin squinted, but the hills around them prevented even the impression that a coastline to the west might be obscured. But even if this stretch was wholly flat with clear skies, the western forest that abutted the northern portion of Danica would prevent the sea from being visible.

"I know I'm wearing the sentiment thin, but if war is the answer—"

Denro chimed, "It's not."

"Then we need to marshall troops. The bird I sent is good, but I *have* to deliver a real report. And having the two of you with me would only help that."

"I'm not a soldier. Haven't been in a long time," Denro said.

"Don't feed me shit and call it honey," Pael retorted. "Men like us don't make it to be as old as we are without knowing how to fight. How to *survive*."

The glance Denro gave Pael was familiar, comforting even, at least to Lin. It was the look the man gave when he wanted to appear reproaching but agreed with whatever the other person had said.

"Denro's been through more than most of us," Lin said through a yawn.

"Bah. Ain't been through more than me. And honestly, boy, what you went through this last year is worth three lifetimes. Just remember, I've lived more lives than most. Seen more things than most. So as much as you think you've been through—"

"Pael. It's just us. I get it. I do. You're tough and a good shot and have slept with more high-class women than Denro and I have seen."

The fact that Pael's dark, sun-loved skin reddened even a shade proved that Lin got him. Denro chuckled, which brought a good laugh from Lin. And finally, grudgingly, Pael cracked a smile.

"Was worried you forgot my dice were *well-loved*," Pael tapped the side of his nose and turned to the road ahead. "Well... if you won't come with me, I need a promise. One you won't be willing to make."

Lin rubbed the crimson bludwieve that twined around his ring finger. He knew it meant he was tied to Erias, even though he'd fulfilled the Uethe he'd given. "What is it?"

"If you can't get her back and our people don't get there in time to help you..."

"I won't promise to kill her," Lin snapped. Any jovialty gone, blown away like wispy clouds in the sky.

"Promise you'll *stay* with her."

An argument rested on the tip of Lin's tongue, then when he broke down the man's words he held it in. What Pael meant clarified. If Lin were to get stuck, trapped, or captured, he needed to stay. Handle whatever torture, pain, or even death might wait for him there.

"You'd ask him to die, then?" Denro asked.

"I'd ask him to wait." Pael twisted in his saddle and rifled through the satchel over his shoulder, pulling out a small container and stuffing something into his mouth. "But waiting could mean dying."

Lin listened to the two men bicker, but it was clear that the vehemence they seemed to show each other when first meeting had faded to merely a soft dislike. The stars overhead were clear, and the sky was free of clouds. Staying in the tower, his view of the sky had been dominated by the occasional storm. But when the clouds were clear, he wasn't sure there was a single view across all of Danica that might steal his breath the way the first time he saw the stars above the ocean had. A smile tugged its way to the corner of Lin's mouth as he heard Pael recounting one of his tales. This time about a duke's daughter.

Away from the restrictions and confines of the scholars, atop Nebra with the wind blowing against his face, he felt more and more like himself. That was really why he'd smiled. Yes, he'd lost himself in thought a bit, picturing the cliffs below Fentis and the docks as a storm cleared to show the sky, but he hadn't disappeared into his mind as he had been doing at the Tower. He might be able to forgive the scholars for stealing his ability to bind, but how could he ever forgive the people who might have poisoned his mind?

It might not be the scholars. More than anything, that thought haunted him. What if it were the Inlays and stitches poisoning his mind? He'd been so wary of Binding until Tylle convinced him otherwise. Though, she had told him untethering was a very real issue, hadn't she?

Lin took a sip from his waterskin and eased back into the saddle, letting Nebra have free rein of the road. The book in his waistband dug into his spine. *Right.* He hadn't had a chance to move it into Nebra's saddle bag yet. Guilt hadn't stabbed into Lin when Denro asked about it at the inn, but now it did as the corner of the squared edge pressed against him.

"Thinking about all the horrible torture that might befall you in Ladrica?" Denro called back.

"Or wondering if you were in my shoes if you'd be able to not only seduce the daughter but have the duke shake your hand afterward, none the wiser?"

"Neither," Lin said softly. "Just wondering if I'm staring at the same stars that those who came before us did. That Mellyr might, once she'd old enough to do so."

Pael snorted, and Denro hummed. "They're as old as the world. Older even. Some cultures think they're souls. Embers from pyres, stitched permanently into the night sky. Others, simply watchers."

"It is good, I think, that I'm no Emissary," Lin said. He sidled Nebra up alongside the other two horses. "If only we could have you both meet the members of the Free Nations. Surely, between the two of you, they'd see we are more than the monsters they'd have us believe we are."

"You'd trick them with two old men?" Denro arched a brow.

"I'd show them that we are more than the violence we might inflict. That the minds of our people are as sharp as our magic and just as bright."

"Bad analogy," Pael chided.

"How so?" Lin asked, a defensive note creeping into his voice.

"See... a good analogy requires a few different components. Most important being commonality." Pael touched the tip of his nose the way he so often did when imparting his tiny grains of wisdom.

"Commonality," Lin said flatly.

"Commonality." Pael nodded. "Don't feed me shit and call it honey, for example. You've seen shit, smelled it too. Same for honey. Both are brownish, depending."

Lin frowned and waved a hand at Pael, deciding he was far too tired for this conversation. "Enough," he pleaded.

"My main complaint is that not everyone *has* the Sight. Myself a perfect example. Is the magic bright?" Pael shrugged. "Perhaps. But it's lacking the commonality. I've not seen it cut, but I've seen cuts appear and things held in place. Watched a Nooseman seemingly try to stop a wagon barehanded."

"Did he?" Denro asked. He'd been listening with a smile that dimpled his cheeks, his gray beard not thick enough to hide it.

"If he had, neither of us would be here. This lad, as misguided as he seems to be at times, saved us. Held his own against the Nooseman."

"Somewhat," Lin said, thinking back to the mud and muck he'd crawled through when the Nooseman attacked again. If he thought about it, he could taste the grit on the apples he had struggled to eat. He scraped his tongue against his teeth and shrugged.

"Somewhat," Pael agreed.

"I've been meaning to ask. You said Tylle had a request for me. You started to explain, but cut off."

Pael scrunched his brow and then nodded as his eyes opened wide. He slowed his horse even more to an easy walk. "I mean, it doesn't matter so much now. But, she asked if you'd take the front lines against quelling the untethered problem. Undoubtedly important."

"Not as important as saving Mellyr," Lin interjected.

"Which is why he said it doesn't matter now. It's clear swaying you from the course you're on now is something better left to the Gods than two old men," Denro said from Lin's left.

"Right." Lin's cheeks flushed. As pleasant as the conversation had been, a part of him still resented them. Denro, for the past few months of indifference, Pael for firing a bolt aimed at Mellyr. Each was a splinter under his skin, keeping him on edge. Keeping him ready to snap and bite.

Pael spat off to the side. "So doesn't matter now. But, depending on how things go up north, you might be asked to help with that."

Lin stared down at the reins in his hands. "Denro. Do you know anything about the untethering process? Anything you might've gleaned from your time in the Tower?"

A short exhale, then Denro was staring at the sky. "I wish. I've spent most of my life hunting them. Over the last decade, the problem has only grown. And it makes me wonder where the fault lies. It may seem like the sightings and attacks have grown worse since the shift in power at the Ferrucium. But if I'm being honest? I'd wager these things have been escalating long before the Fall."

They crested the top of the hill the road cut across, and Lin's breath caught. Water, still and shining with the stars, stretched far until another hill met its furthest border.

"Wakewatch Lake." Denro's voice brought Lin's attention back. "Used to be an outpost atop that far hill." He squinted. "Might still be there."

"Wakewatch itself, on the southern part of the lake." Pael pointed down at the city. It looked quiet and dim, which made sense, given the late hour.

"What if... what if there is nothing that can be done to stop the spreading untethered problem?" Lin asked. "What if Danicans, trained or not, will all eventually go mad?"

"You ask me," Pael started. "I think it's the Ladricans. The Northern Kingdom. Who stands to gain the most if Danicans are constantly attacking each other?" Pael spat off to the side, whatever dark glob he was sucking on still tucked against his lip.

"The Accords don't allow for Ladrican intervention on that sort of scale," Denro said.

"But they allow for testing? For them to take Danicans and turn them into weapons like Noosemen?" Lin countered.

"Not... necessarily."

"So there are Accords in place, meant to define when and how we let them tickle our sacks?" Pael grumbled the question out, apparent news to him.

"No," Denro whispered, but his tone seemed like that of a defeated, tired man.

"Somewhat. But what you're suggesting makes some sense. Think, if there is no one left to overwatch, who would this land go to? The Accords might be a noose around Danica's throat, but it also tied Ladrica's hands in a way. There was no way for them to fully encroach on our border, our land, without breaking the Accords."

No one spoke for a long time, the weight of the suggestion heavier than Lin first thought when speaking.

"They wanted this war. Resources, maybe?" Denro asked.

"Danica is nothing if not bountiful land. Good harvests, forests, all of it. Not that Ladrica is bare, but the winters are harsh," Pael said.

But as much as it made sense that land might be King Lodram's incentive, more so was the fact that they might view the people themselves as resources. Like how High Scholar Anya was able to use a vial of Danican blood to form a Binding.

"Stop the horses," Lin said, stopping Nebra at the plateau of the hill. Denro and Pael had continued for a moment before seeing that Lin was serious. While they turned back, Lin dismounted on the opposite side and shifted the book from his waist to the saddle bag.

"If you wanted to piss from the highest vantage, the outpost up there would've made for a better view," Pael spoke, finally spitting out the wad of dark mossy-looking gunk he'd been nursing near his lip.

"That's not it." Lin wanted to tell them about the blood vial before it slipped his mind again. "All this talk about resources reminded me of something High Scholar Anya showed me. So Pael, you can't see Wievings."

"Couldn't see them even if you still called them Bindings," the man cackled. He dismounted, stretched, and pulled his cloak closer around his shoulders. "But, if I'm paying attention, I can feel the hum of them. Like a beast's growl."

"Right. And you've tried to work the magic?"

"Where are you going with this?" Denro was the last to arrive and seemed to stiffen at the mention of the High scholar.

"Can't say I have," Pael said.

"Most Danicans can. If not all with the right coaching," Lin said.

Pael sucked his teeth and turned to stare out over the lake.

"Full-blooded ones can," Denro said softly.

Pael scratched his stubbled chin and shook his head. "Might not be. Duccal families weren't necessarily chosen for their strong roots. Might be part Belanian, if we dug far enough back."

"One of the Free Nations?" Lin asked.

"Mother's side, way back. Doesn't mean I'm not Danican through and through," Pael said, eyeing Denro and Lin skeptically. "I've done more—"

"That wasn't where I was going with this. No one is impeaching how much you've given this land, these people. What I'm getting at..." Lin formed a Weft.

Alone, atop the hill, it seemed like starlight itself had formed into a blade. Locked away in the tower, unaware that he couldn't work the magic had left him eager to make Weft after Weft. Or find a way to Inlay himself so that his power could never be secreted away from him again. But those thoughts were just as bad as the moments he'd lost in the tower, mind drifting from point to point.

"Is what?" Denro whispered. He'd dismounted and had a hand cautiously outstretched toward Lin.

"I… What… Pael come here and cup your hand under my arm."

"Why?"

"Just do it," Lin snapped. He hadn't meant to, but Gods, he'd lost himself again. Just slightly, but not even in thought. A whole section of time seemed missing from his mind. Denro had been atop his horse one second and the next he'd been beside Lin whispering. The Weft shimmered, edge sharp. Lin clutched it like a knife, held to the flesh of his forearm. He twisted his arm so that the Inlay along the top of it wouldn't spark against the blade of light.

Pael moved slowly but cupped both hands under Lin's elbow.

Lin slashed, quick and shallow. The blood trickled down Lin's arm, warm and wet. It was enough for Pael's hands to fill before Lin shattered his Weft into motes of light, and Lin pressed the wound with his sleeve.

"I'm no stranger to bloody hands, but care to tell me what to do now?"

Wind blew hard and sent ripples across the wide lake below. Denro moved closer, brow furrowed and head cocked at an angle.

Lin licked his lips, applying more pressure to the cut. "Feel the hum, here. Then Wieve." He pointed above Pael's navel, where the spul was alleged to reside.

"If he can't, then it's not possible," Denro said.

But it was. Lin had watched Anya do it. And while Fentis was a city more than a country, and it rested on Danican soil, the scholars not from the Ferrucium were not Danican. And even if they were, Anya certainly wasn't.

Pael frowned, clenched his jaw as if straining to lift something heavy, then smiled as a thread of light materialized. It was thin and delicate and fluttered away with the wind. "D-Did I do something? It felt like I did something." An uncharacteristic giddiness sounded in the man's voice and his face lit like a child's might.

"Yes," Lin and Denro said simultaneously.

The thread floated further away, shifting like a snake might swim underwater until it was wholly gone from view. Pael shifted and let what remained of the blood drip from his hands. He'd lost some between his fingers already, but it looked like even less remained. Slender tendrils of steam drifted up from his hands as if the blood had evaporated.

"The resources are... us?" Denro sounded mournful.

"Anya showed me with a vial of blood. Stoppered and sealed. It let her form a Weave. In all the confusion I'd forgotten to mention it. But it's the only thing that makes sense. King Lodram doesn't want land. Doesn't want any of our mines, lakes, or forests. He wants our people. Think of the Noosemen. Danicans taken."

"No," Pael spat. "Like a farmer who forgets how important a cow is to getting milk. He and his want our *blood*."

Crushed Blood

"Let us base our decision then, not on their lack of violence, but on the chance for it. The inevitability. Given the numbers, given the leaders we've met with who are willing to concede that their people are a danger to themselves and others if left ungoverned, we have a chance to stem the bleeding before it begins. I say to you, as I have many times over, let not our fear of curtailing the unknown keep us from embracing the known. You've all now seen one of them, mind lost to their unusual magicks. And trust me, the monster saw all of you. Restrained only by the Gods-given metals bestowed on the land of Ladrica." Argument presented by Lord Pollan Strat, a representative of the Ladrican Kingdom, given at a conference to discuss the burgeoning conflict at the southern border of Ladrica.

Wakewatch bristled in the early morning breeze. They'd arrived before the sun rose and from the lakeside piers had been able to watch the shadow of the northeastern outpost stretch closer and closer across the rippling water. It wasn't half as lively as Fentis had appeared on even its slowest days, but where Wakewatch lacked the bustle of a port city, it had men and women moving about typical business. Less chaotic. Less frantic. The majority of the homes and buildings were low, one-story affairs that looked like they'd been built decades ago and upkept thoroughly.

Lin chewed on the slice of ham Denro had pushed his way. Remains of the plate the older man hadn't the stomach to finish. Any doubt that Denro hadn't known about Danican blood and magic washed away by the man's immediate reaction, and his pallor since.

Smiling as wide as Lin had ever seen him, Pael took a seat across from Lin. He held a scroll in his hand and tapped it against the table several times before nodding at Lin.

The place they'd found to sit was outdoors and despite the cool breeze from the lake made colder by the shadow of the Ferrucium outpost, it felt pleasant with the sun beaming down on them. It was a table along an uncovered patio on the outer section of the inn. Northern Danica didn't have many cities as large as this, aside from those the Dukes resided at, and even imagining a village like Lyre with an area like this was difficult.

Denro rubbed his eyes and leaned back with a sigh. "Good news?"

"Better than good news," Pael waggled his eyebrows. "Map."

Lin raised his brows at that. He'd used a map in his early days escorting, but he'd never bothered to get an updated one like what Erias had displayed across his desk.

Pael unrolled the vellum and laid a flat disc atop it.

"Hmm?" Lin narrowed his eyes.

"Compass too?" Denro asked, leaning forward.

Chewing paused as Lin copied Denro's posture. He'd heard of the small devices. Used to track direction. But he'd never seen one and hadn't felt like he ever needed one to know which way north was.

"So. The way I see it you need to get up here as quickly as possible." Pael shifted the compass and tapped his finger at the edge of the map. Mountainous terrain was depicted with crude lines and in a sprawling script the words, 'Vellia's Fingers', layered over it.

Before seeing the map, Lin thought he had an idea of how far it was to traverse. Danica itself wasn't large. Not compared to what he'd heard of Ladrica and some of the Free Nations over the last few months, but looking at it put into perspective made it feel like he'd already lost. He could ride Nebra until she broke and likely not get there before the ship did.

"This might be a stupid question…"

"No such thing," Denro said, clearing his throat.

"Yes there is," Pael chided, glowering toward Denro. "But ask and be judged."

Lin couldn't help the smile and pointed down to the chunk of Danica where Fentis was labeled. Dark lines blocked it off as if differentiating it from Danica proper. "How fast can ships actually go?"

"Depends. Is it manned to row, or are they trusting the winds? Are they pressing hard and fast or going leisurely? Course, they aren't like to have stopped the way we have, but for us, it's been necessary."

"To an extent."

Denro and Pael both nodded.

"Let's assume the worst, and they're traveling at the fastest pace they can manage," Lin said.

"I wish I could say. Really. Not enough experience. But fast enough to make me worry about you beating them there." Pael picked at his teeth and looked hungrily at the remnants of ham on the plate between Lin and Denro.

"Any ideas?" Lin looked at Denro.

Denro stared at the map as if he might be lost in the simple lines marking it. "If we barely stop after this, we might catch them. We'll need to cross the lake here, not go around. They'd have a ferry. And the horses might have a rough time of it."

Gods, in all the time Lin had known the man, he'd never looked so uncertain. Not even in that moment when he first spotted Lin covered in Inlays.

"I crossed one time from here..." Denro touched the expanse of a wooded area marked by thick pockets of trees near the northwest edge of the map and dragged his finger rightward along the page until he hit Townsbridge. "To here. And it took the better part of a week. With you strapped to my saddle, sick with fever, and barely stopping. For us to get there, it might be about the same if all goes well."

Lin nodded slowly. If Nebra lamed... No, he wouldn't let that happen. If he needed to let her rest, he'd run on foot the rest of the way. He'd managed a horse's pace on foot heading to the Ferrucium after Aemun had abandoned him. He could do it again. He wasn't even injured this time. All the wounds he'd endured since Lyre had healed. His shoulder was still stiff at times where the untethered had sunk its teeth in, but there wasn't a single piece of him still bandaged or bound.

"We can make it."

"We might be able to make it," Denro corrected.

"*You* might be able to make it," Pael pushed the compass to rest in front of Lin. "Me. Well, if you're crossing here, then I'll be going east." He traced his finger along the paths that stretched from Wakewatch to the Ferrucium. "No sense crossing just to double-back southward."

"So this is goodbye?" Lin looked up at the lithe man. Sitting there, hat pulled low over his brow, he looked even leaner than he had when they'd first met.

"Bah. Wasn't long enough ago that you wanted to punch me in the face. Don't get to act all sad that I'm leaving now."

"I still want to hit you. Just a little less so." Lin managed a smile and craned his neck to watch the city moving around them. Staying angry, as much as he enjoyed the man's company, proved a challenge. A soft smile crept up and stayed there as he watched the children running through the crowd. Likely picking pockets.

"Take the map and compass, and try not to get lost on the way up. I sent word ahead of me back in that other town, but I'll see if I can't drip honey into Grovetender's ears with my tongue."

Denro furrowed his brow in disgust, and all three of them froze.

"Not the finest mental image, but I stand by it. If I can get you any aid, I will. Thaw is coming. We're most susceptible to the northern passes. Or we were. Now, we need to have forces prepared to deal with the South as well. I'll be seeing you two. Lin, don't let the wrong thing stop you from doing the right thing. Denro, a pleasure to meet another old soldier in the game."

"Be safe," Denro said. A diplomatic farewell. But Lin could see it on his old mentor's face, that familiar look of respect, regret even in the deepest wrinkles around his eyes. Once Pael had left, slinked into the crowd, and become a shadow, Denro whispered, "You old fuck."

"Black kettle, pot calling?"

"He's got me on years. Now, we should be leaving as well. No clue when the ferry runs, and we may be waiting for a time if we don't head over now." Denro moved to stand, but Lin held his hand out placatingly.

"What if you didn't come with me?" Lin said softly, tapping the map. "You didn't want to in the first place. What if you didn't?"

Denro sunk back into his chair slowly. "You'd be alone."

"I'd be free... to do what I had to do without disappointing you."

They sat in the silence for so long that flies buzzed about the scraps of ham. A bell tolled through the streets, likely a signal for the ferry's departure.

"Remember when I said I wished you could be an emissary? What if you could?"

"We need to go," Denro pleaded. And they did. With time as close as it seemed to be, Lin couldn't afford a single delay. But Denro didn't need to make this trek any more than Lin needed to be among the scholars.

"You are a scholar. Maybe not a Fentian one, but you've got the mind of a learned man."

"And the heart of a fool," Denro said. He reached across the map and slipped his hand over Lin's.

"If there is one man in all of Danica that might convince them to abstain. Not to even fight with us... but to remain neutral, it is you.

And… and I feel so at fault for all of this. I've already lost you in spirit. Don't deny it. I can't lose you in battle. I can't tell you how terrified I was that you'd be among the dead at the Ferrucium."

A second bell tolled. He still needed to get Nebra from the stall Pael had left her. He didn't *have* the time for this, but he needed to get it off his chest. Denro took in heavy breaths and seemed to stare at the back of his hand. His fingers didn't grip. Gods, when had his hands grown so soft?

When Denro didn't find his words, Lin continued. "I am at fault for all of this. Aemun was… Aemun seemed to be a wicked man, but he had plans. Allies. Connections that his death cut away from Danica. Perhaps you can fix it."

"No man can control the outcome of lighting a blaze even if he stacks every stone and shears all the grass before striking a match. The wind might still blow an errant ember."

"And if I'm the ember?" Lin's voice didn't want to escape. A lump had started painfully at the base of his throat and seemed content to sit where his neck met his chest, choking him.

"Then be one that doesn't fear to burn." Denro squeezed his hand. It was a small act, barely more than a twitch of his fingers, but it meant the world. As much as any one of Mellyr's tiny squeezes.

Lin wiped his eyes with the back of his free hand and pulled away from Denro's grasp. He needed to leave at the first bell. He should have left by the second. If it rang a third time and he was still seated here, he didn't know that he'd ever move. "I'll burn it all down if

I have to. And when I arrive, soot-stained and ash-coated, will you promise to still recognize me?"

"I promise. But you need to promise me you'll bring that sweet child back, wholly herself."

Lin froze at that, then nodded. "I promise."

The bells were simply signaling the ferry's approach. It seemed a large ship for a lake, but Lin's frame of reference was understandably skewed. Binders didn't do boats. He'd always wondered at the superstition or perhaps the truth of it. The cynic in him thought that perhaps it was simply a way to keep Danicans capable of wielding their magic proficiently from traveling away from Danica.

As Lin leaned over the rail and a sense of unease rose from within him, he thought perhaps water truly did something to Binders. Wievers. He groaned and put his hands on his head. He still had a hard time picking one term over the other. His training and upbringing told him he was a Binder through and through. But his heart and rebellious spirit said that term was created to shackle him and his kind. He was a Wiever.

Leaving Denro had been hard. Even if they hadn't spoken like old times, even if they hadn't necessarily been close, it was Denro. And that wasn't even considering the truth about Lin's parents the man had revealed.

Lin stared out across the water toward the shrinking Wakewatch. Denro and maybe Pael were in that town and about to leave for very different reasons. Pael had a longer distance to travel but an easier task. From what the man had said, troops were already strengthening the northern border in preparation for the thaw.

But the real question was whether or not Erias or Azhura would send aid in rescuing Mellyr. Azhura likely would want to. She'd been none too pleased that Tylle told her she wouldn't have a thing to do with her great-grandchild. Erias was still an enigma. Lin shifted his chin so he could see the crimson ring that marked his Bludwieve. Erias seemed like he had Danica's best interests at heart, but he'd been played so easily by Aemun. They all had, though.

Denro's task was a bit harder. He was only days away from Fentis, but they likely would lock him away again. If there was a single man who might convince them toward peace, now that he seemed willing to try, it would be Denro.

On the way to the pier, they'd discussed what Denro might say. The Empire of Elodis seemed sympathetic to the Danican plight, at least according to documents discussing the creation and rectifications of the Accords. But that was ages ago. And Denro didn't know the first way to contact them.

Truth be told, Danica's hope rested solely on the other Free Nations deciding to let Danica and Ladrica resolve this themselves.

Lin swallowed back the queasy, greasy wave that rose through him and decided with his whole heart that Wievers weren't meant for water. Lin blinked several times and tried to focus on the land. It didn't feel like they were moving faster than a horse might run, but when they reached the dock on the other side and merchants began unloading before the sun even descended, Lin understood they must have been going far faster.

With a map, compass, and Nebra, Lin was ready. He felt for his spul. It seemed full. If he never had to eat the green paste the scholars had fed him again, he'd be a happy man. There had been an occasional fish, but as he looked back on it, the diet itself seemed to lack meat.

Lin looked back one last time, staring across the lake as if he might link eyes with Denro. He hated the man for letting Mellyr be tested. Loved the man for everything else. Sending him back might have been a mistake considering the Bound Metal tests and his lack of will to fight before they'd escaped, but Gods, Denro seemed sincere now. Lin just had to hope Denro remained the man Lin thought he was.

The sun, settling into a comfortable place just at the horizon, lit the book in Lin's hands. He hadn't wanted to pull it out around Denro and hadn't been able to look at it on the boat without his stomach insisting on painting the deck. But now he held it. The cover was smooth, the pages crisp as if flattened, pressed, and made seemingly unblemishable in the process.

Lin took Nebra to the main path, mounted her, and pressed her north. With the little bit of sun painting the air, he read. Luckily, the months spent with nothing to do but read or argue with a baby had prepared him for this. Danicans had trace metals in their blood. Most people did, actually, but Danicans somehow used that to fuel magic. Iron mostly. But there were other metals. Lin's stomach sank as if he were still on that boat. Gods. The author listed the tests done. The side-effects. Illness. Bleeding from pores. Death. Of course, death. Not all the metals had adverse side effects.

Some, in the right doses, granted other forms of Wievings. Lin licked his lips and flipped the page and was glad he hadn't given this to Denro. When a... this section of the book referred to them as Binders. When a Binder consumes and attempts to Bind with Bound Metal in their system, they enter a deep sleep. When they awake, *if* they awake, they no longer can draw on these trace metals from within. But forcing a Binder to draw it out from their spul seems nigh impossible, almost as if the strange metal has a mind of its own and doesn't *wish* to be drawn upon.

Reading that, Lin was suddenly thankful that the scholars had only altered his meals to remove the fuel for Wieving and hadn't introduced Bound Metal into his diet. Lin shuddered and, with the sun fully escaping the horizon, settled into the saddle. If the map was to be trusted, he had a long way to go.

Ceasing Hope

"Many might note the similarities in the names, Danica and Ladrica. This is due to the early Ladrican King, Jeof the Bountiful, staking claim of the land south of his own. Ladr, meaning woman but in the sense of their language referring to a mother or Queen. Ica, in the Ladrican tongue, means land, though as you might imaginc now there is more meaning than just the simple word usage. And it should be noted, that the Northern Kingdom doesn't recognize a woman's right to rule. But that is neither here nor there. Danica is then the "father" land. I should also note that in the earliest accounts, far removed from the time of the Accords, it was Dranica. A more literal definition being, Godsland. While it is exciting to speculate the meaning, King Jeof the Bountiful's steward clarified the name before his passing. Not because it is the land of Gods, but because King Jeof believed the land was granted to him by the Gods and it was his and his kin's right to rule." Excerpt from the Histories of Southern Danica, removed and redacted due to the Danican Accords.

Two things were missing as Lin rode Nebra past farmlands interrupted by the occasional patch of forest. Mellyr and Denro. Lin stretched in the saddle. Maybe it was just *one* thing. Family. Soon, Tylle might learn of Lin's failing if she was around when Pael found the Grovetender. She might not have wanted to raise the child, but she sure hadn't wanted her endangered. If he didn't die in the crazed rescue attempt, Tylle just might kill him. No. She likely wouldn't do that, not if she wanted him leading the force against the growing untethered problem. Lin frowned at that. It didn't make sense how things on that front were worsening. Unless the Ferrucium truly had kept the monsters in check.

Lin chewed at the inside of his mouth and stared up at the darkening sky. Storm clouds swelled on the northern horizon like gray blisters waiting to burst. With any luck, those same storms might slow the ship.

Days of eating a Binder's diet and riding on the roads at a good pace unmolested had Lin brimming with energy. Brimming with trace metals. Lin didn't like the thought of it. Magic fueled by blood. His blood.

One passage he'd read stayed with him, playing through his head over and over. Of the metals tested and ingested, zinc and copper in high doses seemed to affect the most change in the subjects. Copper-fueled Wievings gave off a green-hued glow to those with the Sight and kept things from decaying. Zinc-fueled appeared as a crystalline blue glow and aided in healing. But the scholar penning the book never tested it on an untethered. Not once the individual was wholly lost to the madness.

Lin let his arms drop. Somewhere within him was his spul. He felt it, centered near his chest like a knot of energy with threads waiting to be unraveled. Pulling from it, he formed a Weave. Over and over, try as he might to produce a green or blue thread, he failed.

A shudder twitched Lin's arms and he looked around. Despite Inlaying himself. Despite all that he'd done leading up to the Fall, playing at ripping forth this magic felt *wrong*. But how right had forming Bindings first felt when he was a child learning? The uneasiness wasn't helped by the chill wind intent on rattling his bones. The thaw might be happening soon, but as far as the weather was concerned winter still grasped tight to the middle band of Danica.

"I need a cloak," he said as he huddled down to Nebra. Perhaps he'd just practice at the other magics during the day when the sun could warm his soul a bit. Luckily, they kept each other warm through riding and the only wounds he had this time were to his pride and heart. It would be Danica against the world. Unless they had a way of proving they weren't a threat or that Ladrica was breaking the Accords and couldn't be trusted as warden anymore.

Before the sun fully fell, he spotted distant lantern light. Based on their pace, he'd make it before nightfall. Smoke curled up in long, lazy stacks, and even as far away as he was, the scent of spiced meat hung in the air like a banner waving its colors proudly.

"Think they'll have us?" Lin asked Nebra. Her ear twitched. "I hope so too," he said softer, stroking her neck before running his fingers along the coarse ends of her mane. He needed to redo the plaits he'd done months ago. And give her a good scrub. This was the closest they'd been to riding hard and alone like he'd promised her during the chaos after Lyre. Even now he had to keep her from exhausting herself too soon.

Lin beat his approximation by a breath, the sun's dying light painting the trees around the village with a light touch. *Drekinsburg?* Lin frowned. The name sounded familiar. He itched his chin, the scratch of his thin beard loud in the surrounding silence.

He'd managed to keep clean-shaven in the Tower. More for Mellyr than himself, but now back on the road it seemed his face was doing its best to catch up to Denro's.

"Hold," a young man's voice carried.

Nebra slowed at Lin's gentle tug to her reins and Lin scanned the path ahead under the sign. Normally once he got this far north, the villages were surrounded by short, knee-high walls. Aged stone, worn and gray, lined the bottoms of the wall but there were fresh stones stacked atop, less weathered with sharper angles. And peeking out behind the stone were sharpened wooden spikes. Perhaps they'd been trees at one point as thick as they looked.

"Greetings."

"Greet yourself," the young man said, peering out from a platform higher than the wooden stakes and stone wall.

Seems I did. Spending so much time with the scholars, he'd become used to apathy. Cold, but not outright rude.

"Gates are closed at night," the young man said once Lin hadn't moved.

Lin frowned. There wasn't a gate. Just a path, with a barricade of some sort and a platform just behind it. He didn't need to stop in town, but the smell of that meat had caught his attention and he'd hoped he might procure a thick enough cloak if he stopped here.

A bell tolled and another. Then, like the shout of a dying moose, a horn bellowed through the air. Nebra kept calm, as any Ferrucium-trained mount might, but the young man visibly paled. He'd stuck his head a bit over the wall to get a better look at Lin but quickly backed up. He couldn't have been older than fourteen passings.

"What are the alarms for?" Lin asked.

"Get back!" Wood dragged and in a blink, a metal-tipped spear caught the lantern light, not far from Lin's face.

Lin raised his hands. Shouts and screams and *rust*. The scent of rust danced under the mouth-watering spices that cloyed the air. "Untethered?"

The spear tip lowered enough that Lin could see the fear on the young man's face. He needed to save Mellyr. But if he thought he'd had time to eat and find a cloak, he had time to save these people. Flashes of Fallo still haunted his sleep when his dreams didn't consist of him being beaten and smelted into a dagger. That particular dream hadn't gone away, but it had become less frequent.

Waiting for an answer from the terrified young man wouldn't do Lin any good. He slid from Nebra. Moving without his cloak and blade felt strange, even though it had been months since he last wore them. But without them, he was quicker. The clothes he wore weren't tailored and hung off him awkwardly. He'd tied twine around his waist to keep the pants from sliding down days ago in place of a belt.

"Stay near my horse, she'll keep you safe," Lin shouted as he vaulted the barricade, mantling the spikes with ease. It sounded like a ridiculous statement, but it was true. Nebra might not have been able to outpace a Nooseman flying from tree to tree as they fled Wellgrove, but she'd never be taken down by crazed untethered. At least, that's what he had to tell himself. Fallo never was far from his mind and those monsters had been brutal. *They'd laid traps.*

And then he recalled why Drekinsburg sounded familiar. The man he'd pulled out of the river. Untethered had attacked this place already. Months ago. And they were back.

The alarms continued but most of the shouting came from the north side of the village where the smoke was the thickest.

It felt good to run, even if it was to a potentially terrible scene. But as Lin pressed through the well-worn paths, off the bricked main road, he was surprised to notice the number of armed individuals holding the perimeter.

Ochre Wefts more brittle looking than dried reeds flew through the air. One woman, old enough to have been born the same year as Denro, whistled two short bursts and waved a bright scarlet flag in two short horizontal swings. An arrow crashed into the Weft and burst into sparks. Another sickly Weft sliced over the broken wall and the woman whistled again. Her makeshift flag sliced the air horizontally, then vertically.

Whatever system they were using worked. The woman leading it all likely had the Sight, and they had prearranged tactics to deal with the longer-ranged attacks from the darkness.

When Wefts weren't flying, she squinted, whistled, and swung the flag. Archers loosed arrows into the trees.

There was no movement in the woods, no reply sent in a dinghy Weft. As Lin approached and several of the armed individuals turned to him, he raised his hands. The woman whipped around, eyes going wide as she took him in.

Never had he heard a whistle that sounded so much like a declaration of death. Her aged face showed fear and fury in equal measure.

Lin broke the two arrows that would've taken him in the chest with a well-placed Weft. "I'm not untethered!"

The second whistle died at her lips. A sharp tweet sounded as a Weft took her in the shoulder from behind, spinning her as she collapsed on the platform. A younger boy who had been standing just on her other side didn't move to help her. Instead, he took the makeshift flag from her grip and faced the woods. The boy whistled. Not as crisp as the woman's had been and his flag movements were tremulous, but he directed arrows at oncoming Wefts all the same.

"Has the One Shadow granted you a tongue, monster?" A lithe man, all thin corded muscle and shaggy hair asked. He held a blade that looked suspiciously like Ferrucium steel. And he held it like he knew how to use it.

"Let me help."

"The last ones to come help were Ferrucium and they didn't last long."

Lin tsked. "You've got a system in place. But if those untethered can think..."

"Those monsters don't think. They kill and rip and—"

"All the more reason to trust me then. How many surround you?" There wasn't time to sit here and debate the man, but he also couldn't walk past and not expect a blade in his back for the trouble.

"Always seven. Manage to kill one and the next time they attack it's seven again." The man turned, sweat covering him despite the cool air from the north.

"Tell the boy," Lin looked to the platform where the boy had steeled his nerves and rid his movements of the shaky, hesitant jerks. "Not to signal at me. Please. And see that the woman gets aide."

"Gran will be fine. Not the first bit of magic that's bit her flesh. And I'll tell Irvin." The man didn't take his eyes off Lin but shifted aside and gestured at the other men to do the same.

Lin moved faster than he had in a long time. This was what he'd dreamt of when he was told he'd be a soldier. Saving others. He bounded the wall in one leap, scanning the sharpened spears as he did. A body or two rested unmoving among the stones and wood. *Kill one and another replaces it.* What if Lin killed all seven of the attackers? Would seven more really come back in a mindless attempt to take this town?

There wasn't a forest surrounding Drekinsburg. Instead, it was more like sparse, scattered trees similar to the stretches of the hill-lands southeast of Wellgrove. Except with more brush, thick and scratchy. A ravine cut a cliff into the land yards ahead and flashes of Stitched flesh blurred on that elevated ground.

Like a spider dropping from a web, an untethered landed in front of Lin. They fell into a crouch jerking like a corpse controlled by a puppeteer. Even in the dim light of the lanterns, their flaking flesh and stringy brittle hair marked them truly untethered.

Brush rustled as two more approached from Lin's right.

Hesitation meant death. Lin knew that. But Gods, what if these people had been like him once? The scraps of cloth they wore could have been Ferrucium cloaks.

Rust-colored Wefts ate the air between him and the approaching untethered at his side.

Lin unraveled them with a thought, shattering the magic and sending out a long sweeping counterattack. His Weft, brightly pure in the darkness, caught both of them in the temple as they ducked to avoid it. They wore Inlays, far uglier and asymmetrical than what Lin possessed, but those did little good when Lin's magic touched their flesh. He turned to face the one in front of them, not looking when the sound of corpses crashed into the brush feet from him.

The untethered in front of him launched at his throat like a cornered animal, dirty cracked nails scraping at the air and sending out wisps of magic as they did. A whistle shrilled from the town's edge and more arrows flew into the darkness around him. He tensed, waiting for an errant arrow to take him in between his shoulders. Thuds sounded all around, each one causing Lin to flinch slightly.

Dodging the creature was easy. He'd replayed the fights with Noosemen over in his head, thinking of the few clashes where he'd been out-skilled. Untethered were like untrained children with dull knives compared to them. But that wasn't entirely true. Even if they'd been unprepared, he struggled to picture Fallo falling to monsters like this.

Lin stepped in as the untethered overextended. The creature smelled like rancid meat and, of course, rust. A blade of light erupted in the darkness, as Lin stabbed the untethered's chest. The monster reached sad, grasping hands out toward him. Growls and nonsense escaped dry cracked lips.

Three.

Skittering sounds carried through the underbrush. Two pairs of steps, far quicker than the rest. Lin braced himself, turning to face the source.

The pair of untethered moved in tandem, erupting at waist level from Lin's left.

Lin leveled his blade and froze. His gut twisted on itself as he saw the soft features, leaned out by whatever harsh circumstance had created them. Both the untethered were only as tall as his hip. *Children?*

Together, they moved preternaturally quickly. One was on him in an instant. Weft after Weft slashed up at him, broken as quickly as they were formed. But Gods. Lin pushed down the sickness. He'd pray for forgiveness later. He'd have to. They couldn't have been older than Roge. Covered head to toe in some of the most intricate Inlays Lin had ever seen. Each band of light seemed to start at their navel, expanding out on them in eight different directions across their torso and down their arms and legs. And of course, they bore a single, crimson band around their left-hand ring finger. Lin narrowed his eyes. Across their throats, at the base of their clavicles, was Velkath's Sigil. Stitched into their flesh.

Foot by foot, Lin was forced back. "D-do you speak?"

Throaty, pitched growls escaped both of them.

"Damn it. Damn you!" Lin spat.

One circled him and attempted to grab his knees in a tackle of sorts. Lin pivoted and brought his knee up at the untethered—they were untethered *not* children— and struck it in the face. Sharp teeth dug into the meat of his thigh and the other one jumped on him. Whether they'd been capable of it before seeing Lin's or they'd mirrored Lin's blade didn't matter. The little fuck had created a Binding Blade. Shorter than Lin's, but the edge and tip shone just as deadly.

Lin spun, the untethered biting him hanging on and spinning with him. Their hands raked through the fabric of his trousers, leaving warm streaks of irritated flesh. His blade caught the other untethered's and clashed for a moment before shattering the monster's Binding and taking their head in the process. Without hesitation, Lin stabbed down through the top of the other monster's head. Its jaw went slack as it collapsed.

"Just... mindless monsters," Lin exhaled.

A horn bellowed through the night air. On the ridge of the ravine, wrapped in Stitches that glowed as bright as a full moon, stood a lone untethered. They held a ram's horn in their hand and seemed to wear a headdress. Green-hued bindings and bones, worn like a crown. Lin shuddered.

It makes six. Unless they'd already killed one. But instead of pressing the attack, the untethered turned, back just as bright as their front had been, and walked away. Lin grimaced as he stepped forward, the wound at his thigh throbbing with the pressure. Lin lowered his hand and dug within for his spul. Searching for some other thread than the one that came readily to his fingertips. He imaged the crystalline blue described in the book, wishing it into existence to quell the pain throbbing through his thigh. Something was there, alongside his "iron" threads. Like a darting fish, unwilling to be caught. Every time it felt he got close, it slid away from his grasp.

Lin frowned, empty-handed, and decided to limp back. Giving chase with a sore leg wouldn't be a smart decision. And there had been something about the way that untethered on the ridge had held themselves. *Confident.*

When he reached the wall, bits of it now broken, he was surprised to see the people surrounding the town already rebuilding it. He'd doubted the strength of the walls and their spikes initially, but clearly, it did enough to delay the untethered.

"How many?" Lin asked the first person he came across. A thin woman with more bones than meat on them. She was clearing stones and broken wood with all the rest of them.

She looked toward the platform and nodded at the young man and old woman atop it. Gran and Irvin.

Lin grunted and moved through the crowd, made easier by the villagers actively moving away from him. Two men stepped in front to keep him from climbing the platform but Irvin waved them away.

"How many untethered did you kill before I got here?" Lin asked.

"One," Gran said. Her voice was like the sound of wind blowing against the cliffs of Fentis. "At least one always dies taking down the wall. How many did you get?" Gran straightened her back and slid the edge of her top down. She already wore bandages along her torso and back, but grimaced as a fresh cloth was pressed to the wound across her shoulder. It seemed she struggled to move that arm now and having taken a similar injury not long ago, he understood why.

"Five."

Gran's eyebrows went up and she turned as if Irvin might contradict what Lin had said.

"Five," Irvin confirmed. "You're one of the Duke's Web?"

Lin snorted. "Gods, no. But I've met them. Helped them once. I'm heading north but hoped..." Lin winced as he put too much pressure on his left leg. "Hoped to buy some supplies and a cloak for the cold."

"As much help as you've given us, we'll give you the damned cloak. And have a physiker take a look at your leg."

Lin smiled and leaned against the edge of the platform, the thin rail complaining at his weight. He could Stitch his wound closed. That wouldn't be a problem, but he was sure the magic didn't defeat infections and a bite from one of those twisted One-loved monsters was more likely to get infected than even a blade wound.

"I appreciate any help you can give. How long have you been defending yourselves?"

"Months," Irvin said. "We had a nasty attack six months ago that we almost didn't make it back from. Lost too many good people. But some of us... most matter of fact... came from the surrounding steads. Just not safe enough to be out there alone." The way he spoke implied he'd been one of the ones to come to Drekinsburg but after this conflict, no one came to stand beside him.

"Y'all have done better than other villages I've seen. But the Ferrucium is working on this."

"They've been working on it. Just keeps getting worse and worse," Gran said. She'd shifted back into her tunic, her hair in a tight, gray bun.

Lin nodded. "Now that they're working with the Dukes, it should get better."

"No offense, on account of you helping us, but I doubt it." Irvin shrugged as he spoke, then stared into the distance where the untethered had walked away. To be so young and so full of doubt had to be hard.

Lin followed his stare. "Does that one always blow the horn?"

"He seems to lead them," Gran said. "They send a messenger. Ask for an offering. And when they don't get it, they attack. If you'll excuse me, I've got some tea to drink and some sleep to get. Irvin, take him to the physiker, please."

Lin paled. Surely the woman was messing with him. To think that the untethered might send a messenger, might ask for an offering? That was unheard of. Lin shuddered.

"You saw them?" Irvin asked as she walked away.

"Them?"

"The children," Irvin clarified.

Lin met the young man's eyes. "Killed them."

Irvin's eyes watered and he gave a single, defeated nod. "I saw them approach with the first one that attacked the wall. I'd put my life on it. They were twins near my pa's stead. Neighbors."

"Anyone can untether," Lin said. It was a truth he hadn't been forced to consider in a while, but it was true. But those children hadn't simply gone mad. They'd Inlayed their flesh and had some sort of training. They bore Velkath's Sigil and of all the untethered, he'd never seen that before. Hadn't seen one with a crown before either though. Lin shuddered again, eager to get ahold of the cloak they planned to give him.

Ceasing Bone

"Taking agency from the tribes and pockets of people across Danica is akin to killing kings and sundering democracies. How can any of us in good conscience say that stripping freedoms and the right of self-governance from a people we know so little about is the right thing to do?" Excerpt taken from the counter speech given by Speaker Pat Miche, from the Empire of Elodis.

Leaving Drekinsburg felt wrong. Lin knew he didn't have the time to stay and ensure that the untethered assault ended once and for all, but abandoning them to fend for themselves didn't sit well on his heart. Still, they'd managed until now. Even bouncing back after that initial devastation he'd heard about. At least that's what he told himself as he left the walled town behind. They'd survive. Their system seemed as good as it might get. At least until the untethered found a way to break through the walls. Or if they attacked in greater numbers.

As wrong as it felt, leaving was what he did, with a pack full of salted meat, a handful of fruits, and a hand-me-down cloak that seemed two sizes too large, but matched his other clothes the better for it.

The physiker had treated his thigh easily, smearing a poultice over the wound and swathing it with a tight bandage shortly after his talk with Irvin. More than anyone else he'd spoken to there, he felt most bad for that kid.

Sure, at his age, Lin had been years deep in his training at the Ferrucium, but that had been different. Or at least, it seemed different. Irvin was forced into his role. Denro had done a good job of making it feel like being a Ferrucium soldier had been a choice even if it hadn't. Especially considering it hadn't.

Try as he might, no memory of his time before the Ferrucium would come to him. Not his parents, their faces, or the sounds of their voices. If he never saw Mellyr again, she likely wouldn't remember him either. And more than the subtle pain of not recalling his parents, knowing she'd never even think of him stabbed at his heart. He wasn't the guardian she deserved. Deep down he knew that. He'd failed Margaret. He... Lin sighed. He'd helped kill her father and someday, once he did rescue Mellyr from the Ladrican fucks who'd taken her, he'd have to have that conversation with her. Holding it in like the truth Denro had held from him... it wasn't something Lin would do.

Lin licked his lips and stared at the clouds still forming on the horizon. Dark and roiling, like all the shadows in the world were trapped in them, struggling to escape. As warm as the thick oversized cloak was, the material wasn't rainproof and if Lin was caught out in the storm, he'd soak.

Before nightfall, the storm was on him. Cover had been nonexistent, caught on the main road as he'd been and the wind howled while the sheets of rain slammed down. Nebra, never much of a complainer, quickly made her discontent clear. A flash of lightning illuminated a pair of trees just over the nearest hill.

Lin steered Nebra and soon they were under the sprawling branches. The nearest ones were low and wide, the sort of tree he'd always dreamed of climbing when he was younger. Admittedly, not the best cover, but more than the open road would offer. The two trees looked like they were stuck in a struggle for the hill, branches intertwined near the center, massive trunks pressed together as if they might push the other away.

Ancient as they seemed, the trunks and branches were large and knotted. An old war then.

Lin shivered and huddled closer to Nebra. The wind pelted the rain sideways, but despite the massive trees both missing foliage, the breadth of the branches kept the worst of the rain from bludgeoning them. If it was any colder or he'd made it further north, he wouldn't have been surprised to see snow. Even if they were worried about the thaw's quick approach, that didn't mean winter might not keep its grip on the area longer than it seemed.

Rivers of rain ran down the bark puddling into a hallow between the two trees. Lin realized they were dead. Or dying. Maybe not both of them, if the other had died soon enough. But they'd likely killed each other in their struggle. Nebra stomped the ground and nickered, her ears swiveling for the source of whatever sound she'd heard.

"Shhh, we're fine now." Lin moved around the tree, staring at the roots. He hoped for honeycaps, even if the area wasn't nearly as humid as the things preferred for growth.

Corpse seeds, three of them, budded from the muck at the base of the wider-trunked tree. The smell still stung like rotten meat, but his mouth watered at the thought of the sweetly sour juice the fleshy fruit offered.

"You know, I missed you. Someday, you, me, and Mellyr might ride together. Not chasing after something stolen, or in a rush, but just to ride. You'd like that wouldn't you?"

Nebra's tail swished irritatedly from left to right, more due to the rain than Lin's words. He pressed open one corpse seed and placed the other two in the packs on the saddle. White had begun staining the coat near her face. Like Denro, age was getting the better of her. When the time came, no matter what, he'd give her a proper pyre. One deserving of her.

Lin shook his head as if the simple action might shoo away such sad thoughts from his mind. "I still wish there was a magic that would allow me to speak with you."

Her big brown eyes seemed to lock onto his for a moment, then she nuzzled his hands and her searching tongue licked at the juices he hadn't wiped away yet.

"Do you actually like that? I suppose you do like apples." Though corpse seeds were far sourer than even the bright green apples he'd tried once.

Overhead, the storm continued. The thinnest branches above rattled with the wind and must have formed a funnel of some sort as a low, throaty growling came from their highest reaches.

Lin squinted up, blinking as droplets struck his face. It took several steps to round the trunk and find the origin of the noise. He froze, eyes fixed on the dull, ochre Inlays marking the flesh of a ragged, mud-stained untethered.

The untethered dropped in a blur of gangly ashen limbs and intricate Inlays interrupted by crude Stitches. Low guttural noises escaped it, as if it tried to speak but its thin cracked lips couldn't form the words. Clumps of hair hung to their scalp but like most untethered Lin had encountered they seemed to express the worst of a Binder's ailments.

Which, according to the book Lin had taken to reading during the day, was from the excess metals in their blood. And in some cases, the lack of metals. But this untethered, as dangerous as it looked with its brittle cracked nails and expressionless, groaning face, wasn't attacking him. They reached a single, shaky hand out toward Lin as if touching him might set their hand ablaze. A bludwieve caught his eye. Why was it that nearly every one of those One-loved creatures had one?

Lin lashed out, knocking the monster's arm away with a wild swing and following it up with a Weave for each limb, sticking the untethered to the wide trunk of the tree. The bands of magic sparked and clashed against the creature's flesh, but they held in place.

The thing strained against the magic, wrists twisting and cracking. Its face distorted as it growled and hissed.

Killing it would be easy. A Blade or Weft across the throat. Quick and painless. But what if this was the chance he needed to better understand the other magics allegedly within him? He'd felt something when he'd reached for what the book named, zinc. Whatever this monster had come to these two dying trees for, it seemed a blessing of a sort. *Or a curse.*

Struggling weakly, the untethered was like a bird with a broken wing that didn't understand what once gave it flight had become a hindrance.

Nebra nickered off to the side and Lin scanned the area. The monster's presence made her uneasy. It made him uncomfortable simply staring at the wet, ill-looking creature. Inlays and stitches covered the monster from head-to-toe and its dirty rags hung from it like sloughed flesh.

Lin calmed and thought back to the way they'd trained him to draw on Bindings. Back then, he hadn't even known of the spul. Reach within. Place intention into the world. Even recently he'd still had to use a focus. All sorts of different chains to keep Binders in line and weak. But... what if it was a necessary part of understanding the magic?

"Gods, forgive me," Lin said, steeling himself. He formed a Weft, the golden arc of it splitting the gray flesh of the monster's forearm. It bled a dark brown ichor more like syrup and jostled against the tree with more vigor. A scream tore from the thing's throat.

Stitches could close the wound imperfectly. Flesh puckered and irritated compared to the notes in the book. When all he had was an invisible knot of magic, how was he meant to differentiate it? Lin closed his eyes and focused, starting from the first step of what he was taught as a child.

Form a focus. Thread your intention.

With the dappling rain and the growling untethered just inches away smelling of rancid meat and saccharine rust, keeping his focus proved a challenge. But if he could Inlay his flesh in a wagon, he could reach within himself.

On the tenth try, his chest numbed, right above his navel and the sensation spread to his fingertips. A translucent azure string coated the seeping wound on the untethered's arm. Lin hadn't directed the magic, but it pulled to the injury the way Wievings were to Bound Metal.

And the injury closed. Flesh mending without scar. It looked like a thin, flat Weave, crystalline blue.

Lin's stomach twisted as his hands trembled. He'd done it. Pulled at a different thread within. But he couldn't be sure exactly how. Couldn't replicate it.

"I'm sorry," Lin said, slicing the untethered again. Six failures at pulling out the stubborn magic.

On the seventh attempt, the wound sealed. Taking notes wasn't possible, and even if it were he doubted he would. He wasn't a monster like those who had tested on actual people, he didn't need to record any of this for future Wievers.

Lin drew his Weft across the creature's other arm. Finally, mercifully, as the storm scattered above leaving only cold air and disparate droplets, Lin *felt* the difference.

If traces of zinc were what he pulled on from within, it was more malleable than a traditional Wieving. Easier to slip from his grasp and that was why it felt so untouchable in the first place. As if that sort of magic was a fish and he was trying to catch it bare-handed in a river. But in truth, it was there, just under the current of his blood waiting to be caught. At least for now, it seemed a focus was absolutely necessary, lest the magic evade him.

Gnashing teeth and groaning, the untethered continued to struggle against its magic bindings, but the Weaves wouldn't break and the tree, as dead as the corpse seeds implied, wasn't giving.

Lin squinted up through the branches at the clouds and licked his lips. He tasted iron and when he pulled away an inquisitive finger, he noted his nose trickled blood.

"One left," he whispered. Nebra had wandered off. Not far enough to cause worry, but she'd taken to some dead grass near a wide puddle of water that reflected the starry night in its ruined, rippled surface.

His Weaves weren't likely to break, but he reinforced them anyway. With the rain letting up he felt rushed, as if the blowing wind itself whispered the urgency of his task. He should be on the road, not testing strange magics he barely understood on an untethered. But if any of this could be used as a weapon, he needed it.

Lin sought copper within him like he had the other magic. If the thread of power fueled by zinc was a fish waiting in the water, copper was the hardened seed in his blood eager to bloom. He formed a focus and stared through the circle he made with his thumb and forefinger.

A weariness began weighing on his limbs and as he stared through the focus he made, it was hard to keep his hand from trembling.

A sickly green Weft crackled into existence at his third attempt.

If Wanderer's Ore did damage a person's vision, Lin only imagined how poor his eyesight would be after looking at the flickering shade of ghostly green he'd conjured. His stomach knotted tight, but he brought the Weft to the side of the untethered's face, near its temple.

Like a thorn, it pierced into the gray, rash-patched flesh. No. It didn't pierce, it *planted*. Embedding itself under the surface. It crawled along the bone of the thing's temple, wriggling under the skin like a grub under the bark.

As sick as it looked, Lin felt he understood. This magic was described as stopping decay. And what was more decayed on an untethered than their mind? Tylle had touched her brow once and mentioned working Inlays to strengthen more ephemeral aspects. She hadn't mentioned the ghastly glow. But she didn't have the Sight like he did.

"K-ek-i..."

Lin jerked his hand back. It wasn't a word. But it was the closest thing he'd heard from the brain-addled monster.

"Keh-ell..."

The string of sounds almost sounded like a name. Did this untethered remember its name? Lin shuddered and took a step backward, stumbling on a root but righting himself before he could fall. He'd done this... but why did it fill him with so much dread?

"Keh-ell-me."

"Kill you?" Lin whispered.

"Puh-leee-suh." The word dragged out as if buried under years of rust and ruin. There was pain in the request and sorrow but above all of that, unbridled animalistic rage. This was a glimpse beyond the veil of madness that all untethered seemed steeped in. And the person underneath wanted to die. Gods. What if they were always there, just under the surface? He pushed the thought down with all the other things he didn't feel he had time to think back on. Maybe if he reached Denro's age he might come to terms with some of it. Maybe.

Lin studied the jittering, clenching jaw of the untethered. Underneath the grime were soft features. Likely this had been someone's lover, mother, or rival. Fresh streaks of tears made muddy tracks down their cheeks, but it didn't wash away the gray skin, cracking lips, or snarl that twisted free of both.

With a wave of his hand, heavy from the damp, draping cloak, Lin broke the Weaves keeping the creature to the tree.

The monster lunged forward, hands clawing at the air, Wefts stained the color of dried dirt following in the wake of the motion. Lin caught them as they jumped. He wrapped his arms around the untethered as if to embrace an old friend. He conjured a Needle. Golden, delicate, and lethal. They rolled across roots and mud and landed near enough to Nebra that she reared up and would have stomped down on both of them if Lin hadn't eased her with a command and raise of his hand.

Lin rose and checked himself. Bumps and scrapes only. The untethered's Wefts had been so brittle, they'd broken against his Inlayed limbs.

The Needle stuck out from the back of the untethered's neck, right where he'd seen Tylle do it to the soldier on the road. If that Thorn had helped bring the untethered closer to the person they were before the madness took them, what might it do for a person who hadn't slipped over that edge yet?

It wasn't until he'd moved the corpse, dragging it to rest curled among the roots of the dying trees, that he noticed the clouds had abandoned the night sky entirely. Even the storms themselves wanted nothing to do with the inky, moonless expanse above.

Ceasing Hate

"I didn't set out, at first, to light the world aflame. It merely caught from my stare, like kindling eager to burn from the glance of an errant ember. I'm sure someday my sister will forgive me, but it was her love that caused me to come alight." V.S.

The next few days passed without incident, other than the occasional sneezing fit Lin found himself suffering. Each morning he'd taken to forming a focus and conjuring both strands of magic from within. Their glow, much like what he considered a standard Wieving, waned if he attempted it too much. It seemed even a night's rest didn't bring back the same vibrant glows he'd witnessed when conducting his tests.

By the fourth morning, a light fever warmed his brow despite the cool winds, enough so that despite not needing to stop and restock he'd found the prospect of a physiker's concoction enticing when he saw the thin trails of smoke that marked a village.

After seeing the walls and defenses of Drekinsburg, this quaint patch of homes seemed bare and eager to be assaulted. Lin wiped the beads of sweat from his brow and shivered. It was common sense that wet and cold made for a terrible combination, but Lin couldn't recall the last time he'd gotten sick. It was probably that One-loved untethered's fault.

One-loved. Lin struggled between calling himself a Binder or Wiever. He even struggled at first to consider the lot of them as Gods, as opposed to Six. But something was all-encompassing about cursing with the One Shadow's epitaph. Wicked Tel-Myr.

Aside from the knee-high stone wall, there weren't any visible defenses. But that didn't mean the village wasn't on guard itself. A man and a woman approached him. They wore simple clothes with furs hung across their shoulders and carried long walking sticks. The woman's smile wilted, severe brows over sun-kissed cheeks pressing together.

Lin coughed. "Just passing through. Do you have a physiker?"

"Taulia is as good as we got." There was visible relief in the man's voice as he spoke. "Ain't ya, Taulia."

"I'm better than some villages are like to have. Not one of those One-loved monsters are you?"

"Can't say that I am." Lin nodded. "I've got two hares I caught from a night ago that I could trade, but my marks are running low."

Taulia shrugged. "Good enough. Miche can take care of your horse."

Lin took his time exiting the saddle and stretched his lower back stifling a cough as he did. "Just came from Drekinsburg, they've had a hard time of things. How has it been out here?"

"Fine. Mostly. An occasional patrol of Redrobes still comes through, haven't seen them in weeks now though. And the mad ones tried trading once, didn't like our offer, and have raided once or twice. Feral fucks," Taulia spat off to the side and lowered her stick.

Mad ones. Lin still tended to forget that those without the Sight only saw people. Deteriorated people, but a person all the same. "Untethered might looked harmless..."

"Don't have to tell us how bad they are. We get it." Taulia led him to a simple shack, dark furs hanging in the doorway in place of a door. The scent of sage and thyme danced through the air with honey and a spice Lin couldn't place. His sense of smell had been waning since the night under the tree and he knew if he was smelling anything, it must be potent.

Once they'd settled in, Lin blinking at the overwhelming warmth coming from the hearth at the edge of the room, Taulia stared at him, then said, "Strip."

"Excuse me?"

"Your cloak and robes underneath are coated in mud and dirt and reek. You might have gotten a cut or infection and not realize it. Strip, but keep your small clothes on." She turned, though it didn't seem it was to save his modesty.

Lin sloughed off his layers, conscious of how warm his cheeks felt but unable to stop shivering all the same. Taulia busied herself grinding what looked like seeds and flower petals into a paste, but with her back turned it was unclear exactly what sort. Her hips swayed as she worked and Lin averted his gaze to the flames.

"Why'd you want a physiker?" She stared at him, eyes scanning his throat specifically and running a cautious hand over the base of it.

As if to explain itself, Lin sneezed, turning to avoid sneezing on the woman.

"Turn in a slow circle," She said, moving to the center of the tiny room and pressing a little bit of the paste she made anywhere that she deemed necessary. "A few cuts. Old scars. Magic."

Lin turned in a full circle and stopped once he faced her, staring into her eyes. "I used to be a Red."

Taulia snorted and brushed a hand along his collarbone again. "Didn't know that was something you could stop doing."

"Used to not be," Lin said.

"And the rest of us? Children still going to be taken?"

A sigh escaped Lin. He didn't know, but the odds were yes, they'd still evaluate and take promising children.

"You don't have to talk about it. Better you take them than the Mad Ones. Open your mouth and stick out your tongue."

Mad Ones? Taking children?

Lin opened his mouth to ask but she stuck a stick in and pressed his tongue down with it. Taulia's nose crinkled and a frown tugged at the edges of her lips.

"Balance on your left foot and hop." She added a, "please," when Lin gave her a dubious look and coughed.

Shifting his weight was easy and so was hopping, but keeping his expression neutral as a giggle slipped from her wasn't. Steps came from behind and Lin stopped hopping as a lop-sided grin came fully to Taulia's face.

"Taulia doesn't treat anyone without a little tease or two. Some people can't even hop," Miche said as he joined them, giving Taulia a gentle kiss on the cheek. "Need these scrubbed, hon?"

"Please," she said with a wink. "And you lay down. I'm mixing a tincture of ylari root, venti seed, and sprygal herbs."

"Here?" Lin turned a half-circle in the tight quarters. He didn't even see a pallet.

"Or outside if you want, but I can't promise you won't get disturbed by the little ones come morning. Strange half-naked man with magic on his flesh sleeping like a goat and all that." Taulia brought a hand up to her face, covering her mouth and raising those severe brows of hers. "You aren't secretly a goat are you?"

Lin lay with his feet near the hearth and his head almost to the doorway. Miche came in with a blanket that looked like it had been quilted ages ago. It smelled of the woods, but for some reason that made Lin feel more comfortable.

Another coughing fit racked Lin and his ribs ached from the force. Asking what she meant about the untethered taking the children was fresh on his mind, but as he grew comfortable, a weariness settled over him. He still shivered despite the heat near his toes and the thick blanket Miche had laid on him. It reminded him of Binder's sickness, but he hadn't thought he'd overused his spul.

Sleep took him in waves as if he were a boat, slowly filling with water as he sunk below the surface. Lin woke once when Taulia knelt beside him and placed a stopper at his lips. The liquid stung his lips and tingled cold on his tongue, eliciting a cough loud enough to wake the village.

But soon he was back to sleep, any aches from his travels long forgotten. Lightning crashed overhead and Lin thought he'd woken, but in moments he knew he was dreaming. Fear settled onto his chest, a heavy worry that he'd be back to the night terrors of forged steel and shattered blades, but as the world clarified around him, he calmed.

Lin's back rested against the bark of a tree, scratching at the smallest movements. Large roots broke the surface at his feet and his toes dug into the mud. His arms were stuck to the tree, golden Weaves pinning him in place. Whatever fear had fled him moments ago rushed back double-fold. Screams tore from his throat, guttural and nonsensical even to himself.

And Tylle stood before him, looking the same as she had the day he'd left her. Sharp, fair features. Dark hair braided in one long, military strand. Anger and rage just under her placid expression. She worked a Weft, a cruel edge to the light as it sliced through the flesh of his forearm without resistance.

Lin screamed and thrashed but the Weaves held. The Weft didn't break against the Inlays that should have lined the flesh of his arms. But when he looked, all he saw were multiple crude, dark Stitches like dried blood.

Knowing it was a nightmare, a hallucination brought on by the fever, medicine, or both, didn't stop the pain. Tylle cut him. She healed him. Cut him again. It lasted far longer than Lin thought it possibly could have with the actual untethered, but eventually, she stopped.

Words were buried in his chest, waiting to come out past his dry, cracked lips.

The ghostly verdant glow flashed into existence beside his head, then the pain tripled as something stabbed its way under his flesh, grinding against the bone of his temple.

"T-tylle," Lin groaned.

Tylle stumbled back, staring at him.

The untethered had asked to be killed. Lin understood why now. Trapped in his own body, unable to speak, unable to do anything but press forward and howl. But Lin didn't want to die. There was still so much left to do. "Tylle. S-save me."

The Weaves pinning him to the tree sparked away and Lin surged forward, attacking Tylle despite his words. She'd kill him and he'd deserve it. Somehow, despite everything, despite all the warnings from anyone who'd ever seemed to care about him, he'd untethered.

Lin's Wefts, frail and lined with cracks, shattered against Tylle's flesh. Then he was on her, nails raking into flesh. Teeth biting. Why hadn't she stabbed him with a Needle? Why was he tasting blood and feeling trails of skin under his sharp, dirty nails?

Lin pulled himself up, horrified. Tylle was gone and in her place, Margaret lay dying. Except, it was someone who looked like Margaret but different, with lighter hair, and slightly finer features. "Mellyr?"

Lin jolted up. His throat was sore, his limbs heavy. The light of dawn pressed in through the hanging furs and the scent and sound of sizzling fat filled the air.

"Who is Mellyr?"

Lin jumped at the soft voice. Sitting in the space between him and the door were three children, all staring at him with a mix of interest and caution.

"You kept mumbling the name. Then screaming it." The child in the middle looked to be about ten passings old, darkly curling hair cut short to the scalp. He shrugged and pulled the two smaller children closer to him when Lin groaned.

"Shoo, little flies. Told you to leave the corpse be." Taulia was seated on a stool in the corner that looked made more for a child as low to the ground as it was. She had dark circles under her eyes that hadn't been there the night before.

"Ain't messing with him," the youngest child said. Her eyes were the color of clay and the way her light brown hair twisted reminded Lin of Jules.

"It's alright," Lin said, struggling to sit up. The cool morning air blowing by the children was all the sharper for the layer of sweat that soaked Lin and the blanket he'd slept under. "I was having a nightmare. Mellyr is…" Well, she was his responsibility. Lin licked his lips and Taulia raised a brow.

"One of you make useful and get water." None of the children budged until the oldest in the middle nudged the kid on his left. They scurried out as if they were afraid they might be missing something exciting.

"Mellyr is my daughter," Lin finally said. "Or the closest thing to it, anyways. And she was taken."

"The mad ones?" the young girl whispered.

"Untethered?" Lin asked. "No. Ladrica. The Northern Kingdom."

Breathing like he'd been running for his life, the other boy rushed back in with a bulging waterskin.

"You three out. Got to tend to him a bit more. I promise I'll tell you whatever he tells me. I swear it on the Six."

A rooster sang in the distance and Taulia stared at him from her stool. She made the symbol of the Six in the air and rose, one knee popping as she did. "Sometimes living out here, it's easy to hear rumors of awful things. Are the Dukes going to war?"

"Seems like it."

Taulia sighed and knelt beside him, pressing the back of her hand to his brow. "You're fit enough to get on the road again, so long as you eat plenty and rest. Take this with you, drink some twice a day." She handed him a stoppered vial filled with a green fluid suspending swirling chunks of brown *things*.

"Will it give me nightmares?"

"Nothing I mixed for you would've caused the sort of terrors you were having. I promise. Anyway, Miche left your clothes here by the fire. Seems it'll get colder before it gets better so take the blanket with you. You ruined it with all that sweat anyhow."

It had seemed like another life that he'd been an Escorter, and even then he hadn't been treated with the sort of kindness on display here. "I really can't repay you," Lin said.

"Save that girl of yours. Bring her back one day. Keep the war from tearing apart small places like this. Please." Taulia rose and walked through the door, leaving Lin to dress. "And if you've got any connections with the Reds left, see if they can send someone up this way to deal with the Mad Ones."

Lin blanched. "Right. You've implied they've been taking children?"

Taulia's shoulders fell and she nodded. "We've— Miche and I— fought them off when it was small numbers. But... Something has changed recently. And our children aren't allowed out beyond the stone shroud."

"Shroud?" Lin asked, glancing out the flaps of the door.

"When the ones who walked before come hunting, cross river or shroud for hiding."

Ones who walked before? It sounded familiar, but perhaps the fog around his mind was making it harder to recall.

"The stone walls. They're stone shrouds and they keep away bad spirits. But the Mad Ones, they've grown bolder. Crossing lines they shouldn't. So, if you have any way to send aid to this part of the world, we need it."

"I'll do my best," Lin said. But doing his best would mean quitting his hunt for Mellyr. It meant dealing with the untethered now, as Tylle had wanted him to. And after everything he'd been through, he wouldn't abandon Mellyr to the Ladricans— no matter their intentions.

Leaving the small village felt oddly disquieting.

In the light of a fresh sun, there were only five or six homes and it seemed everyone had come out to see the stranger off. The three children waved vigorously until Taulia stalked over to them and scooped the tiniest one up. It was places like this the scholars and

King Lodram wanted to punish. Good, kind people who didn't give two marks about the power resting at their fingertips. And it was a place like this that seemed most susceptible to an attack by the untethered.

A frown crept onto Lin's face as he left. Gods. Danica deserved better. The people deserved better. Lin wrapped his cloak tighter, dug through his saddlebag, and pulled out the compass. Odd, he'd never considered using it before, but after waking he'd been unconfident he was heading the correct way. He was heading northward and the clouds had settled into a thick, gray blanket.

By nightfall, he'd passed two abandoned homesteads and a wagon deserted on the side of the road, boards broken and wheels off the axle. It had set him on edge, but the area wasn't heavily forested and he hadn't seen tracks in the brush to signal what had caused it. Bandits and brigands were still real threats on the roads, especially this far north, but ever since Fallo months back, it had seemed untethered were far more real, pressing concerns.

The wind blew hard between the thin, tall trees that marked what Lin considered the edge of the north. This was the area where he'd done most of his escorts. Lin pulled the cloak tighter around his shoulders and blinked at the thin particles that floated through the air. Snow. Or what Southern Danica might call snow. It was more like flakes of dandruff shaken from the needle-like leaves of the tallest trees. But in no time, it could coat the ground in a slush.

With every setback, Lin hoped, prayed that the Ladricans who'd taken Mellyr were facing twice worse.

Ahead, in a clearing, was a Ferrucium outpost. It, like the homesteads he'd passed earlier, appeared abandoned. Windows little more than dark recesses in the cold stone. But there was no scent of untethered on the air, no sign of violence on the building.

Lin slid from the saddle, slippers crunching the barely there layer of frost on the ground. His breath came out in puffs and he strained his ears to hear anything. The forest was silent. Frozen. Nebra snorted beside him. It could be, with all the changes at the Ferrucium, that they'd decided some outposts weren't worth maintaining. It made sense if they were taking the spread soldiers and moving them to the northern passes near Talm's Peak or amassing one solid army in the south.

Rubbing his hands together helped, but Lin had been a fool for not getting gloves.

"Best we get going girl," Lin turned and blinked. From the corner of his eye, the grass behind Nebra had seemed pressed with Bindings, flattened and glowing, looking everything like Velkath's Sigil. But as he looked again, it was clear it was just reeds, not even close to resembling the shape of that symbol. A symbol Lin had thought twisted and grotesque once, but now knew was a way to remember the first Wievers.

Lin rubbed his eyes, looked around one last time, then mounted Nebra and left the cold, quiet outpost behind. None of it was sitting right with him. The increase of untethered activity. The Ladrican Kingdom stealing Mellyr. The fact that Lin had been born up here to two parents who'd run away and somehow ended up working in the same area decades later.

It was all too much. And that was before considering that Aemun had been up this way with Margaret before Lin had been assigned to escort them back south. Nearly as close to Ladrica and the hub of untethered activity as one could get.

Ceasing Blood

"The Faceless Six. While the Ladrican Kingdom has always been a highly religious one, King Jeof the Bountiful's reign showed an increase in their belief in divine intervention overall. What they could claim, was their's to do so, because The Holy Mother, granted Ladrican's that right. The Six, a faith that later would become the primary religion across most of Danica, was a faith partially practiced in the Ladrican Kingdom and which took zealous hold when King Gunthyr took control. It was easy enough to force this new religion over the top of the Danican people's existing beliefs in Velkath and his kin. What King Gunthyr and his astute advisors failed to realize, was that the Faceless Six, while seemingly spread throughout the southern pockets of Ladrica, originated in Danica. It is speculation, but it is wholly my belief that the belief of the Six was simply a branching off from the Six Wievers, and that was why the Danican people were so willing to accept it as a "new" religion in the first place." Excerpt from A Study of Religion, author unsigned.

Lin was officially in Duke Errond's territory. Normally, he wouldn't consider something like that at all on his travels. But Pael's news that Duke Errond was the only Duke not to respond to the summons of Erias and Azhura put Lin glancing over his shoulder more often than not. Somehow even more so than when he thought he'd broken the Binding Tenets back at Fallo. Lin frowned and looked down at his Bludwieve. At the scholar's tower, he'd learned a lot, mostly that the Binding Tenets were simplified aspects of the Danican Accords the Ferrucium were given jurisdiction to police.

It made him sick and angry and... he exhaled. It didn't matter. None of it did until he got Mellyr back.

He'd left Denro and Pael nearly a week ago. Denro should have made it back to the scholars already and Gods willing, they would listen to him. If Denro could beg for peace, and speak on behalf of all the sane-minded citizens of Danica who were guilty only of being born in this One-loved land, then they might stand a chance.

A part of Lin, a tiny seed that threatened to bloom and choke out all the lingering love he had for the older man, resented Denro. Not so much for Denro keeping Lin's past from him, he understood that to an extent.

No, he resented Denro for not putting his voice toward peace sooner. Denro had been too hung up on how the revolution happened to see that the fallout would be far worse if the scholars wouldn't listen to reason. So he bided his time and let them do their testing without speaking from his heart. Gods, Lin hoped they'd listen to the man.

And Pael. Well, Lin knew what sort of pace that man set when he was driven to get somewhere. He'd likely made it to the Ferrucium before Lin had even left Wakewatch.

Lin smiled and straightened in his saddle, the sound of breaking twigs drawing his attention. A startled bird flew off and a ruckus like a deer bounding away broke the silence of the white wood. As cold as it was, the pale trees weren't nearly as frozen over as Lin had expected. The thaw, while slow, was happening. Just as winter had come earlier than expected, so too was it leaving.

Comfortable that he wasn't about to be ambushed, Lin let his mind drift back to Pael. Whether Erias or Azhura were fully in charge now didn't matter. The only difference might be who they sent to aid Lin. *If they sent anyone.*

Pael's words had worried him. 'Promise you'll stay with her.' As if Lin would leave Mellyr alone with those snake bastards of the north any longer than he had to. Part of him still didn't understand why she'd been taken, but the possibilities played through his head. All the reasons he Denro and Pael had surmised could be at play. *Or worse. None of them.*

Nebra picked her path between the trees, the thin layer of snow crunching under her hooves. It hadn't happened more than a handful of times, but Lin blinked away the brief image of Velkath's Sigil he'd seen burning into the snow. It had looked like someone, or something had pissed it into existence, steam curling up and the dark gold eating into the barely-there snow.

When he looked back at the bank, it was gone. He'd seen it once in the strands of Nebra's mane, which had resulted in his very cold fingers working her mane into new braids. Perhaps it had been because he drew on copper. That specific Wieving hadn't sat right with him. Bodies were one thing... but magic that affected the mind had to be blessed by the One, the Shadow, the Wicked. Whatever dark God conspired against them.

A stream burbled near the main path and Lin stopped Nebra to take advantage and refill his water. A thin clear coat of ice covered the closest edge and the stones surrounding it were slick and dangerous. Nebra drank the cold water and Lin filled his skins.

As an Escorter he'd never visited Duke Errond's estate but knew it was to the northwest from the main path. His people, these people were hearty and not likely to suffer an invasion. But, if he hadn't replied to the summons, it could be that he'd already been invaded and not necessarily by the Ladricans.

Untethered seemed to be a larger and larger problem and if they'd been building their forces— Lin shuddered. The thing that had always seemed to make untethered truly terrifying to him, was how chaotic they were. Dangerous monsters with wicked magic without intent behind their maliciousness. But, if they were organized by someone or something?

Terrifying.

Once they were back on the main path, partially obscured by the thin dusting of snow that quickly melted and muddied the road as the sun rose, Nebra made good time. She raced through the forested path until the tree lines broke around her and she had a stretch of fields and farmlands as far as Lin could see. A wall of trees, shades of verdant green brushed and blown with patches of white, stood guard on the horizon. The path split. To the left, Duke Errond's holdings. To the right, Lyre. Nebra kept her pace until they'd crossed through the frosted farmlands, not nearly as expansive as the fields around the Ferrucium.

Nebra huffed and snorted and as she slowed, shadowed trees flanking them, Lin worried for the first time. There had been enough rest along their trek, hadn't there? He needed to get to

Mellyr, but letting Nebra push herself to exhaustion or worse wasn't something that sat well with him.

"Woah, girl." Lin stroked her neck, focusing on her heavy breaths and the slight lather that had begun building on her coat. Despite his words, she sped ahead, pushing herself harder.

"Nebra!" Lin said, pulling on her reins. He couldn't recall the last time she'd ignored him. But, he'd changed since leaving the Ferrucium, so it only made sense that she would've too. In her own way. "If you keep going you'll hurt yourself. Lame a hoof or ride to exhaustion and then you'll never be able to run the same again! Is that what you want?"

Nebra slowed, not a lot, but enough that she seemed to catch her breaths.

"Gods, girl." Lin looked behind them, wondering if perhaps she'd rushed through that field for a reason that he couldn't tell. They would've been easy targets for anyone waiting to ambush. But he hadn't seen anything and even if he had there shouldn't be anyone expecting him. Unless the scholars sent birds of their own. All anyone would need to mark him was his description and the scholars, thanks to that High Scholar Anya, would know where he was heading. *Shit.*

Lin needed Denro or Pael. Tylle flashed through his mind. He needed anyone really, just to help calm his tattered nerves. Ever since that nightmare with the tree, he'd felt more and more frayed. When he did sleep, it was in short intervals. Not even considering he saw Velkath's fucking Sigil in the branches, the clouds, the snow.

Slowing his breathing, Lin stared at his hands. They trembled from more than just the cold. Lin pulled the slim book from his back, Velkath's Sigil in gold leaf laid over the suggestion of a person's body. He picked up where he left off. Inlays. Inlaying with the less common Wievings showed no *visible* effect. If blue Wievings could heal without Stitches, perhaps an Inlay could be done that allowed for continuous healing, of a sort. Flipping through the scratched-out text didn't do any good. The book was more ramblings about a physiker's testing than it was information about the magic.

What was a Bludwieve? More than anything else the question haunted him. A Wieving of course, but what was it? He'd now seen first-hand the colors caused by rarer magics. And the book, as of yet, hadn't answered that.

What it had answered, on this most recent page, was the truth that you could Inlay someone or something other than yourself. Strengthening it. Lin swallowed and thought first to Ferrucium-steel. Were those blades forged and then somehow Inlayed? They didn't glow to his Sight, so Lin doubted it. He lowered the book and stared at the back of Nebra's head. Could he work an Inlay into her muscle? Give her strength and resilience to keep going at the pace she wanted.

"Would you want that?" Lin asked.

Lin put the book away with a sigh. The sun had begun to set and he didn't have it in him to strain his eyes against the text. For the next while as the thin sliver of the moon broke through the clouded sky, Nebra continued to slow.

A pit of regret, doubt, and shame grew in him, left ignored it might bloom into a tree rife for dying under. Nebra wasn't going to make it. Not at the pace he needed to keep going if he planned to beat the ship to the Fort. For all he knew, the Ladricans had avoided the storm entirely and were already at the Fort replenishing before they departed again.

Lin weighed his options. Stay with Nebra at her pace, work Inlays into her flesh, unsure of how long or how drained he might be, or race ahead on foot. Leaving her in the woods might not be the worst option, but with the chance of wolves or even bears this far north it was far from the best. And if he stayed at the pace she was now going, it would take an entire week to scale the pass beyond Talm's peak.

"I feel like the Gods are constantly testing me," Lin said. He ran a cold hand over Nebra's neck. The braids he'd reworked into her mane looked nicer than the old ones. More befitting to a creature of Nebra's caliber. "And I'm constantly failing." Lin slid from the saddle, legs aching but not nearly so bad as they'd be if his limbs and body weren't magically strengthened.

The scent of smoke hung in the air, enough that Lin's heartbeat quickened. It wasn't the easy, lazy columns of cookfires. A village might be burning.

"One last run, girl," Lin said, sucking in a smoke-hazed breath and deciding the direction.

In the dark, it was hard to be certain where they were. But as the two soft lights glowing like a predator's eyes resolved into lanterns and the low stone wall clarified, Lin was positive it was Lyre.

Behind the physiker's home, a pyre burned into the night. And on the wind, crisper than winter's slow dying grasp was the Mourning Ballad. It was a song Lin hadn't heard since the night Margaret died, and it stabbed into him with all the force the sweet, sad song was meant to.

Lin dismounted and made his way through the village.

Leading Nebra forward, Lin steeled himself for the worst. Odds were good there had been an untethered attack. Good people he'd met here had likely been lost. He steeled himself for that news, hoping it wasn't true.

When he got near enough to the pyre that people might notice him, he added his voice to the song. He hummed more than he sang. It took some time for anyone to approach him, and once they did, Lin breathed a sigh of relief.

"What brings a stranger— Well, wait a moment," the Physiker's son, still larger than most fighting-aged men, looked down at Lin. "You're one of the Reds."

"Was," Lin said softly. "And you're the Physiker's son?"

"I am," he said. He'd lost some fat around his face and nodded to the older man leaning on his cane surrounded by a group of those who'd been singing.

More people had begun drifting his way, curious eyes, some with mournful expressions. A woman with a small child clutched to her chest hovered two arm lengths away.

"You know this man, Herm?"

Herm nodded. "He came through back before the autumnal festival. What brings you back to Lyre?" There was suspicion in his eyes and he kept his chin high and shoulders back like he was ready to strike out at any given moment.

Lin stood awkwardly as the gathered people moved aside and the Alderman approached, head hung low, eyes wet with grief. Not that he'd looked well before, but the man's expression wrung Lin's heart. Perhaps there had been some great loss. The closer the man got, the more the stench of a pig pen traveled with him. The Alderman stopped between Lin and Herm.

When the man didn't move to speak or shake Lin's hand, Lin said, "I'm not here for children or anything like that. I'm just passing through to the north," Lin said.

"Oh," the Alderman said, face twisting with confusion then hurt. "Thought you might be here to give your respects to Lenpy." He rubbed his hands together and blew into them

Lin narrowed his eyes. Was that what the pyre had been set for? A *goat*. Being able to sense Bindings or not, a pyre for a goat was wasted meat. Lin touched his hand from his heart to his brow and whispered, "I'm sorry for your loss, Alderman."

"Means much, coming from a man like you."

The Alderman smiled weakly, revealing a gap of teeth. From someone like Aemun, Lin would've thought that a back-handed compliment. But there was something in the Alderman's expression that seemed earnest.

"If it wouldn't be too much trouble, could I rest my horse here through the night?"

Herm seemed poised to say something, but a soft tapping on his shoulder by a cane interrupted him.

"Ferrucium soldier, Lindel," the Physiker said. He hobbled forward and pulled his cane from his son's shoulder to lean on it. If Lin had doubted the sharpness of the man's wit months ago when they'd first met, the fact that he'd retained Lin's full name removed it.

"You'll have to forgive me," Lin said. "I don't recall your name."

"Pyter Collier. My son, Herm. Alderman Pryor." He seemed to suck on his teeth and then stared at Lin under heavy brows. "I'd be happy to have you in my home for a time if you'll share news of Danica. I'm sure you've got it."

"I can..." Alderman Pryor cleared his throat. "I can see to the mount if you wouldn't mind."

Lin let go of the reins and Nebra took to the fragrant Alderman without hesitation. He hadn't noticed it when the man first approached, but Lin saw he'd formed a sort of belt from a hempen rope with a bell on it. Gods, the man had truly loved that goat.

"Please feed her and give her water, if you've the oat to spare. I've got some few coins I can give."

"Ain't worryin' about coins right now. But I do have to ask," he stopped moving and turned to whisper into Lin's ear. "You swear you ain't here for no children, right?"

Lin held his breath and shook his head, exhaling a soft, "I swear."

Alderman Pryor wiped his ruddy cheeks with the back of his hand and seemed to stare into the heavens for a moment before stroking Nebra's neck in gentle, easy pats.

Cleansing Hope

"I've witnessed now, on several occasions, the overuse of drawing these trace elements from within. The most common threads of magic are colored golden, turning to an ochre, ugly rust when overdone. Each person seems to have unique limits impacted only by diet and health. Ocean blue and forest green are also possible shades, turning a deep, muddy brown and necrotic black when overdone, respectively. I've only seen the crimson magic once and don't know what hue it turns to when overdrawn. I am not proud, as I record this, to admit we pushed some of the early subjects into over-calling their innate magic. In doing so, oft the symptoms were a fever-like illness and, of course, an immediate exasperation of any symptoms related to "Binding" in the first place. It seems even when the liquid metal mercury is avoided similar symptoms can't be evaded forever." Records from the personal diary of Physiker Sichael.

Pyter Collier had left Lin alone in the adjoining room where Margaret had died while he brewed a pleasantly scented floral tea, and spoke to his son and son's promised bride in private.

Lin stared at the cot where Aemun had taken Margaret's life. All because she wanted the man to abandon his crazed desires and flee with her. But Aemun had known about the Accords, seeing as every action he'd taken seemed to ensure that Danica would break them. It sickened Lin to think about the lives lost to that man's ambition and the lives yet to be lost but well on the way.

The cot groaned as Lin shifted. It had been the start of it all, Margaret's death. At least from what Lin had known at the time. But what were the odds that an untethered would attack the very night they made it to Lyre? Or that Fallo would be massacred as it had been. Aemun had played King Lodram's forces, Noosemen included, Erias's forces, and the Ferrucium's forces all against each other. There very well could be a fourth party, or even more, tangled in Aemun's web, like a group of unified untethered. Lin shuddered.

"Dark thoughts?" Pyter Collier's soft voice carried ahead of him as he hobbled with his cane in one hand and a tray with a kettle and cups in the other.

Lin moved to rise, but Pyter shook his head and set the tray down on the cot beside Lin. "How... how many untethered attacks have you had here?"

"Recently?" Pyter shrugged and took a seat, leaning his cane against the wood frame of the cot. "The one with you lot. Before that, can't say I remember. Certainly few and far between. Rumors, more than anything."

"Rumors," Lin echoed. "I'm worried that perhaps the picture is larger than I ever imagined."

Pyter chuckled and, with hands steadier than Lin expected, given the man's seeming brittleness, poured two cups of steaming tea without spilling a drop from the tin kettle. The steam smelled rich and earthy, with a finish of mint. "Most pictures are. Even the simple ones. Though, I'm afraid I'm not sure what you're referring to."

Lin took the cup the Physiker proffered him and blew to cool it. The warmth radiating through the tin cups tingled his cold fingers, and the fragrance eased some of the tension in his shoulders. He stared at Pyter from behind the slowly dying curls of steam.

"Danica is about to be at war. The man I was here with last seems to have started it... but now he's dead."

Pyter nodded, face passive but for a slight raise to his right eyebrow. "If anyone I've ever met seemed capable of starting a war, it might very well be that man."

"Well, it might've been coming either way. Maybe in ten or twenty years. I don't know. So perhaps he sped it up, but now we have Ladrica, potentially pressing down past Talm's Peak once the thaw fully hits."

Steps sounded from the hall that led from the room, and Herm emerged looking as broad as an ox with a grim expression. "And that is the King the dukes report to?"

Lin nodded and finally touched the tea to his lips. Gods, it was refreshing. "Of the four dukes, only one hasn't responded to the call to arms the Ferrucium and Duke Wellgrove have made."

"Duke Errond," Pyter said. "So you're here to get an answer from him?"

Lin blinked at that. It was a logical leap, but furthest from what Lin had in mind. "No. Admittedly, not having his support would be a bane to any hope Danica has of preventing the pass from falling. But I'm on a mission to rescue the child that you helped birth."

By the time Lin shared everything he knew and explained exactly what he meant to do by being this far north, Herm had found a seat beside his father, and the tea had cooled. Lin knew from both men's expressions they sympathized with him.

"And the woman, Tylle, she truly didn't want to raise the child with you?" Herm asked. It was the sort of question that stung each time Lin considered it and one he had wrung on his own often. But Herm couldn't have known that. Pyter winced at the question, a look of regret flashing in his wrinkled features.

"Mellyr, in the early months, reminded her too much of Aemun. Or so she said. But she trusted me enough to leave her in my hands, and that gives me hope." *Hope that someday, all three of us might be a family.* But asking Tylle to set aside her duties would be like asking Lin to set aside his oaths. Lin didn't want to think about how Tylle *had* done that to him. Even if she had been somewhat right in her reasonings, it wasn't fair that she hadn't given him that same chance. He hoped she was well, training and teaching the truth of Danica's history to those who would hear it.

"While I do appreciate you sharing this information with me, there is only one man in Lyre who needs to know these details."

Lin scrunched his nose and frowned at the physiker's words. "Surely you don't mean..."

"I do mean Alderman Pryor. He is a good, kind man and leads Lyre in all things." Pyter yawned and tapped Lin's knee several times before rising. "And he is trusting and listens to counsel. Something many men in his position wouldn't do. Tell him what you told us. He might have a better idea of what to do moving forward than I ever could."

Herm grunted, and a sly smile flashed across his wide jaw. "If only Danica could be fixed with a…" The young man wiggled his fingers the same way he had when asking why Lin didn't just Stitch his flesh.

"It might not heal Danica, but if words won't work, then weapons will be all we have left to prove our point." Lin didn't much like that possibility. The Ferrucium had been thinning for some time, and the disparate ducal forces weren't so much an army as it was an unorganized militia. At least so far as Lin was aware.

"The only thing weapons ever prove is who the better bleeder is," Pyter said softly. He grabbed his cane and leaned on it. "For what it's worth, I think you and that Tylle woman might make a good pairing, and I hope you find the child unharmed."

"Thank you, physiker."

"Please, Pyter is fine. Now, if you'll excuse me, I've got some seeds to grind before sleep takes me, and it seems awfully eager tonight."

Lin yawned and nodded. "I've stayed longer than I intended." His throat wasn't sore, thanks to the tea, but he couldn't recall the last time he'd spoken so much in one sitting. There had been too much to relay. And the fact that so much of it *hurt* to recount didn't make it any easier.

Herm slapped the top of his knees and rose, his dark curls bouncing at the motion. "If you plan to leave, you should talk to

Alderman Pryor first. Pa wouldn't have mentioned it if he thought it was a bad idea."

"I'm not sure I'll be able to find him without that chortling goat." Lin was joking, but when he noticed the mix of disgust and anger on Herm's face, he wished he hadn't.

"Lenpy was around for ages. And well-loved. I knew her since I was a young lad, running amok and avoiding chores. Alderman Pryor will be in the church."

Lin managed to walk away with all his limbs attached. Of course, he could take the young man in a fight. Probably. But all it would take to lose a fight like that was overconfidence. Bindings didn't mean everything, just a whole lot. A knife drawn across the right place or a bolt through the eye would kill just the same as a Weft. Not that he wanted to fight Herm, but these were all things to consider.

Outside, the pyre dwindled to ember and ash, flakes rising, mixing with the light powder falling. It sounded like the dropping of a soft cloth over and over again. Lin listened to it for a long moment, just outside the Physiker's home. His breaths came out in clouds, and the world around him seemed to slow to a crawl. It had felt good to get all of that off his chest.

Lin clenched his jaw and wiped the beginning of a tear from his cheek. The thin layer of snow underfoot crunched at his steps, and all the simple, scattered homes of Lyre were like small islands of wooden refuge among the muddy white expanse.

The church of the Six was just as Lin had left it months ago. Except back then, he hadn't noticed the detail put into even the simple benches. The three benches on either side of the aisle were all hand-carved and looked to be hewn from a whole trunk a piece. Solid polished wood lacquered a dark amber. Stained glass windows depicting the Six Founding Weavers caught the flickering candlelight as if each candle had been placed specifically for that. Which it likely had. And because of the dancing flames, the portraits of the Six looked to be casting magic. Each one Weaving a different part of the mark of the Six. It took Lin's breath to see it this way. Perhaps back then, he'd been too jaded. Too hurt and sad over Margaret's loss. Too tired. Too focused on Tylle and whether she was praying.

"Beautiful, ain't they?" Alderman Pryor's heavy accent brought Lin's attention to focus on the window he knelt in front of. The Faceless Aspect of Mournfulness.

Even without a face, there was something wholly heartbreaking about the way that figure held itself. Hunched shoulders, slouched and kneeling, with streams of cerulean that were likely meant to represent tears. Lin couldn't recall which of Velkath's siblings it was meant to represent. Tylle would have, of course. Ve-something or another. But in every faceless depiction, Lin saw shadows of Velkath's Sigil.

"I think last time I came through, I was too preoccupied. Didn't see how much care was put into this little church."

"Care put into the whole of Lyre. Every bit of it. And now..." Alderman Pryor let out a low, exhausted breath. He inhaled, which made a sort of high-pitched whining sound, then exhaled. "Your horse is in a stable we have just behind the building here. She'll be warm and rested for the night."

"Pyter asked me to relay some of my news to you."

Alderman Pryor waved his thick dirt-stained fingers. "I know dark days are on us. I'm just thankful that you were a good enough man not to come back looking for children to be taken. Don't know that my heart could've handled it."

"Oh," Lin said, taking a seat on the pew nearest the kneeling man. Truth be told, that had slipped his mind entirely. He'd seen young faces amongst those grieving the goat, so the Alderman had lied to him even back then. "You're right about the days ahead. And even if you won't say it, the days behind." Lin placed a hand on the man's shoulder. "I'm sorry for your loss."

There was no doubt in Lin's mind that if he lost Nebra, he'd feel a similar, haunting remorse. The largest difference was Alderman Pryor hadn't been dragging his goat, Lenpy, into danger at every turn.

A broad, rough hand rested on the back of Lin's and the man's shaggy beard trembled with his lips as he turned to look into Lin's eyes. "I appreciate that. She was a good girl. Best."

They sat there together for a long moment. The Alderman mourning, Lin allowing the man and letting that pain seep into him. After several heavy breaths, Lin closed his eyes and prayed.

Gods. Six, or Velkath and his kin. Forgive me for failing Margaret. Forgive me for failing Mellyr. Grant me the strength needed to protect those I cherish.

"One of the most important things a man can pray for is the ability to forgive 'imself," Alderman Pryor whispered.

Lin opened his eyes and saw the Alderman, and his flat nose, near eye-level with him. The candles continued to burn, the fragrance of wildflowers and berries somehow coming from the curls of smoke. But Gods, the Alderman still smelled near unbearable. But in speaking with the man and Pyter, Lin felt he better understood why. He gave everything to Lyre and it's people. Likely hunted and foraged and was as true a wildman as one could be. It was a small miracle the man hadn't ended up massacred by a stray untethered. "I'll try to pray for that, next time I find myself at a church."

"The Six don't care iffen you're under the moonless sky or the tallest roof ever built. They don't care if you come on your belly like a snake or tall and proud like an elk. All they care is that you come."

Lin licked his lips. *And if they don't care at all?* The books he read agreed that Velkath and his kin had existed. Vellia was the first to Wieve and the Six were eventually a branch off of those who'd dedicated themselves to Velkath's family's way of life and virtues. But that didn't make them Gods. "I think it's my turn to thank you," he said, instead of burdening this man with his doubts. "Twice now you've tended my horse."

"Twice now it's been my pleasure. Sweet as she is."

That made Lin smile. "I'll be leaving before the sun rises. You wouldn't happen to have some furs or a heavier cloak I might borrow?"

"Might. I can rustle something up If you'll give me a few moments."

"I can," Lin said. The Alderman rose, traced the symbol of the Six in the air in front of him, and made his way from the church.

Left alone, Lin stared at his muddied, dirt-stained slippers. What came next would be the hard part. Lyre was the last real village marked on the maps before he'd make it to the pass. Well, aside from Fallo, except there was no way it had rebuilt since they'd passed through. With the rest Nebra had gotten, Lin doubted he'd need to Inlay her, but the thought still stuck with him. What if it would be for the best? He looked up at the stained glass panes and turned as boots crunched to the door from the outside.

"Herm had an extra cloak he outgrew. Thick enough." Alderman Pryor shook out a light brown fur hide that had to have come from a young bear based on the size and lack of stitchings. "Pyter said you're planning on going through the pass into the Northern Kingdom."

"I am."

"I've been up there once when I was younger and dumber. Thought I'd see the Peak for myself."

"And?" Lin asked.

"And I was stopped and beat near to death by scouts. Even in the dead of winter."

Ah. That could explain the man's broken, flat nose. "I'm not worried about the scouts. In fact, there may be an entire army getting ready to stage and press down into Danica."

Alderman Pryor nodded and folded the cloak over the pew Lin sat on. “I ain’t concerned so much about you.” He licked his lips and worried at the chain around his neck. “It’s barely a path for a man before the thaw and it ain’t ever a path for a horse, no matter how steady on her feet she is.”

“And if I magicked her? Strengthened her bones and muscles as I’ve done my own?” Lin asked.

Alderman Pryor’s lip curled up and he clenched his fist. “If you’re joking, it ain’t funny. And if you’re serious, I’d die keeping you from doing that to the sweet beast.”

Lin’s brows shot up at the ferocity in the man’s voice. “It wouldn’t hurt her.”

“You don’t know that.”

“It didn’t hurt me,” Lin said flatly.

“You carry more pain in the way you walk than any other I’ve seen. Maybe it’s from everything else, but I bet the markings making you hum like a wound-up string didn’t come easy or painless. Doing that to another living creature… especially when it can’t say no ain’t right. Maybe if she had a choice. Maybe.” Without another word, the stocky man stormed out. Lin waited, soaking in the silence of the holy house.

Cleansing Bone

"Tel'Myr a wicked moniker for a wicked person. You might ask why someone so vile was whispered in the same breath as Velkath and the other revered kin. Simple. Because nothing and no one is safe from corruption. Her "One Shadow" stretches further for her initial proximity to Vellia's light." V.S.

With the fur cloak pulled tight around his shoulders, Lin stepped from the church and into the chill late-night air. He stared up at the ruffled cloud sky, a sliver of a moon so thin it barely showed, and decided it was early morning. Another village and another stretch of wasted time. But the Alderman's words had been something he needed, solidifying his resolve.

Lin took slow steps to the stable behind the church where Nebra rested. True to his word, the Alderman had cared for her. The simple, well-worn saddle hung on the wooden beam that divided the stalls and the bags were set on the ground beside it.

Nebra snorted at him, large eyes catching all the stray light from the candled windows. All the light from the Stitches on Lin's left hand. He'd always wondered at that. If those without the Sight couldn't see magic in general, was it possible to see it if it were reflected from a source that could? Probably not, but there'd been more about Binding— Wieving he corrected himself— that he hadn't known about than it turned out he had.

"Shhh," Lin leaned over the gate and took her large face in his hands, pressing his brow to hers just as Denro had done to him after the Ferrucium fell. "Shhh." He repeated, the sound coming out in stuttered breaths. "Usually when we separate, I don't get to say goodbye. I think... I think I've done that out of fear of not having the right words."

Nebra's breath puffed in short, huffs.

"But I'll be back. I'll always be back," Lin held her and let his tears sting his eyes. "But where I'm going is too dangerous. And if I'd had the option of leaving you somewhere safe before Fallo last time, I would've. If I'd have been able to keep you from the Noosemen, I would've. I should've spent more time with you in Fentis. But the Scholars...." A warm, wet tongue caught Lin across his cheek and he smiled. "Want the salt, eh?"

Lin took a deep breath and pulled away. She'd be safer here. He wouldn't be running her half to death only to stumble and hurt herself in the mountain pass. She'd.... She'd be taken care of. They'd been together so long, she deserved a break.

Nebra's eyes tracked him and she used her mass to nudge his side. She'd more than earned her rest, whatever shape that might take. It was hard to picture her happily grazing in a meadow, but it would be even harder to see her injured or worse on account of him. More than anyone else, she'd been his sole companion on those long rides.

Lin hefted the saddle bags which felt heavier than they should have. When he looked through them he saw a full water skin that didn't belong to him and the three vials of an inky, black fluid nestled beside the single vial left from what Taulia had given him. He pulled the compass out, checked it against where he'd been expecting to go, and nodded. *Fallo* to the pass. He'd go wide of what had once been the town. Visiting Lyre had already reminded him enough of his failures so many months ago.

The physiker's home looked dark, but on the porch, two shadowy silhouettes stood waiting. Lin made his way over to them.

Pyter and Alderman Pryor stared at him, the only light on the porch cast from the candle in the window behind them.

"Thought you'd be asleep," Lin said softly.

"I thought so too," Pyter replied. "Couldn't. I had Herm put some vials in your pack there. Good for Binders. Might taste a bit like blood and I wouldn't drink more than one vial at a time, but the seeds I crushed will help with your magic. Far as I know."

Far as you know. Lin narrowed his eyes but chose not to press the matter and instead said, "Thank you."

"Where's the horse?" Alderman Pryor asked. He'd crossed his arms and had a grim expression on his face.

"I've got a favor to ask. If you wouldn't mind," Lin knelt to be closer to eye-level with the squat man. "Would it be overstepping if I asked you to watch Nebra for me? I... where I'm heading is dangerous. What I'm doing doubly so. And you made some compelling points in the House of the Six."

Lin waited and, when the man still hadn't answered, said, "Please?"

A sniffle and the slight ringing from the bell at his waist was all the warning Lin had before the man, stench and all, took hold of

Lin. "Six, I knew you were a good man the moment I met you. I said it, didn't I?"

Pyter chuckled and patted Lin's shoulder. "If something happens to your horse you know exactly who to blame. But as I said when you arrived, it's been quiet. I'm sure the children would love tending to a horse as well-mannered as Danur here says she is."

Danur. Alderman Danur Pryor. Hesitantly, Lin brought his arms up and patted the man's back several times. "Then we have a deal. If it's alright, we can discuss payment when I return."

"Sure, sure. Did you need to say farewell?"

Lin licked his lips and pulled away from the man, not sure that the odor would ever leave him. "I... I already did. And if I don't make it back—"

"She'll be cared for. But broken hearts work both ways. You don't return, she'll mourn you." Alderman Pryor said as he fingered the rope tied around him. "So you best return."

They wished him well and Lin left Lyre, feeling only slightly better about his choice. If he knew Nebra half as well as he thought he did, she'd be fine. But she might not ever forgive him for leaving her. Better left alive than out there facing Gods know what.

Lin frowned as he reached the main path. He couldn't shake the sensation of being watched. He checked the strap on his pack, took several deep breaths, and rushed along the lightly powdered trail. It was odd to have the memories of those first few days leaving Lyre bob to the surface of his mind. Holding Mellyr well before she'd formed any personality. Needing, hoping really, to find a wetnurse. Aemun's silence and Tylle's anger. But he ate at the road with ease despite the thin dusting of snow. He didn't have a crying child and he wasn't slowed by anything.

The wind bit at him, lips chapping, eyes watering, but Gods it felt good to flex his muscles in ways he hadn't since readjusting to his Inlays. Lin blinked. Velkath's Sigil seemed to burn against a wide-trunked tree, but as Lin passed it, he saw it was simply a string of honey-caps growing in a V shape. Maybe he needed more sleep. Maybe less.

By sunrise, he'd made it to the deserted steads that marked the outer edges of Fallo.

Looming in the distance, just over the treeline, the slow-sloping mountains of Talm's Peak caught his eye. He hadn't even paid it a second glance the last time he'd been here. For good reason as with everything that had been going on a pass to Ladrica had been the least of his concerns. Snow-capped tips spoke of the coldness of the area, but Lin knew there would be sheets of sloughing ice collapsing if the thaw was happening as early as Erias believed.

Lin had initially planned to avoid Fallo, but despite his intentions, he felt drawn to the place. His legs, not yet tired, carried him into the still center of the town as if on their own. The remains of the pyre had been disturbed long ago, bones pulled from the ashes and scattered through the center of the town. Whatever dusting of snow had fallen on Fallo had melted underneath the sun's gentle kiss and the town's center was nearer to a mudfield than anything else.

Wolf prints were pressed into the drier sections, tracks old but not yet faded. Even months later, the place smelled of decay and death.

Lin crept through the town. A bird cawed and he jumped. He passed the shack Tylle had mended him in, the door still hanging half-broken on the hinges. A lone white flower petal, shriveled and browning at the edges skittered across the ground as a breeze picked up. The ceremonial flowers Tylle had used on the Pyre. Lin bent and picked it up.

A cracking of wood sounded off in the distance between him and Talm's Peak and a host of birds took flight, crying and cawing in distress.

Was this devastation really what Ladricans wanted? The contrarian in Lin said no. *This* was explicitly what they were claiming to want to avoid. Untethered running rampant. But under that thin veneer of righteousness, there was greed. Wasn't that how it always went, though? Like the Weavers and the Ferrucium. Danicans restricted their own people to make sure Danica remained free. Yet they weren't. Not anymore free than Lin had been with the scholars.

But if this is what true freedom grants our people?

It made Lin's stomach twist, a pain that was becoming all too familiar. He ignored it as he moved through the skeletal, meatless remains of Fallo. All of this was secondary if he couldn't get to Mellyr. He'd let all of Danica untether if it meant keeping that sweet child away from the Ladricans and their unknown plans.

And if her life with them would be better than anything you *might give her, Escorter?*

Lin froze at the thought. He'd been doing well with not becoming so lost in his thoughts that Denro or someone would have to shake him from it. But this was the first time he'd felt like someone else's cruel words were mingling in his mind. He was sure the voice had been Aemun's lilting, venomous tone. He rubbed the bridge of his nose and stared up at the peak.

"M-maybe I am losing it," Lin stammered, surveying the rest of the empty shacks. The wind howled and whistled through the bones of the town, setting his hair on end. Or perhaps wolves howled in the distance, preternaturally noting a disturbance from a place that had undoubtedly fed them over the last few months. "More likely, it's this One-loved place doing this to me."

Another flock of birds broke the canopy ahead, shrill cries reverberating over the empty corpse of a village.

Lin pressed to the northern edge of Fallo, keeping his eyes on the tree line. He'd been a whole fool letting his intrigue carry him to this cursed place. With death hanging in the air like fresh, windblown seeds.

There was no path visible, thick trees and thicker brush all burdened and limp from the steady dripping water that came off of them. Running from Lyre hadn't made Lin's legs burn half as bad as the steady-sloping march up toward the pass now did. He'd never come this way. Never had a reason to. All he had to go on was that the pass supposedly sat just east of the peak. Or just east of Vellia's rightmost finger. But knowing that and *seeing* it, were two very different things. Maybe if he… Lin licked his lips, tightened his pack across his shoulders, and stretched.

Climbing the tree in wet, ruined slippers proved more difficult than he'd thought. Needle-like leaves stabbed at him and a sticky sap coated his hands and tugged at his poor choice of footwear.

The idea had been simple. Climb up and get a better view, and once that view was had, run on the wind the way Dennick had when he'd chased them through the forest. But now leaning on a branch that swayed as much as a drunk after festival night, Lin reconsidered. Climbing back down seemed like an option just as poor. He shimmied back to the center of the tree and pressed his back against it. Gods, it was harder to breathe up here.

Talm's Peak stood against the horizon. A sea of trees between him and it. Just visible to the east, the stone seemed to bend in on itself. It was clear why the place had earned the name Vellia's Fingers, the grooves in the mountainside looking like a somewhat pinched hand. Or it did if Lin squinted hard enough. Lin took another deep breath and removed his sticky slippers, the residue on them leaving multiple needles stuck to their sides.

The branch was cold but better than tripping if the soft material decided to stick as he ran. When he'd had the idea, he hadn't considered how *different* the trees of northern Danica were compared to those south of Wellgrove. It felt like he had the One's own luck sometimes.

Lin picked off the needles and crammed the thin slippers into his pack before he adjusted his straps one last time. Then he ran.

Leaping from tree to tree proved a terrible idea. While he covered more ground than he thought possible, he fell twice, catching himself on a branch each time, and got more scrapes than he had even as a child. Perhaps this was a young man's game to play and people, even Inlayed ones, should stick to the solid ground below. But eventually, wounded and all, he made it to the far end of the forest. The trees still dotted the slopes but weren't nearly close enough to leap across.

Lin looked at the stony ground below. Then blinked. The glow of Bindings caught his eye from up the path. Too far to tell what they were, but they were stationary. As close as he was to Fallo, a fear settled into his gut heavy enough that it might plummet him to the ground below if left unchecked.

Two possibilities. It was a group of untethered, like what had attacked Fallo so many moons ago. Hiding in the pass between the two nations. Waiting. Or… it was bodies strung up. Corpses of Ladricans caught unaware. *Which could be a boon, all things considered.*

Lin dropped to the ground, crouching as he landed. He slipped on the thin-fabric shoes and wiggled his cold, sticky toes into them. The next pair of boots he found were his. Socks too, no matter where they were sourced from. Think what he wanted about the Ferrucium before the Fall, he'd been clothed and given good quality materials at that.

As he climbed higher up the slope, the path widened. Whatever Bindings he'd spotted still weren't visible, but the ridge above looked familiar and if his memory held, it hid whatever he'd seen just behind it. Wind howled and carried the soft hush of voices on it. Lin grit his teeth and focused. There was also the crashing of a waterfall in the distance, likely made all the fiercer by the thaw. *Shit.*

Lin blew into his hands and rubbed them together. From here on out, it was attack first, ask questions later. There wouldn't be Danicans in the pass. Except... Lin frowned and looked around the path. He'd thought there was supposed to be a Ferrucium Outpost around here. *That* could be where the voices were coming from. If only he could hear the speakers. Or see them. Lin stalked forward, at least glad that the slippers kept his footfalls silent compared to crunching boots.

The sun had dipped below the trees to the west and the cold was eager to seep into Lin's bones with its absence. If all of Ladrica felt like this, it was no wonder they were cruel, spiteful people. Lin shook his head. What was it Pael had said months back? Don't judge all based on one or something like that. There were likely decent enough people among the citizens of the Kingdom. But good people didn't mean they wouldn't attack him if they thought him untethered. Aemun had said the Ladricans considered all Danicans as monsters, hadn't he? It all blurred together, like a fever dream.

By the time he'd crept his way along the bottom of the ridge, he was able to fully hear the voices coming from above. Northern by the chopped words and stilted speech. Some words didn't make sense at all, sounding like a bastardization of their mother tongue and common Danican.

Lin peered over the rocks at eye level as the path cut back. The clouds had decided to let loose a light flurry and the wind picked up at this bluff. Lin could see the glow of the Bindings, but only partially, and not what was causing them.

Not far away was a group of lightly armored soldiers. Their fur-lined gloves and boots sent envy rushing through Lin's bitterly cold digits. Of the three soldiers, two had long bows and the other had a looking glass in one hand and a horn in the other. Scouts. Ladrican scouts. But if they had scouts here, it might mean they didn't have an army. And that was a boon, wasn't it? Lin ducked back down. He could likely take them in a fight. Target the one with the horn first, then deliver sharp Wefts to the other two. Except the armor was likely Ferrucium Steel. Or whatever Ladrican fucks called it. Lin was sick of things he'd known his entire life being considered other things. It was annoying and confusing and...

Lin jolted back as he saw the thick-robed, lithe creature rushing toward him. *Untethered*. Stitches and what once were Inlays traced along the monster's face in skewed, uneven rows. And Gods, they moved so silently even when they were upon Lin, vicious smile and... Lin blinked in shock as the robed figure silently embraced him. One lone arm wrapped around his shoulders. With a thought, Lin broke the Needle he'd formed, motes crumbling like rusted iron.

"Shhh," Denny mouthed, wild eyes looking up at the sliver of the ridge above them.

Relief preceded embarrassment. For a moment, he'd thought of Tylle. But of course, she hadn't come for him. Of course, she hadn't come for *Mellyr*. Lin was thankful he had to remain silent, as he wasn't sure he could have forced words past the tightness in his throat anyway.

Cleansing Hate

"All those in favor of allowing the Kingdom of Ladrica dominion over the land known as Danica, raised hand in unison. Of the many, counted fifteen kingdoms and powers, and those gathered peoples representing them, ten were shown to be in favor. Two abstained. Three were opposed. The listing is as follows." Excerpt from the Histories of Southern Danica, removed and redacted due to the Danican Accords.

Denny appeared just as wild and dangerous as when Lin had first met her. Moreso perhaps. He had questions with hopes attached but knew better than to voice them now, not with the three soldiers above them.

An uneven smile graced her face, the lines of Stitches across her cheeks exasperating the lopsidedness. She raised her brows and nodded her pointed chin up at the ridge. Apparently, losing a limb hadn't dulled her wicked sense of humor as she dragged a finger across her throat.

Lin raised a hand to slow her, but she was already flipping up and over the lip of the ridge. Her dark cloak was rough near the bottom and tattered, looking like the garb of the Noosemen. And it enveloped her, two to three sizes too large. *To cover her missing arm?* Whatever the reason, it made for a sight as she flew through the air.

Darting up just behind her, Lin watched as the soldier brought the horn to his lips. The call died with the man's breath as the horn split horizontally in half.

The Weft did the same to his face. Magic caught at the soft sides of his mouth and cut until his jaw hung by shredded, bloody tendons. To the soldier's credit, he dropped to his knees with barely a scream. Or, more realistically, the blood he gurgled prevented any scream from escaping.

Lin sliced two arrows from the air, ruining their trajectory. Denny spun in a flash to the remaining soldiers, who readied to fire again. They died before their fingers fully tightened around the bowstring.

Denny shifted and seemed to be scanning the surroundings. "So this is Ladrica?" She spat toward the closest corpse. "Thought they were 'sposed to be big bad enemies of Binders?"

"I did too," Lin said. He smiled despite himself. "But these were probably just scouts. Not fully armed soldiers. And we caught them by surprise."

Denny blew a strand of hair away from her face and gave him a look that suggested he'd fed her spoiled food. Then her lips quirked and her eyes drifted down his torso and settled onto his bare toes. "Work any interesting Inlays lately?"

"I've been busy." Lin ignored her roving stare and moved to examine the bodies. Of the three fresh dead, one had a near enough size that it wouldn't be unbearable. He ungently stripped the socks and boots, whispering a prayer as he did. "Who else is coming?" He asked over his shoulder.

When there was no reply, he turned, boot half on.

Denny's footprints led to the outpost's door but no sound came from within.

Once laced up, Lin followed. "Denny?"

Signs that the outpost had been Ferrucium maintained once showed in the crumpled crimson banners at the walls, now coated in dust. Lin followed the footprints until they disappeared in a dark doorway, the stench of spoiled goods hanging in the air.

Lin adjusted the straps over his shoulder and stepped through. Silence pervaded the outpost as much as dust did, settling into everything. Not even the scuttling of mice carried. Lin swallowed. Denny was somewhere. Guards had been—

"Ahhhh!" Denny screamed as she lunged. Wrapping her arm around his neck.

Lin yelped and nearly fell back as she hung onto him. She beamed a smile up at him, Inlayed eyes bright and terrifying from the darkness.

"Gods woman! Are you trying to scare me to death?"

Denny giggled and pulled away. "No need to act like a baby. I'm not an untethered, even if I look like one. It's a larder, by the way."

Lin shook his head and moved past the lithe woman, a smile coming unbidden to his face once she couldn't see him. If Denro or Pael had seen that, the teasing would be endless. But Gods, she moved so silently it was a marvel she even left footprints.

The room was narrow and shelves with sad remains of salt blocks, venison, and spoiled fruit lined the walls. Only one real prize existed and it was a jar of pickled honeycaps that faintly glowed behind the salt block.

"Are you done pouting?" Denny asked. She'd come to stand beside Lin and was poking the fleshy, rotted fruit.

Lin lifted the jar, examining it to make sure the contents hadn't spoiled. "Is anyone else coming?"

Denny spun to face him. "Oh yes," she snapped. "Carine, busy as she is, has stopped all the preparations for war to infiltrate what is likely the enemy's strongest border to rescue a child of no consequence. Tylle, the rude bitch, has dropped whatever she was doing and is just behind the ridge. Ah yes, and Jun decided his time would be better spent joining you than teaching combat skills to the few Binders we've been able to recruit."

Rude bitch? Lin frowned. "You don't—"

"In fact, as you can see with your own, Inlay-less eyes, I've brought an entire army. Danica moves at your very breath. I forgot that you were Velkath Reborn, mover of mountains, slayer of shadows."

"If this is how you plan to be—" Lin started, setting the jar down.

"Me? You didn't even ask me how I'm doing. How hard do you think I pushed to get here and you practically ask if it's just me? Well, nooooo, Erias himself is moving from the Grove to aid you in this." She stared at him for a moment, the Stitches across her face evening out. "I'm all anyone thought we could *spare*. More will come, but it won't be before the assembly takes place." She snatched the jar and, one-armed, slid it into the pack over her shoulder.

Lin let his head hang. "Denny. I didn't mean to imply that I wasn't grateful. I was prepared to do this alone if I had to." He looked up at her and stared into her bright, Binding-laced eyes. "What assembly?"

Together, they moved through the outpost until Lin was sure there weren't any other scouts or soldiers hiding. The small flurry of snow that had come down earlier had already stopped, and it left the path forward coated in slick, wet patches. Denny moved around them as if it were a game, jumping from point to point soundlessly.

Finally, she turned and said, "A group of them. Leaders of some sort to discuss the Accords."

"So they mean to hold a conference before they'll move?" Lin asked.

"Dunno." Denny turned and hopped another patch. Her shrug was lopsided, but she landed gracefully. "But I do know that our people weren't invited. And Erias has it on good authority it's taking place on an island just off the coast of the fort you're planning to visit."

Lin snorted. *Planning to visit.* "How can he be sure?"

Her blank stare said all it needed to.

"So Pael made it back?"

"With bells tied to his nethers."

Lin shook his head. Denny continued walking backward, facing him. There was a foreboding presence in the air. As if the land itself didn't want Lin here. He still hadn't seen what might've caused those Bindings he'd spotted from the treetops before entering the pass. That likely contributed to what he felt. But part of what Aemun had said long ago didn't sit right with him either. *Bound Metal.* Ancient. A gift from the land meant to punish Binders. And he had to have sourced it from Ladricans. What if the earth underfoot was laced with that noxious metal?

"He didn't really have bells tied, so far as I know." Denny had stopped moving, and when Lin looked up, she was within arm's length of him. "You alright?" She raised her brows at him.

"Thinking about Bound Metal and Ferrucium Steel and… how it all comes from here."

"Oh."

"And I'm worried about Mellyr."

"Of course," Denny nodded. "And you're wishing I were Tylle?"

That was like a punch in his gut. "No. I already told you, I'm thankful you've come at all." And curious why she thought Tylle was rude, but his head was already starting to throb from dealing with the wild woman, so he'd ask later.

She narrowed her eyes. "But you're wondering why they thought I would be a good fit compared to Tylle. Erias wants that child rescued. He feels your pain. Truly."

"But?" Lin asked.

"But you and I? We're expendable and dangerous."

Lin licked his lips. "I don't think you're expendable."

"I'm so close to untethering I can taste it," Denny leaned in and whispered. "One bad day…" she looked down at the space her missing arm should've occupied. "One *worse* day, and I'm snapping. I feel like a cord wound too tight. I know you know what I mean."

Gods. She meant it. Denny thought Lin was as near to untethering as she seemed. But he didn't want to make her feel alone out here. Didn't want to give her a reason to consider him any less on her side than he was. "Sometimes. It gets hard. I feel like I've been lost in thought more than I used to be. And recently," Lin walked past her so they weren't just standing on the rocky pass, "I've been hearing voices."

"Oh wow," Denny said, skipping to take the lead. Not even skittering a pebble as she went. "You really are cracking, huh? I was joking." She giggled and as the path rounded into a bend she slowed, stones and bits of ice crunching under her feet.

Lin snapped his attention to her and then saw what had caused her to finally make a sound.

The road looked like it had once been cut through the trees, but whatever foliage had flanked the path appeared long removed. Stripped bare. In the place of trees were metal stakes. Countless numbers of them, large and small. Countless bodies impaled upon them. Lin's stomach turned at the sight and threatened to rise from it. Flashes of Fallo danced across his vision, but this was different. The bodies weren't strung up with Stitches, though each tortured soul bore them.

These were numbers of untethered on a scale Lin had never dreamed of. No blood, dried or otherwise, coated the ends where the stakes protruded from the corpses. And the lack of smell or carrion didn't make sense even in the cold.

Lin stumbled forward and Denny tugged on his arm, her grip gentle but unyielding. With a jerk, Lin ripped his arm free and took three unsteady steps to the nearest untethered. He fell to his knees. Stared up at the creature.

The metal didn't give off a nauseating presence but it reminded him of Bound Metal in the draw he felt toward it. It didn't have the sharp sheen of Ferrucium Steel. But it did have a layer of green rust that spiraled upward in unusual, swirling patterns. He'd never seen it before. Lin narrowed his eyes as he examined it.

"Gods," Lin whispered. If he looked for too long, he saw Velkath's Sigil flashing behind the bodies, in his peripheral, disappearing when he sought it.

Denny grabbed Lin by the shoulder and looked down at him, rage and pain twisting her expression. Her jaw clenched and she shut her eyes. "We should go."

"Why aren't they rotten?"

Denny opened her eyes and stared at the nearest body. "Real untethered are rotten long before they decay. I... I don't know."

"But..." Lin shook his head, unable to put thought to words. There was something else going on here. Perhaps a different sort of metal reacting with Danican blood. He hadn't felt comfortable giving the book to Denro, he sure wouldn't give its secrets to Denny. "This... This had to be a warning for Danicans and untethered who crossed into the north."

"Not all of them could have been mad monsters. There's no way. There's no..." Denny's words faded like her breath in the air. "When we come back, let's give them a proper pyre."

Lin nodded. Those metal stakes made him uneasy. It all made him *fucking* uneasy. As quick as the scouts' deaths had been, perhaps they deserved worse.

They ran in silence for a time, the air slowly becoming easier to breathe. Once they crested a lopsided ridge that overlooked a dip in the wide path they slowed. If soldiers were staging, they were hidden off the main road and entirely silent. The lack of troops and the slow understanding that the path, while wide and viable through the pass proper, wasn't upkept nearly well enough for a full army to make any sort of breakneck pace made Lin doubt the pressing urgency and claim of the Ladrican Kingdom's armies invading Danica.

"Denny," Lin said softly.

"Lin-del," she replied. She shifted to face him from atop the log she'd climbed. If she had one of those flat, metal masks she'd have looked just like a Nooseman with the dark sky behind her.

"What if they're taking Mellyr to that island? What if she never was being brought to the fort?"

Denny looked like she was sucking on the inside of her cheek. "Then we invade the island and take her from there."

Lin shook his head and looked down. The sky had grown too dark to see much, but they were almost beyond Talm's Peak and he knew the fort likely laid down there in the darkness, just out of sight. "Aemun played us, played everyone."

"You're worried about plans a ghost might have made?" Denny snickered at him. "You're a coward, aren't you?"

Lin furrowed his brow, eyes drifting to the sound of owls crying. "No. I just mean what if it's all a part of *someone's* plans? What better way, after centuries, to remind the world that we are monsters than to have me, or us, attack a gathering of leaders of the world?"

Denny's head shook, her wild eyes tilting up as if she were trying to count the stars. Then her movements slowed and she stared at Lin. "You might be right. If that were the case..."

There was a question to her tone.

"I'd go anyways. I'd save Mellyr, no matter the cost."

Denny moved so fast Lin barely tracked it and almost stumbled back as her lone hand grabbed his chin. She kissed him on the cheek, so soft and cold and passionless that Lin wasn't sure she'd even done it. "*We'll* save her. No matter the cost. Now quit gawking and let's at least get down to the fort. Here." Deftly she untied the sack around her shoulder and pulled out the jar of honeycaps.

Lin watched her move, mesmerized at how proficient she'd become in the last few months. "I'm sorry."

"For?" She smiled up at him.

Lin took the jar from her and uncorked it, the scent sweet and spiced. "Not asking how you were. How *you've* been." He ate one of the honeycaps, the taste not nearly comparable to the pleasant scent, then chased it down with one of each of the vials he'd been gifted. Neither tasted enjoyable and both were gritty, but he took a pull from his waterskin and swished the fluid enough times to get the worst of it down.

She eyed the vials with a frown. "Well... I've been worse. And better. And... Exhausted. Erias has had me running messages more than anything else. Worried about my mental state and all that."

"You're still more than capable," Lin started.

"Never said I wasn't. Some things are harder, but still doable. In fact, I learned a neat little trick that maybe you'll get to see if you're lucky." Denny winked at him.

The blush that took Lin's cheeks felt like it might light the entire path and Lin felt guilty his mind had gone there. All from what... a kiss on the cheek? No. It was more than that and he knew it. She'd been the first one to ask after him after Aemun abandoned him. In her way at least. And now she was here.

"I meant... I meant I'd still be terrified to fight you one on one."

"I'm sure," she said, the saccharine tone not leaving her voice one bit. "As you should be."

As they continued down the path, trees eventually took to their right side while the left sloped more and more into a cliff face. The path rounded unevenly but in the distance, the fort broke through the darkness. Pits of lanterns or torches flickered warmly. So far away that they were barely more than dots, like stars.

"Smaller than I expected," Lin said.

"I still can't believe there were so many untethered... so many people staked like that."

Lin blinked and turned to look at Denny. "I... Me neither."

"And they looked old and healthy, somehow. Healthier than possible with the weather and wolves and..."

She was right. He'd tried not to look at the untethered closely, but not one of the bodies had looked weathered or disturbed by predators.

"What if they were cursed? Or some strange magic was used on them?"

Lin licked his lips. Hadn't the High Scholar mentioned other, smaller magics throughout the world? Binding wasn't the only magic. "What if they were alive? Frozen there in time and place to suffer?" His mind unwillingly went to the untethered and the trees, working Weft after Weft against the monster's flesh. Cutting only to realize the creature... *the person* within felt it all. Or had that just been an element of his dream? A manifestation of his guilt?

"Six, I hope not. The One's Shadow is long enough without dark thoughts like that adding to it."

Cleansing Blood

"It is with heavy hearts and unashamedly high hopes that we take full on our shoulders the burden of keeping the Danican people safe. In the sheets before you, you will see King Gunthyr's plan in all its glory. Laid out before you as our God laid it out to him. We expect resistance. We expect there to be pain and hurt as with all forms of growth. But in the end, as this assembly has voted, we expect it to be for the best of not only all the Free Nations and those powers gathered, but the blood-tainted Danicans themselves."
Statement presented by Lord Pollan Strat, a representative of the Ladrican Kingdom, given after his promotion to vizier following the final vote.

Fort Talmsdale was composed of thick gray stones and appeared as if it were hewn straight from the surrounding cliffside. It loomed squat and wide like some great beast that had given up as it crawled from the dark depths.

If all of Ladrica was as dreary and bleak as this stretch, it was clear why they might want Danican land. A gray-chopping sea cut the coast, and couldn't have looked more lifeless if it had been an actual corpse. There was no comparing it to the Pellic Sea he'd just spent months beside. Even the waters near the Ferrucium, dark like a night sky, didn't feel *lifeless.*

"Is that the ship they took her on?" Denny asked. She was squinting, making the Stitches along her cheeks skew further. She raised her right hand and cupped it to her eye as if peering through an invisible spyglass.

Lin watched her for a breath, unable to hide the grin she brought to his face. "No. Or at least I don't think so. I can't be sure."

The ship in front of them looked too short and low to the water. But he'd been closer to the Pollsh trading galley and this ship was lined up against the fort, making an accurate estimate of scale more complicated.

"We'll ask. And if they don't want to answer, we'll make them." Denny spoke so matter-of-factly that it made it easy for Lin to nod in agreement. She might be odd, a dash unpredictable, and downright terrifying at times, but he was glad to have her beside him.

No matter what, it was better than attempting this alone.

"And if she is headed toward the island?" Lin asked. He squinted through the hazy air, a thin fog obscuring the horizon off the shore. Try as he might, he couldn't see the land Denny insisted was there.

"Then I think that should count as an invite to this super special meeting they didn't want our people at. Maybe we can show them we aren't the monsters they think we are. Or make them regret stealing her away."

"Maybe," Lin said. Picturing the lightly armored Ladrican emissary who had held Mellyr was pointless. No matter how hard he tried to envision a peaceful resolution, the images of slit throats, severed hands, and corpses surfaced instead.

"You need rest."

"I'll have it when either I'm dead or the bastard who took Mellyr is."

Denny's lip twitched as if there was something more she wanted to say. Instead, she shook her head and they crept forward.

Not a single sentry seemed to shadow the top of the fort or the windows along the highest floor. Torches were inset along the path leading from its eastern and southern sides, the northwest pressing against the shore and not visible from the angle they approached. Flags whipped along the turrets atop the fort. The Ladrican serpent coiled into a knot depicted on the fabric danced in the wind. A wolf's howl cut through the early morning air and Lin would've jumped if Denny hadn't been staring at him.

"What?" Lin asked when she didn't pull her bright eyes away.

"You're breathing loudly."

"Am I?" Lin whispered.

"Yes. Shh. Move like a breeze."

Lin frowned. "Breezes aren't silent."

"No, but they sound natural." Denny continued forward, soundless as always. It had to be magic, the way she moved, but there wasn't anything in the stolen book he'd read that might explain it. Even if her legs and feet had some sort of Inlay, it wouldn't explain the phenomenon.

Lin stepped where she did, matching her pace, and soon they were against the flat of the wall. Danica had some buildings made of stonework, but most were wooden structures and compared to those, this fort felt ancient.

Denny pressed the side of her head against the wall and held a lone finger to her lips, listening through what had to be stone as thick as three men lined up. Lin followed suit, the cold wall stinging his ears. Unintelligible muffled voices carried. Without a word, Denny pulled away and gestured for him to follow her around the exterior.

Scratchy, thin-limbed scraggly bushes and sharp, flat stones comprised the walk, and with every crunching misstep, Lin expected the soldiers within to swarm out. But none did. Not a torch or lantern came out to shine on them from overhead. Maybe Denny's unnaturally silent steps had made him overly concerned about his perfectly natural *quiet* steps.

Now that they were closer, it was clear the ship wasn't the same one that had spirited away Mellyr. Where the Pollsh trading galley had an insignia on the side and a name, this ship appeared battered and worn by comparison. The dock it rested at seemed just as worse for wear, the wood darkly stained and warped in places.

"Two armored men." Denny nodded toward the rear of the ship.

Lin squinted. It seemed his eyes were getting worse and worse with each passing year. Gods, they were there, just blending in with the backdrop of the sea. Lin blanched. What if there *had* been sentries above them this whole time and he just hadn't noticed? No. Denny would have said something. But now that he was looking for them against the dark sea, he noted more men aboard the ship. Ten or so, not in armor. Sailors then?

"I don't see any other boats, aside from that sad little thing. If we want to make it to the island, we take that ship," Denny whispered.

And if she isn't even there? "And if we ruin whatever plans Erias and Azhura might've had with the Ladrican Kingdom in the process?"

Denny slowly turned and stared straight into his eyes. "If Erias was worried about relations... he... well, he wouldn't have allowed me to come."

That made sense. But there was something about the way she'd said it that didn't sound right. The pause. She always spoke so assuredly even when she said the most ridiculous things. "Denny... earlier you said he sent you. Now you're saying he allowed you. Did Erias send you?"

Her reply was a twist of emotions across her face at once. "Yes. And no. It's complicated. But I'm here for you, aren't I?"

The first time they'd ever really spoken, she'd essentially told him she'd kill him if he didn't meet expectations. Was this like that again? Had she been sent to stop him if it seemed he couldn't achieve the desired outcome? Lin shivered and considered that even Pael had taken a shot at Mellyr to keep her from Ladrican clutches. "Complicated how? Complicated like you were sent to keep me from saving Mellyr or?"

"Complicated as in no one knows I'm here. Or they likely do now but..." Denny blinked away the start of tears. "They wouldn't let me be me anymore. It was like I'd been leashed. Pael came in and started mentioning what you were doing and it sounded like *freedom*. It sounded like... like I'd be able to be me again. Erias and that old bitch and everyone else can act like these aren't our enemies, or that they won't be our enemies until they press their boots on our throats in our own homes, but I won't sit idly. I won't. Carine and Erias found me and sharpened my fangs, and helped make me who I am, and once I lost my arm and the Ferrucium was 'restructured', I was told to stop baring my teeth." Denny chomped at the air between them. "I refuse to let them dull. I won't ever be made to think I'm weak again."

"Alright," Lin whispered, raising his hands and gesturing for her to calm down. "I understand." He did. In a way. It had been clear that Denny had some sort of trauma in her past and Lin wasn't about to kick that viper's nest, but he'd felt the same fury when Pael and Denro hadn't wanted him chasing after Mellyr. He hadn't chosen to be her protector, not fully at first, but the world would be taken by Wicked Tel'Myr if anyone thought they would stop him once he'd fully embraced the role.

"Keep up. Try to keep one of the armored ones alive for answers."

"Right," Lin whispered. Before he'd fully finished the word, she was off. He'd grown used to his Inlays, to the extra strength and speed the magic granted him, but he felt like a toddler when watching Denny move. There was a reason, other than the cloak, that she reminded him of a Nooseman. Those northern monsters had trained extensively with Inlays and Bindings of all sorts for the sole purpose of keeping normal Danican Binders in line. Denny had that same lethal athleticism to her movements.

Keeping up was possible, but not quietly. The hard, flat stones that shifted and clattered against each other sounded like alarm bells in Lin's ears. But by the time anyone seemed to notice them,

Denny was already on the dock, Wefts flying in wide arcs at sailors and soldiers alike. They shouted in Ladrican, which still sounded like broken Danican to Lin, but one word was clear.

"Untethered!"

A bell at the front of the ship clanged even as one of Denny's Wefts took the upper forearm from the sailor ringing it. Lin joined in the assault, catching up to her moments later. She'd pivoted once jumping onto the ship and had barreled toward the nearest armored soldier.

Lin sent a Weft ripping through the air. It crashed, then exploded into sparks against the soldier's breastplate. Not even a scuff on the metal.

Both armored soldiers drew two weapons apiece. A sword in one hand, similar to what Ferrucium soldiers carried and likely made of the same steel and a baton in the other.

Weft after Weft flew from Denny in a flurry. Her attacks were reckless, as if her spul was endless—volume over accuracy.

"Denny stop!" Lin called. He watched in horror as the soldier the Wefts had been aimed at raised his baton, the tip off-colored compared to the rest of the tool. The Wefts cut the air toward the soldier, then stalled out as if they'd lost all momentum. With a flick of the baton, the Wefts ricocheted out into the early morning sky to dissolve into motes of light.

"Bound Metal!" Lin felt nauseous even thinking about the cursed stuff. With armor and blade made of Ferrucium steel, he doubted the batons were meant as defensive tools. "Don't let it touch you!"

The look Denny gave implied he was an idiot for even suggesting she might get touched. Which was all well and good but he had been there when she lost her arm. He'd heard her scream.

An arrow thunked into the deck, too close to Lin's foot for comfort. Torches flared to life on the ramparts of the fort and several archers were sighting in on them.

"Archers!" Denny said. *Gods,* she'd rolled her eyes.

Lin rushed forward, and a Blade formed in his right hand. Most of the sailors had left the deck at the call of 'untethered' but some few stayed with unsteady blades or boltshooters. They hid behind barrels and along benches fit for rowers, but Lin ignored them. Odds were, this would be far harder than it seemed.

Neither of the armored soldiers seemed to possess the Sight. Their eyes stayed trained on Lin's center of mass, but as Lin closed the gap between them, it seemed they sensed the humming energy of the Blade in Lin's grip. Simultaneously, the nearest one shifted their stance and attempted to stab Lin's sternum with the baton.

The closer the weapon came, the more it felt like stepping through those damned doors of Erias's. If he hadn't experienced that before, and Erias's One-loved ring pressing into his brow, and Aemun's strange Bound Metal bracer, the unnatural pull from the tip of the weapon would've stolen his footing.

Lin slashed horizontally, simultaneously sending a Weft aimed at the soldier's throat. The Blade fuzzed as if losing substance as it clashed with the baton. The armored soldier counterattacked immediately, their sword arcing to take Lin's head. Pulled off course by the Bound Metal baton, the Weft crashed into the soldier's helm. It was knocked askew, clattering to the deck.

Under the helm was a fair-skinned woman, and her glare was as sharp as her blade as she pressed the assault. At the sound of the helm crashing, the other soldier pivoted and flanked Lin.

Denny appeared between Lin and the approaching soldier in a blur. She'd stopped slinging Wefts and had drawn a long, curved dagger. As fluidly as she moved, there was a hitch to her steps that proved the Bound Metal affected her.

"Untethered," the helmless soldier growled.

"Fuck you," Lin replied. With Denny to his back, he moved to get within the soldier's range. He sidestepped a sweep of the sword just as a bolt cracked into the deck beside him. Looking at whoever fired it would leave him vulnerable to the sword-swinging, baton-poking terror before him, so he pressed in even closer. Denny had the right idea, underarmored and quicker than the soldiers, they needed to press their speed and flexibility as an advantage.

Lin stepped in, broke apart what was left of his Blade, and shifted the magic into a smaller, more compact weapon. His first instinct had been to make a Needle in each hand, so thin it was hard for him to even see it. He crashed his left forearm against the soldier's sword arm to block a strike and shoved the needle up toward the woman's chin.

The baton swung up and under, the tip almost thrusting into Lin's chin, the shaft cracking into Lin's right arm and sending his attack wide. The strike reverberated through Lin's bones. It had been too long since he'd had to worry about bruising, but he was sure only the Inlays kept the counterattack from breaking bones. Lin let the momentum of the attack swing him around and he jumped into the air, twisting the soldier's gauntlet. They tumbled to the ground together, armor clattering as they rolled. The sword stabbed into the deck and Lin cranked on the soldier's arm. The goal was to release the woman's grip on the baton, but she wouldn't let go.

Shouts came from around the ship and the woman snarled curses. Armored soldiers had a variety of advantages, but pinned on her back, the armor's weight had to be working against her. Lin leveraged his hips and slammed a balled fist over and over into the bracer protecting her wrist. Pain lanced through his hand. Then, after the third strike, the armor dented. It caved ripping a howl from the woman as the baton finally rolled out from her grip.

Lin untangled himself from the soldier and rose on unsteady feet. His hand complained as he grabbed the baton, fingers not listening to grasp it entirely. But he picked it up.

The soldier beside him struggled to stand and Lin kicked her across the chin as hard as he could manage. She collapsed and he wheeled to where Denny and the other armored soldier clashed.

Denny had come to a similar conclusion as Lin and had coiled herself around the armored soldier, stabbing and slicing into the cracks between the armor while avoiding the soldier's slowing strikes.

Lin rushed in, using Denny's black cloak to hide his approach, and thrust the baton into the breastplate. It dented the steel right away and the soldier staggered back from the force, stepping so as not to trip. Off-balance, the armored soldier stumbled until their back was against the rail of the ship, the baton crunching and bending the steel as Lin put all his force into it. With a final exertion, Lin felt another crunch as something underneath the armor gave way with a sick snap.

"Fuckers," Lin wheezed out.

"If... if all their soldiers are like this..." Denny let her words fade as heavy steps crunched along the shore leading to the dock beside the ship.

Lin knew what she had been about to say. He felt it in the bruised bones of his hand and the throbbing of his forearm. If all Ladrican soldiers were armored and with weapons that effectively made Binder's tools useless, Danica didn't stand a chance at surviving. Lin followed the sound of the steps and his heart dropped so far that it might've sunk below the sea if the ship weren't there.

The flat, metal mask only had thin slits for the eyes and the cloak they wore was darker than the night sky, with hints of scarlet in the cuts of it. A Nooseman. A One-loved, fucking *Nooseman*.

Congealed Hope

"It is with a heavy heart and much deliberation that Emperor Kan has declared that Elodis will no longer openly trade with the Kingdom of Ladrica due to the harmful nature of the Danican Accords. This embargo will affect the following, but not be limited to. A list to follow." Excerpt taken from the counter speech given by Speaker Pat Miche, from the Empire of Elodis.

Denny struck out, three Wefts slashing the air between her and the Nooseman. As hard as it was to imagine, she seemed to form Bindings even swifter than she had back before she'd lost her arm. Doing a Binding without a focus was one thing... doing it without a hand to guide it seemed like another level of skill entirely.

Lin blinked away the afterimage of Denny's Wefts, so close in structure to Velkath's Sigil that he wasn't sure she hadn't done it on purpose.

The Nooseman was a breeze on a silent night. The Wefts warped around them and were redirected at Lin as if taking control of another Binder's magic was as simple as breathing. It brought back memories of Fallo, when the untethered had taken Lin's Binding from him and used it to snap back his fingers and wrist.

Lin rolled to the side, swept up the soldier's lost sword, and broke the Weft about to bite into his arm.

Cowardly archers who had hidden earlier took shots anew. A barrage of arrows biting into the deck around them. Perhaps they hadn't wanted to shoot toward the armored soldiers but had no qualms about accidentally striking the Nooseman.

Nooseman are just Danicans, like us. Except Lin didn't fully believe that. These men and women were trained to be better, to explicitly be stronger and more capable than even the most adept Ferrucium soldiers.

Lin took a step forward and tightened his grip on the sword. Sweat beaded his brow, stinging his eyes and his knuckles were white. As he was now, he should've been at least as capable as Tylle had been back then when she'd defeated not one, but *two* Noosemen. And hadn't they said Dennick had been the best of them? Lin and Denny shouldn't have an issue dispatching this single one.

"Why are you here, untethered?" The Nooseman spoke in that same halting, broken dialogue Dennick had spoken with. There were plenty of names he'd lost along the way, but Dennick still sent a shiver down his spine just thinking about the man. The monster. But this Nooseman was a woman, voice harsh and pitched.

"Baby," Lin said.

Denny didn't seem to have the patience for even the broken conversation the Nooseman attempted to have. She'd given up on sending the arcing, sharp Wefts and had moved in, dagger in her lone hand cutting the air.

The Nooseman wasn't keen on blocking. They shifted just out of reach of each strike, pivoting on the balls of their feet. They swayed like the mass underneath the cloak was incorporeal.

Denny slashed, finding only air. She shifted her weight, spun, and missed again. Her strikes looked hard to track and impossible to predict. But the Nooseman moved as if Denny announced each attack.

Lin pressed the assault, sword in hand. He wouldn't create Bindings, not if this Nooseman excelled at taking control of them. Or at least, that's what he wanted his enemy to think. He was at her side, swinging opposite of Denny. The Nooseman was a shadow, their cloak tattering but neither blade finding purchase.

"What baby?"

Lin stalled his overhead swing. Then took a boot to his chest for his troubles. The blow felt off-balance but it knocked the wind from him all the same and sent him tumbling to where the armored soldier he'd kicked across the face had been. Her eyes were open and she growled at him through a bloody nose and teeth painted with a deep crimson. The sword had slipped from his hands in the tumble and had clattered to the deck underneath one of the rowing pews.

From the deck, it looked like two Noosemen were fighting each other. Both the real one and Denny were moving like shadows, but it was clear which one had the upper hand.

Lin scrambled to his feet, the ship rocking underfoot. Before he could take a step, he felt a strong tug on his ankle and his cheek greeted the wood of the deck with a hard thud. There was no doubt it would bruise the way he landed. The soldier, Gods take her, was on him. Even with her dented armor and likely shattered wrist, she crawled onto him. Striking down, slamming both gauntleted fists like hammers. She cursed and spat and no matter how Lin kicked, wouldn't come off of him.

The one benefit was that the archers had slowed their incessant firing toward him.

Denny grunted, and Lin laid flat to see her.

How had this all gone so poorly? Lin formed another Needle. Whether the soldier had the Sight all along or just felt the pure humming of power, she slammed her armored fist into his wrist. Over and over. The third blow broke the Binding as her Ferrucium steel armor crushed the magic into motes of light.

On her fourth swing, Lin managed to use her momentum to roll her off. With him on top and his back exposed, it was only moments before an aspiring archer made him into a pin-cushion.

The woman under him didn't look fearful. Her jaw was set in a furious, blood-spattered grin. She swung up at him, gauntleted fist connecting with his chin. Lin took the blow, then the next as he formed a Weft at her throat. It sunk in as his weight pressed down, but she pulled her head back unnaturally, shifting and rolling to the side enough that the Weft bit deck instead of neck.

She howled and his Weft collapsed.

Lin rained blow after blow down on her face and arms, the armor preventing the worst of it from connecting. But he could tell she was overwhelmed and when he was sure he had her disoriented enough, he formed a short, thick Blade and stabbed down. She managed to catch it in her hand, the Ferrucium Steel of her gauntlet shrieking against the magic in Lin's grasp. It was shrill and pitched and at some point, she added a deep guttural growl to the sound as Lin tried to force the Blade into her throat.

A howl, choked and pained came from behind. Lin looked up. Knew he shouldn't have and did anyway. Denny dangled from the Nooseman's grasp, their hand clenched around her throat. Gods, they were holding her up with one hand.

"Fuck off me!" The soldier howled. Her face had gone a deep red and spit and blood clung to her bruised lips. But all her screaming didn't stop the Blade as it found purchase in her throat as it screeched along her gauntlet. She continued to burble out curses as she choked on her blood.

Lin struggled to his feet and sprinted at the Nooseman. The short distance seemed to stretch further and further away as he formed six Wefts, like a line of sickles, all slashing toward the Nooseman's side.

In a blink Denny's squirming, writhing back was in the way. Lin broke all the Wefts at once, lighting the area around the deck in a flurry of motes. Then he was on them, sweeping a kick low that the Nooseman easily avoided. He followed it with an upward strike aimed at their forearm, but they moved Denny into the way again and Lin stopped his attack short and took a punch across his chest.

Denny's strangled breaths were loud as she struggled. She kicked and clawed with her free limbs.

"You come looking for baby, but you are children yourself. Weak, like babies." The Nooseman chuckled as they blocked another flurry of blows from Lin. "Your blood makes you weak. Weak blood-tainted-babies."

"Let her go!" Lin screamed. He'd avoided the last few counter-attacks from the Nooseman and had angled in close. Denny continued kicking and then the space where her missing limb should be glowed an ochre-gold. It looked as if she'd crafted a limb out of Bindings. It only lasted for a split second, but sparked and hissed as it drew a gouge across the Nooseman's flat, metal mask.

The Nooseman spun, like a leaf blown by the wind, ending with Denny slammed into the deck, the wood cracking at the impact. Maybe more than wood as Lin watched her twitch.

Lin moved to take advantage of the Nooseman's poor posture, bent over Denny as they were when a weight like that of a stone slab crashed into him from the side. His vision flashed and he bit his cheek but he regained control of himself just as he hit the low rail of the ship. The breastplate pushing him overboard was dented and crushed, the face hidden by an armored helm stained with blood. As they tumbled the armored soldier wrapped their arms around Lin and squeezed.

Falling into the water was like hitting the ground after falling from a high tree. Not that the ship itself had sat high off the dock, but the water was flat and cold and the soldier's weight pressed them both down.

Lin's first instinct was to exhale, but he held his stinging breath down. Gods, it was his nightmare made manifest. He was a blade being forged and this was what would temper him. *Or kill him.* He struggled, his fur cloak just as heavy as his boots. The soldier squeezed with seemingly everything they had to try to break bones and press the air from Lin.

Opening his eyes stung, the water dark and deeper than he'd expected as close to shore as they were. His Inlays made the water near him glow slightly. Lin tried to form a Weft, but it was like the threads of power couldn't sustain themselves. They sparked into creation and then drifted apart, floating away on invisible currents like strands of seaweed.

Lin blinked. Bubbles escaped the helm as they continued to sink and the crushing pressure on Lin's chest ceded while a new pressure built within. He'd lost up from down and his limbs felt far heavier than they should. Of all the ways to die, he hadn't seen drowning being the thing that finally ended him. He'd survived Noosemen, untethered, Aemun, all to be dragged overboard and pulled to the bottom of the sea.

Stroke after stroke he clawed his way back to what he thought was the surface. It hurt. His muscles ached, his lungs screamed, heart throbbed. No matter how hard he pulled himself to the surface, it didn't seem like he made any progress.

Purple flashed through his vision and the hammering of his heart in his ears turned into the steady beat of metal being struck. Over and over. Lin was the blade, he always had been. Shaped into the mold those holding him wanted. But metal sank. It was hard and even Ferrucium steel could be inflexible. Lin was hammered until he was raw, and it still wasn't enough. He still wasn't pure.

Another strike, no harder than the last few, no softer, hit him in his core and he exploded into hot embers. Velkath's Sigil burned bright in the sparks. There was a symmetry to it that Lin hadn't considered before. A beauty. It shifted into Mellyr's smile. Cute, innocent. He'd failed her.

Lin reformed, smelted down. Reworked. Broken. This time his embers and sparks formed Tylle's uneven frown. The disapproval on her face was so heart-achingly familiar. Then it shifted and he stared at Aemun's arrogant grin. Lin could hear his voice. *Escorter.* Such disdain. Why did Lin think he was capable of anything? The last thing Lin saw was an untethered. Stitches and Inlays along their flesh. They were beautiful. Horribly so. That was what a real blade was meant to look like. Sharp edges, sheen, and all. *Escorter.*

Congealed Bone

"The transition to a central rule wasn't easy on Danicans. Many died in the early years of the newly named Ferrucium's rule. The ducal houses were chosen due to some local prominence and sworn oaths. Not the magical oaths, mind you, making them far easier to break. Those Wievers who agreed to turn on their brethren were given special designation once they'd proved their worth, and soon, Danica was in the firm grasp of Ladrican rule."
Excerpt from the Histories of Southern Danica, removed and redacted due to the Danican Accords.

Lin choked out a breath, then another. He coughed until he could breathe and rolled onto his side spluttering water and sucking greedy breaths. The stones under him clattered and the slow lapping waves steadily pulled at him, unwilling to let him be fully free of their cold caress. His soaked clothes weighed on him like a heavy, wet blanket. Shivers racked him. His teeth chattered and his fingers and toes ached with an icy numbness. Staring up at the sky was all he could do for a while and no matter how many breaths he sucked in, his chest didn't stop stinging.

When he finally felt like he had the energy to sit up, he saw Fort Talmsdale far off on the shore, like a pyre against the backdrop of the range they'd crossed to get to it. Talm's peak loomed.

Lin blinked and wiped his damp face, pulling away a blood-streaked palm. Made sense why his brow throbbed, he must have smacked it against a stone.

Lin narrowed his eyes. It looked like there were people with lanterns walking this way. Probably soldiers searching for him. *Fuck.* He forced himself up, fell to a knee, then crawled away from the rocks and into the tree line. Frost coated the ground and crunched underfoot. Gods, it was cold, but it seemed another snow flurry wasn't on the wind. *Yet.*

With his back against a tree and shivering, Lin waited. From where he crouched, there wasn't any sign he'd been sprawled out along the dark shore. Not that he was familiar with this sort of terrain. He slid down, huddling and breathing into his hands. They weren't warming and he wasn't sure his flesh had ever looked so pale. He sucked in uneven breaths and forced down the thoughts of Denny that flashed through his mind.

Add her to the long list of those he'd failed. *Fuck.* He needed to calm down. But the Nooseman would have killed her by now. Those merciless monsters were as bad as untethered. *Worse.*

"I'm sorry. I f-failed y-you." Lin choked out the words and clenched and unclenched his hands several times. He was always too weak, too slow. And now he was stranded. Surrounded by enemies, with no allies, and no clue where Mellyr was.

Lin stared out across the dark, still water. The island Denny confidently stated should be hosting the assembly stood out dark against the lightening sky. There was no way he could swim across the gulf.

With the tree at his back, he sucked in six calming breaths. Then a seventh for the good or ill of it. There was a chance, slim as it was, that Denny was alive. Until he saw her corpse, he had to hope. He used the tree to stand, then hobbled from trunk to trunk until he was as close to the fort as he could get.

Between him and the fort was a field cleared of all foliage, much the way the Ferrucium's surroundings were kept. He glanced at where the soldiers had been patrolling along the shore. No sign of them. The ship was gone. Lin scanned the water and spotted it. A lone lantern lit its rear and it looked as if it was heading to the island. So, assuming the Nooseman was aboard, they'd be at the isle. Lin frowned. He couldn't see the docks from the angle he stood at but Denny had mentioned the shitty little boat that had rested there.

A shiver rattled through his bones and Lin took a deep breath. As bad as things were, he'd been through worse and saw the other side of it. He'd make his way to the docks and he needed to move quickly before the sun rose. But before he left, he'd need to check the fort itself. There was no guarantee Mellyr hadn't been brought here, even if the Nooseman had seemed confused by the mention of a baby.

Lin skulked, clothes wet and heavy, going back toward the shore to avoid the hooded lanterns lighting this side of the fort. A path carved through the wilderness from the north and it looked well worn with heavy ruts.

You expected an army. What is a fort full of soldiers compared to that?

The sound of running water, like a lazy stream, trickled from a pipe set into the base of the fort. Lin looked up and pinched his nose at the foul odor. A well-rusted grate, coated in slime and some thick mold-like substance, rested just above his eye level. The tunnel was slim, but still large enough that Lin was sure he could squeeze through. And more important than all of that, it was in a shadowed recess where the light of lamps didn't reach. A discolored waterline along the stones implied the sea rose to meet that tunnel.

"If a God or Gods is looking down on me... please... please see me through this," Lin whispered. It took most of his strength to climb the wall. His numb fingertips slipped on the cold, damp stone more than once and his cheek and brow throbbed in unison.

He held himself up and the edge of his boot gripped the inch of stone-lip from the uneven building.

With a heft, the grate shrieked aside. Lin's first instinct was to freeze and hope no one would spot him hanging there. He squeezed into the odorous tunnel, stifling his reflex to gag, and pulled the grate full-closed behind him. Of course, it sounded as loud as an alarm to him, but there was a chance nobody had heard it. And if he'd learned anything over the last few months, sometimes chances had to be taken.

Sloshing through the tunnel on all fours was the only option, especially as the tunnel narrowed deeper into the fort as he progressed. The surroundings were only lit by the Stitches of Lin's left hand, casting everything in a muddy brown shade. Splatters sounded from ahead and then a surge of waste and water crawled past him.

Gods. It was fragrant and foul and Lin would need ten baths after this to ever feel clean again. A bit of something warm stuck to his hand. *Eleven baths.*

He looked under his armpit to glance behind him, face coming closer to the trickle of water than preferred. More light was shining through the grate and it looked like his guess was correct, the water from the sea was slinking in behind him. All things considered, good. He'd need the salt to clean whatever wounds he had after creeping through this gunk. At this point, he was sure he was well within the bowels of the fort as much as it smelled of shit.

Every few feet there were narrow slits above him, too small to climb through. Ahead, light signaled the end of the cramped tunnel. It opened above him but not into a privy as he expected.

Crawling out was easier than getting in, especially since the grate here moved as if it was shifted often with barely a complaint. The room was lit by oil-burning sconces and looked spacious, with numerous adjoining cells. Each cell seemed to have a table in the middle and chains attached to the walls. *A dungeon?* If so, it was far larger than Erias's dungeon back in Wellgrove. The stonework around the exit of the pipe seemed designed so that fluids and anything else spilled might angle into the pipe with minimum assistance.

Lin wasted no time stripping from the layers of his foul-smelling, wet clothes. He kicked them into the hole he'd crawled out of and shivered as close to one of the oil lamps as he could. It rested above one of the long tables and highlighted an organized row of several tools including a scalpel made of Bound

Metal that looked like it belonged to a physiker, if that physiker had a panache for twisted, cruel experiments. His mind jumped to the sort of tests the Fentian Scholars might've done to Mellyr and his stomach spun on itself. It was the spark needed to move away from the slight warmth of the lamp and assess his situation.

Only one door leading out of the main area stood out and beside it sat a long plate of polished steel and a cabinet as tall as Lin. Seeing a flash of himself, pale and sickly looking, with Stitches along his torso where Tylle had saved him and Inlays running down his limbs, made him do a double-take.

Gods, he did look like an untethered. He ran a hand through his hair, thinner than it had been when Tylle braided it, then down his torso as he touched the soft hum of the Stitches that had saved his life. His cheek was bruised and swollen and the cut on his brow was caked in dried blood. A streak of blood crusted the side of his face and the wound itself oozed a bit.

Even if he looked untethered, even if he heard every voice in the world inside his mind and saw drifting signs of Velkath's Sigil, he knew he wasn't untethered. He couldn't be, not until he found Mellyr.

The cabinet opened without resistance, and inside were several changes of clothes. The third set he tried fit Lin well enough given the circumstances. Tighter than the draping clothes Pael had found for him. Slim-fitted and overly constricting in the Ladrican fashion. Aside from the clothes, the cabinet held a rack of empty, stoppered vials and sheets of notes written in an illegible scrawl.

Seeing the scratched-out writing made Lin realize he'd lost the book he had taken from High Scholar Anya.

Lost when he was thrown overboard.

Likely sunk to the bottom of the icy sea. Anya said the answer to removing his Stitches and Inlays wasn't in there, hadn't she? But what if there were more Wievings that Lin hadn't discovered, lost in those pages? Book aside, the last vials of the medicine he'd gotten had been in there as well. The last thing he needed was his bout of fever to return given the plunge he'd taken.

Lin shut the cabinet and crept to the door. Steps came and went, boots scuffing the stone. As much as this space looked like a dungeon, it seemed it wasn't set so far from commonly walked paths. How tall was the fort? Two, maybe three, stories. But it was elevated above sea level and this section could be a fourth, lower level. *Fuck.*

The door groaned as it opened and Lin froze. He'd been prepared to fight an entire army to rescue Mellyr. *One fort won't stop me. One man won't stop me.*

He didn't have time to hide and there was a puddle near the hole where his damp clothes had rested. Lin pressed flat beside the cabinet and mirror.

A heavy-set man with thick, wavy hair and a scowl that could scare a Nooseman stepped through the door. He wore a pair of focals and was thankfully alone as the door closed behind him.

"Interrupting important—" Whatever mumbling the scowling man was doing was cut short as Lin grabbed him from behind, squeezing his arm around the man's thick neck.

"Scream and I slit your throat. Do you understand me?"

"Danican," he growled.

"Do you understand?" Lin's Blade formed against the side of the man's cheek, and he tightened his hold so the tip pricked under the man's right eye.

"Yes," he strained to say, tone softening. "How say... Enough bloodshed has been had."

Lin tightened his grip and pulled hard, bringing the man's center of gravity back and putting him off balance. The man smelled sterile.

Lin walked him forward away from the door and ended the forced march near the wide drain in the floor. "What do you mean?"

"P-ple-ase."

He didn't want to loosen his grip. Not if this was the man in charge of this room with its tools of torture and chains. But he did. Just enough so the man could take in a full breath.

"Explain."

"I-I am Physiker Yurell. I was assigned to Fort Talmsdale ten years ago. As punishment for disagreeing with one of King Lodram's trusted advisors on how disease and waste relate." His words weren't entirely broken, not the way some Ladricans spoke and he knew enough Danican to sound more fluid than an actual foreigner. But he had the same, naturally fair complexion of most Ladricans.

Lin pushed him away and stared at him, Blade in one hand, Weft formed and ready to fly from the other. "And?"

Yurell turned and looked like he was attempting to smile. "All that to say, I can aid you."

"All because you were sent to this fort?" Lin frowned. He didn't trust the man. It might be because of nerves but the thick-necked man's beady eyes moved around the room far too much.

"All because I've seen the way you're people have been mistreated. You are untethered, no?"

"No," Lin snapped.

The heavy-set man flinched. "A-apologies. You look like the ones I... I tested. Was forced to test, I mean."

"Tested?"

If there was ever a point that Lin had watched a man weigh his own words, it was now. "I was ordered to experiment on the ones captured who'd crossed into our territory. Forced really." He licked his thick lips, his mustache twitching. He kept his hands up and glanced from the open grate to the nearest cell, and back to Lin.

Lin's first thought went to Mellyr, then to the corpses staked and displayed in the mountain pass. "Did you test a child?"

"Oh no. Never a child. I'd never."

"What sort of tests?" Lin asked.

"A number really. How did tainted blood react when mixed with certain reagents? What happens if a Binding is swallowed? How long can an untethered survive without food or water? Various things that... for the advancement of curing the disease... had to be done."

"Disease?" Lin leaned forward, bringing his Blade nearer to the man's neck.

Yurell shifted. "The blood-taint. Some believe it is a curse. Others, simply a fact of life. But learned men, like myself and others who have spent their lives unlocking the mysteries of the world, understand the workings of the human body. Danicans aren't cursed. They just bear an affliction. One that, hopefully, we can eradicate someday."

Gods. The man meant what he was saying. But if he was incapable of eradicating Binding, what would keep his ideology from murdering every Danican out there?

"You seem like a reasonable man." Yurell's eyes continued to dart around the room in uneven intervals.

"I can be," Lin said. Though if he was standing in the Physiker's shoes, he was sure he'd disagree.

"And you must know the terrors of the untethered."

"I do."

Yurell nodded vehemently. "Wouldn't it be better if they weren't able to go mad? If they didn't have the power to kill indiscriminately?"

Lin stared at the man as he finally made and held eye contact. "It could be."

"Then please understand that the tests performed, even the active test in the southern pass, are not meant to be cruel. A little pain now to save the future from so much more."

"Wait." Lin tried to straighten out his thoughts. "So the untethered there *are* still alive?"

"Oh very. The metal they are staked upon is sustaining them. The catch is that they're frozen in a sort of... stasis."

"They can feel it," Lin said.

"Oh no, they..."

"They *can* feel it. They're aware." Lin growled the words and took a half step forward. "It... it is a bar of Zinc? Copper? Some sort of amalgamation?"

Physiker Yurell's eyes narrowed and he rubbed his hands together as if warming them. Lin realized the clothes he was wearing couldn't be this man's. They didn't match, size-wise. So he had a partner or someone else that might be coming in. *He's stalling.*

"Bound Metal laced with copper. I was under the belief that Danicans didn't know what fueled their magic?"

"Is it magic or a disease?" Lin replied. He shifted to launch the Weft toward the door if need be.

"Both."

As interested in this man as Lin was, he felt like time was running out. If Physiker Yurell's goal was to stall him, he'd succeeded. "There was a boat here."

"It left," the Physiker said quickly. "Shortly before the alarms finally subsided."

"Are there more boats?"

"Ah... I doubt it. We don't keep ships here, though the occasional one might come along. It's typically a rare occurrence."

"What do you keep looking at?" Lin shifted and spared a glance behind him.

Yurell lurched. Swift despite his size, the man slashed at Lin with one of the tools that had been laid out on the table. Lin flinched his arm back, but the blade, a scalpel perhaps, drew blood. It burned white-hot and his entire arm numbed. It was a temporary lack of feeling, one that faded almost as soon as it began. The Weft he'd been holding dissipated as if someone had unwoven it. This man wasn't a Binder, even if he had the Sight.

"Stupid blood-tainted pig. As if I'd help a monster like you." He spat the words as he tried to rush past Lin, aiming for the cabinet where Lin had stolen the clothes from.

Lin snorted and let his Blade turn to disparate threads like the Weft had. The slash along his forearm stung and bled, but more worrisome than that, his Inlays where the blade had marked him had dulled, the color slowly coming back to them.

Feeling for his spul, Lin formed a focus and pulled at the thread he'd found that darted like a fish. A blue Wieving formed, like a patch, as Lin pressed his hand to the wound. The more he used these unfamiliar magics, the easier it was to draw on them. And seeing the shocked expression on the Physiker's face made it worth it.

"So you do know of the various trace metals you draw on? Do others know? And you can do it at will?"

"It doesn't matter." Lin shifted to stop the man's advance. Now that he looked at it closer it was obvious he'd grabbed the scalpel made from Bound Metal. That partly explained why the wound had stung so much, as it wasn't nearly so fine an instrument as the standard one's he'd seen physikers use.

"Of course, it matters."

Lin snapped his fist forward, punching the stout man in the chest.

Gasping for breath, Physiker Yurell stabbed forward but Lin moved past the clumsy strike and punched him again this time across the chin. The stout man stumbled, catching himself on the table and scattering various tools in the process. They rattled to the floor as the physiker wheezed.

"W-wait."

Blow after blow saw the man crumple. Lin kicked the Bound Metal tool away and stood over the cowering Physiker. The man's lip had split and a gash across his chin bled heavily.

"I will escape here. And soon, before I leave Ladrica, I will free those untethered you've bound. For better or worse I will loose them on your people."

"M-monster," the man whined.

"These markings aren't what make me a monster, what I will do to anyone who stands between me and rescuing the child stolen from me is." Lin grabbed him by the blood-stained front of his tunic and lifted him from the stone floor enough that he was on his knees. "Explain the layout of this place to me."

"No," he said. His face twisted as he sucked in a breath to yell and Lin moved on instinct, snapping the man's neck.

The truth was, despite healing his wound, when he searched for his spul to form Wefts and Weaves, he couldn't call them forward. It wasn't clear whether the Ladrican soldiers fitted out with those damned batons knew that cutting a Binder with Bound Metal was enough to disrupt their connection to their spul, but as the color slowly returned to the Inlays in his flesh, he was thankful all they'd had were the dull-tipped batons and not blades of the One-loved stuff.

But he'd realized something through this. Bound Metal didn't seem to affect the other sorts of Wievings the way it did the basic ones. Which made sense. Lin shuddered, mind drifting to the untethered staked like scarecrows in the pass.

After what happened at the tree, Lin was sure the untethered, if they weren't dead, could feel it all. The cold. The metal. Everything. To push the man into the hole seemed unnecessarily cruel, and not at all something that the Gods would likely smile upon, no matter how detestable he seemed. It took a few extra moments, but Lin dragged the body and put it in the furthest cell.

Congealed Hate

"Many historians incorrectly assume Verbanth was the first to break the Accords, but those few recorded accounts that remain clearly state his incursion into the heart of Ladrica was the cornerstone of Ladrican insistence that the Accords be necessary. One cannot break something that had yet to be formed, no matter the savagery behind the act. No, the first true breaking of the Accords came when an entrepreneur merchant thought to build a ship and sell his goods across the Pellic Sea, despite the Ferrucium decreeing through the Binding Tenets that the seas were not to be traveled upon. Of course, there were accounts of Danican citizens sneaking under Talm's Peak, eventually living among the Ladrican people in the early days of the Accords. These instances would be quelled nearly immediately by tests on children's blood." Excerpt from the Histories of Southern Danica removed and redacted due to the Danican Accords.

Knowing that Ladricans could have the Sight, even if they had no affinity for Binding made Lin feel exposed in a way he hadn't before. Not since first waking in Fallo and seeing the Stitches lining his arm and torso.

If one wrong person spotted him, he'd be done. Any chance of being stealthy would be gone in a blink. It was a miracle no one had heard the clatter and commotion as he'd dispatched the physiker.

Walking like he belonged proved challenging as he wasn't entirely sure where he was. That combined with the ill-fit of his top and the constant fear that every sound he heard was the rushing of soldiers to find him and he wasn't feeling confident he'd get out of the fort in one piece.

Lin crept through the bowels of the fort, the surrounding dark stone oppressive. Steps sounded from various corridors that Lin avoided, but the further he crept the clearer it became that the only way out he'd find, without pushing his way through a score of soldiers, was back through the waste hole he crawled through originally.

Lin clenched his fist and rubbed the irritated flesh where the Bound Metal blade had cut him. The color to his Inlay had fully returned, but there was a heaviness to the limb that lingered. He tried to form a Weft and though his intention seemed to cause a spark, the magic blinked out of existence as quickly as it came.

Maybe the shit hole is the right choice. No. Even if it meant cutting his way through all the soldiers in the fort, he didn't want to go back into that foul-smelling tunnel. That, and the fact that the tide had likely risen into it by now.

A corridor intersected and led to his right, the hall lit by the same iron-wrought sconces that the original room bore. Two voices carried. Both were unintelligible but deep and guttural.

The best place to find a weapon would be on a soldier, assuming he couldn't stumble his way to an armory of sorts. So, Lin headed toward the voices. The closer he got, the surer he was that it was only two people and they were involved in a heated debate, their dialect clear enough that both had to be at least possibly fluid in Danican. Not that the languages were so different, but the northerners often stressed sounds in odd ways.

Lin pressed flat against the wall outside the doorway. A smile came unbidden as he considered how easily a person like Pael might find his current task, slinking around and going unspotted. Especially considering how the satchel the man carried always seemed to have exactly what he needed in it. Wanderer's Ore, a spyglass, maybe a boltshooter. Pael never did explain where he'd pulled it from that one battle. Maybe it was one of those other magics the scholars had mentioned. Or maybe the old bastard really did hide the thing in his pants.

The tone of the conversation grew more heated and a thud preceded the sound of a chair sliding across stone flooring. Steps sounded, and they were heading his way.

Lin jerked away from the wall. He'd wasted too much time not moving and listening, and now he was stuck in the corridor with the enemy regardless. He kept his head down and walked past the door, doing his best to make it look as if he not only knew where he was going but was meant to be there.

If they stopped him, he could pretend to be on an errand. He could ask about Mellyr. There was too much he didn't know about the inner workings of the fort. If only he'd been able to question the physiker before snapping his neck.

Halfway down the corridor was another intersection. Lin ran a hand along the wall as he walked. His fingers were still numb, but the feeling was returning slowly. He was sure he could Bind soon and any need for subterfuge would be gone. The men didn't have Mellyr and when he'd walked past the room it was a small barracks of a sort. No crib or child in sight. Four steps to the intersection. Four steps to freedom.

"You there. Physiker, where are you headed?"

Lin took another step and looked over his shoulder. There wasn't anyone else in the hall and he had stolen these clothes from the physiker's cabinet. In the flickering hall light, there was a chance he might pass as a Ladrican. If they squinted and didn't pay much attention to the ill fit of his clothes. *And if they didn't have the Sight.*

Lin pointed up, hoping that conveyed all the two men might want to know. Sweat stuck the clothes to him and his heart pounded in his ears.

Of the two, the shorter man was dressed in the same dark clothes he'd seen the other unarmored soldiers wearing. The other wore much the same, except his pauldrons, a cloak, and an insignia on his lapel. Both men had blades sheathed at their sides and the one that seemed to be a lightly armored officer also had a baton. He carried a helm between his arm and side and had a thick beard that made him look older than the lack of age on his face would have otherwise shown.

Worst of all, both men had a dangerous look in their eyes. Whatever they'd just been arguing about clearly still hanging over them. Perhaps that was what they'd called after him for. *Hopefully.*

"Take a message to Commander Delrose for me then since you're heading up. I've got to make the rounds or I'd march my tired ass up there myself, I assure you."

Lin pulled his hand from the wall and nodded. This man didn't sound Ladrican. Despite his fair complexion and dark hair, he didn't really *look* Ladrican either. A foreigner among the army?

"Here. And be quick about it, she expected me well before the fifth bell, but with all the ruckus. Let her know it comes from Sergeant Royce and she'll forgive the interruption." Royce held out a thin roll of parchment between them.

Lin forced a smile and reached for it with his right hand.

The Sergeant pulled the scroll just out of reach. "And just so I know who to blame if this gets lost, your name?"

Lin swallowed. He could feel all his fingers now. Odds were, he had full access to his spul. Two swift Wefts and the men would drop.

The shorter soldier beside Royce chuckled and leaned against the wall. "Physiker Yorell is always getting new assistants down there in the depths. Not surprising to see another new one so soon. Physiker Yurell has an itch to bring in the pretty ones too. Can't say they fit the clothes on you too well." There was no doubt that this man was Ladrican. He watched Lin. Studying his face. The knot and bruise and blood. *Shit.* "Must have caught him on a good day then, to get me the position." Lin shrugged and turned his face away, feigning shyness regarding the injury. Anything to take the attention away from his poor Ladrican imitation.

"Ha! Got that right. Good thing too. Didn't hear it from me but if you were an extra pretty one he'd probably put you in more positions than you wanted, catch my meaning. Though wounded as you are, maybe he already did?"

Royce's face darkened and he shook his head, frowning at the soldier. "Enough. Spreading baseless rumors about a man, no matter how soiled his reputation was coming from the capital, when he isn't present to defend himself is moralless behavior. And you." He turned his attention fully back to Lin and frowned deeper. "Repeat what you heard Soldier Femor say at your own risk."

"My lips are sealed," Lin said. He stared into Royce's eyes. The blue hue to them was like a dull Wanderer's Ore. "The scroll?"

Gods, he just needed to leave. He swallowed and reached out toward Royce again.

"If you're lucky, they'll stay that way," Femur said under his breath, glaring from the wall at Royce.

Lin waited with held breath. There was still a chance to get out of this without killing these men. Royce seemed like a decent man, all considered. But Royce kept the missive a hair's breadth out of reach. "Name?"

"Physiker Collier."

"Collier?" Royce rolled the name off his tongue and stared flatly at Lin, letting the scroll pass to Lin's outstretched grasp. "I knew another Physiker Collier once. Last I heard he'd—" A boy ran full speed into them. He couldn't have been older than twelve years and wore a cap that barely covered his blonde hair spilling out at the sides. He carried a bell in one hand and held it as if debating whether to ring the damned thing.

"Slow child, lest you trip and break your neck!" Royce wheeled out of the way just in time.

"Physiker Yurell has been murdered! We've got an intruder!" The boy yelled, not slowing at all as he passed the trio.

Lin took the interruption to turn around. The boy outpaced him, but Lin walked quickly hoping to be rid of Royce and his companion, Femor.

The bell clanged loudly as the boy found his rhythm. Lin stared after him. At this rate, he'd wake the whole fort. But he was just a boy, a message runner.

"Collier, hold!"

Lin didn't stop. He rushed ahead, catching up to the boy. He could do what needed to be done. *Had to be done.* Anything to get to Mellyr, wherever she was.

"Collier! You just heard the same news as us. No feelings for the murdered superior?" Royce shouted, heavy steps following.

Lin grimaced. *Gods forgive me.* With a lunge, he snatched the message runner from behind. He wheeled around, his fingers tightening around the child's slender neck. "Not a step closer!"

The boy kicked and choked out a scream, his bell clanging and crashing to the floor. An alarm that might wake the dead. "If you quit kicking, I'll loosen my grip." Lin squeezed tighter to accent his growl and the boy slowed, then stopped.

"He's just a child. Let him go." Royce's helm clattered to the ground and rolled to a stop near the boy's swinging feet. The man and his companion had chased him and they stood just at the other side of the four-way intersection. Other soldiers had likely heard the bell, if not the shouting.

"I can't."

"You and Physiker Yurell get into it, eh? Made some advances on you and you snapped. I get it. We can work through this. He hurt you and you hurt him back." Femor's left hand brushed his cheek and he raised his other palm out toward Lin. He sounded genuine.

Royce's sword sounded smooth as it pulled free of the sheath. It glistened like good Ferrucium steel should. But his other hand went to a cord around his neck, not to the baton. "Six, you're an idiot Femor. He's clearly part of the group that assaulted the ship earlier. His clothes barely fit him and look closely at his skin. Gray and ashen in places. Maybe not an untethered, but a damned fool near enough."

Lin turned the boy so that he was solidly between Royce and himself.

"You mean he's a tainted blood? Femor's face shifted from shock to disgust, to horror as he looked at the child with fresh realization. "I... I didn't think they looked so much like us, so normal. Saw a member of the King's Noose once, but the mask and all."

"Shut up," Royce snapped. "Let the boy go. You aren't getting out of here and there is no reason to add his death to your list of trespasses."

"Was there a baby here?"

"Baby?" Royce inched forward, his boot kicking aside his dropped helm.

Lin lifted the boy higher. He yelped and kicked but struggled to keep hold of Lin's forearm, trying and failing to pull himself up. "Was there a Danican baby brought here? I won't ask again!"

“No! No child. Please let him go.” Femor had paled and his hands trembled.

“Are there any other boats?” Lin took a half step back and considered his next move. He could probably outrun both the men. But if he couldn’t get answers, it didn’t matter. He’d come in knowing that he’d fight if he were caught. Kill if he had to. What sort of cruel trick were the Gods playing that this messenger had to run through when he did?

“Please let the boy go and we can talk.” Femor seemed at a loss, failing to say anything new. Royce looked like he understood the situation far better. There was no chance Lin would set the squirming messenger down before leaving.

“I’m not a fool. Tell me what I need to know and the boy will be released after. If I wanted to kill him, I would’ve.”

“There is usually a skiff or two, no better than fishing boats, at the docks,” Femor said. He’d moved off the wall and had circled an inch or two to Lin’s left. These men were ready to attack him at the first sign of weakness.

A glance left then right confirmed the stretch of hall intersecting was free from flanking soldiers. But he was running out of time.

Lin sent a Weft just in front of Femor’s boots, chipping the stone. Then did the same to where Royce stood.

“You *are* untethered!” Royce yelled.

Femor flinched back, jumping as debris launched into the air.

“Take another step past that line and find what lines I’m willing to cross. A child very important to me was stolen away and I need a boat.”

Royce licked his lips and slowly sheathed his sword. "Proceed down the right hallway. Take a left at the fourth turn, up the stairs. Go now and if anyone asks, I swear I won't tell them we saw you."

"S-seargent Royce?" Femor shifted and scowled at the man. "You can't be serious. One messenger boy isn't worth letting an untethered run amok in the fort."

"Go," Royce repeated.

Lin stared at the pair, then took a shuffling step back. Without another word he turned right and away, shifting to hold the boy by his underarms so he didn't accidentally break his frail neck. He got about ten steps before he heard the bell the boy had dropped ringing. Glancing back he saw Femor had picked it up and was running down the opposite way, shouting unintelligibly.

A Weft colored a dull, rusted orange, cut through the air toward Lin. He unraveled it with ease, the magic shattering.

Royce's hand was splayed out, much the way High Scholar Anya had stood when she sent a Weft. So that was what he'd been playing with by his throat. A corded vial of Danican blood.

There had been empty vials in the physiker's dungeon. By the time Royce had conjured another Weft, Lin was far enough away that the impotent, stolen power wouldn't reach him. But that had likely been Royce's plan. Let Lin run, then take his head from behind.

"You're lucky that Sergeant valued your life."

"You won't get away," the boy coughed. Seemed perhaps Lin had squeezed too hard. If he were in the boy's position, he'd already be screaming his head off, or dead. "That foreigner might care about me, but true-blooded Ladrican men won't let you escape. I'll gladly die to make sure a blood-tainted monster like you goes with me."

The boy's words came out shaken and sounded scared, but Lin believed the boy meant what he said. Gods, it was like what he'd been taught at the Ferrucium. Told that all with Stitches broke the Binding Tenets. Except this was worse. It wasn't just untethered or Tenets. It was all Danicans viewed as monsters, even when it should be clear to anyone with a brain that Danicans and Ladricans shared some common ancestry. Their languages were too similar to be otherwise.

Lin rushed down the hall, more shouts echoing from behind. He could toss the boy aside now, but if worse came to worst, he *might* make for a shield. *At least from arrows*. A dark consideration to be sure, but he'd meant what he said. There were no lines left he wouldn't cross. Losing Denny... it had done something to him. Failing yet another person.

Following Royce's instructions led him to a door guarded by two soldiers on the exterior. They had spears and turned, eyes wide as he rushed at them with a child held aloft.

The boy stiffened and the little shit shouted, "Untethered escaping!"

Keeping the boy close to his chest, Lin barreled through the gate. As he passed he sent two Wefts outward, taking the heads clean off the guards before they could impede him. Blood sprayed and bodies crumpled.

The dock was just ahead but so were a handful of armored soldiers. Most of them with lanterns and bolt-shooters.

Fuck.

There was no way he'd get past all of them while clutching the child, so he tossed him. The boy hadn't been ready and hit the ground hard, rolling to a stop along the gravel path.

"Run and hide," Lin ordered.

"Fuck yourself, blood-tainted monster!"

Not striking him took more restraint than Lin possessed. Before Lin could take a step, bolts shot towards him from the soldiers on the walls above. Lin spun and broke four of them with a long, well-placed Weft. He avoided two of them by pivoting away. Caught one in his right hand before it could puncture his shoulder. And watched from the corner of his eye as a bolt rocked the young boy backward.

Lin dashed back to the kid and turned away, seeing him splayed out. Blood pooled from the wound and his limbs twitched. The bolt stuck from his clavicle, deep and angled and not at all something Lin trusted to not kill the boy if removed.

"M-mo..."

Hearing the boy's dying breaths calling Lin a monster would be too much to bear, so he turned away. Steeled himself. He couldn't tend to the boy's wound. Even if he'd seen flesh pull together through Wieving with that blue magic in a way that normal Wieving could never have hoped to achieve. He didn't have the time.

True to Royce's words, a skiff knocked along the dock. Just behind the line of soldiers.

"Mo-mma."

Fuck. He wasn't calling Lin a monster. He'd come to save a child. What type of man would he be to let one die?

Lin scooped up the boy. If he could make it to the boat, he could try to save the boy's life. He'd been the one who dragged the lad out here, knowing there might be a slew of soldiers waiting.

The boy weighed so little that Lin rushed at full speed. But the soldiers didn't seem to care that Lin was trying to save a life. They fired indiscriminately and when the bolts stopped the soldiers on the docks charged with Bound Metal tipped batons in hand.

A soldier clad in full armor led the charge and stabbed at Lin's center of mass with the baton. Lin side-stepped the attack despite the boy under his arm and grabbed the base of the soldier's neck. He wore a helm that overlapped the metal of his chestpiece, but Lin squeezed it and pictured the magic spreading along the surface like a mold. Like the untethered had to his sword back in Lyre. Using his momentum, Lin spun and slammed the charging soldier's helm against another's shoulder chest. Lin let go and moved past, the soldiers screaming as they struggled to free themselves of each other. But the Binding had stuck them together.

Swords swished through the air as they sliced and slashed at Lin. A dodge, a duck, a forearm strike. All tools he used to bleed between the soldiers. They were organized and Lin was tired. But all he needed to do was get to the skiff, not fight an army.

Stray blows landed. A cut along his calf sparking. A slice caught across his back when he didn't move fast enough. Gods, he was growing tired. And more soldiers were pressing in from the fort itself, though these men seemed to have the restraint not to pepper their allies with bolts.

Lin rolled under a horizontal slash and slid to the edge of the dock. With a flick, a Weft shorn the rope tying the small, dingy boat to the post. More soldiers pressed in, short blades once again traded for bolt-shooters. He tried to toss the boy in as gently as he could while kicking and keeping the nearest soldiers back.

"Stop him!"

"Untethered!"

"He's taking Little Leo!"

"Monster!"

With a flurry of motion, Lin created a cocoon of Wefts. But instead of staying inside it, like he always had before, he made it wide enough to slip off the dock and into the small boat while it obscured the view. Cold water lapped his ankles as the less-than-sturdy thing rocked with his weight. He kept his focus on the cocoon, swelling it as large as he could. He could feel bits of it being destroyed. Bound Metal tugged at the edges, slipping his control on swathes of Wefts at a time.

Unfair fucking metal.

Shouts chased him. Bolts swished into the water, some thudding as they connected with the front of the boat. Or was it the back? Lin shook his head and pushed his arms to row. It was slow going at first until he found a rhythm.

With all luck, the dock itself was ruined. By the end of his escape, he'd let the Wefts loose to slash in all manner of directions. He was sure more than one soldier would find a fatal wound from it.

But Gods did Bound Metal weapons seem to make things wholly unfair.

Lin had the advantage of actually experiencing it before, but fresh Ferrucium soldiers? They could be warned and taught, but the experience was something a person needed firsthand. *Bound Metal. Ferrucium steel. Binder's Blood.* What other tools might these Ladricans, might the world, have that Lin was ignorant of? Maybe Danica didn't stand a chance. Newly united under Azhura and Erias or not.

A groan escaped the dying boy. Lin had slapped a Weave across his neck to stem the blood loss, but he hadn't tried to pull at the deeper magic within. Not yet, but now that he was far enough from shore not to take a bolt in the back for his troubles, he planned to try. Prick or not, the child was trying to be a hero.

Congealed Blood

"While it is unclear why, as many things with these Danicans, there is a noted aversion to water. And not even among just the mad-ones, no. What was initially designed to be a measure of controlling the people quickly became accepted and commonplace. It was all too easy for Danicans to give up the sea and avoid flowing water altogether. The untethered truly can't stand it. Some say the progenitors of Danican magics, Vellia, and her ilk, had a dispute with the ruler of the seas, though this is wildly unsubstantiated, like most things involving that family." Records from the personal diary of Physiker Sichael.

Bolts and arrows stopped piercing the water some time ago. Once they'd gotten far enough that Lin was sure a stray attack wouldn't still catch them, he slowed his rowing and focused on the child. They'd called him Little Leo, and little was right. Even though he'd carried him to the boat, if he couldn't staunch the boy's wound he might as well dump him overboard. Let the current take him and do with him what it would. Give the boy the same chance the Ladrican soldier had given Lin when knocking him over the rail.

But Lin had never been that type of man and even as the world wholly conspired against him he couldn't do something so cruel. So he stared at the shaft sticking from Leo's shoulder, golden threads of Lin's Weave seeping with the boy's blood.

To staunch the wound, he needed to pull out the bolt, and then find that elusive blue-hued magic from within.

Lin shifted and stared across the dark water. The sky continued to lighten, but that didn't stop the depths of the surrounding sea from looking back into him.

There was a total absence down there which weighed on him when he looked at it. A fear of the unknown that frayed his nerves. It made him constantly look over his shoulder. Every sound was a threat. It didn't help that he'd had all those dreams he'd spent as a blade being dunked over and over into pits of water just as black. No. He'd die a happy man if he never had to be on open water again.

His cheek throbbed and all the cuts along his limbs ached. There was time to rest before arriving at the island, especially if the boat continued to be pulled along on its own.

Leo groaned and Lin flinched at the sound. The Weave on his wound wouldn't hold much longer.

With trembling hands and a steady worry that one wrong move would flip the small boat over, Lin hovered over Leo. He rolled the boy onto his side and broke the tip of the bolt that stuck through his back. A tug pulled it free from the other side and the Weave he'd placed flat dissolved as the boy's blood began spilling in earnest. He'd never considered how unsteady magic became when mixed with fluids.

Lin formed a focus, index finger joining his thumb as he stared through the hole. He'd done this so often in the Ferrucium during training. Envisioning his will entering the world. Lin pulled at the magic inside, finding the thread that darted underneath it all. Like a fish just under the surface. Visualizing it helped him grab hold of the hidden magic and the glowing blue Wieving crystallized at his fingertips.

As he worked, it occurred to him that he was doing the very thing he'd been upset at Tylle for. Sure, this was a different sort of Wieving. But surely it left a mark all the same. Any with the Sight would know this boy had been stained by magic. Lin watched the blood pulse from Leo's wound with every beat of the boy's heart. Lin directed the magic over the wound, sealing the injury with that cerulean, crystalline glow. Tears dotted the edge of his eyes and a smile came unbidden. Aemun couldn't have known everything, or he'd have stemmed his lost limb with this.

Underneath the crystalline shape, the flesh pulled together, the wound puckering closed and leaving a scar the size of a Ferrucium mark. The only sign was the blood staining the boy's tunic and the pattern of blue threads across his shoulder that looked pulled from quartz.

Lin shifted back to his original seat and took the oars back in hand. He'd much rather be on Nebra, riding than coaxing this boat across the dark water. As he looked down, he wondered if Denny had been tossed overboard into those churning depths and regret swelled in his chest. What if she'd been down there with him and washed ashore elsewhere?

Why was he always failing those who seemed to care about him? Not that Margaret had cared about him. But he'd let her down most of all. She'd asked him to stay close. But even if he had witnessed Aemun attacking her, would things have changed? Tylle had opened his eyes to so many things and yet, even she couldn't be bothered to stay with him. Every dip of the oars splashed water and the constant, slap, slap, slap of it took Lin deeper into his thoughts. Lin stopped rowing and stared. He'd heard a whisper, he was sure of it, but now that the water stilled there was only silence.

A thick fog rolled across the water in smothering sheets that obscured the island ahead.

"W-where are we?" Leo's harsh voice cracked out.

"Island," Lin whispered. Gods, he was tired. He hadn't healed any of his wounds after working Leo's for fear of overdoing his spul.

"You... You saved me?"

Lin sighed and looked at the boy's dark eyes. "Marked you. Anyone with the Sight will know you for having the Binding Tenets broken."

Leo's face, youthful and round, twisted with disgust. "You tainted my blood?"

Lin narrowed his eyes at that. He'd heard many things over the last few months, but he didn't think a non-Danican's blood would become tainted by contact. But it made sense that it might be taught. If all the rules and superstitions from inside Danica were meant to keep them in and keep them docile, then similar things were likely taught to keep others out.

"No."

They sat in silence for a time, Lin rowing again once the fog cleared enough for him to see the shoreline. There were docks of a sort ahead, appearing just as poorly maintained as the one he'd fled from. Moored were several ships of various sizes, from small rowboats to galleys like what Mellyr had been stolen away on. Lin gritted his teeth and glared. It was true, a meeting was being held. A gathering of the very nations that had long ago agreed Danica should be cordoned off from the world. To be treated like dangerous animals, all while being watched by foxes as if they were chickens.

But why here of all places?

"Why'd you save me?" Leo whispered. He'd pulled himself up, tunic sticking to his shoulder where the blood had dried. He was as pale as freshly fallen snow and his hands trembled.

"Never intended for you to get hurt."

"You grabbed me and—"

"I know!" Lin snapped. "I... I just want to rescue someone I care about. A girl, far younger than you. A child. I didn't plan to get you involved"

"And the woman you were with?"

"What?" Lin let the oars slip a bit and leaned forward.

"The King's Noose took her when they left the dock. Figured you wanted to save her too."

Lin licked his lips and shifted his focus back to the island resting beyond the boy. The closer they got, the larger it loomed. A neutral territory allegedly. Yet one that he was sure a Danican like him— a monster— wouldn't be welcomed warmly at. He steered the boat to the side, wanting to come ashore far from the docks where he was sure soldiers would be waiting.

"Did you... not want to save her?" Leo stared up at Lin, eyes alert, what little color the pale Ladrican boy had coming back to his cheeks.

"I do. She's only here because of me."

"Ha. So she's like me."

Lin sighed and pursed his lips. "Once we're on the island, you can take the boat and flee. You're marked, but maybe it won't matter. Maybe."

Leo traced the blue-latticed magic. "I can feel it there. Like a blade of grass humming in the wind."

Lin studied Leo's wound and exhaled. He pressed toward the island, even his Inlay-enhanced muscles complaining at the action. He was sore and tired and felt like he hadn't had a full night's rest in weeks. Plus he was hungry and the boy, since coming awake, had only stared at him, aside from the few words they'd shared.

"You look like you want to eat me," Leo said. He leaned on the left side of the boat, hand dragging in the water as if it weren't icy cold.

Lin shook his head and blinked away the sweat stinging his eyes. "I might."

Tall trees clarified on the island, far wilder looking than any he'd seen across Danica. As if the forest had come alive and consumed everything else the island had to offer.

"What do you plan to do once you get to the island?"

"Find my friend, if she really is there, and daughter." There was no better word for what Mellyr was to him. The moment Tylle hadn't wanted to raise her with him was a wound that wouldn't heal and it had festered. But that didn't make him any less like a father to the child. In fact, it stoked those flames. Feeding the desire to do this one thing as well as he could. And still, she'd been tested on. Stolen.

And see how well that's done for you, Escorter.

Lin jumped. Like a knife from his blindspot, Aemun's condescending voice stabbed him. He settled the boat flat and righted the course, looking away from Leo's confused stare. But as he looked into the woods along the shore, he saw flashes and hints of Velkath's Sigil in his periphery.

"Gods." Lin let loose the oars and leaned forward, doubling over. Like a needle being driven into his skull from the other side, a pressure had built behind his eyes and pressed out. The voices, the signs. It was all becoming too much.

"From where I'm sitting, there are no Gods. Not the way the preachers claim, anyway. But I've seen monsters." Leo hadn't moved to comfort him, and his hand still dipped lazily over the side of the boat. When Lin managed to look up at him and the piercing sensation dulled, it was clear the boy was watching him from the side of his eye. He rested his chin on one folded arm and when he saw Lin look at him, his gaze drifted out across the water.

"So have I. I'm sorry that I used magic to save you. I had to. But even if you hate me... curse my name until I die... I'd rather know I tried doing everything I could to save your life."

Leo shrugged. "You speak just fine. You really from the other side of Talm's?"

Lin nodded.

"Is everyone down there a monster like you? Like the priests and soldiers say?"

That was a harder question to answer and Lin stared down at his ill-fitting boots. "I was told once, by a man far wiser than me, that lumping all of any one thing together and treating it like a whole often leads to misunderstanding. Apples for example."

"Apples?"

Maybe Lin was too hungry, his mouth watering at the thought. "Apples. Some are sweet. Would you say all apples are red and sweet?"

Leo brought his attention to rest fully on Lin's face. "I've seen green ones."

"And are they sweet?"

His face screwed up and he shook his head. "Sour."

"Right." Lin nodded. It was an analogy he thought Pael might be proud of. Not the waxing poeticism the old man so often seemed to use or even half as clever as what Tylle might string together. But it got the point driven home. "So we are like apples. Some Danicans don't even have a real affinity for the magic. Most never untether."

"But you did?"

Lin took a deep breath and raised a finger to his lips as the boat grew closer to shore. "No."

"Only someone gone mad would cross through the pass. That's what the soldiers say."

A chuckle escaped from Lin, aching his side as it did. "A fair point. But believe it or not, I used to think a lot like you. I still do in some ways." Lin sighed and closed his eyes. "Please believe me. If I could get my daughter back without anyone else getting hurt I would."

Leo was young, younger than Lin might've first thought considering he was a message runner at a fort, and he had a look in his eyes. A desperate desire to believe and trust the man who'd saved his life. "If you didn't want anyone getting hurt, you wouldn't have come at all. It doesn't matter. Our soldiers are always ready for you blood-tainted monsters to attack. Even if..." He grew silent and seemed to shrink into himself.

"Even if what?"

Leo shook his head and shuddered, spinning to look over his shoulder at the looming island.

Perhaps it was the cruel testing of Gods, or something far more mundane, but Lin hated that he constantly found himself empathizing with the people who pressed a boot to the neck of his home. It was easier for him, of course. He'd been there, helping police his own. He ran his right hand over the Stitches of his left and took in the reassuring hum that had brought him comfort over the last few months. What came next would be blood. Whether it was something Erias had planned somehow... or King Lodram... it didn't matter. If whoever pulled Lin's strings like a puppet wanted a monster, they'd earned one and then some.

Even without Lin rowing, the boat seemed content to press toward the island. He'd noticed it before but had continued rowing to keep the pace. Some form of invisible pull that didn't bring Lin any comfort as the bottom scraped onto the rocky, uneven shore.

"Those are Pollsh vessels. A Fentian one too— you can tell 'cause of the prow. And Elodian. And Nacodonis. And maybe Belanise, but most of the free nations have similar ships so you can only really tell by the color of their sails, and most of those are furled." Leo seemed insistent on talking, likely due to nerves, as he leaned over the side of the boat, squinting at the moored ships near the docks.

From where they sat in the water, soldiers were visible as vague shapes. It didn't seem as if they'd spotted their craft and Lin looked from them to Leo. His knuckles tightened on the oars and he waited. If the boy made a sound, a scream, a sudden movement then Lin would knock him unconscious. But he didn't want to if he didn't have to.

"What're you waiting for?" Leo whispered.

"Hmm?"

"Aren't you going to go?"

Lin licked his lips. "Are you going to take the boat like I suggested?"

"I might."

They stared at each other in silence for a moment, then Lin moved.

Getting out of the boat without tilting it over one way or another proved more difficult than Lin imagined even with the bottom scraping rocks. Leo shifted to the opposite side and steadied the boat. It helped Lin to only get his boots and shins wet and not stumble and fall in entirely.

"Drag me ashore," Leo said.

Lin was about to argue then decided against it. Whatever way this child felt he hadn't asked to come to this island and certainly hadn't wanted to be struck by a bolt in his shoulder. But what was in store wasn't something a child should be a part of.

With a single kick against the front of the boat, Lin pushed it and Leo away. Whatever current had brought it to the island once it was closer still seemed to be affecting the small boat, but it had given Lin enough time to make a headstart. At least he hoped.

"Hey!" Leo said in a hushed, irritated voice, hands reaching out to grab Lin but missing. A thud sounded as the motion of the boat caused him to land on his rear.

"Take the chance to go." Lin waved a hand and turned his back on the boy. He'd done what he could to save him and if something happened to him on this island, he wouldn't forgive himself. What mattered now was finding the castle in the thick pocket of vegetation and rescuing Mellyr. *Denny too*. If she was actually here.

In all the time spent over the last few months, nothing had made Lin feel more like an untethered than how he crept through the trees. He imagined this was what those hate-filled monsters often did when scoping out a village to attack. A shudder racked him as his mind drifted to the untethered children that had assaulted the village and that odd one with those damned horns.

Bird calls carried through the air, a gray-clouded sky eager to appear as dreary as possible. A mist, cold and heavy, crept across the island. He hadn't been on the island long at all before a light pattering of rain began falling.

Lin continued inward, stepping between trees, and more than anything, listening. He hadn't heard more voices, but Velkath's Sigil, or something eerily similar, still floated in his periphery. Every time he looked, it danced away as if it were a bashful sprite.

"Why do you keep stopping?"

Fuck me. Lin turned, stifling the urge to jump in surprise. Face drawn and smeared with mud, visible just behind a large-fronded plant, was Leo.

"To listen."

"Rain makes that hard," Leo whispered.

"So does a child I've asked to stay behind."

"You didn't ask that."

"It was implied when I told you to take the boat."

Silence, interrupted by the steadily louder pitter-patter, stretched out between the two of them. Crouching, Lin moved forward. Now that he focused on it he could hear Leo's movements and the young boy's strained breathing.

"You're going to give me away. *Go.*" Lin tried to sound menacing. But truth be told he was miserable, now soaked to the bone and exhausted. Inlays only did so much, even when his body was fully adapted to the changes they offered. He'd fought, drowned, fought some more, rowed, and didn't have it in him to sound snappish.

"You want to save someone? That's fine. Even for a tainted-blood. But I won't. I... I won't let you hurt anyone. If you try... I'll yell. I'll scream and fight and you'll have to kill me."

"I could just kill you now before it even got to that."

Uncertainty flashed across the boy's face and his lip poked out a bit. "You could," he said. Even his words were laced with doubt.

"And no one would know. You'd die out here among these tall trees and gnarled roots for what?"

"For my country," Leo whispered. "Do it if you mean to. And if you're not prepared to hurt me now... Just me here between the trees, then don't hurt anyone else."

It was a child's logic. But the boy had a point. Wasn't it Aemun who had talked down about Lin's convictions? Lin licked his lips and met Leo's eyes. He'd taken lives before. Killed children. *If those untethered counted*. If it meant saving Mellyr he should be ready to take Leo's life— anyone's life really. And he would be. If it came to that.

"Don't slow me down."

Calamitous Hope

"Danislan. Island of the Gods. Or Island gifted by the Gods, if you still believe the explanation for ancient Ladrican naming conventions. Ladrican scholars point to this isle as proof that Danica and those that came from that isolated place, owe fealty to Ladrica. Any learned person knows it proves otherwise. Why would an island exist, with Danican architecture and symbology so close to Ladrica, while the opposite cannot be proven?" Excerpt from the Histories of Southern Danica removed and redacted due to the Danican Accords.

Perhaps if it weren't surrounded by trees eager to choke the light from the world, the castle would have stood as impressive as the Fentian towers. It certainly took up as much space, larger even than the Ferrucium Hold. But for all that, it was overly weathered, as if the trees and stones were the only thing keeping it held together.

Lin and Leo crept along silently. A stretch of path visible from where they stood pressed into the tree line.

There was the chance the doors wouldn't be guarded. Not with the numbers he'd seen still at the pier. A chance slender as a thread.

"Come on," Lin grunted. If Leo planned to follow him the entire time, he'd have to move quicker. Lin pressed to the edge of the castle and stared up. If he were alone he could climb one of the trees and vault his way onto one of the ledges overhanging the exterior wall. Or he could scale it the way he'd scaled the Ferrucium walls.

Leo came to stand beside him and Lin sized him up. He'd carried him easily enough through the halls of the fort, this should be no different. "Climb onto my back."

"To go up there?"

Without answer, Lin patted him down, roughing the boy's trousers and shirt.

"Hey—"

"Shh." Lin pushed both of Leo's sleeves up and when it was clear the boy didn't have a blade hidden anywhere on him, Lin nodded and knelt. *Unless the boy is like Pael.*

Leo's arms wrapped around Lin's kneck tightly and it made Lin think of Mellyr. Not that she'd ever been old enough to hold him so tight, but she'd pulled his hair and ears hard enough that it wasn't hard to imagine.

"You stink." Leo's voice was soft at his neck.

"Hmm. I was dumped into the water. Crawled through a pipe that waste and blood seemed washed down. And rowed for the last few hours. I might stink."

Lin waited for a comment from Leo, but when none came, he rose to his full height. "Don't let go. I don't care if you're scared, your arms get tired, or anything. Hold on tight. I mean it." His words came out as more of a growl than intended and then he was off. His first thought had been to climb the nearest trees but after examining the branches, they likely wouldn't bear his weight. Then his mind went to Denny and how weightless she'd so often appeared. But no. Even if he were as light as a leaf, the trees here were slim at the trunk and worn smooth of bark.

The needle-like leaves shifted and rustled from a biting gust of wind. The thaw was coming, even this island was evidence of that. He'd expected snow-dusted shores, powdered trees, and slick ice. What he got instead was muddy ruts, damp roots, and a pervasive chill that didn't quite numb him.

If the trees weren't the path, then the walls would have to work.

Lin's boot connected with the stone and he propelled up, each kick thundering in his ears and launching him further along the wall. He formed a pair of short Blades, one in each hand, and stabbed into the stonework. Each Binding sunk into the face and anchored him in. Hand over hand, he pulled the two of them up. It was just like when he'd scaled the Ferrucium, except this time he didn't have the guise of a Nooseman to carry him past questions.

The ledge he'd thought to enter in clarified into a decorative stone-casting opposed to an actual opening and Lin rested there as he surveyed the wall from this new, windy vantage.

"Woah," Leo whispered.

A smile crept onto Lin's face. With everything it was easy to forget how amazing this was. How, as a child, he'd always dreamt of climbing those great tall trees near the Ferrucium. Now look at him, a damn near professional climber. The smile dropped as if it had teetered on the edge and the wind finally took it. Would he have had the same dreams if his parents had actually raised him? Or would he have wanted something more?

"Do you see anything?" Lin asked.

Leo wriggled and writhed. "I think the stones collapsed at some point. I could squeeze through."

Lin shifted. True enough, what he'd assumed was a wall was a collection of rubble in the recessed shadow. A pocket of blue light shone through. Wanderer's ore. "So you can sneak in and warn them I'm coming?"

"No." Leo didn't sound keen to explain himself further but his hands tightened around Lin's shoulders and he stilled.

"Then we continue up. Even if you did get in, you can't push those stones and I don't want to risk the noise even if you could. Listen, Leo, there are two ways this might go. One, they don't know I'm here and aren't expecting me. I get Mellyr, in and out. Two, they wanted me to come here."

"Whose they?"

Lin licked his lips and looked over the edge. With his Inlays, he'd probably survive the fall, even if the crowded rootwork surrounding the base of the wall would make the landing highly uneven. *Highly painful.*

"The Ladrican King, maybe. Someone else. But the point is, if they're expecting me things will get bad in there. If they do... if they do please hide. Or side with them and make it clear you aren't my ally or friend."

A snort escaped the young man like a thrown dagger, catching Lin right where he wasn't expecting it. Certainly, he didn't think he and the boy were friends or allies, but Gods, Leo hadn't needed to snort like that.

Without giving Leo a chance to explain or the silence to settle, Lin turned and began the climb again. These stones were similar to the shoal on the shore and seemed almost eager to take in the

Wefts he stabbed. Wholly dissimilar to the walls at the Ferrucium. More than anything perhaps that truly did age this structure. Or this far north they were so unworried about Danican magic that they didn't think to use Bound Metal in their buildings. Images of the strange spikes pinning the untethered in the pass flashed through Lin's mind and his hand nearly slipped from the lip he'd grabbed.

"I can climb up you and help pull you up." Leo's voice brought his focus back to the immediate. He'd cleared the entire wall and now hung from the edge of a window.

"No. A window like this... might have quite a fall inside. I'm alright." Leaving the Fentian scholars, he thought he'd truly outpaced the small moments lost to him where thought overtook common sense. But every time he called on the other types of Wievings, he felt more of himself coming unraveled. *Untethered*. He shuddered and clenched his jaw. By the end of this, he would be many things. But he'd never be an untethered. Never.

With a grunt, he pulled the both of them onto the window sill, centering his body weight to be right on his haunches. The interior was dark, with no ore or lamp lighting what looked to be a narrow stairwell. Flashes of Velkath's Sigil out of the corner of his eye made staring into the dim-lit space a struggle.

"When I drop, hang on tight."

Leo had held on tight the entire time. But it would be just Lin's luck to get into the interior of the castle and have the boy break his neck on the landing. Lin shifted his weight, turned as he dropped, and hung like a tapestry against the wall. He strained his hearing, listening for steps, voices, for anything that might signal someone was coming. But the stairwell, more obvious now that he was flat against the wall and could feel the intentional curving of stones, was empty.

Dropping didn't hurt, but he landed on the side of his foot more than he intended and would have rolled the ankle entirely if he hadn't caught his weight against the side of the wall.

"Can I let go now?"

Lin knelt and Leo stumbled off of him. "Up or down?"

The castle had loomed large, even with the wild overgrowth surrounding it. But if it was anything like the Fentian towers, sprawling as that place was, most meetings would be held in a large communal hall. And for the consideration of the elderly and others who didn't envy climbing scores of flights, those were often on the first floor.

"Down. Keep close and quiet." The castle was cold, the halls empty, but the further down they went the warmer the air became. Tapestries hung along the walls, mostly moth-worn to the touch and the images were impossible to decipher in the dark. Eventually, they reached a hall that broke away from the stairwell. It was well lit and the scent of smoke hung in the air. It should have made Lin think of a hearth, but all that came to mind was Fallo and the Ferrucium, and the pyres that had been made of both. The corridor opened into a grand hall with a second level connected by twin staircases on opposite sides. Servants dragged carts of goods, food, and clinking bottles of wine, and at the doors under the steps, two soldiers stood with spears crossed.

Clothed in a deep black cloth, likely velvet, with fur lining the neck and wrists, the soldiers were pale and looked every bit like the other Ladricans. Which at least proved that this meeting at minimum, had someone of import to the Kingdom.

"Are those the King's Noose?" Leo asked.

Lin's heart dropped and he pressed flat against the wall, before realizing what Leo was referring to. Similar to the tapestry that hung in the Ferrucium, three sprawling images hung against the far wall and depicted individuals fighting shadows with threads of light. One looked to be a young woman, hair cut short to her shoulders, hands displayed in a curious pattern.

"No," Lin whispered. Each tapestry had a familiar mark near the bottom, one that he tried and failed to blink away several times. "They are Velkath's Kin." Lin shivered and stared at what he assumed was a depiction of Vellia. He'd always assumed she'd been old, like Azhura. But this was a young woman. Possibly younger than Margaret had been. And what of the rest?

"You there! Stop!"

Lin cursed under his breath and formed a Weft, ready to hurl it towards the guard. Leo squeezed his elbow and he hesitated.

"Sorry sir," a man called, bowing his head subserviently. He was a tanned-skinned man, likely from one of the island nations. He spoke with no accent but it sounded obvious he was forcing the language. A bottle had fallen from one of the carts and a blood-hued puddle was slowly forming in the center of the hall. Lin had heard of the other nations' peoples, but imagining them and seeing them weren't the same. Wherever this servant called home, it didn't matter. All the other Free Nations had allowed the Ladricans to rule Danica. Not one of them was innocent.

"While they're distracted." Lin jerked his head to the door the chastising guard had stepped away from.

Lin walked with his shoulders back and chin up, steps echoing across the stone floor. Columns rose to support the second story that overlooked this entire area and Lin walked alongside them. When he reached the door, one guard had remained while the other had moved to aid the servant.

Whatever the power structure here was, these Ladrican soldiers acted as if they ran the place. Perhaps they did, seeing as it was so close to the Ladrican shore.

"Until the first hiatus, nobody enters or exits." The guard's rough voice came out as if he were reciting from a script. "Especially someone that smells as foul as you."

Lin stared at the man. "Urgent."

"Clearly. There is a servant's queue along the left stairway. Get in line and wait like the rest too incompetent to act without their master's orders."

A glance over his shoulder revealed the other guard ready to turn back but the servant, still on their knees cleaning the wine, continued prolonging the exchange. Gods. If Lin didn't know better it was like the man was *trying* to help Lin.

"Understood." Lin turned as if he was planning to leave, then jabbed out his right hand and caught the guard in the throat. Prick or not, he knew if he killed him Leo would start causing trouble and if he couldn't bring himself to kill the boy out there, he'd rather not be forced to do it within these walls. The guard choked on his reply, throat crushed, and fell against the door. Lin palmed his temple, the man's head thudding against the door like a rude, oversized door knocker. Lin caught the man as his knees gave out and leaned him against the wall.

"Hey!" Leo started.

"Knocked him out, didn't kill him," Lin said, setting the man upright so he quit falling over.

"The other one is coming back," Leo said from beside the nearest column.

"What's the meaning of—"

Lin didn't wait for him to shout and bring more attention. As soon as he was to the alcove under the stairs, Lin grabbed him by the shoulders and slammed him against the wall. The thud echoed through the expansive room and the guard struggled to pivot and use the spear in his hands. But in three strikes of the man's helmed head against the wall, the man looked unconscious, blood dripping from his nose and ears.

Lin snagged the spear and tapped the butt of it twice against the stone, feeling its weight and balance. The weapon felt like it was more for show, the tip not even Ferrucium steel, but the wood of its shaft felt light and even somewhat flexible.

"You said you wouldn't hurt anyone," Leo said, fear and anger boiling up in his voice.

"Kill. And I never said I wouldn't. How else was I meant to get through? Go." Lin opened the door and before looking within, pushed Leo ahead. Whatever argument the young man might make died on his lips.

The room was large with brightly lit sections of the wall accented by angled Wanderer's Ore so that specific designs, all too similar to Velkath's Sigil to be coincidental, stood out in bright blue relief. Aside from those stylized symbols, oil paintings of various important-looking figures were interspersed along the walls on either side of the entrance.

Voices carried then stilled as Lin stepped forward. He scanned the faces of those seated in the center of the room. Two rectangular tables, about ten people at each facing the other, and not one of them looked concerned at his entrance. Gasps of surprise and shouts of fear soon broke. From the edge of the room, several chairs screeched against stone and more figures became visible. Guards, weapons at the ready. At least twenty-five of them on each side, and more along the back wall. Still a far cry from a gathered army, but not good for Lin.

"What... what is the meaning of this interruption?" A pale man, as old as Azhura, with a severe brow and graying hair asked.

Lin wasn't sure but he thought he saw a sparkle of jewels adorning his brow. He spared a glance at Leo, then tightened his grip on the spear. The door had a beam that would lock the entrance if lowered. Without a word, Lin lowered the bar, metal crashing as it slammed down.

"I don't mean any—" Lin reeled as a shadow grabbed Leo from beside them. A soldier stood there face twisted in disgust, dagger held to the child's throat.

"State your business!" The guard screamed.

The light from the Wanderer's Ore accenting the symbols had pulled his attention and he hadn't noticed the many soldiers seated along the perimeter. *Fuck.* But this had always been a possibility. Wanting to do something peacefully and not being prepared for war were two very different things.

Leo screamed as a line of blood dripped from his throat.

"State. Your. Business." The soldier accented his point by jostling Leo at every word.

"I've come... I've come from Danica." Lin hoped those gathered would understand him. Judging by the number who raised a hand to mouth or shrunk back, they did. "Not for war. Not to lay blame for the state of things within my home. But to rescue my daughter."

"Is this... wild one your daughter?"

The hair at the back of Lin's neck rose as a Nooseman stepped out from behind the further of the two tables. They dragged Denny by her hair, her cheeks bruised and swollen.

"No. But I'll be taking her too." Lin tried, and failed, to keep his voice level.

"Calm yourselves. He means this little one. Don't you?"

Lin's throat tightened. Mellyr was there swaddled in what looked to be silk stitched with gold. Her eyes were closed and the woman holding her, possibly the emissary who'd taken her in the first place, cooed as she looked down at her. Armor glistened under the emissary's robes and she cocked her head to the side as she examined Lin.

"But she isn't *truly* your daughter. Is she?" The woman asked.

Lin took a step forward, eyes shifting from the lightly armored woman to the Nooseman. "It doesn't matter. Give her back to me or I'll take her back."

"Elicia, don't speak anymore to this blood-tainted monster." The gray-haired man rose and clapped his hands. The angled Wanderer's Ore seemed to shift and in moments the room was lit so brightly in that sickly blue hue of the ore, that Lin felt he might vomit. "This proves without a shadow of a doubt..." he rose to his feet, two others at either side of him taking the same action. "...exactly my point on the Accords. They're dangerous, capable monsters!" The man's jowls shook as he slammed the flat of his hand against the table.

"If it is as he says, King Lodram, he was brought here through subterfuge. He even speaks and asks for peace!" A thin waif of a man, the one on King Lodram's right, pointed at Lin.

"I've seen trained dogs beg when it was convenient for them, *Elodian wraith.*"

Lin struggled to take his eyes off Mellyr. She was there, not more than ten meters from him. Of course, if he fought to take her, Leo would likely die. He should've left the boy. And not only was Mellyr there, but King Lodram was too. Lin's knuckles whitened on the spear. One well-placed throw. That was all it would take to end the life of his people's largest oppressor.

Lodram was gray and old but certainly not bent of back and senile. Nor did he look particularly wicked. Gods, the man looked downright kind when he wasn't grimacing. This man upholding ancient, cruel rites, looked like he might play cards with Denro. Now that he was risen to his full height, Lin saw the circlet he wore was dotted with glittering jewels but the metal itself wasn't gold or silver. *Bound Metal.*

"This is why they must be contained," King Lodram shook his head and scanned the faces of those around him. "Monster, do you plan to attack me? If so bare your teeth and show all those gathered what you're capable of."

Lin shifted his weight and Leo yelped beside him. Denny wasn't moving, but her chest rose in a slow, unsteady rhythm.

"This is why the resisting dukes claim that Ladrican rule isn't the way. Self-governance would have kept this man in check," the Elodian man said. Lin was sure he hadn't seen anyone from the Elodian Empire before, even among the servants in the hall. He was paler than Lin would have thought possible, as if all the blood had fled his body, and his hair was a faded black tone. His clothes were plain compared to the King's garbs beside him, but the man carried himself well.

"Answer me this untethered." The speaker was the woman who'd risen beside the King. Her robes were different, more showy than the last time Lin had seen her. But there was no mistaking the hard eyes or the shaved head. *High Scholar Anya?* "Why did High Scholar Dellis have to die?"

"T-that isn't fair. You aided them in stealing Mellyr. I-I didn't know anyone would die."

King Lodram snorted. "I'd expect such weak drivel from the boy with you... not one of the very untethered who has sunk Danica into chaos. Tell me who is it really behind the machinations in Danica? The Dukes, the Ferrucium, or that horned untethered?"

"What? None of that matters. I don't want to hurt anyone here. So many of you..." Lin raised his voice. "So many of you probably only know the stories you've been told. I was like you. I worked with the Ferrucium, policing my own. Then... then I broke the Binding Tenets."

Disdain flashed across the king's face as his lip curled.

"At first, it was to save my life. Then I did it to save others. We are not monsters any more than you."

"Says the Danican who likely killed many good soldiers to get here, snuck into this very secure meeting place, and is staring at me like a fox might a hen." King Lodram shook his head.

"Of course, we know *all* Danicans aren't monsters. But your actions and the actions of your people, no matter the reasoning, state otherwise." High Scholar Anya lowered her eyes. "This child is Danican. But she is more than that. She is what will save these Accords. A marriage, predetermined long before you claimed custody of her, that when she comes of age will allow both sides of this conflict to see peace."

Lin frowned. "She is a baby. And you'd speak of marriage?"

"Her father's lineage dates back even further than the Accords. She will have a suitable member of the royal Ladrican family when she comes of age." High Scholar Anya's chin dipped a bit. "She will have a good life."

Lin looked to Leo, then Denny on the floor. How had he thought this would go? Why did he think himself capable of anything? He couldn't save Margaret. Now Mellyr. Perhaps he'd been clinging to the idea of proving himself to Leo. Proving to a random Ladrican boy that Lin *wasn't* a monster. But it seemed that was exactly what this was calling for. Violence. Lin's head throbbed.

You can't achieve anything, can you Escorter?

"Shut up!" Lin snapped at Aemun's cruel, chiding voice in his mind.

"I really can't imagine what you hoped to accomplish coming here, but you've failed. You won't be leaving here alive, much less with a future member of my family." There was a stinging finality to the king's voice.

Lin formed a sharp, flat Weft and pointed his spear toward the king. "Last chance to give her back to me." His voice strained, shaking from frustration and pain.

"See. All that talk of peace leaves the table when something stands in your way. Do it, untethered."

Lin blinked away the tears and looked at Leo one last time. "I'm sorry," Lin whispered. And he was sorry; to Denro who'd wanted peace, to Leo who might just be the bravest young man Lin had met, and to Mellyr who would once again be bathed in blood.

Calamitous Bone

"The earliest sign that a person might untether, is that they are Danican. The second sign is that they wield the magic of their people and show the tell-tale symptoms. Thinning hair. Brittle nails. Ashen, graying skin. The third and final sign is the hallucinations. Voices, sounds, and in rare cases sights. One reason some delusional people claim untethering to be a curse bestowed on the children of Velkath is that the sigil of his house is often what these mad people see, even having no frame of reference for it before the hallucinations. And that leads to the question, what if they truly are cursed?" Records from the personal diary of Physiker Sichael.

Lin hurled the spear. Flashbacks of the assault on the Ferrucium only empowered his throw. His momentum carried him as he unleashed the Weft. Leo screamed, his voice echoing off the walls, begging Lin to stop.

The Nooseman caught the spear like it was a stick thrown by a child, broke it in half, and tossed the two uneven lengths back. One caught the Weft, slicing the shaft in half longways. The other would have taken Lin in the shoulder if he hadn't charged forward.

Blade forged from threads of bright gold blinked into existence and Lin vaulted the space between him and the tables where the delegation had debated. Chairs crashed to the floor, papers scattered, and screams sounded as Lin cleared the first table. Tears stung his eyes. Mellyr was so close. He had to save her. Get her back. Hold her.

"Kill him! Take his head, Gritt. Do it!" King Lodram had been one of the first to back away, his dark beady eyes focused like he could see right through Lin.

"Tell me," Gritt said. "Were you one of the ones who killed Dennick?" Her flat, metal mask seemed just the same as all the others, but he knew underneath it there would be sunken cheeks, chapped lips, and pale, gray flesh. There was no doubt this Nooseman was the one he'd fought on the docks alongside Denny. They met Lin's Blade with their own, bright and slender.

Guards pressed in, circling. The cowards waiting for a chance to attack him when he was distracted. And behind them most of the leaders cowered. So many disparate faces and features but the fear they shared was evident.

Lin slashed down, the blow parried easily. The wounds he'd suffered running from the docks pulled at his stolen clothes, tugging with each movement."I survived Dennick and watched him die. But I didn't kill him."

Gritt's head lowered and she seemed to shudder, her black robes with crimson stitches fluttering as if a wind had blown through the room. "When we fought aboard the ship, I didn't think you could have been. Or her. Any of your kind really. He was strong. He was loved."

Gods. Her voice was soft and steady but it sounded as if she was mourning the man.

"Gritt. I ordered you to kill him, not converse. Do as I commanded. Guards, either slit the boy's throat or release him. I've heard enough of his incessant howling."

Lin wanted to turn to the guard, but he knew this Gritt wouldn't wait to take advantage of his distraction. But he could hear Leo scrambling away, slipping on the floor, and crashing into the nearest table. Apologies came out from the boy, muttered and tearful.

Lin pivoted, avoiding the Nooseman's strike. They circled each other between the two gathered tables like fighters in a pit for the King's entertainment. But at least he could see Leo now. Mellyr too. Just right there. The only threat in the room right in front of him.

Leo tried to pick himself up and flee from the table but a hand shot out. The Elodian had circled the end of the table while Gritt moved and had removed one of his gloves.

"Shh, it will be okay." He brushed his bare hand across Leo's cheek, consoling him. In a breath Leo froze, body growing rigid, then unnaturally limp as he collapsed into the man. "Could we not talk without violence? Please."

"Leo!" Lin screamed. He lunged forward, unsure of what the man had done to the boy.

"The boy is fine," King Lodram snorted, waving a dismissive hand toward Leo and the Elodian who'd touched him. "Petty magicks from a petty man. Gritt— if that monster leaves the tables there will be repercussions. Now kill him!" King Lodram's face reddened and his thin lips had curled.

The surrounding guards pressed in closer, steps shuffling and giving them away.

Gritt stepped in front of Lin. She moved so deftly it was a wonder her feet touched the floor at all. Her Blade barred Lin's path.

"Correct me if I'm wrong, but we are here with the powers of the world gathered in one room. Are we not?" The Elodian said. Whatever the man's game was, he spoke slowly and clearly. "If I had to guess, even this little disturbance was planned by Good King Lodram here."

Lin stared at the Nooseman, waiting for them to move. There was no missing the saccharine spite in the Elodian's words.

King Lodram sneered, cast a side-eye at the now gloved hand of the speaking Elodian, and stepped away, towards High Scholar Anya. "Yes, I orchestrated for a deranged monster to break into this assembly and try to kill me. Say your peace, *wraith*, but do try to keep your foolish accusations grounded in reality."

"I'm not here for you!" Lin snarled.

"Please," the Elodian said, dark eyes locked onto Lin's. "Before this dissolves into further violence, please listen to me. For those of you who don't know me. I am the Mouth of the Emperor. Speaker of the House of Silence. I am, as King Lodram so cruelly stated, wraith-touched. But more than that I am a man, a father, a son, a brother. Those other titles may define me, but they don't encompass the entirety of who I am. I am Julius."

King Lodram feigned a large yawn and sat back into his chair— well away from Lin's reach— with his arms folded. Some of the leaders slowly returned from the side of the walls, though they stayed well behind the bristling soldiers.

"I say all of this to say, how likely is it that on the very day of our meeting a Danican, embossed with their magic and on a mission to rescue the very child confirmed to have been taken, would come here if not goaded to do so?" He slammed his hand on the table as if knowing it wouldn't disturb the unnatural rest he'd affected Leo with. "What better way to make the powers of the world fear Danicans than to see their might and fury firsthand? I mean stars above, look at the man. He's clearly been through hell and back to get here. For what? As a father myself, I can say with my whole heart there is nothing that would keep me from mine."

Lin searched the faces he could without looking away from the Nooseman. Confusion, fear, apathy. All these different people and none looked him in the eye, save Julius.

Gritt lowered her Blade a hair, stalking him like a trained wolf waiting to be told to attack. But the King had ordered her already, hadn't he?

"You say your daughter, this child, was stolen from you. Recount your tale. Please."

It felt like Lin was being called to the center of the Chamber of Judgment, and his heart beat furiously in his chest. Purple spots danced in his vision and a heavy, pungent incense of sage and chamomile was all he could smell. He stared at the bundle that was Mellyr. How had she grown so large already?

"I was a guest, a prisoner really, with the scholars for months. Locked in a room for my foolishness in asking for their aid. They chose to uphold the Accords and leave us to the wolves once the thaw began. It was at this time that a Pollsh trading galley arrived and spirited Mellyr away. I was told that the only logical place the ship might dock was Fort Talm. Once there I found Mellyr gone but was led to believe she may be on this island. That is why I'm here. That is the only reason I'm here." Lin's voice broke. "Please... if you give me back that child I can leave. We can pretend like I was never here."

A throaty laugh escaped King Lodram. "Y-you think the learned leaders of this wide world will just forget that you assaulted an assembly discussing the Accords? Something you've admitted to breaking in spades? I knew your stock was barely better than animals, but I've severely underestimated just how stupid you are!"

Lin formed a Weft, bringing out fresh gasps from those gathered who must have had the Sight. But as quick as he'd conjured it, the Nooseman took control of it, breaking it apart into separate threads of magic. Her head shook, face hidden behind her mask, and her Blade angled to point at Lin's chest.

The door behind Lin rattled, but the bar didn't give way, and soon knocks and shouts sounded from the other side.

"Along the way, I found Danica in disrepair. Untethered attacks have grown more rampant, and somehow more organized. I learned the Fentian scholars conduct tests on our people. The physikers at Fort Talm did much the same. We are treated as cattle. Our blood is stolen and used as a fuel source for magic that doesn't belong to them."

"Is this true?" Julius, already pale, turned a horrified expression toward Anya.

"Tests have been conducted. Always with consent," Anya said.

"How can a child consent?" Lin yelled, causing the encroaching guards to flinch.

Anya sighed. "We went through this before, Lindel. Denro consented to the tests. And Mellyr wasn't harmed. Now it's clear you came all this way for something. I'd be willing to speak toward a motion that would see you able to leave here under the stewardship of the scholars."

"A prisoner you mean?" Julius scoffed. "If anything, this is plain to see that the two powers closest to the Danican people have been abusing their roles as guardians."

"Please," Lin whispered. "I— I was prepared to come in here and do whatever I had to to bring Mellyr home. I don't care about the Accords. So often I've found myself lodged between the machinations of people who want more than they're capable of holding. I didn't even want these One-loved markings! These were to save my life." Lin ripped open the tunic he'd stolen, revealing the Stitches down his abdomen. "These patterns grant me strength and speed." He ran his left hand over his right arm. "But I would remove all of them gladly if it meant taking that child back with me. I am no avaricious monster, seeking death and power. I just want to hold that sweet girl again."

"He... he speaks well for a blood-tainted monster, no?" King Lodram chuckled and clapped slowly. "But my previous point stands. He has no love for the Accords. Let us recall why Ladrica was granted the authority by our forefathers over Danica."

"Because our forefathers were afraid of what they didn't understand," Julius said.

"Because Velkath and his kin were inconsolable," Anya retorted.

"I think it is prudent that we speak with Erias and Azhura. Clearly, this man shouldn't be seen as a representative of the Danican people. Grief-stricken and... unbalanced as he seems." A man Lin hadn't heard speak yet, but who did so with an even, flat cadence. The words weren't harsh, but neither had they seemed kind. His shoulders were narrow and he wore a slim-fitted vest with velvet cuts down the side.

Another woman stood, red hair cut short to her shoulders with golden loops in her ears and a gown that looked cut from the night sky itself. "If it is as Julius posits, and you've intentionally lured this...man here hoping to cause irreparable relations between us and the Danican people, then as a representative of Nacodon, I must denounce you."

"Denounce me?" King Lodram shifted in his seat, straightening the cuffs of his robes. "You'd have to have a real say in these affairs to be capable of *denouncing* me. You are but one of the many Free Nations. I am a King. Lineage ordained by the Gods themselves."

"I second Lady Aurell's point," A heavy-set man broke past the row of soldiers. He was draped in enough silks to make a bedspread and held his hands in each other, jeweled rings alight on his knuckles. His voice came out high and pitched and as he turned to stare at Lin, it was clear he wore no small amount of blush on his cheeks.

"If these schemes end up being true, it puts to question everything our forebearers were led to believe related to the Accords."

Lin swallowed the lump in his throat. Gods. These people, disparate and as different from him as any Danican he'd met, were thinking logically. Some undoubtedly viewed him as a monster, he could see it in the way they averted their eyes from his or cowered beside others. But there were people here willing to listen.

"I… I am not the man to represent my people. I've never claimed to be. But… I could list at least two I think who would not only be willing to speak to you, but also listen."

"Enough!" King Lodram rose back to his feet. "Believe it or not but I do not need to pull strings in the background. Working in the shadows is not something a person anointed by the light does. It simply isn't done. We can discuss how or why this tainted blood man snuck into our meeting place at a later date. But as it stands there is a very real threat in this room. Those with the Sight saw him conjure his wicked magic. Those without the Sight felt it surely. I can provide proof that I've been far too busy to conspire to bring about an untethered's wrath upon this council. That being said, this threat is tangible and must be dealt with. Over my writhing corpse, he will take Lady Azhalia now that she has finally come into my custody."

Murmurs of confusion, approval, and dissent came from those gathered. King Lodram was one of the only persons in the room with a crown and he carried himself fully aware of that fact.

The bar rattled again, the sound of steel pressing between the wood to pry the doors open.

"By order of the King's Guard, open these doors!" Came a shout from the other side.

It didn't matter if they opened the doors. Not now. But Lin hadn't dispelled his Blade and neither had Gritt. But this Nooseman, so skilled in taking control of other people's Bindings, hadn't taken his Blade. *Why?*

"If it is true that you wish no harm upon any of those gathered here, then surrender." It was the large, blush-cheeked man speaking. "The Free Nation of Belanise will ensure no harm will come to you, lest Ladrica wishes to face an embargo unlike anything they've seen in their kingdom's history."

"An embargo?" Lin narrowed his eyes at the man, sending him a step back into the table. "He has taken my... my daughter and you claim he will face an embargo? Correct me if I'm wrong, but hasn't Danica technically been under a centuries-long *embargo*?"

The man stuttered and took another step back. The pale Elodian, Julius smiled. It was faint and seemed to stretch his cheeks a hair tauter than natural, but it was there. "Our new friend here makes a point that shouldn't be ignored."

King Lodram hung his head, shaking it back and forth for a moment as he touched his brow. Then he slammed a hand on the table and looked up. Eyes narrowed, jaw clenched, fury flush across his face. "Tighten." The word was a curse and spit flung from his thin lips.

Tighten?

The leaders at the table flinched back and several soldiers wearing various colors pulled from the approaching circle, clutching at their dignitaries like beggars might bread. They pulled them away, backing them to the wall, blades drawn. These were their men and women, and they were terrified. It had to be a phrase related to the Nooseman, but as Lin looked at the expressionless mask, he saw no movement. Even the Blade stayed flat at Gritt's side.

"Have you lost your hearing as well as your senses?" King Lodram growled. "I tell you to kill him and you toy with him. I tell you to tighten and you stand motionless! It is like with the monster's arrival you forgot *your* place!" Spittle flew from King Lodram's thin lips.

"I said no!" Gritt screamed.

Lin didn't think she had said anything but her voice came out from behind the mask timid and rattled, as if it had been hiding there all along. It was a far cry from the confident, woman he'd heard moments before.

"Stupid girl."

Gritt used her free hand to slip the mask from her face. She looked somewhat like Denny, at least if Lin squinted. Wild curls of limp strands where her hair wasn't shorn hung across her brow and her eyes were golden with Stitches. "I won't kill this man. And I certainly won't kill these gathered leaders. Dennick struggled so that we might find a path and I believe this is it." Her jaw clenched, chapped lips tightening.

"To disobey my order is death. You know this?" King Lodram didn't smile but his eyes seemed to dance with joy as he watched Gritt suddenly spasm.

"If fulfilling my Uethe means attacking people during a time of parley, then I don't want to fulfill it. I've seen these Uethes broken firsthand. I've heard enough to know that despite my many failings..." tears streaked her cheeks and she fell to one knee. "I was right to always ask questions. I was right to think that Dennick hadn't needed to die far from me when he was the best of us all!"

Gritt tossed her mask to the ground, the metal clanging sharply. "He was loved." Her words came out choked and tears came fully down her ashen face, the glow of her Inlayed eyes making it look like cracks of light shone in her face.

Lin watched in horror as the Bludwieve around her finger grew larger, waves of heat spiraling from it. He glanced at his own and his stomach twisted as if in time with the twining magic thread. Gods. This Nooseman was willing to die for him.

Even if that wasn't true, she was willing to die for her beliefs, her secret convictions not consumed by the King's. And here he'd thought they were all brainwashed monsters. He'd decided they were all the same flavor of apple, hadn't he? He dispelled his Blade and was at her side in a breath, clutching her shoulders. Her body radiated heat and it was growing warmer by the breath.

Julius moved away from the King and Leo and was to Gritt in an instant, hand free of his glove. She bared her teeth and growled at him until he caressed her cheek. All the color building under her skin drained in a moment, the heat with it. Then she was unconscious, twitching on the floor. "When she wakes, I will have to touch her again."

Lin flinched back away from the man's exposed hand.

"I am wraith-marked... not so different from you and your kind. It is a sleep and nothing more. This affliction of mine is why our Empire is so understanding of your people's plight." Julius smiled and brushed back the strands of pale black hair that had swept across his face.

Denny groaned and her eyes blinked open. She touched her head gingerly, then shifted to sit up. "Wh—" Her voice dropped as she scanned the room, eyes coming to rest on King Lodram. Without hesitation, she threw a Weft colored like dirty water. It carved through the air at Lodram. Then it went wide, angling away from the man and slicing toward Mellyr and the woman who held her.

It hurt to unravel like he was trying to pry apart iron with his nails. The Weft shattered, spraying Mellyr in dingy motes.

"Denny, I'm here, don't fight right now," Lin said, struggling to keep the fury from his voice. She'd almost killed Mellyr and barely seemed to register it.

Her bright eyes still locked onto the King. A smile twisted the Stitches into uneven lines across her face as her gaze rested on Gritt. "I hope you didn't kill her. She's not that bad."

"She was dragging you by your hair," Lin said.

Denny shrugged. "At least my body is still attached to my head to be dragged by." She groaned and rubbed her side. "She got me pretty good though. I'll have to pay her back."

At the side of the room, Mellyr's cries sounded like an alarm. Lin shuddered at the sound and rose to his feet, still wary of the

Elodian man beside him. Denny's smile dropped, shattering like frail glass.

With his biggest threat unconscious, confidence flooded into Lin. Confidence and a realization. He *had* barged in, no better than a monster. And just now, Mellyr almost paid for it. Sure he hadn't thrown the Weft, but it could've been his if he'd aimed one at the King. *Bound fucking Metal.*

"I am open to the idea of *Mellyr* helping us find a truce. But until she is of age to decide that for herself, please give her back." Lin hoped he sounded half as measured as Denro always did when speaking. He'd even settle for a fraction of Aemun's unearned confidence.

"He's being too polite. If you don't give that child to us... No one will leave this room alive. Not a single damned soul!" Denny stumbled to her feet, cloak fluttering.

"Denny!" Lin snapped.

"And the blood-tainted monsters reveal their true intentions." King Lodram's voice dripped with enmity. "Kill us all. Prove yourselves the monsters we've known you to be."

"Gladly," Denny growled. She lunged forward, another Weft forming in a blink, and slung it at King Lodram.

Lin broke it, shattering the Weft before it reached the king and redirected again. With Mellyr so close it wasn't worth it."Denny stop. If we can help it, we don't want to kill anyone."

King Lodram scoffed. "Once a bitch snaps at your hand, it is better to put it down lest it think it can do so again someday."

"Denny, please. Give me a chance," Lin whispered. He'd stepped forward to be beside her and placed a hand on her shoulder. The room had grown quiet and the sigils along the wall seemed to flash, Velkath's Sigil transposed across them every time Lin glanced away. His head swam but he felt so close to a peaceful resolution. So close to giving Denro and Erias a reason not to be furious with him once it was all said and done. *And Leo.*

Calamitous Hate

"Ferrucium Steel. Bound Metal. Both ores are mined from the mountain range dividing Ladrica from Danica. Both are supposedly magical. The Bound Metal is far easier to explain as the ore it comes from is naturally either attracted or repulsed to iron. Which is often what the average Binding is believed to consist of. Add intention to it, and suddenly you have a tool that nearly neutralizes Wievings entirely. Ferrucium Steel is less straightforward. We believe, with iron at its heart, that it is essentially a solidified Binding. Capable of withstanding the magic, seeing as it is nearly identical to say a conjured Blade." Excerpt from a tome entitled, "Minerals, magical and mundane".

"A chance? It seems you've misjudged many things. I'd no sooner bring you to this island than I'd bring a hound not trained to hold its piss in the house. Now, I think you've prattled on quite enough about peace and all that. You will not be taking this child. You will not be *leaving* this island. But what you will be, the both of you, is an example to the traitorous dukes." King Lodram's jowls shook and he pressed back a slip of gray-white hair that had fallen from the Bound Metal circlet he wore.

"I'm no speaker. I said as much. I'm no emissary meant to sway the hearts of those gathered. I'm simply a surrogate father wishing to save his daughter. Please... stay your hands. Calm your hearts.

Can't you set aside considerations for the coming war and think of the plight of the people."

Lin rotated to face the wall of soldiers, gesturing at Leo with his left hand. "How many more children must be dashed against the rocks to feed the hungry Gods? How many... how many more people have to go through life enslaved by our past?"

"For someone claiming not to be a speaker, you've done quite well for yourself," Julius said softly, nodding towards the faces of some of the less cowed leaders along the wall.

"Speak with Danica's leaders. Postpone any decision to punish Danica as a whole until you've given us a chance to plead our case. Ladrica's cruel reign should be limited to its citizens, not those of a nation who owe nothing to a king who cares little for them."

King Lodram's cheeks had grown pink and it seemed if he ground his teeth anymore he'd have none left. Lin studied the soldiers, trained and hardened and ready to die if it meant killing him. Then he glanced over his shoulder back at the king.

"Cruel?" King Lodram's voice swelled. "You want to see *cruel*? Take that tainted infant and show him how cruel we can be."

"No!" Lin turned and he heard the sound of boots on stone as the soldiers who hadn't taken their delegates to the wall pressed him from behind. The door had been opened at some point and more Ladrican soldiers had joined the ranks. But Denny was quicker than the footsoldiers and formed an ochre-hued Blade, darting to cover Lin's rear. She moved with a limp, dashing to the closest soldiers and slashing at any who got near.

"Don't let him goad you," Julius said. Lin yanked his shoulder free from the man's gloved hand, a slight ping of terror that he might be trying to put him to sleep as he had the Nooseman and Leo.

The Ladrican Emissary, robed in dark sheets of velvet with plates of Ferrucium steel protecting her throat and wrists moved in front of the king. She looked ready for war in her own way, her severe expression as hardened as the bits of armor she wore.

"As you wish, my liege." A dagger flashed into her hand and Lin threw two Wefts at her. One struck the edge of the dagger, shattering into motes of light and spraying across Mellyr while the other sparked and raked the armor at her throat. Her eyes grew large and her nostrils flared but even as the magic crackled under her chin, grazing up against the steel, she pressed the dagger down.

Anya was there in an instant. She grabbed the woman's arm, twisting it back and around behind her, disarming her. Another scholar, one not clothed in the station of a High Scholar, moved in tandem with her, taking Mellyr in her arms as the woman struggled.

"The Fentian scholars move against the Accords?" King Lodram asked. Disbelief graced his wrinkled face and he'd taken a half step toward the scholars.

"While immediate rectification is impossible, it is my opinion that perhaps we at Fentis were too hasty in deciding not to at least listen to the Danican leaders."

"I *am* the Danican leader. As was my father and his father's father. One... *monster* comes in here begging like a starved mutt and suddenly this collective of people grows bleeding hearts? Do each and every one of you not come from sturdier stock? They are monsters!"

"I only see one monster in this room." A thin, near gangly man peeled away from the wall of guards at his back. He wore neutral tones and the look of disgust on his face made it clear where he stood, even if his words sounded as neutral as the colors he wore.

"The Accords were drafted for a reason. Perhaps Ladrica is the only one close enough to see the danger these people still pose. Perhaps my forefathers were fools for trusting in the common sense of the Free Nations."

Lin rushed to Anya, listening to it all unfold, uncaring. He reached for Mellyr but the High Scholar stepped between him and the woman holding her.

"Just because we don't wish to allow Lodram to kill an innocent child, doesn't mean you are the best guardian. Look at yourself. You aren't thinking clearly if you thought coming here was ever going to result in saving her."

Lin's mouth hung open and he stared at Anya. "Y-you told me where they'd be taking her!"

"I wanted you out of *my* room." She straightened her back and pressed a trembling hand forward while the other rested near her throat. Her fingers tightened and Lin saw the glow of a Binding begin to form.

"You denounce the king's actions yet still wield the blood of my people as a tool!"

"We're all tools," she said.

"So we've come to an impasse," King Lodram's voice rose over the murmuring of those gathered. "Bring it to a bloody vote then. Guards, stand down from that wild bitch lest she bite more of you."

Lin blinked and raised his hands, palm out to Anya. "I don't want any trouble. I told you as much in your room. Please, let me at least see her."

The sound of weapons lowering came from the center of the room and the leaders of the various nations slowly made their way back to the tables, giving Lin and Anya a wide berth. Sweat mingled with perfume and for a brief moment, Lin thought he smelled an untethered, the acrid rust of one hanging in the air. But then it was gone, swallowed by the burning incense.

Anya nodded at her lesser, and the scholar undid the silk shawl covering Mellyr's face. She still cried, soft whimpers that crescendoed into wails every so often, but it was her. She looked healthy, her eyes bright against her rosy cheeks. Lin hovered there, every bit of his body telling him to snatch her and never let go. He tensed and Anya moved to stand in front of him.

"This might end up not being a total disaster, but if you force this, there are no guarantees." Anya stared at him, face unreadable.

"Fine." It hurt to be so close yet unable to take her in his arms. After how far he'd come, he still couldn't hold her or let her tiny fingers wrap around his hand. And maybe it was his imagination but she seemed to calm at spotting him, her cries changing. Her hands reached, grasping. Even after everything, she still wanted him.

"This meeting was originally called to give approval and consent for Ladrica to quell the rebellion in Danica through force. Our mediary within the Ferrucium was confirmed murdered, as well as two of the Weavers put in place to govern, and all attempts to reach the four dukes have been met with resistance.

"And now it is clear that the honey dripping from this bear's lips has convinced you he and his people are all bees, not to be feared.

"So let us vote. All in favor of the ratifications of the Accords allowing for immediate use of force to reinstate Ladrican control over the land of Danica, say aye." King Lodram paced as he spoke, hate wrinkling his face and bringing a sneer to his thin lips.

Lin watched the leaders. Some looked back now, locking eyes with him, studying him. Odds were he looked as horrible as he felt. He kept his palms up and out and even lowered himself to a single knee. "Please," he mouthed to any still observing him.

Denny slumped to the ground beside him. "I got three of the guards," she whispered. "They don't seem to be the same as the soldiers on the ship. Something feels off. Most are young, like fresh recruits."

Lin nodded and swallowed hard as he pulled his eyes away from the leaders' faces to look at the corpses. It was true. Most didn't have Bound Metal batons, and while the majority of blades were Ferrucium steel, some lacked even that. Not to mention the disparity of armor amongst these men and women. Gambesons and cloth did very little to stop honed Wefts. But perhaps they hadn't expected assailants as skilled as Lin and Denny. None of it made much sense.

"Aye," Five, no six people said simultaneously with varying accents.

Hope, something Lin thought had long died within him, swelled in his chest, like a seed growing. It hurt, pushing against the bounds of his ribs, pressing out from his heart.

"And those opposed to ratifying the Accords to allow for immediate use of force to reinstate Ladrican control?"

Of the twenty or so leaders gathered, eight raised their hands and said, "Opposed."

King Lodram seemed to be counting, his wrinkled face passive until he licked his teeth and hung his head. He leaned on the table, hands spread to support his weight. "That leaves five abstained votes. Clearly state your choice."

Anya was one of those who hadn't voted. "The scholars will wait to vote until we can speak with the real Danican representatives."

Calls of assent came from the velvet-clothed gangly man, the perfumed, heavier-set man, and a woman Lin hadn't seen speak. Whether it was reassuring that the leaders of the Free Nations didn't all agree or not, Lin felt he understood where the hesitation was coming from. If he had been in this room and asked to vote months ago, before meeting Tylle in Lyre, he would have argued for the king's point. And even now... he wasn't sure that Erias and Azhura would lead their people to something better. But anything had to be better than the cruel tests and unfair treatment from the scholars and Ladricans.

That's right. He couldn't let the High Scholar's current attitude change the fact that she knowingly performed tests on Danicans.

Not any more than he could forgive Denro for assenting to it. Or Pael for trying to shoot Mellyr. Hate was easy to harbor, an easy source of fuel. But love? He looked back at Mellyr, wishing more than anything to hold her and ease her whimpering cries.

King Lodram drummed his fingers on the table, a vein at his temple pulsing in rhythm. "I feel like I've made it abundantly clear that… for all intents and purposes… I am the representative of Danica. *Me.* All of you… are separated by seas and oceans from the blood-taint. You don't understand the threat of it sleeping under Ladrica's border. The assaults from the south on our border. I'm the Danican leader!" His fist slammed and he huffed up, glaring at anyone who might look at him.

"Then what is the point of this vote?" A dark-skinned woman asked. Her hair was set in braids with beads and jewels framing her face.

"He hoped," Julius and shook his head. "To sway the room so as not to appear a villain. Let us not be tricked by his calm demeanor. Ladrica and the royal family will do anything to keep Danica under their stewardship."

"Wraiths shouldn't speak to their betters, empire ghoul," King Lodram spat.

Some gasped at the blatant insult, but most murmured to their neighbors behind flat hands. Lin watched it all. Is that the future Danicans could expect for simply being different? Insulted to their face and expected to take it?

Gritt mumbled something then shot up screaming. Sweat beaded her brow and her black robes clung to her. She clutched her left hand as if she might stop the flow of blood to it.

Lin flinched and shivered at her howls. "Can you ease her pain?"

"If she already woke, it won't work again so soon," Julius said. He looked genuinely remorseful as his lips twitched and he folded his hands into each other.

"The only ease she will have, since she decided to disobey me, is to follow my original orders or kill herself. It isn't my fault she was swayed by a small, insignificant speech from filth like you. One shouldn't abandon their duty quite so quickly."

Lin fought the urge to jump across the table and strike the man. King or not, he was arrogant, rude, and more than that, clearly cruel. No wonder Aemun had somehow earned his ear. They were more alike than they were different. A realization dawned on Lin as he stared at the king. Even now, months after his death, Aemun's actions rippled through this gathering.

"Who offered Mellyr as an eventual bride?" Lin asked.

Like a wounded pet, the wetnurse had circled back to stand beside King Lodram and curled her lip as she answered the question. "The child's father, of course. Her *real* father. The one, I have on good authority, you murdered."

"He betrayed Danica. Betrayed Ladrica too as far as I can tell. He was—"

"He was a man with ambition and plans and thought further than trying to rush into a place he knew nothing about, surrounded by people who viewed him as a monster, to save a child who wasn't his to save," King Lodram waved his hand as if dismissing Lin entirely. "A monster of course, but a semi-competent one."

If words could make a man falter, those nearly did. How often had he heard Aemun's mocking voice over the past few days? Chastising him. Deriding him.

"No," Lin muttered. Gods, his voice sounded choked by gravel. "He was a man that brought the might of a rebellion into the Ferrucium at the same time as he brought down the wrath of your Noosemen. And at the end, he said it was so his daughter might have a better future. I struggle to imagine all his twisted plans would have left her in Ladrica's care."

"This is getting us nowhere." Anya interrupted. Her eyes constantly darted to Gritt, whose howls continued to grow increasingly animalistic.

"Cut it off," Gritt said between screams.

"It won't—" Anya started.

"Do it!" She cried.

Lin struck quickly, sending more than one soldier stumbling back and reaching for weapons they'd let go lax during the conversations. Gritt's hand fell to the ground, even the bones of the wrist not offering resistance against the honed edge of Lin's Blade.

Her screams continued. The glow of her Bludwieve flickered, and as if there were an invisible string connecting it to her pulse, faded out like the dying beats of her heart.

Lin blinked. He'd done it. "Come here. I can—"

"Aggghhhhh!" Like a viper striking, a red thread jumped from her hand. It twisted and twined, wrapping up and around the stub of Gritt's hand. She clutched her wrist with her right hand, blood spilling between her fingers. Then the crimson thread was looped around her wrist, writhing and twisting until it rested where a bracelet might.

"An Uethe isn't so easily undone," Anya said, barely audible over Gritt's wailings. Mellyr joined in, screams echoing off the sigil-covered walls.

"Help her!" Lin snarled at Julius. The thin man had moved and rested his ungloved hand against her brow. His lips moved as he muttered to himself, almost like he whispered a lullaby only he and her could hear. The color drained from her slowly and when he pulled away, he looked sickly with pronounced circles under his eyes that hadn't been there before. "Next time she wakes, I can't help at all."

Lin glanced down at his own Bludwieve. There was a chance he might still be able to remove his, but if one thing was for certain it wouldn't be by chopping away his finger or hand.

Calamitous Blood

"Elodian magicks— They're called wraiths more due to their unnaturally pale complexion than their magic. They make Ladricans look like members of the Free Nations by comparison. But their magick is just as off-putting. A single touch, one gentle caress is enough to put a person to sleep. Certain events seem to wake them, but when all factors are normal, the sleep can hold until the Elodian chooses to wake those they touched. The Elodian Emperor mandated long ago that Elodian citizens traveling abroad must always wear gloves, and all do unless they wish to be branded criminal." Excerpt from A Study of Religion, author unsigned.

"So a formal truce of sorts?" Tessia said. She was the tall, dark-skinned woman with beads in her hair that had spoken earlier. It was clear that other leaders of the Free Nations looked to her for strength and solidarity, if not for some semblance of leadership itself. "A ceasefire of all these wild occurrences in a room meant to broach the topic of peace."

Was this always how leaders worked? They'd spit at you with venom and then stare as if it were meant to salve a wound. Not that Tessia had spoken cruelly to him, but there was something in how she looked at him. Listening to the gathered leaders made Lin's skin itch. Just across the table, the lesser scholar with Anya tended to Mellyr.

All of it was too much, the noise, the stares, the damned sigils on the wall overlaid by Velkath's damned sigil.

So close. Lin clenched his fist, closed his eyes, and exhaled. He might not have Aemun's snake tongue or Denro's calm countenance, but he could do this without more violence. The only thing that had achieved so far was nearly killing Mellyr.

King Lodram's vein under his circlet looked as if it were barely contained and at some point, Denny had slunk over to Lin and leaned her entire weight on him. At first, it had felt like a bird had landed on his shoulder, the touch was so slight. Lin stared down at the top of her head. Gods, she looked so frail. Brittle, in the overly blue light of the Wanderer's Ore.

Leo stirred, his fingers twitching, then his eyes opened and he moved lethargically away from Julius and the soldiers nearest him. "W-what happened?"

"Young man," Julius paused. What little color the ghost of a man had still hadn't returned to him and he rubbed his gloved hands together as if to warm them. "I can't apologize enough. You came in with him you see... and you headed straight for the delegation of my fellow leaders. Sleep was the better alternative." Julius's head tilted to the side as if pointing with his eyes at the nearest guards who still hadn't yet sheathed their blades.

Leo's brow furrowed and he shuddered, pulling his knees to his chest as his eyes locked onto the sigils cut into the walls. "Thanks, I suppose."

Lin thought he recognized the expression flashing over Leo's face. Confusion, distrust, *uncertainty.* Clearly, Elodians were allowed to exist among the others, but by King Lodram's words and actions, there was no love lost. And Leo had been saved twice now. Once by a tainted-blood monster and then again by a wraith-touched.

"If you'll excuse me, I've been missing out on the proceedings. And like or not, I am a mouth of the Emperor, among other things." Julius straightened his robes and rose, chin up. His first few steps were steady, but he stumbled and had to use the table to support himself.

"Know anything about him?" Lin asked.

Denny made an incomprehensible noise and shrugged.

Lin watched after the thin man, then glanced at the standing members of the Free Nations. "If his people can put others to sleep with just a touch... What other sorts of magicks are out there?"

Denny grunted. "Dunno. Don't care."

Lin snorted. *Fair point.* "I'm gonna get up... and try again to take back Mellyr. Please remain calm. It seems at least some of the room isn't against us, if not on our side."

Another grunt, maybe a nod. She shifted off and sat beside Gritt. Looking at the two of them, they could've been related. Distantly maybe. But all Nooseman *were* Danican. It was hard to believe his words alone had convinced her to break her Uethe to the king. Maybe in the time he'd spent reaching the island, Denny had somehow tainted the woman's mind. Or maybe there were some deeper feelings there for Dennick. Lin shook his head and rose.

"High Scholar, a word." Lin moved with his shoulders back and chin up like the room hadn't slowed to stare at him. The guards and soldiers who'd pressed in, those that still had all their limbs and weren't casualties of Denny waking, shifted uncomfortably.

"Lindel. I can't express enough how unwilling I am to let you take the child." Anya stepped from the table to again stand between Lin and the scholar struggling to ease Mellyr's discomfort.

The thieving bitch— Elicia— who'd stolen Mellyr in the first place stood beside the king, nursing her arm and glaring as if she wished herself capable of slaying them with her eyes alone.

"You and that Ladrican emissary stole her out from under my nose. Can your conscience allow this?" He wanted to sound placated, and neutral, but he knew fury slipped into his words.

"My conscience has allowed for many things. As I've said there were arrangements in place long before she came into your care." She leaned in and narrowed her eyes. "Think for a moment. Who do you think sent that ship to Aemun?"

Lin blinked. The man *had* said something about the scholars and Accords near his time of death, hadn't he? *Gods.* "Even after death, I find myself tangled in his web."

The High Scholar leaned in and Lin jerked his arm up, but her palms were up toward him and her eyes were wide, as if asking for trust. "Do you still have the book you took from my office?"

"If I did, what makes you think I'd give it back?"

"A trade might be possible. At the very least, we could bring you with us. It is becoming increasingly clear that leaving her in the custody of King Lodram might not be in the best interest of anyone gathered. Least of all her. You could swear another Uethe. To her if not to me. To be her protector."

Lin glanced over his shoulder at the faces of the leaders gathered. Then at Leo who sat there trying to make himself look as small as possible.

"Quit staring at me like I've taken the spoon from your babe's mouth," King Lodram hissed.

Lin focused his eyes and realized he had let his eyes linger on the man, staring lost in the folds of silken robes.

"We will have to gather again, already the night grows long. I would've sent a representative if I thought this would drag on as it has." The heavy-set, heavily perfumed man said. He'd risen and stretched and seemed eager to pace. "Not to mention the interruption that has yet to be settled."

"You complain too much, Donus," Tessia chided.

"I complain exactly as much as I need to. Squeaky hinges, oil, and all that."

"If anyone knows about excessive oil, it would be you," the thin man with velveted clothes said.

"Then let us agree to reconvene, with Danican representatives in attendance, in say three months?" Anya said. She'd been leaning away from Lin, one ear turned to the conversation.

"Three months?" King Lodram slammed a fist against the table. His circlet appeared as if it might slip from his brow. "The thaw is upon us. I demand temporary permission to enact a quelling of the uprising. I don't seek aid. I don't need assistance. But old rites do require that I seek approval. In three months, without intervention, it may be too late. It is all well and good to say you want to meet with their 'leaders' but in the meantime, their assassins will be after my head!"

"A point I don't think should be made lightly," Julius said.

"I don't make it *lightly*, wraith."

"Word will be sent to Erias, I can promise that," Denny whispered.

"What?" Donus asked, turning to glance down at her between the two tables.

Denny stared at Gritt for a long moment, then down at her hand and the Bludwieve that circled her finger. "We can get word to Erias and Azhura swiftly. He will be happy to meet with the many leaders gathered here."

"Then it is decided. Let us reconvene at the Towers in three months' time," High Scholar Anya said. Her voice carried a weight of finality to it that seemed like it might break King Lodram's back.

Lin scanned the room. It felt odd to imagine that someone like King Lodram, a ruler in name and action, could be quelled and routed by a group of others. He never could have imagined, not so very long ago, that the person the Weavers answered to, would have such limited power.

"Again you stare. Congratulations, tainted-blood. You've swayed the soft, malleable hearts of some of those gathered here. But some of us are made from sterner stuff than clay."

"And some of us are blades that have been tempered, broken, reforged, and sharpened," Lin said, an edge to his voice that he hadn't meant to form.

King Lodram scoffed and turned to the woman at his side, whispering something in her ear.

"Let us—" Tessia's words shook from her lips as the room rumbled. A second, closer explosion sounded from outside. Lin stumbled. The shaking was underfoot and in his gut. It was like the world was erupting. Dust rattled loose from the eaves and slowly hazed the air.

The Wanderer's Ore lining the walls rattled loose, shattering and casting broken light in various directions. Blue sparks erupted where the One-loved material struck damp patches.

"What is the meaning of this?" King Lodram straightened his back and scanned the room. "Another plot? You already gained what you wanted, no?" The man's ire was directed at Lin, accusation in the tone like spit clinging to his lips.

The soldiers who'd been nearby, clearly not wanting to give Lin and his companions enough space to act freely, shifted to face the ruined door. A third, further explosion sounded and the scent of smoke steadily inched into the room.

"What have you done now, tainted-blood?" King Lodram's voice was calm. Even. And he pointed a knobby, ringed finger at Lin.

"I've been in here this entire time!"

"You've interrupted this meeting well past the initial commencing of this council. Only God above could tell us what you were doing before then. Confident as I am that the truth couldn't be pulled from your mouth as easily as your pathetic pleas."

Lin clenched his jaw. "I had nothing—"

Another nearer, rumble sounded. Servants who'd been forced to wait outside pressed in clamoring about smoke and explosions ruining the harbor. Some soldiers, those smart enough to realize Lin wasn't an active threat, pressed out through the ruined doors.

A crash echoed through the expansive room as one of the tapestries of Vellia's kin collapsed to the floor.

"Nothing to do with this," Lin finished. It was clear by the way those nearest gathered stared at him, they didn't believe him. Painted on their faces like the gaudy blush and lipstick some seemed to wear. These people. These leaders hadn't struggled the way Lin and his people had. They saw him as a monster and even keeping his calm hadn't swayed some of them.

You could kill them all. One swift strike to the throats of those that step on our peoples'.

"We practically already adjourned. Flee if you wish. We will reconvene in a few months. I'm sure by then, this will be settled," King Lodram snorted and waved a ringed hand. The man appeared eager to have the other leaders exit the room, despite the unknown occurring outside. Either he was behind it somehow, or he was being cautious and using the others to test the waters.

"I can't prove it..." Lin whispered, pulling close enough to the king that he hoped his voice wouldn't carry.

King Lodram held up a hand, stalling the emissary as she drew another knife from the sheaths at her waist.

"But I know you're behind whatever this is."

To Lin's surprise, the king leaned even closer. So close that the man's short-cropped beard tickled the edge of Lin's ear. Lin pulled away slightly, expecting a dagger to find his neck.

"I'm sure, one way or another, you are responsible. You wretched creature. Long my family has reigned as wardens of your little land, and long it will continue. Whatever that is— do not think me weak just because one traitorous bitch tried to bite my hand." His chuckle was wet and throaty. "And really, you're as malodorous as you look. Foul-fool."

Lin would've lunged at the man if he hadn't felt Denny's hand on his shoulder. She'd risen and once again leaned on him, as light as could be except where her hand rested. When Lin looked at her, she shook her head. A curt shake.

"Someday, you'll get what is coming to you," Lin snarled.

King Lodram pulled back and smiled, accenting the wrinkles around his eyes and brow. "Aren't you tired of making promises you can't keep?"

Gods. This man's tongue was barbed. "Tell me something. Where are the rest of your troops? Surely those few handfuls of soldiers and a Nooseman aren't all the force Ladrica has left? That destruction... it wouldn't happen to be your troops, would it?" He wanted the last question to carry over the din of chaos spreading outside and the soft conversations of the remaining leaders in the room stall completely.

"My troops? Ahh... haha. Didn't see them when you came across the pass, did you? All those warnings your Grovetender has been preparing for? The great threat of the thaw?"

"That's enough my liege," Elicia hissed.

King Lodram studied his underling the way a hunter might observe a deer he stalked. His lips trembled for a moment as he seemed to weigh his words. "Brilliant counsel as always. I do tend to prattle more in my age than many might view wise. Though, even a bear with claws and fangs like this one, or a bird that flies quickly like that one would struggle out at sea. Who could have imagined that you two would be safer than those you left behind? Ha." Another wet, throaty chuckle, like the man was choking on his spit as he laughed.

"What does he mean?" Denny asked. The bruises on her face and dried blood made her look like a talking corpse. Her left eye wouldn't wholly open and the socket looked far more swollen than it should have been.

Lin shivered as he played back the man's words. He could attack the king. Take his head from his shoulders. But that would only fuel the rest of Ladrica's rage and it would tell all the gathered leaders here that he was the monster King Lodram claimed he was.

"Lin!" Julius, voice near to trembling, called. "I tried to sway some of the other leaders from venturing out, but my words hold as much as a bottomless bucket to the ones who listened to that weasel Lodram. I fear what awaits those gathered out there. This island isn't prone to natural eruptions. And the smoke. Clearly sabotage of some sort."

Lin narrowed his eyes and took it all in, shifting his attention from the king and his knife-wielding wetnurse of an emissary. "And what do you want me to do about it?"

Julius rubbed his hands together and held his gaze. Gods, even the man's eyes were pale, near gray. "If this is some sort of assault, show them your heart. Show them why Danicans shouldn't be feared but sought after as an ally!"

"He has a point," Denny said. "I can help."

"No. You will rest. Keep an eye on the Nooseman. If she wakes and decides following the king's command is better than the incessant pain she seems to be experiencing, we want to be ready to deal with her. Tylle told me once... not to accept quick words of apology any more than quick words of anger. Or something like that. I think actions should be counted doubly so."

"She knew what it would mean to disobey him," Julius said. "Even those of us with no gift for the magic you do know of Bludwieves. It was actually one of the first ideas given to the Accords when it came to..." He trailed off and looked away.

"When it came to isolating and turning my people into glorified cattle?" Lin asked.

Julius nodded. "Unfortunately so."

"Probably where Lodram's forefathers gained the idea of servitude for the Noosemen." Lin shook his head. "It doesn't matter. Let's see what sort of commotion could shake an island. Tell me, was this place once part of Danica?"

"That is a difficult topic to tackle..." Julius murmured.

Before he could say more, High Scholar Anya approached and raised her chin to the door. "Julius spoke to you already, yes? This could be an opportune moment to help shape the way members of the Free Nations see you and your people moving forward." Her brows raised, wrinkles coming to her forehead.

Lin took a deep breath. "And if this is some sort of trap, to let me become someone else's problem so that you don't have to deal with me wanting to take Mellyr?"

Anya shook her head. "You spent months with my people at the tower, did you not?"

"I did."

"Was anything ever so simple there?"

She had a point. A very good one at that. "Fair. Promise me that if I go out there and we learn that the Gods themselves have somehow awakened to punish the people on this island, and I die, you'll take care of Mellyr. You can't let that bastard have her. Even if you think her life would be wholly improved from it. Please."

Anya's lips tightened into a line but she nodded. "I'll take your companion."

Denny shifted her weight and was supported by the High Scholar in a blink. "If anyone tries anything in here. They'll regret it." Denny's words were weak.

"I just noticed your eyes, they're fascinating," Anya whispered. "Wholly blind without the Inlays, no?"

Denny growled but nodded without further comment.

"Promise me you won't let him take her."

Anya licked her lips and shifted Denny on her shoulder. "I'll do everything I can. It's clear by his earlier command that he doesn't care about her safety, let alone the previously agreed betrothal. But

I do think uniting the two lands through a marriage might be for the best."

Another smaller explosion shook the world. It clipped the end of the High Scholar's sentence as Lin turned and exited the room.

In all likelihood, someone was attacking. He didn't know untethered to use explosives and King Lodram was right, Lin *hadn't* seen the troops Pael and Denro had been so sure would be waiting in the pass. Unless he counted the paltry number stationed at the fort. Could they have been out at sea, now attacking? Possibly. But what would they have to gain by attacking this island of all places, especially with their king here as well?

Who'd have thought you'd be safer than those you left behind? Lin swallowed and took a deep breath. The only thing separating him from Mellyr now was whatever was causing the explosions outside. All he had to do was prove to the gathered leaders that he was a hero, not a monster. And if they still didn't give him back Mellyr, he'd show them how terrible he could be.

Choking Hope

"The dangers of Wanderer's Ore can't be understated. Cheaper than oil and, when placed behind the correct glass, just as bright as an oil-burning lamp. But any contact with moisture causes the material to spark, burning through stone and bone alike. Many tales of terror are told of children mistakenly putting a shard of ore into their mouths. The mines near the western side of Pollsh are home to the bravest of scavengers, seeing how often rainfall occurs." Excerpt from a tome entitled, "Minerals, magical and mundane".

Terrified, quaking servants were corralled and protected by various guards, as well as a handful of the gathered leaders who'd actually left the room at King Lodram's behest. Each face was painted with worry, even the soldiers.

Not a single sword or shout came Lin's way to stop him from leaving. Perhaps fear rooted those with the Sight in place, or the fact that he was leaving out the front door unmolested implied to them that he wasn't to be bothered. Either way, he wished entering had been half as simple as exiting. The two guards he'd knocked unconscious were still laid out by the columns.

Finding his way out through the front proved easy enough. He followed a group of soldiers to the entrance where doors the size of boulders stood ajar. Grand things, the doors were. They looked carved from stone and if they somehow fell over, there was no doubt they'd crush even the strongest of men.

Cold, biting gusts of wind carried the scent of smoke. And from the gap in the doors, the burning ships were brightly visible.

With as little experience as Lin had with boats and traveling by water in general, he was caught off guard watching the ships be consumed by the hungry flames so easily. For some reason, he'd imagined they wouldn't burn quite as easily as a pyre. The smoke was dark and had a pungent, malign odor to it.

Another explosion off to the side erupted from a smaller vessel. There was no initial sound of warning prior, but gouts of purple-hued flames erupted out.

Pieces of the ship turned to shrapnel and blue and orange sparks guttered from the devastated opening. Screams, nearly as loud as the explosion, came from the shore.

Sabotage? That was the only answer. And Lin was confident he'd seen sparks like those before on a smaller scale. Wanderer's Ore once it was wetted sparked and hissed but this? Ore and oil perhaps. Lin shuddered and took a faltering step forward.

Between the fog rolling on the water and the smoke drifting up from the docks, the shore itself was entirely obscured. Silhouettes were visible, the ships that weren't yet burning looming like hulking monsters half-submerged.

The path was clear of debris and foliage— well-kept despite the state the castle itself was kept in. Perhaps the Ladricans liked it that way. A standing monument to Danica's decline. Assuming this place had once belonged to Velkath and his kin.

Lin approached the burning ships, Blade in his right hand and his left prepared to throw as many Wefts as needed. Something felt wrong about the entire thing and Lin couldn't shake the feeling as he stalked down the path. It didn't sound like any of the soldiers who'd come out were fighting. No steel on steel. No martial grunts. Nothing. All of that combined with what Denny had pointed out, that the soldiers inside hadn't been nearly as capable, or outfitted, as the ones at the fort. Why wouldn't King Lodram have the best of the best with him? Even the Nooseman he'd brought ended up turning on him.

He wasn't near the ships yet, but the heat emanating from the boats came in waves, burning away the cold air.

"Untethered!" The voice was familiar. Not an ally but the foreign-looking sergeant from Fort Talm. *Royce.*

Royce, armor bright with the reflection of flames, stood strides from the dock, which had caught fire as well, a contingent of six other soldiers with him. Four of them held Ferrucium steel swords in one hand and those damned batons in the other. And all were outfitted in full suits of armor, helm and all. The soldiers on either end each carried a spear, but the honed tips still reflected light the way good Ferrucium steel did.

Fuck.

Screams continued from the shore, the source invisible with the fog, smoke, and flames. If any ships made it free of that fiasco it would be a small miracle. Heat, intense as any Lin had felt before, roiled from the docks in waves and shimmered behind Royce.

"Royce. There is an active truce. The delegation here has agreed to meet with Danican leaders in three months' time at the Tower of Fentis!"

"As if I'd ever believe the words of a tainted-blood untethered."

Lin took a step forward, leveling his Blade. "I think you're a good man. Leo is alive because of you. I saw the child I'm after because of *you*. Now you're here and boats are exploding all around you. *Why*?"

Royce's blade lowered a half-inch.

"People were on those ships. Luckily all the leaders were meant to be inside, but servants and family! How can you call me a monster if you're capable of something like this?" Of course, Lin was assuming the man responsible, but what other answer was there?

"Because," Royce's voice was half-muffled by the helm he wore. "When we kill you, everyone will know that you planted bombs on the ships when first reaching the island. We tried to stop it, but we were too late! Much like the massacre you left behind at the fort."

Massacre?

Lin took a deep breath and steadied himself. His hands might be tied when it came to King Lodram, for now, but more people had to have seen these soldiers on the ships. Had to have seen what really happened. All Lin had to do was survive.

The soldiers pressed forward, closing the distance as more geysers of purple-hued flame shot into the air, disrupting the smoke. Shadows of people jumping from ships showed in the brief illumination.

"Turn yourself in, monster," Royce called. He raised his blade, the tip pointed at Lin as if it were a bolt-shooter. "You will be tried and executed, but it will be painless."

"Make me," Lin growled.

In there, in that room full of leaders who might think him a monster, he had to be something he wasn't. He had to consider how the people who seemed to truly want the best for Danica might not just want but *need* him to act in that moment. But out here, surrounded by soldiers he was sure had destroyed the ships of said leaders, he didn't feel inclined to act properly.

Royce had seemed like a good man. But that had been surface level. Lin spat to the side and leveled his Blade, all light and wisps of gold, at the man.

The soldiers moved with precision. If they'd been stationed all together at Fort Talm's for some time, odds were they'd have fought against untethered crossing the pass. Maybe they'd even been the group that had helped the Physicker mount them on those metal spikes.

From either side, the soldiers with spears pressed in. They wielded the weapons deftly, using the length to keep their distance as they stabbed in.

Royce hung back, sheathing his baton to clasp something around his neck. A vial of blood. *Danican* blood.

Lin sidestepped the first spear thrust, catching the shaft under his arm and twisting. He'd hoped to break the wood, but it was more flexible than he expected and the soldier pivoted with him. Lin let it go before the sharpened edge of the tip could slice his ribs. He'd seen the flesh of Nooseman and untethered covered in Bindings spark with Ferrucium steel, but his limbs were the only places with Inlays, and his Stitches only crossed his torso.

Royce shouted something incoherent and an ochre-hued Weft sailed his way. It was odd that every single Binding he'd seen generated by non-Danicans resembled a Binding cast when the spul ran out, but Lin didn't have time to think more about it. He barely had time to consider it as he broke it with his Blade.

Alongside the spearmen, the other four soldiers pressed in.

Lin studied them and found himself backing up more and more. Soon he'd be back to the castle entrance if he kept giving ground, but in a flash, they flanked him in a half circle and pressed to take more room. Four swords, four batons, two spears. Royce with his stolen, weak magic and sword. Lin sent a Weft, low and wide, cutting toward the two swordsmen flanking his left.

The batons they held pulled the Weft. He'd seen the Bound Metal redirect Bindings before, but this time with this many soldiers wielding the awful weapons, it was like the Weft was pulled apart into multiple strands, unraveling in different directions. But that solidified it. He needed to steal one of their weapons.

Lin let his Blade disintegrate. "One of you wouldn't be willing to give me one of those swords, would you? Make this a fairer fight?"

He hadn't expected a reply, but the fact that all they did was tighten the half-circle around him without a pause to register what he'd said surprised him. A stab from a spear to his right made him spin. He caught the shaft firmly in both hands and yanked. As he did, the other spearman lunged on his left, thrusting where he'd just been. Lin had fought Nooseman. Untethered. Preternaturally swift enemies. The only advantage these soldiers had was their numbers.

That and the fact that the Bound Metal, even limited to the tip of four batons, made his stomach queasy and skin itch if it got too near. It wasn't even half as bad as Erias's One-loved door, and marginally easier to bear compared to the way Aemun had worn it.

Lin looked for the silver strands he'd seen when fighting Aemun and speaking with Erias, but none were visible. Perhaps a difference between a Danican wielding it and someone without the blood. Or intention.

For all of Lin's wandering thoughts, he took a slice to his left shoulder. He'd avoided the spearman's thrust and had even gotten close enough to yank the spear he'd been grabbing from the soldier, but one of the soldiers with a blade between the two spearmen had taken the opportunity to slash down at him. Lin mostly avoided the blow, taking a flesh wound and spinning behind the soldier he'd stolen the spear from, slamming the shaft into the back of the soldier's knees, and tripping them.

One down, but not out. Armor or not, they'd rejoin the fight and pull a baton from the sheath at their waist. Lin stabbed down as he stepped back, spear tip crunching into the meat of the soldier's face as it slid through the slit in the helm.

Gods. If there was any doubt before, it faded away with the slow clearing fog. Lin had killed more people— more normal people— than untethered.

Either unaware or uncaring that Lin fought for his life, a tide of people, servants, sailors, and families rushed up the path. Some carried dead and dying, the scent of smoke not covering the stench of wounds. Gods, one man's face was charred so badly that the bone showed. They surged past, knocking into the soldiers and screaming for help.

The remaining soldiers didn't wait for the dust to settle before pushing in. But now Lin had a weapon. The spear felt weighted well and even though he had limited combat experience with that type of weapon, he'd trained with axes, spears, daggers, and of course, swords. He'd even been one of the better archers back when Denro was still an Educator.

Lin spun away, careful not to clip any stragglers, the tip of his spear glistening but the nearest soldiers harried him.

More explosions carried from the docks— sparks of light cracking and bouncing from a slow-burning barge.

Swords flashed near him, inches away and a breeze followed. A spear was a good step, but what he wanted was a sword. He couldn't block a Ferrucium blade with the shaft of the spear he held, it would slice through. So he pivoted on his back heel, fighting to keep his eyes off the chaos behind.

"You fight like a coward!" Royce called from behind his fellow soldiers.

Lin nodded. But his movements had achieved what he intended. He had two soldiers in front of him, both with swords. The others were behind them and struggling to regain some semblance of a formation as more people stampeded from the docks.

As they pressed forward, Lin shifted his tempo, stepping in and stabbing with the spear. He used his offhand to guide the thrusts, stabbing, stepping, and stabbing again. Not every strike landed clean, metal armor screeching at an off-hit, but the blows that did land bit into the seams of the armor. One of the soldiers choked out a word or two before dropping. In Danica, they didn't have the luxury of armor, let alone full suits. You'd think these bastards would consider a piece to protect their throats more.

Stone crunched behind Lin before he could take up the felled soldier's blade, he ducked and darted back as a diagonal chop cleared the place he'd just occupied. But now the remaining soldiers hounded him. Pressing in, slashing, stabbing. The spear was an effective weapon for measuring and keeping distance. It did less well as the soldiers cleared and passed his defensive stance.

Sparks flashed as the sharpened edge of the soldier's blade ran along the Inlays of Lin's left arm. It was only a matter of time before they realized they needed to attack his torso. At least if they had any sense left between the four soldiers and Royce.

The nauseating pull of Bound Metal drew his attention from his right as if the blood in his veins struggled to escape.

Lin pushed his left arm up and out, pressing the blade wide. He stepped in, stabbing the spear down into the soldier's boot, then placed his palm against the front of their visor. Wefts found their way through the crevices under his touch and in seconds blood exploded out from under the helm. The soldier collapsed backwards and Lin swept up the sword they dropped.

The weapon was weighted nearly the same as a Ferrucium steel sword and the blade shone with the same sort of vibrant sheen, but it was clear these were different to the weapons the Ferrucium kitted out their soldiers with. The hilts were missing the circular bottom, and these felt a hand longer.

Lin spun on the two soldiers pressing him, barely parrying a well-placed thrust from the last remaining spearman.

Royce circled, closing the distance. Lin hadn't noticed it before but the man had a slip of a cloak hanging from his shoulders. Perhaps that was how the Ladricans designated sergeants. Lin parried another strike, wondering if the other man, Femor, was amongst the dead or soon to be dying.

"If..." Lin growled. "If this is the strength of Ladricans, maybe my home has less to fear than I first worried."

Lin parried again. With the numbers reduced to two swordsmen and one spearman, Lin tried Bindings again. But this time he used the same principle he'd tried to best Aemun with. He conjured a thin, weightless thread. It floated in the air like silk from a spider, drifting closer and closer to the batons every time the soldiers moved.

The spearman didn't seem to react to it, but both swordsmen did. The one on Lin's left pulled away while guiding the ethereal thread, letting the spearman take their position.

Unless they dropped the baton soon, it would be too late. At a minimum they'd lose an arm, at most Lin would add another life to his tally.

"No response? Hmm? I'm not even the best fighter we have and I've taken out what... four fully armored soldiers?"

Provoking them wasn't working, but the situation was better than it was at the outset, so Lin just needed to breathe. His shoulder stung but aside from that he didn't feel any other wounds. Royce hanging behind the others was worrisome, but odds were the man didn't have any tricks or he'd have used them to save his allies.

Lin dashed forward, ducking under the spear tip and slashing upward with all his might. Armor shrieked against his blade but held firm. He used his momentum to spin, thrusting the tip of the sword into the swordsman's chest. The steel plate dented, but Lin hadn't thought the weapon would pierce through.

Right arm limp at their side, the spearman dropped their spear and pulled out a short, dark-bladed dagger.

Lin blocked a horizontal sword slash from the other soldier and spun to the limp-armed soldier. Royce was there in a flash, blocking Lin's strike with his sword and ramming his helmet into Lin's brow, pushing him back.

Shouts sounded from the castle. That Elodian man, Julius perhaps. But it was hard to tell with the way Lin's ears rang. Chaos continued as the smoke crawled to where they fought, thick and heavy. But the time since the last explosion gave hope that whatever mechanisms were triggering them had finished.

Lin disengaged, sending a Weave at Royce's feet to slow him.

"You will die on this island, untethered." Royce's voice was a hoarse whisper, but he enunciated every word as if biting them off. He clasped the vial near his throat as if attempting to unravel the Weave with the stolen blood.

Lin blinked away the stars swimming in his vision. With his left hand, he formed a Blade and blocked the black dagger that flashed into his peripheral. The swordsman Lin had pressed back flanked on his right and stabbed straight at Lin's unprotected ribs.

Like a boat's prow cutting through the water, the black dagger sliced clean through Lin's Blade and carved into Lin's chest. Blood pooled right away and the wound stung. It wasn't Bound Metal. At least not any kind that Lin was aware of.

The sword stabbing for Lin's ribs nicked him as he stumbled back and away. It didn't feel like it had hit bone, but the steady throbbing from the left side of his chest pulled most of his attention. A blade that didn't clash with Bindings and instead sliced right through them. Gods it hurt.

Lin backpedaled, giving himself enough space to level his stolen steel. The three attackers were wreathed in flame, looking everything like what Lin had always thought he'd be. Heroes. And that was likely the narrative they'd regurgitate once they swallowed Lin whole. They tried to save the boats. Lin was the attacker. A monster crossed through the pass. *This* had to be what King Lodram wanted.

"Weapon like that must be rare, seeing as no one else had one. And you thought—" Lin winced as he took another step back, his wound screaming. "Giving it to a random soldier would make me less cautious against it."

"I like you. You think quick on your feet. Capable fighter too. If only you weren't born with tainted blood." Royce continued pressing forward.

Soon Lin's back would be against a castle wall and he'd have nowhere left to run. If he entered the castle now, the soldiers inside, cowed as they might be, would likely aid what they saw as fellow Ladrican soldiers.

Lin stared at the three fighters and sucked his teeth. Finding the evasive, blue-hued healing magic among his spul was easier than ever. Even if it was clear the thread hadn't replenished enough. It felt frayed in a way that overusing traditional Wievings never did. He forced and pressed his palm flat onto his chest.

A deep dark blue glow came from underneath his hand, nothing like the bright crystalline hue he'd conjured before. By the time Lin's hand reached the bottom of the slash, the glow had darkened to the shade of dried mud.

"What did you do?" Royce shouted.

Lin's neck twitched. Fatigue threatened to tip him over the edge of consciousness. But he'd overused his spul before and while he was near to it, he hadn't done too much. He could recover from this.

"Something I doubt that stolen blood around your neck would ever allow." Everything sounded distant, even his own voice, as if torn cloth had been stuffed and twisted into his ears.

First, he had to take that strange dagger out of the fight or take it for himself. If it cut through Bindings so easily, odds were good it did the same to their armor. Even if it wasn't a rare material, which Lin doubted, it was likely a dangerous one. As controlling as the king, and this council seemed to be, there was no way Danicans and their magic were the only things restricted.

Lin stumbled forward, feigning fatigue. The swordsman that nicked him along the side took the bait eagerly, rushing in and slashing up and across. A valiant attempt to take Lin's head from his shoulders and one that failed before it even gained momentum.

As soon as the blade reached its apex, Lin grabbed the soldier's helm. A scream sounded from within the armor, as they struggled to jerk away. Wild slashes followed and then Lin let them go. They tripped backward, flailing the whole way down. He didn't know enough about the different types of Bindings to trust that they didn't somehow pull from the same source and he couldn't risk overdoing it. No matter what that book had said.

Lin stomped down on the soldier's arm and stabbed down into the now-open visor. Femor's eyes flashed with fear and Lin looked up as Royce charged at him. The limp-armed soldier kept their distance, black dagger waiting to take pieces of Lin should he overcommit.

"Royce. Sergeant stationed at Fort Talms. A foreigner, not Ladrican by birth. You don't have to keep this up. Give up. Turn yourself in. Tell the gathered leaders that King Lodram—"

Royce's blade flashed with a quick, horizontal slash.

Lin blocked it, the attack vibrating through his arms and core. Even with Inlays improving his strength, these soldiers had worn him down. All his bravado couldn't keep his limbs from tiring. "—Commanded you to do this!"

"You aren't half as clever as you think you are!"

The limp-armed soldier still stalked off to the side, their dark dagger barely glinting when its edge caught the light of slowly dying flames near the docks. Flashes of movement out there caught the eye, more shadows against the flames, but with luck, it was people working to put out the flames.

"To be honest, I don't think I'm all that clever at all," Lin said. He circled Royce. The last thing he wanted was to be pinned between the two of them and the castle wall, so he crossed the path, worn stone underfoot more slick than the gravel and brush he'd been on moments before.

Royce's hand flashed and two rust-colored Wefts arced towards Lin. Trailing just behind them was Royce's blade, cutting the air to make a cross.

Blade met blade, steel clanging. In a straight contest of strength, Lin knew he was superior. He felt it in his bones and Royce's blade gave inch by inch. Lin pulled his sword away, Royce stumbling forward from the lack of resistance. Lin twirled, forming a short Blade with his offhand and stabbing it in the crevice where helm met breastplate.

Royce dropped to a knee, slashing up and forcing distance.

If the soldier had stripped their armor and stalked about quietly, they might have landed a lethal blow on Lin with that One-loved dagger, but as it were, Lin turned in time as the soldier's heavy steps against the stone underfoot gave their location away.

A single thrust from the stolen sword dropped the soldier. The dagger's hilt bounced against the stonework, the blade itself sparking as it struck the stone, then shattering halfway from its base, leaving a cruel jagged edge.

Lin looked at it for a long moment, then noticed Royce had raised his visor and was doing the same. Gods, the man looked as awful as Lin felt. Like he'd been the one tossed into the water, nearly drowned, and fought his way through several waves of heavily armored Ladricans.

Royce lunged for the dagger and Lin did the same. Royce was quicker, but he overshot and tumbled onto his side as the two of them wrestled for the weapon.

Shards of the broken blade tickled through the fabric of Lin's stolen clothes. Lin had a lock on Royce's armored forearm and pinned it in place. They struggled, and then Royce let go and tried to thrust his hips to move Lin off of him.

"Just give up!" Royce spat.

There was so much rage and pain in the man's face.

"I can't afford to."

Royce punched up with the arm that wasn't pinned, his metal gauntlet bludgeoning Lin across his face and chest.

Lin clenched his jaw and took the blows, forcing the hilt free from Royce's hand. He took what remained of the dagger and thrust it down into Royce's breastplate.

Like drums of metal, Royce's helm and other armor clanged and banged against the stone under him in a chaotic rhythm. He kicked and punched and spat but Lin had spread his legs to keep from being tossed off and now pressed all of his weight down on the dagger.

It was a gamble. There was a chance that the dark blade would break against steel the same as it had against the stone when it fell. But as the jagged tip touched the breastplate, a hiss and sound like tearing parchment came up and then it was as if all the resistance in Royce's limbs gave way the same as the armor. Like a hissing snake, the dagger sizzled against the Ferrucium steel and then sank through, stabbing into the man's sternum.

Royce coughed blood, teeth stained with it, and grabbed Lin's collar, ripping it.

"Why? You seemed so... so willing to listen in the fort. Why attack? Why destroy the ships?" Lin left the dagger where it was and slapped the man's face.

Royce's eyes narrowed and he coughed again, wheezing in a sucking breath. "Always the plan."

"That's no explanation!" Lin screamed at the dying man. "Stay with me! King Lodram always planned this?"

Even dying the man had a way of looking indignant. Royce's head shook in his helm slightly as he exhaled, eyes closing entirely.

Lin stared up at the dying flames. Did that shake of the head mean King Lodram wasn't behind it? Or... with a sigh, Lin pulled the jagged, broken dagger from Royce's chest. What blood would've stained a typical weapon seemed to slip from it like dew from a leaf.

Exhausted, he rose and shuffled over to the soldier who'd originally wielded it. The sheath was a simple thing, wood and leather and perhaps bone. His days of being too proud to take from the dead were far behind him, buried alongside the man he used to be.

Choking Bone

"And so I burned— eager and hungry like a starved flame. How you thought to quench me, dear sister, with your lies. But lies can be like kindling and much like my flame they only stoked my ire."
V.S.

Lin staggered up the path toward the door. More people were coming and going from the entrance, avoiding Lin and aiding those who limped from the docks. Many were wounded, some were dead. As the smoke cleared, bodies clarified facedown in the water. Scraps of ships and other debris smoldered, stray ore still sparking.

Soldiers slowed at the corpses of Ladricans outfitted in full armor, but it seemed at least these men and women had a better sense of duty to aid the injured.

Being trained as a child, it had made sense to Lin when they told him Ferrucium soldiers need not wear armor. Ferrucium steel was too rare to craft whole plates and Bindings, especially Wefts by the maddest of untethered, would cut through anything less. Lin hawked a glob of red-tinged spit to the side, seeing the truth for what it was now. He and the others weren't outfitted in armor just in case of war between Ladrica and Danica.

A thick jowled man intercepted Lin, hands out and up. He wore the Ladrican colors in a waist-hugging vest that seemed far too tight for him. As it were, Lin hadn't considered all the unusual people who'd crossed his path on the journey to find Mellyr. All the things he could think of to tell Denro when next they met were horrible.

Lin raised his recovered sword a hair and the heavy man slowed. "I was sent to ask," the man's voice was deep and confident, even as his eyes and trembling hands betrayed him. "If it is safe to send individuals to the ships? To see what state they are in."

"I can't speak on that," Lin whispered. "Those men who did this wouldn't say why they did."

"Some survivors claim they came across the water from Fort Talms, but I find it hard to believe that our King's own troops would assault this gathering."

Lin let the sword fall back down. "So do I. But... I can't think of a reason for these men to act on their own."

"Who says they were? Steward Bodrose, by the way." The steward extended his meaty hand and Lin stared at it for a long moment before shaking his head, declining to reciprocate.

"I can't imagine your people will think highly of a man who touched someone with tainted blood. If any ask, will you vouch that it was Sergeant Royce and his men who set upon the boats?"

Steward Bodrose shifted and a pained expression lit his face. "I will. We lost good people because of it. A handful of ships... well it likely doesn't matter to you. Not in a rude way I mean, but..."

Lin waited as the man struggled to find his meaning without offense before interrupting, "I'd say, start sending people to investigate if you wish. More wounded will likely be heading inside, and I'll see that no other surprises await us."

"Very good," the heavy-set man nodded. It seemed he was comfortable, even eager to take orders, and turned his attention back to the smoldering wreckage of the docks behind him.

It was hard not to stare. With the smoke clearing, Lin counted as many ships as leaders who had convened. Most seemed sized too small, likely built for speed over anything else and the largest one was familiar as Lin studied its charred sides and the hole in its side. The Pollsh Dreamer. Perhaps its size had helped reduce the overall damage, but the thing hadn't sunk, unlike some of the other ships. Fires dotted its deck, casting shadows through the haze.

With a sigh from the pit of his soul, Lin stalked back to the castle. The sheathed dagger rubbed against his waist, the weight there not heavy, but wholly unfamiliar. Gods, he hadn't carried a knife since his had rusted in Lyre.

Lin took his time up the path. There were burning questions he had for King Lodram, but the last thing he wanted was to speak with the man. His breath caught as he studied the markings along the walls again. If there had been any doubt previously, it washed away as he forced a deeper breath. His ribs ached from the task. Throbbed where the tip of the blade had caught him.

There was no doubt, these were the markings of Velkath and his kin. Or if not his kin certainly his contemporaries. The other persons depicted alongside Vellia could have been any of the brothers except... a smile came unbidden. The furthest one had to be Truthful Vellyr, portrayed entirely nude except for the small cloth, flesh riddled with magical markings. He wondered if Tylle knew about this island.

Wounded on cots lined the walls, the expansive place was now home to the dead and dying and those too stubborn to realize they belonged to either group. A home fit for someone like Lin. Stepping around sprawled legs wishing to use a wall to support himself, he ignored the stares.

You've failed everyone and everything, Escorter. What makes you think this will end differently?

The stairs crossed overhead and Lin stepped through the door leading to the hall where King Lodram and the other leaders had been meeting. Leo sat against the wall, Denny and Gritt beside him. They all appeared to be resting, chests rising and falling at varying tempos. Lin didn't blame them but he did envy them. Soon. He'd rest as soon as Mellyr was back in his arms.

"Lin. It is Lin, isn't it?" Julius's voice whispered from beside the doorway. *Speaker of the House of Silence.* "Did you find the culprits?"

"Saboteurs. Many of the ships are out of commission. And many people survived."

A smile split the pale man's face, straight white teeth fitting in with the almost overly pristine look the man seemed to have. What had the king called him? *Wraith-touched*.

"Good. That is good that many survived. Grand. I'm sure some saw you confronting the saboteurs as well. Didn't I say they'd see a Danican hero? That was the goal, after all. Saving lives I mean.

Who knows what they might've done if you hadn't intervened? Very good."

Lin took a step past and the man's gloved hand shot out, grabbing his arm. Lin kept from flinching but looked down at the man's fur-lined leather and then up into his pale gray eyes.

"These saboteurs, did you happen to find out who they were aligned with? Best to know all the details before we accuse anyone."

Everything pointed to the Ladricans. Royce had been at the fort arguing with that man Femor about something... Lin shook his head before asking, "Why do they call your kind... Wraith-touched?"

Indignation flashed across the man's face, frustration curling his lip. "Small-minded people make up small names for that which they don't desire to understand. And for fear of seeming too large, we accept those names. Danicans, as I understand it, pull from magic within themselves. Certain Elodians, not all, can pull at something within others. Where your power can be seen in some cases and felt, mine is subtle. Sleep. That is it. But only ever by touch."

Lin nodded. It did seem the man had to make direct contact. "They were dressed as Ladrican soldiers. Came across from Fort Talms. Where are the other leaders?"

Several of the Free Nations leaders huddled against the far wall where Lin had last seen them, but High Scholar Anya and King Lodram were notably missing. Tessia stood illuminated against a pillar, surrounded by chunks of broken Wanderer's Ore, her arms folded across her chest and a look of absolute displeasure on her face. An attendant, likely her own by the similarly styled clothes, a coat of short fur and wraps of soft, silken pants that flowed with each step, spoke to her in hushed tones.

Donus, the large heavily perfumed man, had shifted to take up two seats and was loudly complaining about the need for waiting in the first place, especially as his roving eyes landed on Lin. "Back already, see it couldn't have been that bad out there!"

"Ignore that buffoon. Wine drunk before the meeting even started. You say they came from the fort, but more specifically—" Julius whispered.

Lin pulled his arm free and matched the man's gaze. "Where did the king go?"

Julius licked his lips and seemed to weigh whether or not he wanted to say anything. With a flourish, the man straightened the front of his tunic and thin, gossamer shawl that draped his shoulders. He leaned in. "I don't mind telling you. And it's pressing that you stop him from fleeing, especially if my suspicions are correct. That is why I need you to tell me if Royce implicated the king in this!"

What little bits of conversation had spread through the room died.

"I don't know. I told you what I noted and I couldn't possibly put it more plainly! Consider me a baby bird, just learning to fly." Lin spoke slowly, in case any in the room struggled to understand Danican. "They wore armor. They had swords. They came from a Ladrican fort. But they would not plainly announce their allegiance." Lin shrugged and stepped forward.

Julius wanted him to lay the blame at Ladrica's feet. But Lin had been toyed with by a man much better at keeping his intentions hidden than this Elodian. And if he wanted Lin to fault the king so badly, he'd need to pull the words from Lin's Stitched lips.

"So no insignias? No standards? No dying words?" Julius's voice returned to a hushed, chopped tone.

"Not one." *Always the plan*. That was the last thing Royce had choked out between bloody lips. "Look. I appreciate that you voiced in favor of Ladrica not invading Danica en masse. What I don't appreciate is you standing in my way as I return to look for the child stolen from me."

Julius took a step back then lowered his gaze and seemed to scan the room. "Fair. Completely fair. See to your needs and I'll go check the slain for any sort of designation. The scholars that remained and the king and his people took to the back route, through the doorway over there."

Lin looked at the shadows the man pointed toward and grunted. Either Anya had again betrayed him, or she'd fled with King Lodram for a separate reason. He tightened his hold on the sword and pressed onward. Another glance at Denny and Leo showed them leaning on each other. Neither looked comfortable in their rest. The fact that Leo let himself sleep against Denny solidified that he likely didn't have the Sight.

A pang of guilt stabbed Lin anew. If the boy kept up his behavior, his people would shun him even more.

Following Julius's instructions led Lin into a hall with cobwebs running along the ceiling line. They hung in large swathes like moss hanging from trees and were illuminated by dim sconces of faded burnt-orange ore. Whatever this path had been used for previously had given way to disuse. A far cry from the somewhat upkept council room.

Lin considered the island as he followed the hall's outward curve, an isle so close to Ladrica and Danica, with a castle and tapestries depicting Velkath and his kin. Real fucking depictions of Velkath and his kin. Of Vellia and Vellyr. With everything going on he hadn't the time to consider the implication— those names of old had existed. Of all the tomes he'd been allowed to read that discussed the Accords, only one had mentioned the Old Gods. To see them depicted in the same style as the tapestry hanging in the Chamber of Judgement sent fresh doubt rebounding through his thoughts.

It took some time to reach the end of the narrow corridor and when he exited, the air felt fresh and cool. The room was even larger than the hall the leaders had met in but was beyond disrepair. Large broken sections of the ceiling were strewn across the stone floor and portions of the castle's looming exterior were visible against the night sky through the gaps. Puddles of murky water had gathered giving the room a stagnant air.

Thrones hewn from similar stone as the walls lined the far side of the grand room. Six in total. No, seven. What would have been a seventh throne was crushed to rubble under a section of the collapsed ceiling and a long broken column rested near it.

Unease, familiar and queasy itched under Lin's skin. The thrones were lined with golden filigree and carved, detailed etchings accented by various gems. It was a miracle the place hadn't been ransacked. How much freedom could gems like those buy a man out in the greater world?

As chaotic as things had been, he and Mellyr and a bag full of those stones could disappear easily.

Lin turned in a half-circle, examining the expansive ceilings and walls. A doorway was positioned on each wall. They could have gone anywhere, and multiple tracks through the dust led to each door. What bits of the ceiling were missing let in light patches of rainfall, refusing to let the quiet solemnity of the room go undisturbed.

Scuffled steps from the door across from the one Lin had entered through sounded, followed by a groan. "You said that was the exit!" King Lodram's voice echoed out, his tone just as biting as any time he'd spoken with Lin.

"Please listen closely, as this isn't likely something you'll hear a High Scholar express again. I was mistaken."

"Bah, all that time stuck in the tower has weathered what good sense your ilk used to possess."

Lin moved past the thrones and pressed himself flat against the wall. Even that little sprint hurt. The flesh across his torso had healed, but not fully. Something about wielding the magic had felt wrong and time hadn't eased the sensation.

Lin waited, slowing his breaths. Harming the man now would do little good. Even if he had directed Royce to attack the isle. But it didn't explain the lack of troops. Or why Julius had been acting so oddly. When a man wanted one specific answer so badly, well, it didn't bode well. Not that much had boded well as of late.

"At this rate, we might as well have left through the front door," King Lodram snapped as he exited into what had to be a throne room.

"And why is that?" Lin asked. He tried to keep his tone neutral as he peeled off the wall.

"Ahh!" The king, in all his finery, jumped and stumbled back, circlet skewing and robes flaring. "You fool! Trying to make my heart seize?"

"Danica might only be so lucky." Lin bladed himself so that the emissary, her name lost to him, wouldn't press quite so close. He'd had the common sense to keep the sword he'd taken and leveled its tip at the indignant king.

"Lin!" High Scholar Anya's brow pinched, her expression as displeased as her voice sounded. She followed behind the emissary, the lesser scholar robed in light blue following her with Mellyr in hand. "Lower that and be reasonable."

"Reasonable? What if I'm tired of being reasonable? What if before reaching this island to get my child I had sworn off being *reasonable*? That I might rip the throats of anyone and everyone who stood in my way? What if my mouth pools with blood from biting my tongue?"

"Please," Anya's eyes pleaded far more than her tone did. She moved into the throne room so that she stood between King Lodram and Lin. Sweat dotted her shaved head and the faded-out lines of what Lin assumed were once Inlays shone like silver scars where her flowing robes didn't cover. The thick bands of tattoos along her arms showed as her sleeves fell to her elbows.

"Why were you fleeing through back tunnels?" Lin asked, lowering the tip of the sword a hair's breadth.

"Did you not hear the attack? Smell the smoke? You truly are as stupid as you look!" King Lodram folded his arms and shied away as Lin took a half step forward.

"I'm the one who stopped the fucking attack!"

"How dare you speak to him—"

"Elicia..." King Lodram's voice was low. "He has a point. Tell me tainted-blood. Who were the attackers?"

Lin had met dangerous men before, the sort that moved silently and let actions speak louder than boisterous voices. Pael was the sort Lin considered dangerous and until this moment he'd thought the king was a pompous fool but the way he stared into Lin's eyes now made him doubt that assessment.

"Men of yours from the Fort."

"Impossible. Betrayal?"

"Possible," Anya interjected quickly. "Even if, as you say, Lin, the attackers have been dealt with, seeing the king and any of the other leaders we can to safety should be top priority."

Lin shook his head. That very well might be their top priority, but as it stood he stared at Mellyr. Stared at his sole remaining purpose bundled in the arms of the scholar. "Get to safety. Flee from whatever tunnel or hall you meant to leave through, but give me back my daughter."

"No. We've discussed this. You must understand where we're coming from with this." Anya's jaw set and it seemed for a moment that she might lead the king and his group away without another word.

Elicia, that was the blade of a bitch's name, glared and the scholar holding Mellyr hadn't looked more terrified since Lin had first spotted her.

"As I alluded before. It was through a deal that Aemun and King Lodram crafted. Oaths were sworn. Promises were exchanged that would see Mellyr *eventually* betrothed. A deal that would be very good for her and Danica as a whole. A step towards potentially ratifying the Accords. A deal that the good king here decided to uphold despite Aemun's *unfortunate* passing. It is only because of his untimely death that everything is falling apart."

"There is too much uncertainty around all of this," Lin hissed.

"I've found in my many years, tainted-blood, that the easiest answer is often the truth." King Lodram adjusted his circlet and smoothed out his fine robes, now looking far more ruffled and ruined than they had before.

"If that is the case, the simplest answer is you attacked your fellow leaders, hoping to place the blame on my shoulders somehow, and scurried away like a rat!"

Anya threw up her hands and let out an exhausted sigh.

"Rat? Like a *rat*? I thought we were beyond baseless accusations and speaking about Aemun, the rat-faced fool! Ladrica's sigil is a snake. Rats are swallowed bloody whole!"

With the grace of a skilled dancer, Anya was back between them, wrinkles appearing severe in the poor light of the weathered room. "There is no love lost between you two. The scholars... were originally mediators more than jailers. Somewhere along the way, I say with a heavy heart, I think our search for uncovering the mysteries of Wievings took us further from that original goal."

A harsh scoff escaped King Lodram and Elicia moved closer to him, still glaring but this time directing her disapproving gaze at Anya.

"In all of this... I've not attacked you," Lin said. He lowered his voice and winced as the ripped fabric of his tunic pulled at the stab he'd taken to his side. "I may not have held my tongue but I've stilled my blade and fist time and time again."

"As any civil person *should*. Should I thank you for acting as you should? Either way, your very presence is an assault." King Lodram's lip curled as he spoke and he glanced around as if looking for an audience who might applaud the insult.

"I came peacefully, as peacefully as I possibly could, to get that child."

King Lodram shook his head, eyes shifting as if he were doing some sort of mental calculation. He looked like he might say something before shutting his mouth into a firm line, as if remembering who it was, what it was, he was speaking to.

"Fine. If not you trying to play the people— who attacked the harbor?" Lin pressed. "Who would stand to gain from making you look like a monster and me a hero?"

"Any of those fools out there would love to see Ladrica fall from the heights my family has clawed its way to."

Anya snorted and when the king turned to look at her, she doubled down, crossing her arms in front of her and raising a brow.

"Perhaps not heights, but to assume my people are doing anything but thriving would be a grave mistake. But more than any of those scrap-licking imbeciles, that Elodian wraith would be eager to see Ladrica ruined. If not for us, the Empire would've moved against the Free Nations centuries ago. We are the baluster keeping back more darkness than just the night sky!"

Lin was at a loss for a response. He knew in one breath that the man was referring to Danica and his people, but there was so much passion in his exhalation that Lin struggled to fault him. *Flower petals, dagger's edge.*

"Perhaps," Lin said.

"Julius was acting odd. Not that I know him well. Too intense, so to speak," Anya said with a shake of her head. She stepped forward, around King Lodram, and ran a hand along the weathered stone of the nearest throne. "If it is as you say, we should be going. No point lingering around if he's somehow enticed more Ladrican soldiers to his side."

"Impossible," Elicia growled.

"Agreed. The chances of that are slim, to say the least." But King Lodram's expression had faltered, the mask of hubris slipping and showing a frail, tired man underneath it.

"I'll go with you. Protect the retreat if that is the case. But let me hold Mellyr. Just for a moment. Please." The word came out jagged and raw and Gods, the last thing he wanted to do was let the people in front of him think him weak. But he'd come so far and she was so near and if they told him no one more time he was likely to attack them where they stood.

Perhaps Anya saw it in the wildness surely leaking from his eyes, or in the way he'd set his jaw as he prepared for their answer.

"Let him. A gesture of goodwill." Anya nodded. "Then we move."

The king's lips thinned even more, a tremble coming to his face. Rage. Fear. Worry that Lin might taint Mellyr.

Lin set the sword aside and took Mellyr into his arms. Gods, it hadn't been that long but she'd gotten larger. And when he held her, she squirmed and her eyes opened, Aemun's piercing stare doubled on his daughter's innocent face. And the smile as she reached tiny hands up, only to pull on his beard. She slapped him gently. Giggled.

Tears came and he breathed her in. Slow sobs that ached and she squirmed more. They'd been taking care of her— she smelled like freshly plucked clover with a dash of honey.

Her hair was longer and it was darkening to a shade closer to Margaret's and Tylle's raven-colored locks. Lin stared at her, smiling and crying at the same time. He kissed the top of her head and she yanked on his tunic. She'd gotten so strong.

"Let's go," Anya said.

"Make sure the child is scrubbed after this. The monster is covered in grime and blood and now her clothes are ruined." King Lodram's indignant voice pulled Lin back to reality.

Lin blinked through the tears and shook his head softly. "It just doesn't make sense."

Everyone bristled, and Elicia stepped forward with a dagger flashing into her hand. King Lodram folded his arms and a smug smile had found its way onto his face.

"Of course, it doesn't make sense. King Lodram is a liar. Good king, tell him where the Ladrican army is right now! See how long-lived this uneasy peace lasts. I'd wager it would only ever last as long as it took the king to board a boat and return to his throne built on the lives of his betters." Julius's voice carried, echoing off the rubble-lined walls. "Tell him where your troops are."

Choking Hate

"I've not seen one form of Magick aid the common man in any meaningful way. Elodian wraiths shelter themselves from the world. Danicans are a threat to all. And those Belisians claim their unusual, abundant luck isn't magic at all. But what I have seen is God working through his people— granting my forebearers the wisdom needed to make Ladrica prosperous." Excerpt from A Study of Religion, author unsigned.

Julius stepped into the hall, footfalls echoing softly. His movements were fluid as if he were some otherworldly being. But Denny was very much a living person and could be near silent when she wished. He smiled, white teeth too bright against his pale flesh. His shawl gripped tight around his shoulders and he held Gritt's discarded mask lazily in one hand.

It was like all of the king's bluster and animosity had redirected in an instant toward Julius. He stammered, jowls shaking, before Elicia placed a hand on his elbow.

"Let go of me, woman! It's like you've become emboldened by all the idiocy taking place that you think you can quell me with a simple touch. And you—" He'd wheeled to face Julius, one knobby finger raised.

"Me!" Julius interrupted. "Go ahead, Lin, *ask*. Since he refuses to tell," his expression turned smug, flesh pulled taut across overly pronounced cheekbones.

"You dare interrupt me?"

"I very much do," Julius said with a chuckle.

Anya hadn't moved and the scholar beside her had moved to stand between her and Julius.

Mellyr squirmed in Lin's hands and the beginnings of a cry started from her.

All of King Lodram's grandeur washed from him in a moment. His head shook and he stared at the ground between Lin and Julius.

"Tell me what?" Lin asked.

King Lodram licked his thin lips and narrowed his eyes. "There is no reason."

"Have you been keeping secrets?" Anya asked. Her breaths were coming faster and she'd grabbed the cord of leather that hung from her throat.

"Hells with you!" King Lodram snapped. "Damn you all. The leaders of the world will forgive me... I do not doubt that. It may take time, I may be sanctioned and Ladrica might face embargos, but my great country will survive and be the better for it."

"What've you done?" Lin growled.

King Lodram narrowed his eyes and turned his knobby, crooked finger at Lin. "What should have been done from the beginning."

Julius clapped, slow and soft. "There it is. His hatred, the hatred of his people will never quell. But what he neglected to put into words, is that the bulk of the Ladrican army is currently sailing toward the southern coast of Danica. Hasn't it?"

The world fell out from under Lin. They'd been so worried about the thaw and the northern pass that they hadn't considered a fleet sailing from Ladrica. Of course, they hadn't. Ships weren't a factor across Danica. Lin swallowed and tried to shush Mellyr, swaying with her despite the wounds that screamed every time he did. But just because *Lin* hadn't considered an assault from the sea... *fuck*. Had Erias?

King Lodram's hands shook as he clenched them but the man nodded slowly. "Naught to be done now. I'd hoped to be back home before the news broke but the wraith speaks true. Mind you this was in action well before the assembly. I'd hoped to draw out more of you who worked with the traitorous Dukes."

Not a wrinkle of remorse was on the man's face or in his eyes.

Lin tried to imagine what it would mean. From Pael to Denny, both had seemed sure that Erias and his people were expecting the thaw to be the signal for war, but from the northern pass, not the south. Danica wasn't structured to watch for marauders from the south. His knees shook, feeling suddenly weak. "Then all is lost."

"Lost?" Julius asked, leaning in. "Far from it! You are a Danican! Wiever of magicks varied and deadly! Kill him now and this could end!"

Lin clenched his jaw. It felt like bile, hot and stinging, was rising from his stomach and flooding his heart and mind. He *could* take vengeance here. Should. For all the trespasses done against his people.

Denro's voice was a balm, if barely. *'What would that achieve?'*

"Have you lost any sense left to you, wraith?" King Lodram has backed up, grabbing and pushing Elicia in front of him.

"Do it," Julius stepped closer, voice low and dangerous.

Mellyr moved in Lin's arms and he looked down, her bright tear-filled eyes were the only thing worth looking at in the decrepit throne room. "Why?"

"Why kill him? For vengeance," Julius said.

"No… why am I always pressed between men who think they can use me like a weapon? Like a tool?"

"That is all any of them think your people and my people are!" Julius threw his arms up as if encompassing the whole world with one gesture. Gritt's mask still hung loose in his grasp, a splash of blood under the left eye-slit.

"King Lodram." Lin kissed Mellyr's brow and stepped toward the king as Elicia's dagger raised.

"What?" the older man snapped from behind the woman's shoulder.

"I don't have proof and I couldn't tell you what his ultimate goal is, but I'm sure more now than ever, that Julius has coordinated the attack on the island somehow."

"As I thought!" King Lodram seemed to bounce between moods and attitudes more than any person Lin had met before. "Elicia!"

Elicia was a wetnurse, emissary, and by the way she moved, a capable fighter. Her dagger cut towards Julius as if the man were a lamb and she a wolf, plunging from the shadows. Anya had handled her well enough in the room surrounded by other leaders and dignitaries, but it seemed Elicia had taken that loss and let it fester something ferocious within her.

Julius backpedaled, hands shooting up as if to placate the woman and king she served. Like the glimmer of a sheer thread held to the stars and squinted through, something shone near his ungloved hands.

Lin's first thought was a Wieving done without Danican blood to fuel it. And Gods knew he'd seen more shades of the magic than he'd thought possible, but something felt off. Unfamiliar in a way he couldn't put into words. The thread seemed connected to Elicia somehow, and when Julius pulled it, it snapped.

Elicia crumpled at Julius's feet as if she had tripped, her lips turning blue.

"Elicia!" King Lodram's irritated voice grated, then like a stone tumbling down a cliff and sending more after it, King Lodram collapsed.

"Julius." Anya struggled, the gossamer thread connected to her not snapping the way the other two had. She sank slowly to her knees, eyes struggling to remain open, hand clutched to the vial of blood.

The other scholar attempted to run but fell and struck her head against the edge of the wall, blood pooling from the wound immediately.

Lin stared in horror, bracing himself for whatever might be happening. When he realized he was unharmed, he straightened and checked Mellyr.

"You spared me? No. You lied about your magic, didn't you?" Lin asked, noting the strands of twilight that glittered across the shoulders of the collapsed. The strands seemed entirely unaffected by the Bound Metal circlet the king wore, now once again crooked across his wrinkled brow.

"You of all people shouldn't be a child about something so trivial. Imagine... Imagine a world where these idiots didn't know what your people were capable of. You could sail the sea without restriction. See the wide, hateful world in all its glory.

"Vellia, often called wise, was a *fool*. Freely and immediately sharing the truth of her gifts, begging those without Sight to believe her. A simple, foolish girl. Our people watched and learned from her terrible experience. I didn't entirely lie though. We do have to touch full-blooded Danicans to rest their souls. Ladricans resist better than most, but touch isn't required."

Julius sighed and looked down at the others. He stepped lightly, then smashed his heel down on her hand. No cries, no sound of pain, just the crunching of boot onto bone. With a kick, the dagger skidded away. "If I sat in this room until my flesh melted from bone, her soul wouldn't wake."

Lin squeezed Mellyr tight. He'd rested the sword against the wall when he'd taken her and now would struggle to grab it without dropping her. *Fuck.*

"Why look for the blade when words could cut to the problem just as quickly?" Julius's arms swung, mask still in hand as he weaved between the fallen bodies, growing closer.

"Why are you doing this?"

"To give Danicans a chance! We are, if not allies, at least two people who could grow to be that. Most who survived today consider you a hero. A *Danican* hero. The world hasn't had one of those in ages. And they saw the king's trusted warriors, slaying so many of their people."

Lin shifted, blading his body so that Mellyr was as far from the man as possible. "Not so many were out there to see Royce's men. It would be my word versus the king's."

"True. Too many didn't see. But I didn't mean the soldiers at the dock." Julius smiled, then slipped Gritt's mask on. "But everyone knows his most trusted warriors are the King's Noose. Things couldn't have worked out better for us."

Us.

Lin felt sick. Perhaps the title wraith was justified if this was the way all Elodians— Lin stopped the thought, apples and all that. No, this was likely the ravings and actions of a lone man trying to vie for power. Trying to control things that weren't his to control. "You'd pretend to be a Nooseman and massacre the leaders within?"

What Lin needed was someone to take Mellyr. He couldn't set her down, not if meant potentially giving this man leverage. And as much as she squirmed now— she'd be in danger crawling around the throne room.

Julius laughed, a tinny, echoing sound. The mask stifled a fraction of it.

Lin still remembered how constricting the metal was when he'd donned Dennick's. There was no way laughing under the pressure of that metal felt good.

"Did the mask give it away?" Julius snorted then shook his head. "But no. I don't plan to do that. I already did." He waved his hands and waggled his fingers, dark threads shifting as he did. "Sleep for the guards. Blade for those that might side with Ladrica once the Danican hero is found murdered."

Lin looked at the doorway Julius had entered through. Denny had been resting in that room. Leo too, even if the little bastard was a brat he didn't deserve to be killed by a scheming man. "You killed them and you'd make me look like a martyr?"

"So naive. If you die, you *will* be a martyr. And the tale is so touching. Lone Danican comes to the isle to rescue his stolen daughter... ends up saving most of the gathered leaders of the Free Nations in the process. Tragically murdered protecting the child from the King's cruel, uncaring noose." Julius mimed out a knot tightening around his own throat, then straightened. "But know, that I'm truly impressed. This was the backup plan after all. You pushed me to this."

The twilight-shaded threads drifted through the room, none coming close to him or Mellyr.

Julius stepped forward.

"W-wait. What does the Empire gain from deposing King Lodram?"

"Resources. Respect. *Revenge.*" Without warning the man lunged forward, bare hands grasping the space Lin occupied moments before.

Lin backpedaled, back hitting the wall, and he pushed off of it, clutching Mellyr tightly in his arms. She screamed nonsense, terror racking the child.

"Good. *Run.* This needs to seem tragic after all." His voice sounded off, distant somehow.

Even as tired as he was, Lin was the quicker of the two. Mellyr screamed, frantically pushing futilely against his chest. It hurt to scare her so much, far more than the weak pressure from her strikes. He circled the large stone that had crushed the seventh throne and looked for options. If he trusted the wailing child not to move, setting her atop one of the thrones might not be the worst.

Julius vaulted atop the rubble and stared down at Lin. "It does become harder to breathe with this thing. Hmm." He jumped down, right hand stabbing forward with a baton he'd had hidden, aimed right at Lin's chest, left hand swinging a sharp, flat-edged blade. Its curve was deeper than any blade Lin had seen before and clashed against the Inlay along his forearm.

Lin took each hit, angling himself so that Mellyr wasn't close to being struck. Each thrust of the baton made his insides quiver. He needed to work a Wieving without the use of his hands. It should be possible. He'd done it before, hadn't he? And Denny seemed just as capable of sending out multiple Wefts and she was missing an entire arm. He gritted his teeth and pictured a Weft threading from his left side.

The Weft formed, sharp and fast, but as it cut towards Julius, the Bound Metal baton pulled at it like an errant thread.

"Ha! See, that is what really makes you Danicans so terrifying. The ability to adapt. Are your hands full? Who needs them!" Julius's distorted voice peaked as he pressed in, stabbing and slashing.

Each strike sparked against Lin's flesh and he was thankful the man didn't have that awful, dark dagger Lin had tucked at his waist.

Lin angled back as a hot slice ran along the outside of his upper arm. Another strike caught him across the side, near his armpit and it seemed Julius had adjusted his aim to cut at more vulnerable spots.

Another slash sparked along his left forearm. Lin shifted Mellyr so that most of her weight rested against his body and right arm. He spun, taking a stab into his right shoulder, and rushed forward.

The others were sprawled behind the thrones and rubble. Julius stood in front of the nearest exit. The hall Lin first arrived through was across from him, the light pattering of rain cascading from the openings above. If he ran as quickly as possible, he might be able to break across the room and muster assistance.

Lin darted around the nearest throne as Julius lunged. Velkath's Sigil was carved along the back, worn down but clear. If he could slide Mellyr into the nearest throne for a moment, that might give Lin all the time he needed. But "Julius hounded him looking every bit like a Nooseman with his dark flowing shawl and fluttering loose clothes.

Lin's flesh was a patchwork of wounds, every thudding step sending a jolt of pain through him. It was far from the first time he'd felt like a fool, but the Gods must be having a good laugh at him now. If something didn't change, this poor sweet child would bathe in the blood of everyone who ever thought to care for her. He listened, visualizing the way the man moved and stepped and lunged. Lin had seen the entire room, he knew the layout. When he reached for his spul, he held that image and sent out a flurry of Wefts.

Sections of the throne broke apart from impact and skittered, pebbles peppering the far wall.

Julius's steps behind him slowed and Lin hazarded a glance over his shoulder, skirting to a stop adjacent to the entrance he'd been shooting for. The masked man pulled his hand away, slick with blood. His robes, sheer and expensive looking, were open and showed pronounced ribs just above a slash so clean it had to have come from a Weft. He coughed and shook his head. "What aren't you monsters capable of?"

Lin had done it. But Julius was still standing and even though he bled it looked far from a fatal wound.

"I've never been cut by your people's magic. Wievings, huh? Hurts more than I expected." Julius stumbled forward. He managed to limp between Lin and the others still unconcious on the floor.

A scream, high and violent, tore from the main hallway. Lin turned to look and spotted Denny rushing in, hand free of weapons but a slew of dark brown Wefts formed in front of her. She didn't make it wholly into the room before collapsing to one knee.

"You fucking people," Julius hissed.

Denny held a hand to her neck, blood slowly pulsing from between her fingers. Lin's fears proved to be true. When she pulled her hand away, a crude dark Stitch covered the wound. Blood leaked from it as if the flesh hadn't pressed together correctly. Julius had attacked Denny in her sleep. *Fuck*. Her wound didn't look good.

There was a tension in the air now that wasn't hanging before. Julius's mask shifted from facing Denny to looking towards King Lodram. He threw down the baton and it clanged along the stone loudly until rolling to a stop at the foot of the crushed throne.

Julius stumbled at first, moving like he'd forgotten he had a wound across his side, then he was sprinting full speed towards the king, curved dagger still in hand.

Lin tracked the logic. If he couldn't kill Lin, make him a martyr, perhaps killing the king was the next best outcome, even if it meant he died. Maybe that *was* the best-case scenario. Let the mad Elodian kill the ungrateful fucking king. Lin watched, unmoving as Julius approached the unconscious man. Pulling at his spul, sending a Weft to take out his calves would be easy, but Lin didn't. The king and his forefathers brought all this upon themselves, let them weigh whether the blood spilled was worth it once it was one of theirs bleeding.

Julius was two steps away when a crossbolt sprouted from his shoulder. It sent him tumbling, sprawling to a stop by the crushed throne. He groaned through the now crooked mask.

Lin's first thought was to look for Pael— but then he saw Little Leo. The boy had dark circles under his eyes and trembled as he reloaded his weapon with a clawed-shaped device.

Once finished, he leveled the thing at Lin. His expression was far harder than a child his age should ever have to look. His hands shook, Gods, the boy's entire body shook. Likely the first life he'd ever really tried to take.

Lin nodded at the boy, shrugging to show that he held Mellyr. Leo shook his head, lowering the weapon a hair but keeping it trained on Lin.

With Mellyr held tight despite her unsteady complaints, Lin warily moved to Denny. He formed a focus and healed her, pulling on the darting fish of magic in his blood, the way he'd healed Leo. It was closer to a shade of blue than when Lin had pulled that other Wieve for himself, but it still looked foul, near corrupted.

Denny's nose scrunched about as she tried to look down, but relaxed a bit when she touched the wound and felt it sealed. She grunted.

Lin wanted to collapse. Even assaulting the Ferrucium hadn't left him feeling as drained as he did now. Tears came as he pressed his sweaty brow to Mellyr's. She playfully slapped him, hands grasping at anything and everything. This fight had made him realize something he'd already come to terms with regarding Nebra. He couldn't keep her as close as he wanted *and* protect her. Not when she was an infant. His eyes burned as he looked at her.

"Can you take her?" Lin said, despite his tight throat.

Another grunt, no nod, no whisper. Lin didn't blame her. Parts of his body screamed any time he moved, he couldn't imagine a wound across his throat. He handed Mellyr to Denny, kissing the child on the brow and letting his lips rest there for a long moment. Just in case. Plus the longer he stayed in that position, the more time the room had to stop spinning.

Mellyr slowed her wailing for a moment, pulling at Denny's face to force her eyes open more. Then the cries turned to giggles as she stared at Denny's Inlayed eyes and Lin realized she had the Binding Sight.

Lin slowly rose and saw the boltshooter was still trained on him. He nodded again at Leo, turning and hoping a bolt didn't take him in the back while he checked on Julius. He avoided the drizzle coming down from the ruined ceiling and got to the man without sprouting bolts, which was a good sign.

A kick sent the man's wicked, curved blade skidding away. Another kick flipped him fully over to lay on his back. Agonized groans followed as the bolt shifted in his shoulder.

"Sorry," Lin grumbled, careful to avoid the man's bare flesh as he put Weaves along his arms and legs to bind him in place.

With the mask skewed and the robes bloody and torn, Julius looked as bad as Dennick had at the end. Lin studied him. Maybe not *as* bad. But the man looked like shit.

Lin knelt beside him and pulled the mask away, still surprised at how heavy the things were despite their thinness. Never in his wildest dreams a year ago would he have thought he'd be pulling off a Nooseman's mask. Even if Julius wasn't a *real* Nooseman. Not even close.

"K-kill me." The words were soft, pleading. His white teeth were pink from the blood on his lips.

"Wouldn't have bound you up if I meant to kill you," Lin said. Though, he had considered it. For attempting to slit Denny's throat. For endangering Mellyr. Just as he'd stayed his hand when he could have saved what would have amounted to a wholly ungrateful fucking king, he had considered taking this man's life. For petty vengeance. Lin looked down at the Blade he'd formed, short like a dagger, dirt-colored. He was reaching the end of his spul and paying for it. But one cut across this bastard's throat would be worth it.

Lin looked over his shoulder at Denny and Mellyr, and beyond them at Leo. "No. You will answer for what you've done. To people better suited to getting answers than me." Before Julius could protest, Lin ripped the scrap of shawl that stubbornly clung to the man's shoulders.

Julius howled, the bolt yanked askew, still embedded in the flesh but blood pooling fresh.

"Ah, sorry," Lin said, a smile on his face as he stuffed the scrap of torn shawl into the man's open mouth. The last thing he needed was this bastard biting off his tongue the way the Nooseman had when speaking with Aemun. Well, maybe not last. But that was pretty high on the list if Lin wasn't going to kill him.

After another few moments of catching his breath, Lin was on his feet, body complaining at every motion. His shoulder screamed if he lifted his arm too high. Another scar to add to the collection, if he lived long enough to admire it.

Lin walked hands up and palms out over to Leo. The boy had moved so that he hovered over the fallen king like some sort of guardian spirit. "Thank you," Lin said. "For stopping him."

"I watched you let him charge," Leo said, sounding every bit out of breath. His hands still trembled and there was a pain in his eyes that Lin thought he understood.

"I'm at my limit," Lin said. As if that meant anything, or could mean anything to the boy.

Leo shook his head. "If he doesn't wake up, you're next."

Lin nodded and sank to the floor beside Denny. He was too tired to argue. If they didn't wake up, it would be Julius's fault, what with his magic. Not to mention Lin was sure the king wouldn't give two shits about Leo "protecting" him.

Worst came to worst, he'd break the bolt with a Weft. But all things told, he felt he'd managed to prove to anyone that mattered that his people weren't entirely monsters. *Hadn't I?*

Choking Blood

"If I had been smarter, stronger, present, perhaps all of this could have been avoided. Verbanth was unreconcilable. And how could I or anyone blame him? Our dear sister, Vellia, she was the moon. Bright and strong. What is a sky without the moon?" V.S.

Lin's eyelids fought him every other breath, but he stayed awake if not alert. The last thing he needed was an overambitious Ladrican attacking him in his sleep, not to mention if Julius ended up having more cohorts among those gathered. The man had proved himself a capable enough liar, Lin would be a fool to take anything else he'd said at face value.

Denny had kept Mellyr tucked into the groove of her arm and they both rested against Lin. Where her flesh touched him, it felt warm. Unusually so.

Mellyr wiggled free at some point and crawled atop Lin— playing with his beard.

Looking at her, it was hard to imagine the next steps forward. Denny would likely go back to doing whatever Erias allowed, assuming the man took her back. And if Anya had her way, Lin wouldn't be able to leave with Mellyr.

Lin glanced at Leo. The boy had shifted into a position so that the bolt-shooter rested braced against his knees, aimed right at Lin.

Leaving before the others woke didn't seem like a good option, not if he wanted to avoid a fight.

Guards, those that had survived the assault, had at some point entered the throne room. They gave Lin a wide berth and did the same to the stone thrones. But they'd righted King Lodram and the others, resting makeshift pillows under their heads.

Now they stood there avoiding eye contact, waiting for anyone to give a command. Whispers of their conversations carried through the silent room, thankful they were in the throne room, creepy as it was, compared to dealing with the bodies outside.

A chill gripped the air and Lin's breath came out as fog. He wished he hadn't shed Herm's oversized fur coat to at least keep Mellyr warm. Her cheeks were rosy, her bright eyes fighting sleep. Every time he looked at her, he saw *him*. Flashes of Margaret too, of course, but more of Aemun. The shape of her nose, the color of her eyes and olive-toned skin.

Eventually, Steward Bodrose limped in, blood and ash on his face. His velvet tunic was stained and he looked every bit like a deadman walking. He nodded when he spotted Lin and began instructing the guards to take whatever supplies survived the attacks at the docks and place them aboard the king's vessel.

"Elodian magic?" Steward Bodrose asked with a frown. He paced, hands resting atop his head.

Lin grunted, realizing the man had directed the question at him.

The steward tsked and knelt beside the king, checking for a pulse. "We can transport them as is, but it'd be better if they woke. The Nooseman, or, Noosewoman? Or ex, as it were, is awake now and in terrible pain. I don't know if there is a correlation between pain and waking..."

"Could break a bone," Denny whispered.

Lin craned his neck to look down at her. He'd thought she'd been asleep but if she had the sense to joke that must be a good sign. Then he recalled all the times leading up to the Ferrucium that she'd mentioned breaking his bones and he shivered. She likely meant it. "Julius said they'd sleep forever, but I'm not sure there was a single thing he didn't lie about. And seeing as the Nooseman keeps waking."

"I..." The steward flushed. "I was thinking smelling salts or a slap at the worst."

"Or he could just undo it," Lin said. He nodded at Julius sprawled near the rubble of the seventh throne. The guards, wary of the man, had left him restrained and groaning through his gag.

Steward Bodrose shook his head and scratched his receding hairline. "I don't believe they have the capability."

"He implied they did. Did you know that they only need to touch Danicans to bring the sleep upon them? Everyone else— no touch needed."

"Oh. Ohhhh." The man dropped his hand and touched his breast.

But it seemed Julius, with his mouth gagged and hands bound with Weaves, was incapable of conjuring those dark, ephemeral threads of his. The way they moved in the air, the way it looked even, was so reminiscent of Wievings that they had to be related.

In some way. Or perhaps that was what all magic looked like when viewed through the lens of Sight.

They sat in silence, guards coming and going to report to the steward until even that slowed. Soup was brought in, hot and heavily spiced, and everyone awake was offered a bowl with a chunk of bread that had seen better days.

Lin greedily slurped his down and soaked up the bottom of the bowl with the bread, softening its hard edges and making it far more palatable. Then he helped Denny eat. Mellyr whined at being woken and snuggled into the groove of their bodies.

Through the ruined ceiling, the stars became visible and flakes of snow drifted in taking over for the light rain from before, sparking the conversation on whether they should move into the meeting room.

It was debated at length until a guard rushed in, cheeks red, with a stoppered vial in his hand. "The best thing the physiker had compared to what you asked for."

Steward Bodrose stood up gingerly, favoring his left leg, and unstoppered the vial. His nose scrunched as if it might jump from his face and tears dotted his eyes. "Oh my," he choked through a cough.

The man moved like he planned to start with the king, but decided starting with a less valuable person might be in his best interest, pivoting to Elicia at the last moment. To say that she shot up with the most vile expression on her face would imply that she didn't walk around looking somewhat vile at all times. But she jolted up, coughing and gagging, looking every bit like she might stab the portly steward.

It made Lin recall the first time he'd gotten the scent of a corpse-seed and based on the reaction he was sure the nut was part of the concoction.

"What..." Elicia's voice faltered as she seemed to take in the room and the king she served beside her. "Give me that!"

She took the vial ungently and placed it under King Lodram's nose. He seemed to handle the process better than his wetnurse had, but after a fit of painful, lung-loosening coughs, he groaned and deflated into himself. "I've never slept so fitfully. Damned wraith. Where did he and that terrible taint-blood scurry off to."

Lin cleared his throat and watched the king register the state of the room. His eyes eventually landed on where Julius sat, restrained and gagged.

Elicia moved to the others, waking them far less gently than she had the king.

For once, Lin was glad to not have slept, as angry and exhausted as they all appeared. Not one of them seemed happy to have slept on the hard, stone floor. Ungrateful really.

"What are you smirking about?" Anya asked. Her voice was hoarse and she rolled her neck eliciting a loud pop.

Lin thought about sharing his actual thoughts, then shook his head. "What now? Any chance of calling off the soldiers now that I saved your life?"

"Ha!" King Lodram, with the help of his people, rose to his feet. His robes were as wrinkled as his brow and stained in places.

Elicia began wiping away dust and debris from the garments. Dirt had built up in the man's wrinkles. If not for the circlet, he'd look like a mummer playing at King. Even with it really, the way it was skewed on his head.

"Before a hasty reply is made, consider that he and his friend there likely saved *many* lives," Anya counseled.

"It could all be a ruse. Collusion meant to..." he faltered and seemed to flounder for words.

"Meant to see Danica's star rise while the Empire claims a lack of knowledge about their speaker's actions," Elicia finished for the man.

"Exactly." King Lodram nodded at the woman, his lips set in a thin line. "But also, these events notwithstanding, it is too late. Even if the Fentian port thought to rebuff the many ships, the Ferrucium port would make for a prime landing and my forces are aware of that. And besides, the people will be hard-pressed to believe that an Elodian wraith had soldiers infiltrate our garrisoned men. Let alone Fort Talms."

Lin only half-heartedly listened. He'd already assumed the king wouldn't change his stance. That had been part of the reason why he'd been willing to let Julius reach him before Leo stuck him with a bolt.

Steward Bodrose nodded. He'd been standing off to the side awkwardly and seemed uneager to interrupt, but he raised a hand and said, "Your Highness, if I may. Tessia is unaccounted for. Donus was murdered along with Delia, Vana, and Richt. Others are injured but survive and all say it was a Nooseman who attacked."

"Bah. The wraith playing dress-up."

"As we know. But... between Ladrican soldiers attacking the docks and now the assumed Nooseman many of the representatives for the various Free Nations demand answers. It may be, in my humble opinion, in our best interest to somehow prove that we aren't out for a war against the known world. Especially given that before Gritt defected, she was ordered to... *tighten*. So... we might begin by at least showing compassion to those who saved not only our lives, but the lives of many gathered."

"And what would you have me do?" King Lodram's brow, knitted tight at first, eased and he looked down at his hands. "We... I can't call back our forces."

"I know, my lord." Steward Bodrose's eyebrows raised.

"But you can, perhaps, send a bird and tell them to hold until the council reconvenes in months," Anya said. Even after everything, she still sounded so calm. So collected.

King Lodram on the other hand looked like he'd licked the dirt-covered stone and found its flavor wanting. "But if the battle has begun in earnest, so be it. We won't give up any land already seized."

"A wise choice," Elicia whispered.

Anya looked like there was something she wished to add but only shook her head and sighed. Lin thought he understood how she felt. Even after all this... even after Lin risked his life to at least stall Julius, the king acted this way.

"I need to clarify something," Lin said. He shifted, slipping away from Denny and Mellyr and slowly rising to his full height. "Julius attacked me, same as he did you all. But I didn't stop him. Little Leo there took the shot. I just stalled that madman. Leo, a true Ladrican, stopped him. I'm no hero. No savior. If there was an ulterior motive at play— I had no part in it."

King Lodram seemed to notice Leo for the first time, his chin raising and lip curling. "A true Ladrican, hmm? Come here, boy."

Leo's hair and clothes were a mess, disheveled and torn respectively. He practically dragged the bolt shooter behind him, and when he reached the king he gave a salute better than most grown men might. Straight-backed and proud, Leo stared up at the king.

"You stopped the wraith?" King Lodram asked, inflection throwing disbelief like spittle.

"Yes, my lord. Ran messages at Talms, the fort that is, and practiced with bolt shooters plenty. Got him in the shoulder."

"I see."

Lin watched, a sense of pride bubbling up for the young man. The handful of times Lin had spoken with the Weavers in his youth, he didn't think he'd been even half as sure of himself.

Lodram pointed that damned ringed finger of his at Leo's neck. "And that mark right there?"

Leo's face twisted into a frown. "One of the traitors... Sergeant Royce and his men got a bolt into me. He saved me." Leo jerked his chin back and nodded at Lin.

King Lodram looked like he tasted something bitter and his face twisted.

"I didn't ask him to!" Leo blurted. "Sir," he tacked on, realizing he'd just yelled at the king.

"No, of course not. A good, true Ladrican would never." The king seemed to study the room, and the people, and finally, his eyes rested on the bolt shooter. "A good, true Ladrican. Elicia, see this child handled."

Lin bristled and stepped just in front of Elicia. "Doesn't sound like you mean to reward him for saving you."

"You may have won the malleable hearts of some of those gathered here, but do not think to tell me how to handle a child of Ladrica. He, more than anyone in this room, is subject to my will." King Lodram shook his head and crossed his arms. "Freeing him of that accursed mark is a reward any *good*, true Ladrican would want."

"You mean murder? Or removal?" Lin whispered.

"Little... Leo." King Lodram stooped down, resting on one knee to the horror of Elicia and the shock of Steward Bodrose. "Do you really wish to go through the rest of your life marked by this man's tainted-blood? Truly consider this. Any with the Sight will know you for what you are."

Leo's lip quivered and his head shook in one of the most unconvincing displays Lin had ever witnessed.

"Bastard!" Lin growled but Elicia stood firm and stared into his eyes, her pointed jaw set and clenched. She was ready for a fight. She *wanted* one.

"Quite the opposite. I'm acutely familiar with my lineage. My family helped build this hall.

"Before the invaders from the south took it and made it their own. Before Danica, land of the Gods, was beset with tainted-blood monsters." King Lodram looked up at Lin, a smile spreading.

Lin studied the faces of those gathered. "If you hurt that child, I don't care, I'll kill you here and now."

Anya and the other scholar argued softly behind the king and Denny mumbled something from against the wall. Elicia hadn't moved and Steward Bodrose looked like he might faint. Several guards raised their weapons in response to his tone.

"Yes, prove to the few remaining leaders that you are the monster I claim. I've lived a full life. Sired smart, strong children. I even met my first grandchild recently. They say cutting off the head of a snake is the best way to kill it. But I haven't *truly* been the head in fifteen passings. I'm the belly, helping us crawl along, fat and happy."

King Lodram rose and straightened his circlet. He stretched his neck as if offering it for a blade.

Lin clenched his fist and looked down at Leo.

Confusion, fear, and pain all mired the boy's expression. And all sorts of other feelings Lin was sure he couldn't have processed when he was Leo's age.

When Lin didn't strike him, the king leaned forward and opened his arms as if to hug Leo. Folds of stained robes that looked everything like a forest at night, full of terrors. Leo stepped forward and the king's hand caressed his cheek, avoiding the side where the Wieving had healed him.

"I-I'm not ready to die," Leo blurted. "I-I can be a Nooseman. Or—"

"Stupid child, you can't be a Nooseman." King Lodram tightened his grip on the side of Leo's face, the skin near his ear immediately reddening. "And I can't have you coming home a *hero* looking as you do."

"Banishment," Steward Bodrose said abruptly. The words came out loud, nearly forceful, and even the speaker himself looked surprised he'd said anything.

"Yes. I was thinking the same. He would make a fine initiate," Anya said. She'd gone as pale as a fresh moon and stared intently at King Lodram's knobbed knuckles. It wasn't lost on Lin that she had grasped her vial of blood.

Leo's lip quivered, then tears streaked his cheeks muddy. The boy acted like he'd just been told his life was over. Gods, he'd seemed somewhat ready to die if that was what the king wanted.

"This boy *is* a hero," Lin pointed at Leo.

"Would it be that we could all get the recognition we deserve when we feel we deserve it," King Lodram straightened, knees popping under his robes, and leaned onto the steward. "Take me to the ship. See that this boy doesn't try to sneak aboard and give the soldiers orders to kill him if he's found."

Elicia pressed in close enough that Lin could feel her breath, warm and sour. "One day, you'll lose everything you love."

Lin considered how hard he might be able to punch her in the throat. If he put his weight into it. As exhausted as he felt, it wouldn't nearly be as hard as she deserved. Half as much if he was being generous. He could send thin Wefts to her eyes or between her fingers. Though, even the thought of working magic right now made him yawn.

"Untethered caught your tongue?" She asked, a sneer somehow making her expression even uglier.

"Thinking of all the ways I might be able to hurt you and call it an accident," Lin whispered.

"And gather up that insidious wraith. See that his hands remain bound and clothed. Leave the baby and traitor for the time being. They'd just slow us down and if there is more subterfuge awaiting us, I'd rather not deal with them." King Lodram looked down his nose at Lin, something that should have been a challenge considering the king's below-average height, but apparently, he was rather experienced by the slight angle of his head and the lift of his brow. "And don't imagine this is over, tainted-blood. Your people are monsters. You are, without a doubt, a monster."

When the king and his people finally shuffled from the throne room, the steward looking back somewhat mournfully more than once, Anya and her junior scholar, blood matting her hair to the side of her head, approached Lin. They moved softly as if all the previous commotion had disturbed the room enough.

"Let Kayle have the child."

"Leo?" Lin asked. Now that the king and his people were gone, it felt like all of Lin's strength and will to keep fighting had departed with them. Each limb felt burdened. He was exhausted, sick of feeling betrayed, and worst of all, wary of being used once again.

"Azh—" Kayle, the junior scholar let the name fall from her lips at Anya's raised hand. A simple gesture but one that seemed to be another show of good faith by the High Scholar.

"Mellyr. She was gifted a new name at the passing of her father. But yes, both children. Though, I think it would not be an issue for all of us to head towards Fentis together. If our boat survives."

Lin shook his head. Too many had been burned or broken. He'd always been cautious of Wanderer's Ore and the attack seemed to justify his distrust of the strange material. Water brought life, anything that hissed and sparked at contact with it had to be bad.

"No?" Anya asked.

"Sorry. I mean yes. If there is a ship to take us. Leo?"

Leo looked up from his feet without a word and shuffled forward, mouth set into a thin line.

"Give it time. You will see that the Tower of Fentis is a grand place to reside," Anya said with a smile that seemed genuine despite the dire circumstances awaiting them back south.

As they walked through the room, Lin couldn't help but stare at the thrones. Seven. And the tapestries in the main hall. So much loose Wanderer's Ore shaken from the walls that a flood would set fire to the entire place. Denny leaned against his side and limped along, Mellyr rocking in her arm despite Kayle's worried glances.

"High Scholar," Lin said."Is it true what the king claimed, did his family help build this place?"

Anya raised her hands, laced her fingers, and let them fall. Her normally fluid movements seemed forced, like a stiff puppet. "His line has claimed many things, many times. Some say his lineage dates back well before the Accords, much like Aemun's. Others claim any ties he has to the Ladrican rulers of old are circumstantial at best and fabricated at worst. Even others say," she leaned in close, "he is a descendant of Wicked Tel'Myr."

Lin snorted. "Wouldn't surprise me, the way he acts. Six and One."

Everywhere he looked he saw floating remnants of Velkath's Sigil. It was like the symbol had burned into his eyes and though the intensity had faded, the frequency had increased. More than anything, it made his head spin like he was in the middle of a great battle, Wefts and Weaves flying past him.

"What's wrong?" Denny whispered.

Lin looked down at her and saw her Stitched eyes piercing him. He forced a smile. "What isn't?"

"Your heart..." she nudged her head into the side where she'd been resting it. "Feels wrong."

"We can talk more later."

Denny grunted and they continued until they were outside. Anya stopped and spoke with several of the surviving guards who attended with the Free Nations' leaders. None seemed thrilled to see Lin and most looked worse for wear.

It was clear, no one was leaving this island unscathed, even the survivors. *Especially* them.

Howls near the docks announced Gritt's presence. She sat on the shore and clutched a Blade to her throat, rocking back and forth and muttering incoherent things between screams.

Gods. "Anya, please. There has to be something you could do for her."

Kayle shook her head and made a sign in the air that Lin didn't recognize.

"I fear not even sleep can comfort her now. Death might be the only—"

"No! She took a stand against her cruel king. There has to be something we can do." Lin pulled away from Denny and approached the screaming woman. Tears streaked her pale face and her eyes were red and swollen. Her removed hand had looked cauterized and the Bludwieve that should have been around her finger wrapped her wrist like a tight, twining bracelet.

Lin looked at his own Bludwieve and knew his to be a serpent waiting to strike. "Anya!"

The High Scholar came to stand on the shore beside them, waves crashing only a few feet away. Ruins of some of the worst-faring ships floated on the waves or thunked against the stone in a steady rhythm. "Even among the pages you lost, nothing detailed a broken uethe." There was a touch of ire to her tone. It wasn't like he'd meant to lose the One-loved thing.

Anya folded her arms and stared at the wailing woman, then shrugged.

Lin put out a hand, sinking to the ground beside her, trousers wetting in the process. It was cold and a breeze came off the dark water that immediately made his teeth chatter. Ash had mixed with the dusting of snow to make the already bleak vista as bland looking as over-cooked porridge.

Gritt pulled away at first, eyes wide and worried and terrified, but then she let him touch her.

Touching her arm felt like touching a kettle that had been left on the embers overnight. It made sense why she'd left the refuge of the castle to sit in the freezing wind and biting water.

"It burns?" Lin asked.

Through gritted teeth, she nodded.

"Anya, what about... what about copper?"

"What about it?" She asked, brow raised. "Kayle. Follow those men over there and see if our ship survived, if so have them help prepare it and take the children and that woman on board, out of the cold."

"Yes, High Scholar." Kayle led Denny away, the latter not taking her eyes from Lin for a long moment.

"If this is an attempt to strand me here and take away Mellyr," Lin said, raising his voice to carry over the sound of waves and screaming, "I won't let that ship get far."

"Copper. It helps prevent decay. I don't know what good—"

"Horseshit! They've stabbed Bound Metal stakes through untethered laced with copper and it put them into a type of stasis. I worked a Weft fueled by copper... and it brought an untethered's sense back. I think."

"You what?" Anya stepped forward, crunching the shoal underfoot.

"You heard me." Lin licked his lips and eased his grip on Gritt's arm.

Anya was silent for so long that Lin had to turn and look at her. "I believe what you did was put the mind at ease somehow. Untethered go mad. Toxicity of minerals most often, but not always. And you managed to halt that, reverse it even. What did the untethered say when their senses came back?"

Lin looked down at the various stones underneath him and Gritt. "Begged me to kill them."

"Ah."

"Gritt. I can try... I can try to stop it. The pain. But I can't promise it will work. If it doesn't work as intended, I might be able to put you into a sort of stasis with Bound Metal and a copper Weft until we find a real solution. Would you want that?"

Gritt looked disgusted, even through the tears and wails. She nodded, short and curt. If she clenched her jaw any harder, it was like to break, but she let her Blade turn into disparate threads. There had to be other Noosemen left. Maybe even others who'd be willing to turn on their king.

Kayle and the others didn't return, leading Lin to believe they'd found the ship and it was one of the few that survived the worst of the attack.

Lin formed a focus and reached for the strange, unnatural seed in his blood. It took a moment and he withered as it came to life, the magic blooming into a sickly green thorn that stabbed into Gritt's wrist. Her screams slowed, then stopped entirely as she breathed heavily beside him. Then her arm jerked. A hard yank, followed by another. It looked like something warred just below the surface of her flesh, veins moving as thin pale vines and scarlet light shifted. She looked like she wanted to scream, but no sound came from her, until finally, she stilled, motionless.

"Magic has a mind of its own," Anya said. "I'm sure you're weak after that, but do you think you can carry her?"

Lin felt like he'd die of thirst, but he nodded. Gods, his teeth ached and it felt like the stones pressing into his knees might break his bones entirely.

"This is the result of a Bludwieve meeting copper. Having Bound Metal would be best, to stab within her, but I've none. If she wakes, it could be bad. We need to get her to the Tower as swiftly as we can."

"If the Ladricans haven't already razed it to the ground," Lin mumbled.

"King Lodram is many things... but I doubt he'd throw away centuries of camaraderie all because we decided to let you speak."

"Anya... did your people have anything to do with Royce?" Lin asked, winded as he lifted Gritt. Her eyes had closed and her flesh, while still green and red-hued along her arm had stopped burning at the touch.

Anya slowed and turned, eyes narrowed. "What would make you ask that? It was Julius."

"No... you're right." Lin sighed. "Brain gets foggy after pulling copper." He had his doubts but when she was his only way back to Danica currently, it seemed best to keep them to himself. The vials of blood for one. And the fact that she *and* Julius had sent him out there. Both of them wanted him to look like the hero. Perhaps she'd even stalled King Lodram's exit by intentionally leading the man the wrong way.

"You know, you're far more reasonable than Denro led us to believe you'd be."

Lin snorted, regretting the action as his chest throbbed.

Gritt was either heavier than she looked or Lin had used all his strength, but after gaining his balance, he managed to pull her up onto his shoulder. He got a whiff of his underarm at the motion and groaned. If people thought he'd stunk before, he was outright foul now. His shoulder screamed as much as his torso, but if he could sit once they got onto the ship, he was sure he'd be fine. Already it felt like his spul was recovering, even though he had an emptiness where that seed of copper had rested. His fingers had regained their feeling and it was easier to keep his eyes open.

Lin breathed a heavy, winded sigh of relief when the ship came into view and Anya confirmed it was theirs. *Another point to why she might be behind it.* The Scholar's ship had mostly been untouched, furthest from the dock as it was.

"Please, Lin, after you." Anya smiled wearily. "Let us be on our way."

Calloused Hope

"The Accords were never intended to be a long-term solution. The Ferrucium should have been a bastion that could teach Danicans godliness, but along the way, it became far easier to exert control as opposed to compassion. New Ladrican Kings found more reasons to demand obedience— especially after King Gunthyr's Queen was slain. And favor-hungry Dukes and Weavers of the time were more than willing to oblige." Excerpt from the Histories of Southern Danica removed and redacted due to the Danican Accords.

If Lin never had to sail the open seas again, he'd die happy. Or at least happier, everything else being equal. The short row to the island had made him confident that the open seas might treat him somewhat gently, but as waves from a storm crashed against the ship, Lin realized his folly. Days on board had left him rested, if sore, and he'd tucked his head between his knees often enough that he wasn't sure he remembered how to sit upright.

Gritt didn't move. She couldn't, with the magic warring within her. Odds were she felt it all. Odds were, the magic only kept her pain from being a bother to those on board. But he hoped he'd done the right thing.

At Anya's behest, Leo had made himself useful, taking orders from one person to the next. Not that the ship was large enough to need it, but over the days Leo had seemed to find resolve in the task and even smiled when Anya or Kayle spoke softly with him.

Lin looked up from between his knees towards Denny and Mellyr. The two of them slept like dogs might, curled around each other. If Lin tried that, he'd probably crush the child, but Denny was light and lithe and seemed to enjoy the occasional soft kick Mellyr pushed her way. And when the babe cried, Denny was on it, whispering lullabies that Lin only caught vague strands of.

A groan sloshed out from Lin as the ship rocked.

"We could have a physiker brew something for you."

Lin shook his head, letting his brow rest against his knees.

"The good news is, you've kept the sick down. Otherwise, we'd have to put you up there with the swell."

"Hmm."

Anya's steps grew soft as she drew near and then she sat on the bench beside Lin. "I wanted to speak with you when you were feeling better, but it seems the sea has truly poisoned you."

"I've been worse," Lin said, squinting and turning his head to look at her. Not to mention it was just as likely the overuse of his spul making him weak. But he still didn't trust the High Scholar fully and had no intention of seeming weaker than he already did.

"I'm sure you have."

"If it's about Mellyr, it can wait."

"It really can't," Anya whispered. "In a few days, we'll be at the Tower— assuming there is a tower left standing, and you'll be ready to go. You'll want to take her with you. And you can't. Maybe once the meeting finds a positive resolution, but certainly not before then." The High Scholar seemed to fumble her words and Lin listened with one ear in her direction, the other pounding against his forearm with his pulse.

"Have you ever felt like you were drowning? And every time you reached for a handhold, it either fell away or turned out to be mist?"

Anya shifted and sighed. She'd changed into a darker cloak that looked like water might roll right from it. Not quite leather, but close. Gods, it had to be hot. The room had grown muggy despite the cold storm raging outside.

"I can't say that I have."

"Every single time I think I've found my way to land, I swallow more water. And it doesn't get easier. I haven't yet started to think it might be better in the depths, lifeless. But Anya... I am close."

"Madness you mean? The blood taint?"

"No. I'm tired. I've been exhausted. All I wanted was Mellyr back and now that I have her and I'm near her I've... I've realized that as long as I cling to her, she will be in danger. I thought of myself as her land, her safety, but I'm the ocean deep and hungry and if I keep her close, I'll kill us both." Lin didn't try to fight back his tears. There was nothing left for him to prove to Anya, no sense of pride worth hanging onto. Thinking hurt, the steady thrum of the ocean crashing sending waves of pain down his body. Nausea pervaded everything and his wounds ached all over. He ran his hands over his head, the braids Tylle had woven for him grown out and not nearly well-kept enough to warrant keeping. When he pulled his hands away, strands of hair clung between his fingers.

Anya was silent for so long that Lin thought he'd scared her away, but eventually, a light touch rested on his shoulder. "We will watch the child for as long as you need us to."

"As strong as I think I am, I can't protect her if she's with me. A Weft almost caught her when I first attacked. Not mine, but still. And then holding her, Julius nearly killed us both. And he was far from a fierce warrior. But I need to be able to trust you and your people." The last part came out in a growl and Lin tried to soften his expression as he looked up at her through his tears. "Please."

The ship rocked hard to the side and Anya braced herself on Lin's shoulder. "Trust can be a tenuous thing."

"It shouldn't have to be. I just want to know exactly what kind of tests you'll be doing on her, if there are any left to do. I saw..." Lin shook his head and sniffled. "I saw the sorts of things they did at the Fort as tests."

"Like the Bound Metal stakes you described?" Anya asked.

Lin nodded.

"I still can't believe they perfected it." Anya took her hand away and stared at Denny and Mellyr. "Those stakes were something theorized. I never thought the tests would continue. But I can promise you... nothing like that has happened or will happen to her. What we did with Mellyr were simple tests to see if her blood was... if Aemun's blood carried any weight."

"How could you know anything about her blood from tests?"

Anya was silent for a while. "As I mentioned before, Aemun's lineage is quite old. Was old, I should say. Mellyr there is a descendant of who you might've heard named Cunning Velkath."

Lin stared at the sweet, sleeping infant. Cuddled against Denny, she looked everything like a normal, peaceful child. "How does one descend from a supposed God? And what does that mean for her?"

"Because that family wasn't always revered as such. And it means nothing, as far as we can tell. But Aemun left behind a scroll and sent it to us before everything happened. Sealed it with some sort of Wieving. A Seal, for lack of a better name. Very much like a Bludwieve. Damned thing won't come undone and we thought perhaps someone who shared his blood might be able to undo it."

Lin shook his head. "I was there for months and this is the first you're telling me about it?"

Anya squeezed his shoulder. "We weren't exactly on good terms. Plus, all the High Scholars were told by Denro how you snapped and killed the man. Aemun could've been an asset."

Oh. The lie he'd told for Tylle's sake. Lin sighed and nodded. "He might've. Doubtless, he would've navigated... oh hold on." Lin brought his hand to his mouth and choked down a wave of nausea. He squeezed his eyes tight, and after several long moments, opened them. Velkath's sigil drifted at the edge of his vision. "As large of an ass as he was, he likely would've handled all of this better than me. For the good or ill of it."

"I never personally met him, though I've heard tales. Handsome. Charming. Smart but entirely selfish."

Lin sucked in a breath and leaned his head back against the wall. "Entirely. But this Seal, her blood didn't break it?"

"No. Then we thought perhaps it was related to Bound Metal somehow, seeing as he grafted it onto his flesh at the end." Her face twisted into confusion and disgust, so at odds with her usual placid expression.

"I take it that it isn't something typically done?"

Creaks sounded from the walls and calls above deck made it sound as if they'd come through the worst of the storm. All the better for it. He hadn't felt great the first day or two, but this constant rocking had magnified the unpleasantness tenfold.

"No."

Lin waited for Anya to elaborate, but when he looked out the side of his eye, past the floating sigil, she merely stared at the wall, arms tight around herself.

"When I was a soldier, the world was so small. I thought Ferrucium steel was rare. I thought Stitches meant you were untethered. I thought Bindings were limited to Weaves and Wefts and a few other simple tricks. Now I know better. Even the Elodian magic looked like a type of Wieve. Strands of darkness, stabbed through with light like the night sky was woven into a string."

Anya scoffed and nodded. "You claim you haven't navigated this well... but you managed to save many people. Even the king himself. You verified something we scholars have long theorized and your actions kept Mellyr from staying in Ladrican territory. By all accounts, you're a very capable man."

Lin shook his head. "I couldn't stop Julius. I don't have Mellyr. Not really." He looked at her, as warm and comfortable as anyone on the ship likely was. "I haven't stopped the war."

Anya chuckled. "I didn't think that was ever your goal."

Lin smiled. She had a point. "And all I've really learned is that there is still much I don't know. Too much."

"Like what?" Anya asked. She shifted where she sat and pulled a flask from within her tunic. Once uncorked, it smelled sweet and strong. When she took a sip, she exhaled through her nose and melted into the bench a bit.

Lin shifted. He still didn't trust the scholars, but as Anya had said, that was a tenuous thing. And if he needed them to protect Mellyr while he was resolving the issue of Ladrica's invasion and the growing untethered problem, he'd have to trust someone.

The sheath stuck to his side a bit, the sweat collected against it keeping the leather to his flesh. With a yank, it came free and Lin held it to the side, silent for a moment.

Anya raised a brow at him as he pulled it free. "Don't tell me you waited all this time to stab—" Like the dying crash of waves from outside the ship, Anya's voice faded as her eyes rested on the blade.

Lin forced himself fully upright and turned to face her. Her eyes had grown large and her lips were pressed into a tight line. "You recognize it."

"I've never seen it, but I've heard descriptions before. Unlike the narrative you were taught regarding the iron used to craft Ferrucium steel, this is a very rare blade. How did you come to possess it?"

Lin pulled the cracked, black blade free, the broken, jagged edge looking all the more terrible in the half-light of the cabin.

"One of the attackers at the docks. Cut right through a Weft I made."

"Did it cut you?" Her voice had grown timid, a trait Lin wouldn't have thought the woman capable of having.

Lin sheathed the blade and set it onto his lap before lifting his tunic to show the blackened wound running across his torso. He'd kept the wound covered since the first day aboard the ship and the puckered dark flesh looked red and agitated.

"Oh," Anya whispered. Then leaned in and frowned at the wound. "So the blade didn't sever an Inlay?"

It felt like ice ran through Lin's veins and he lowered his tunic. "Can it do that?"

"No. Well, perhaps. It is speculated."

Lin nodded. It made sense. The thing seemed to cut through everything but stone. What was it Aemun said? *Flay yourself*. Is that what he meant? Lin looked at the sheathed dagger resting on his knee. If that was truly the only way to rid himself of these markings...

"And it appears you overused your spul to heal that wound."

"The unusual Wievings... They drain me much faster. Is it bad?"

"Normally no. But with the blade causing the wound it could be severely infected."

Lin shrugged.

"Don't just shrug. You'll need proper care. We'll have a physiker look at it."

They sat in silence for another stretch when Lin interrupted by tapping the sheath against his knee. "So this thing burns through Ferrucium steel and cuts Bindings like it's nothing."

"Correct," Anya said. Her eyes were locked on Lin's hands, staring at the Stitches along his knuckles specifically.

"If it can cut Bindings. Wievings of all sorts... can it?" Lin waggled his ring finger where his Bludwieve twined. "What if this is Gritt's answer?"

Anya frowned. "Perhaps. Legends say this was the weapon Tel'Myr wielded when she cut ties with Vellia. A wicked blade."

"For a wicked person," Lin said.

Anya looked poised to say something when heavy thuds overhead preceded softer, hurried steps and winded breaths down the short stairs that led from above deck. Leo, soaked to the bone and dripping, nearly tripped as he slid to a stop. "Captain says," he huffed a deep breath and frowned when his eyes drifted to where Lin sat. "Says the watchman sees ships off in the distance. We're still days out and it isn't likely it's Ladricans, but the ship is in-dis-ting-uishable." He stumbled through the last word trying to replicate the captain's words.

"Tell him to avoid them." Anya glanced down at the sheathed dagger.

"He is."

Anya narrowed her eyes. "Then why rush down here?"

Leo looked down at the puddle he'd caused. The steady drip from his clothes added to the constant creaking of the ship. Something Lin hadn't thought would be a bother but was. Waves crashing. Wood groaning. People whispering. All of it was too much at once. And now? Drip. Drip. Drip.

Lin leaned forward and hung his head. His hands pressed flat against his ears.

"No reason," Leo mumbled.

"No reason?"

For the most part, Lin had kept to himself the last few days. But as tight as quarters were, it was impossible not to notice little Leo's infatuation with High Scholar Anya. So impossible that she noticed it too and at every turn seemed inclined to correct the boy's mind. Yet, if anything that had seemed to worsen the fervor with which the young man wanted to please her. Like a loyal hound sitting and staying and fetching but in this case, it seemed to be one menial message after the other. As young as Leo was, Lin wouldn't be surprised if he'd made up the story about the other ships just to have a reason to get out of the rain and speak with the woman.

Lin watched them between the gap of his shoulder and forearm. Anya was pleasant-looking. Not in the typical sense, not the way he found Tylle to be, but her complexion was clear of blemishes and the hardness of her features gave her a regal bearing. Even with a shaved head, he could picture her beside any one of the Dukes. Perhaps it was that and the way she held herself that added to the charm. But he'd never have feelings like that for her, not after all the lies and half-truths.

"Would it be rude to ask what you two were talking about?" Leo asked.

"Very," Anya said.

Lin smiled as Leo took a seat on the floor beside Anya, staring up at her as he crossed his legs.

"An inquisitive mind is something we do like in our scholars. And a still tongue even more."

"Not a conversation for children," Lin said, trying to force Leo to look at him. When the boy finally did and saw that Lin stared back at him, he quickly frowned and looked away.

"No, he can listen to this next part. I was about to inform sea-sick Lin here about the story of Vellia and Tel'Myr." Anya straightened her back and took another, longer pull from her flask. She began to stopper it before weighing it for a moment and proffering it towards Lin.

Lin took it and smelled it first, the sweetly spiced aroma not quite stinging his eyes, but near enough that he took the follow-up sip gingerly. It tasted like spiced apples, the tart ones, and burned all the way down. "Pretty good," Lin whispered.

"Belanisian recipe." Anya shrugged before putting the flask away to Leo's clear disappointment. "Vellia and Tel'Myr. Wise and wicked. The Six and their One Shadow. A blemish so to speak. But it wasn't always the case. Tel'Myr was a title given later, not a name. It means *Shadow*. She was Vellia's older sister and fled past the reach of Vellia's fingers at the time of the betrayal.

"Like most things, it all stemmed from love. This was after Vellia learned the ways of Wieving and shared her secrets first with her family, then with the world. Venya, Tel'Myr's true name, had met a man. Mind you, this is all documented in the deepest tomes, buried by the Accords. And truthfully, this is what helped incite the Accords."

Lin was listening. He didn't have a choice unless he wanted to move from the rather comfortable position he'd managed to craft for himself. The storm outside had lessened and with it, the one in his gut. He licked his lips and continued to watch Leo, though more discreetly. It was easy to think he'd done the right thing by saving the boy. A life is a life, after all. But would this child be happy? Would Mellyr, once she was old enough to understand what had happened? Gods. The Belanisians really knew how to make a drink.

He'd heard the name Venya before— but the source was lost to him. Tylle, likely.

"Venya was in love from the moment she laid eyes on the man. Virt, her twin brother, should have seen the signs, but as his moniker suggests, he was dull and failed to notice. Being the only two sisters, Vellia and Venya were close, and Vellia eventually met this lordling. His speech was odd, customs odder, but in time Vellia too fell in love with him. But Vellia was wise. And she loved her sister. So she kept those feelings to herself."

"I thought you were about to tell me Vellia actually betrayed Tel'--Venya."

"No. Though that would make for a compelling twist. All of this was to say that the dagger was a gift to Venya from the lordling. Given in secret, along with whispered promises of power and destiny. Become a shadow, he said to her.

"Vellia, even as wise as she was, didn't see the betrayal coming. Venya was jealous of the way her brothers, and the people, revered Vellia. Jealous of the occasional looks she saw *her* lordling, betrothed in secret, give to Vellia. Perhaps it wasn't *this* blade. But a blade much like this slit Vellia's throat. Earning Venya the moniker wicked. Verbanth loved both his sisters greatly, but the devastation he wrought on the world for Vellia's loss can't be understated. His wrath is ultimately what led the members of the Free Nations to agree to the Accords."

Lin looked at the sheathed dagger and blinked, surprised that the soft beginnings of hard tears were in his eyes. "We were taught, Danicans I mean, that the Six created the world. Faceless Weavers who brought order into existence through the Grand Tapestry. Then... a friend of mine told me some of the histories of Velkath and his kin. Though, it seems her knowledge is incomplete against yours."

"Oral histories likely survived the cleansing that took place. It is easy to see how figures who still cast such large shadows across the land could be misconstrued as Gods."

"Why would someone kill their sister? For a man no less?" Leo asked. He'd inched closer to Anya and looked horrified.

It made Lin think of Aemun and Margaret. The man had done something unspeakable to a woman he claimed to love, all for what? For Ladrica to invade? For Mellyr to be betrothed to a lordling?

"People do unspeakable things for power. And sometimes, for nothing. That lordling would eventually be known as Just King Gunthyr. The ruler of Ladrica at the signing of the Accords."

"And what happened to Venya?"

Anya looked down at Leo and patted his head. "This last part isn't for children. Run along and tell the captain I'd like dinner to be rationed out before nightfall this time."

Leo opened his mouth to argue, then rose with a frown and slowly walked up the steps, fully opposite his energy coming down.

"That boy would do anything for you." Lin chuckled.

"Terrifying," Anya whispered. And it seemed she meant it as she wrung her hands. "It likely wouldn't matter, as who knows how much Leo might believe what I've said, but I'd rather him be an actual scholar before learning more of this sordid past."

"And me? After my stay, am I considered a scholar?"

"An honorary one perhaps, seeing as your child will be a ward for a time."

Lin shrugged and leaned back, the nausea fully abated for the time. A smile coming to his lips fully formed. She'd called Mellyr his child. *His*. "Venya?"

"Perhaps the saddest of all. After killing her sister, wounding her brother, and fleeing to the north, she bore King Gunthyr a few children. Then the Accords were signed not long after and Danicans weren't allowed to leave their country. A small quelling occurred and Just King Gunthyr grew even more paranoid than many reports claim he already was."

"He sent her and the children back to Danica?"

"No. He kept her close. And her children. They were the very first Noose. Sworn Uethes, and Bludwieves, and all. She bound herself to her king and died as his slave and made her children do the same."

“Bastard,” Lin growled.

“A real cocksucker,” Denny whispered.

Lin and Anya turned to look at Denny who’d partially sat up, a smile on her face making the Stitches across her cheeks grossly misaligned.

Anya smiled. “Maybe someday you can read the full histories and see for yourself?”

“I’d like that.” And he would. But between the Ladrican attacks and the untethered, he was more likely to die than ever catch a moment to read histories again. If only he’d been allowed the access he wanted when he was cooped up for months. Lin lifted the sheath, staring at the stitched leather string that danced around the edge of the carved bones. “If this thing is capable of cutting Bindings, why didn’t Venya cut her Bludwieve?”

“She was in love. Didn’t want to,” Denny said, stretching one leg out as far as she could and touching the wall. “Obviously.”

“Should we see if this thing can ease Gritt’s pain?”

“One way or another it will,” Anya said, a grim expression settling onto her face.

Calloused Bone

"What most scholars wouldn't admit, if they even know, is the tower existed on Danican soil long before the scholars took up residence. Tomes older than the Gods themselves could be found there if the tomes wished to be found. No stone shroud protecting it either, but plenty of magic woven into the building of it, if you ask me." Comments on the Tower of Fentis by an Elodian scholar.

It was Anya who suggested they wait to cut Gritt. A sentiment that made sense once she reminded Lin that there was no true physicker on board the ship. Worst case, they'd have an enraged, bleeding, Nooseman. Best case, she'd be right as rain and decide she didn't wish to stay among the scholars anymore. Neither option seemed all that great, so they waited. Two days had passed in discomfort since then, but now with the sun out and the sky clear, Lin felt an ease across his shoulders he hadn't since embarking to rescue Mellyr.

Those ships the captain had apparently seen were well-avoided, given that Lin couldn't spot them anywhere. Not a sail, mast, or prow in sight. Or little Leo had made it up and the captain lied for him. Though, it wouldn't be the first time Lin had failed at seeing something obvious to others.

Men with better legs and stomachs for working aboard a ship moved deftly across the deck. The wind was against them, so a handful rowed and the others kept busy maneuvering the sails in ways Lin didn't think he'd ever understand. They called and shouted and rowed to the steady beat of a drum. Conducive to rowing on time, less to intimate thoughts. So Lin busied himself by staring at the sea, dark even during the day.

"See it?" Denny asked. She'd slipped beside him as silent as a soft gust of wind. *Natural-like.*

Lin smiled. In truth, all he saw was the ocean, vast and hungry. And Velkath's Sigil of course. It teased him at the very edges of his vision, darting away every time he focused on it. He'd wanted to ask Anya about it but had thought better about giving the woman any reason to doubt his sanity. *Any more reason*. "The sky? Or the water?"

Denny bumped her hip into his leg and shook her head. "The tower."

The horizon was a line of angry blue where sky and sea met and, even when Lin squinted, seemed fully free of any towers, cliffs, or sea monsters.

"No."

"Well, it's there. Free of any surrounding ships."

"You don't sound too pleased," Lin studied her. It was good that she'd been able to rest and seemed recovered, but there was a hardness to her movements and voice that didn't sit well.

"If the ships didn't make land here, the only other place is the Ferrucium. No?"

Ah. Or the invasion might've floated a bit up the Telms. Though that was doubtful. "Yes. But if they landed there, they'd have a harder fight than taking Fentis."

A grunt escaped Denny. In the midday sun, she looked paler than ever but the Stitches across her face and in her eyes were washed out and Lin could see her features more clearly than usual. "What?" she asked.

Lin licked his lips and nudged her back with his hip. "Wondering where you might've deposited Mellyr."

She didn't pull away from his touch and even seemed to relax into it, leaning onto him more than the rail. "Kayle."

The thought that the scholars of Fentis were a bastion of learning and understanding had faded long ago, but in the short time spent among Kayle and Anya, and the few others with names Lin couldn't recall, he'd grown to understand them better. Or at least understand the stance of the Council that governed them. By claiming to side with Ladrica when Lin and Denro met with the High Council, they were siding with history, siding with vows and oaths they'd made in the past. But all of that was moot now. If Ladrican forces had truly invaded Danica without a majority vote— the Accords were mutually broken.

Even with the Fall having happened. The Accords didn't hold the Dukes or Ferrucium in check the way it did Ladrica. Anya had explained it as a prisoner having little responsibility to upkeep the chain meant to bind them.

"Think any harder and you'll go cross-eyed," Denny whispered.

"I'm just worried about what comes next."

A war. A bloody affair likely full of soldiers outfitted like Royce. Even if the remnants of the Ferrucium had some kitted with whole armors, a force like what Ladrica could bear would cut through them like a scythe to the field. Not to mention any other members of the King's Noose.

"We could run. You, me, Mellyr. Not romantic or anything, but just get away. Hide out somewhere until it all resolves."

Lin looked over his shoulder at Anya who spoke with the captain, Leo not far from her side. It wasn't lost on him how similar her offer was to his back when Tylle had gotten her vengeance. But going to Ladrica, nearly losing Mellyr had taught him something. There was no more running. There couldn't be.

"We could." Lin's voice felt flat, hollow. He turned and looked first at his Bludwieve, then at hers. "Especially if we can remove these."

"I ran across the border, sort of against Erias's orders. Didn't feel a thing."

A shiver rolled down Lin's back. All that implied to him was that Erias wanted them both to go while having no actual hand in sending someone. He could argue innocence if things went poorly.

"I wouldn't press my luck with this sort of magic..."

"Just admit you're scared. Admit you wouldn't want to leave Tylle behind. Admit a hundred things that'll ease my mind even if it never touches my heart."

Above, under the clouds, birds soared on the wind. He'd give anything to be one of them right now, flying unfettered. "Denny. I've never felt more fear in my life. When I came to the tower with Mellyr, I thought I wanted to run from it all." Lin shook his head and took a deep breath. "But if I run, I can't protect Mellyr. I can't make sure she has a life worth living. Freedom isn't hiding in the woods and hoping a monster or soldier, sometimes the same, doesn't come for you. Freedom is knowing that I did everything I could to make the world just a bit safer for her."

"And if you die in the process?" Denny's voice was as soft as it ever got, like silk drawn across a tree trunk, catching and nearly tearing in the process.

"Then I die. And I just hope whatever Gods exist know that I did so trying to give Mellyr a better life. Give all the children of Danica a *better* life."

Denny sank into him entirely, not as a lover might, but how a child might squeeze a favored doll. Never had her touch, other than strikes, been so firm. Never had he thought to hear her cry the way she did. It was like she expected him to drop dead there on the deck any moment. After a long stretch, she relieved some of the pressure and looked up at him. "You're still the darkest shadow I've ever met, but I think I see the light that makes you. And it is so bright."

Lin sighed. No telling what the cracked woman meant, but he nodded all the same and squeezed her shoulder back.

***

A day later, the Tower and port of Fentis were all Lin could see. From the sea, the Tower was even more impressive than it had been the first time Lin saw it.

White stone, glittering as if the sea spray reached the slanted base of the building, rose twice as tall as the surrounding structures.

And the odd green, blue, glow of Bindings worked around the stone made it shine even brighter. Stasis, reversion, and healing? Perhaps Wievings to keep the Tower pristine despite its ancient status.

Docking took far longer than Lin expected, with linemen tethering the ship, setting anchors, and bringing the remnants of cargo up. All while a cloud of anxiety hovered over everyone. It was clear by the curt conversation, tense expressions, and nervous glances. Lin wasn't excluded from this and stood off to the side, near Kayle, Anya, and Mellyr. Denny was below deck, helping those set to pull Gritt off the ship. She'd taken a liking to the woman, watching over her when not with Lin.

Lined up along the dock were several white-robed scholars, and two of the midnight-robed High Scholars flanked by their guards. The streets behind them seemed empty, save for an occasional passerby. Odd considering the time of day, but perhaps this was some effort at security if Anya had sent word ahead as she claimed.

Leo stared up at the tower, mouth agape, and Lin couldn't blame him. It was funny that the first thing to wholly draw the young boy's attention from High Scholar Anya was the tower in which he was meant to reside.

Lin shuffled up beside Kayle. The scholar had created a sort of sarong from a cloak, much the way Lin had way back in Lyre, and Mellyr rested in it. She wasn't asleep and beamed up at Lin when he grew near, reaching for him.

"She is well."

"I know. Thank you." Resigning himself to letting the scholars watch her until he could care for her hadn't been easy. But it was a decision he'd made and one he needed to stand by. So, like with everything else, he tamped any worry and stress down deeper. All he could hope for was that the cracks he felt forming didn't worsen. Much like his decision to leave Nebra at Lyre with the Alderman, he wished that this would be for the best.

"All set, High Scholar." The captain, a stocky fellow with a beard as thick as his belly, waved a hand at the plank connecting the boat to the dock. It seemed sturdy enough and as Anya and Kayle began walking, so did Lin.

This wasn't a trap. He kept telling himself that as he walked from the ship to the docks, passed the placid faces of scholars, and onto the cobbled road that led through the port. Fish and shit. That's all he could smell after the many days of fresh ocean air. And despite the less hostile welcome, all he could taste was a hint of bile that refused to fade. Last he knew, not one person in that pristine tower wanted him left alive. Pael had killed a High Scholar and broken Lin free. Lin hadn't caused the chaotic scene that unfolded last he was here, but he had worsened it to those without the Sight.

"Lindel."

Lin froze.

Denro, robed in the silken whites of a junior scholar, pressed towards him. His hair had been shaved on all sides in the style of the scholars and his face had grown pale, though not sickly looking. Lin stared. A life indoors actually suited the man.

Words failed Lin. For some reason, he hadn't even considered that he might see Denro. High Scholar Anya stepped aside, nodded, and then, like a storm with no break, Denro was on him, almost bowling him over.

"I am so *proud* of you!" Denro's brow pressed into Lin's so much that he was sure when the older man pulled away his forehead would be flatter for the slim remainder of his life.

"W-what?" Lin managed. Tears stung his eyes and he grabbed the back of Denro's head, holding the man there so that he couldn't look up and see the pain on Lin's face.

Together they shuffled off the main path, the press of crew and those who'd been waiting threatening to knock them over.

"The High Scholar sent word right away. Your actions have given our people a chance. Bought us time."

One of the bells in the tower began ringing out over the port city, like a death knell for everything Lin had thought to accomplish when first chasing after Mellyr. "I didn't do anything," Lin said softly. "I meant to go in there and take Mellyr back by force… and I couldn't. I kept thinking about how… how it would fail you and Erias. Fail the people."

"So instead you saved who you could. Including the Ladrican King!" Denro laughed and twisted his neck to finally break free of the hold Lin had on him. "You should be happy."

Lin wiped his tears away and raised his chin, matching Denro's gaze.

"Happy?" Lin swallowed against the lump forming. He struggled to keep his voice low, but it was like it fought against him, refusing not to pitch upward. “Ladrican forces have likely already made landfall. All I potentially did was convince the Free Nations, those bastards who’ve watched and allowed us to be shackled for centuries, not to intervene. Which they likely already weren’t going to do!”

High Scholar Anya smiled at several of the men passing by with luggage and placed a hand on Lin’s shoulder. “Perhaps this is a discussion to have in the privacy of the tower?”

It was odd seeing Denro bow to her, but even though barely more than two weeks had passed since Lin left him, it seemed the man had already adjusted to the way of things within the Fentian Tower.

“Lin,” Denro said, falling in step behind Anya. “Walk alongside me. Please.”

Denro took his arm the way a mother might an unruly child’s. Lin glanced over his shoulder, spotting Denny and raising his chin at her. Her hand was full aiding Gritt, but she did the same. Kayle and Leo fell in line ahead of Denro. It was a funeral procession more than anything, especially as the city itself, normally bustling, seemed to be in mourning.

“Was Ladrica as cold as they say?” Denro asked.

Lin nodded.

“And Mellyr was wholly unharmed?”

Lin watched Leo’s heels. The boy walked a bit wonky, now that Lin studied him. “Mhm.”

“And King Lodram, was he as vile as many claim him to be?”

A sigh escaped Lin that felt like it had come from the darkest reaches of his heart.

"Really Lindel. What has gotten into you?" Denro hissed. "There was a time, not long ago, that I couldn't get you to stop talking. Now you sigh as if I pester you?"

Lin couldn't stop, not without interrupting the procession, so he continued forward, watching the occasional scuffing step of Leo's. "Normally… I wouldn't be able to keep to myself the strange and wonderful things I've seen. But Denro." It was like his throat had dried, any moisture in it seeping from his eyes instead. "I've seen terrible things. Untethered children. Untethered staked alive in the northern pass, hanging there, undying. Our people aren't loved or wanted. And worst of all I'm…" He trailed off shaking his head.

"If you mean to say you aren't loved or wanted, you're a larger fool than I would've assumed!" Denro snapped. As if the man had forgotten all the painful things he'd said to Lin just weeks ago. But that wasn't what hurt Lin now.

"No. I'm—" Putting it into words stung, but it was the truth. He knew it in the way he knew Velkath's Sigil didn't float around him for others to see. In the way that he'd been lost to thought for no good reason, or that he overused his spul knowing the consequence. "I'm untethering. I feel it. Like an itch just behind my eyeballs. Strand after strand of my resolve, slipping away."

"You've been under tremendous amounts of stress." A point to which Denro wasn't wrong. It was a miracle his hair hadn't grayed from his ordeals over the last months. But it was more than stress.

He'd cut that untethered over and over again, healing it and cutting it again, with so little remorse at the time. Only a monster could do that.

"My skin itches and grows gray," Lin said, sliding the sleeve of his cloak up to show the flaking, graying skin underneath.

"All Binders..." Denro cleared his throat. "All those capable of Danican Wieving, find that their skin might gray. It is not indicative of madness."

Lin nodded and stared up at the sky. "I hear his voice sometimes."

"Whose voice?" Denro asked.

"*His*," Lin hissed.

"Aemun's?"

Lin met Denro's worried look. "Yes. Reminding me that I'll never be half as clever as he was. That I've already failed Mellyr and will continue to do so."

Denro stepped in a touch closer, squeezing Lin's arm tighter. "Aemun was long dead before you settled on that name for her. Perhaps madness does touch you. If there is any place I'd want to be if I feared untethering, it would be here, among these people."

Everything in Lin's bones told him to pull away. To rip his arm free and run.

Cowardly Escorter.

"Early reports are calling you the Hero of Talm's Shadow," Anya said, not turning her head fully to look at Lin. "Those who know the range as Vellia's Fingers are calling you the Hero of the Fingers." The way her head rested, Lin could see her brow raise slightly as if silly names given by people meant anything.

"You just need to rest," Denro whispered. "The Scholars know you weren't responsible for High Scholar Dellis's death. You've come back a hero on *both* sides of the Accords. You haven't lost yourself. You found Mellyr. You should be proud of what you accomplished!"

Funny, how often others try to tell someone how they should feel. Lin sucked the side of his mouth and blinked away the tears. The problem was, he'd done so much tamping down of emotion that there was nowhere else for it to go. No room left in his heart. If his actions and symptoms didn't mark him as untethered, what would? What could prove to them that he needed help, that he was no longer himself? More importantly, why did he feel like he needed to prove his madness to them?

The silence that covered the rest of the procession like a shroud was only interrupted by the occasional tolling of a bell. Scattered few people were on the streets that had been overfull when Lin last walked them, but even so, this march took far longer than when he'd rushed through this area. Amid the shops and stalls were vestiges of nature. Planters with the blooming buds of near spring. Not nearly as grand or sweet-smelling as they'd be in a few months and far from the beauty of whole hills coated in the things, but a pleasant contrast against the white stonework.

Birds flew overhead, floating on winds that seemed far warmer than they had just days ago.

***

When Lin noticed night had fallen, he was drying his hair with a towel that scratched and pulled at his skin. He hadn't lit any candles and, at Lin's fervent request, there was no Wanderer's Ore to light the corners of the room. He pulled the towel away and even without looking, knew countless strands came with it.

With a sigh, he grabbed a brush and began working on the knotted mess that had once been his braids. Mellyr would be with Denro and Kayle. Tylle was Gods knew where. Dead maybe, if the Ladricans had attacked the Ferrucium as King Lodram claimed. But he'd also said the forces might've disembarked here at the Fentian port and that clearly hadn't happened.

Lin yanked a particularly stubborn knot and winced as his hair tore. He threw the brush, the ivory handle crashing and breaking against the wall. Like a taunting, twisting snake his Bludwieve mocked him in the dark. Crimson and glowing. Not the slightest bit warm despite the hue of fading embers.

He rose and walked to the large window, opening it and stepping onto the balcony. From this vantage, it felt like he could see the world. The port was alive now, though still a semblance of what it had been before Lin left. It seemed the city was having a sort of celebration.

Lin shivered against the wind and craned over the rail to see towards the north. Being on the western side of the tower gave him an unhindered view of the city and ocean beyond it. Darkness. All-encompassing.

"You'll catch a cold." Denny's voice carried from the room's main doorway.

As if that was his largest concern.

"I expected you'd be staying with Gritt, seeing as you convinced her to throw away her allegiance so easily," Lin said.

Denny barked out a laugh and slipped up behind Lin, steps as light as always. "You swayed her I think, not me. She barely said a string of words to me when she knocked me out. She had kind eyes though."

Oh. Now *that* seemed odd. He'd been sure Denny had convinced her to betray the king. Lin was pulled from his thoughts as Denny smacked his rear. Blush burned his cheeks at the realization he was nude and he grabbed the towel he'd carelessly tossed over the chair. "Stop that."

"Still sad to see you haven't magicked up your bottom bits. But... I just came to say goodbye. While these louts are relaxing, there is a war happening. By the time they reconvene to talk for peace, it'll be too late. I'm expecting you're staying with the child?"

Lin took a deep breath. "I've got a meeting with High Scholar Anya later tonight. Going to see if Gritt's Bludwieve can be undone." He didn't want to tell her the second part. He'd been weak when seeing Denro again. No one else needed to know he felt he was untethering. It would just make things harder if he eventually did. Wouldn't it? "After that... I'll join you. I decided... I can't protect Mellyr the way I need to if she's cradled in my arms. The scholars and Denro… they'll watch after her."

"You trust them?" Denny asked the question as she sidled up beside him, slipping into the space between his arm and side.

More than I trust myself at this point.

"Enough to know they aren't going to hurt her. I've seen how important she is to them."

"Should I wait for you then? We can leave together." She looked up at him, lines skewed and lopsided from the smile on her face. Her eyes glistened with the Stitches and possibly hope—an eagerness for acceptance.

Lin leaned in, and she snaked her arm up, grabbing his chin. She pulled him in and they kissed. He'd expected a ravenous, hungry kiss from her, but it was gentle, her lips as soft and silent as her steps. She pressed her hip into his side and he relished in the embrace. Denny angled her body to face him properly. But it felt wrong. There was too much to do. And she deserved someone not on the edge of untethering.

Pulling away was possibly the hardest thing he'd done in the last span, but he did, turning his back on her and reentering the main room. Her lips had tasted of wildflowers and her breath had a sour note of that Belesian drink Anya loved.

Lin found his linens and pulled them on reluctantly, his body arguing with his heart. He cleared his throat and wiped his eyes with the back of his hand. "Tell me where you'll be and I'll meet you. No telling how long this might take."

"Townsbridge."

"Thank you, Denny," Lin said. He stared out at the sea and the darkness around it. It looked nearly as dark as the now clean wound across his chest. The salve he'd rubbed on the injury smelled terrible and was as foul-looking as the seeping pus.

She left the room without looking at him, her head hung low.

Lin went to his pack and pulled free the sheath that held the broken dagger. He couldn't replace the book lost to the lake, but he recalled enough of it to start it again if he had a chance. And he planned to add notes about this strange material, and the fuller extent of Elodian magic he had learned. But first, he needed to survive what was to come.

So many months of wishing he could leave the place and get answers, and now that he had, part of him wished he had never left. Lin lingered, thinking of the kiss and how much of a fool he was. Denny deserved more and if the scholars could stall his untethering— stop it entirely even— he'd give her the life she seemed to want.

Lin exhaled, shut the door, and walked down to the dungeons.

A Crumbling Tapestry

"Leeching, as it was, used to be a common practice of removing tainted-blood from a person's being. This quickly revealed a side-effect though. If a person is too far gone towards that inevitable slope of madness, no amount of leeching will save them. And the leeches will die in the process." Records from the personal diary of Physiker Sichael.

Gritt looked peaceful despite the bulging veins of magic writhing just below her flesh. The thick threads of glowing red and green didn't move often, but as Lin pressed closer, they twitched.

High Scholar Yona stooped over the table, checking the leather straps on Gritt's arms before waddling to do the same to the ones around her ankles.

Run, fool.

Lin gritted his teeth and ignored Aemun's snide voice. Apparently, Anya had taken his claims of untethering seriously enough to offer a solution. One that she swore would delay the process long enough that he could aid in the coming war without fear of hurting those he loved.

"The blade?" Yona asked flatly. He took his time moving back to the side of the table where the raging Bludwieve was held in check by Lin's magic and held his hand out. The aging High Scholar, apparently a physiker long before joining the Fentian Scholars, seemed kind, if not overly personable. Perhaps a bit too serious for

Lin's tastes, but even Anya had been that way at first and still was in many respects.

Lin drew the broken dagger from its sheath, the jagged edge catching the light from the Wanderer's Ore across its many crevices.

Yona grunted and licked his thin lips, hand steady as he took the dark blade. "Nearly weightless. Amazing. Tighten the tourniquet."

Taking a step back so that the scholars could work was a decision he didn't make lightly. For some reason, even though she had been an enemy, Lin wanted to stay beside her. Partly for her, but more than any of that, for himself. If this worked, one nick and he'd be free of his own Bludwieve when it came time to remove it.

Then the physiker-turned-High Scholar set to his task while the junior scholars moved with towels, water, and other tools that Lin often saw organized among a physiker's toolkit.

Two smooth cuts and the meat of Gritt's arm lay visible, split from the nub at her wrist. As soon as the dagger touched her flesh, whatever magic had held in her stasis withered, like a root without water. The green strands didn't break into motes of light, as a traditional golden-hued Binding might, but turned into a powder-like ash.

Gritt screamed immediately, writhing against her restraints. Feral howls escaped her, pained and terrified.

Yona continued his work as the lesser scholars surrounded Gritt, adding their body weight to her limbs to aid the straps in keeping her still.

"It burns!" Gritt screamed.

And with her flesh peeled and blood stemmed, the crimson magic burned her. Writhing and twisting, the way a rope might tangle and tighten, cutting off circulation and causing burns along the raw muscle showing.

"Gods man, hurry!" Lin snapped.

Yona shook his head. "The magic... it has entangled her veins, see those small lines like roots? If I'm not cautious, irreparable damage could be done."

Lin paced, craning to see over the scholars' shoulders.

Gritt screamed until her voice went raw, howls turning into frightened sobs after a while. Then mercifully, she quieted. The light and anger and fight seemed to leave her eyes all at once.

"What happened?" Lin moved to the other side of the table, grabbing the woman's hand. Her palm was hot to the touch, but her digits were cold.

"I isolated..." Yona let one of the junior scholars dab the sweat from his wrinkled brow. "The Bludwieve. Sliced it."

Her chest barely moved, but it *did* move. And that meant she breathed. "She'll survive?"

"That is harder to say. We will document this. Stitch her up and monitor her for a time. Incredible, what this tool is capable of." Yona cleared his throat and pointed using the jagged tip of the dagger. "I believe you are next, no?" He nodded towards the unoccupied table.

Lin licked his lips thankful that whatever he was about to go through didn't involve the broken blade or his Bludwieve. Not until they had more time to see how Gritt recovered. If there was to be a war, he'd need his Inlays. "Yes."

The other scholars moved at Yona's command, gut threaded with the needle into Gritt quickly. It seemed all of the scholars down here with the aged High Scholar had aspirations to learn the art of physickry.

"Anya was clear that we should hold onto this, given the nature of the item and historical value."

Lin nodded, giving them what they wanted. Bending so as not to break. He'd survived this long without it. Barely even used it in combat. Besides, it seemed something better kept in a locked chest than out in the wide world. The very idea that Julius might've had it and gifted it to some random thug was absurd.

Yona took the sheath and slid the dagger back in, tucking the weapon into a pocket within the folds of his dark robes.

If anything, the dagger was the sort of thing he'd expect the Fentian Scholars to have squirreled away ages ago. Perhaps they had, only for Anya or someone else to gift it to Julius or Royce. The plot was as convoluted as any he could imagine, and less likely for it.

"Are you alright?" Yona's voice was low, and he'd rested a wrinkled, liver-spotted hand on Lin's shoulder.

No. Fairly far from alright. Lin nodded.

"Good, good. Remove your clothes. Except for your small clothes, those can stay. Then lay there while we prepare."

Doing so meant that his wounds, some blackened and raw looking, were visible to the few scholars who'd gone about preparing.

He caught more than one staring and held their gaze. Some of them seemed to have the Sight and could see his Inlays, or they just enjoyed his physique. But the latter was far less likely.

The table was cold as he lay on it. Forceps, a tray, and a glass jar filled with some sort of writhing black fluid were brought beside him.

"Straps," Yona ordered. An older man, still a junior scholar in his pristinely white robes, stepped forward hesitantly. The way his eyes lingered on Lin's arms and torso told him this man certainly had the Sight.

"No," Lin whispered.

Yona frowned. "Please. It is for our benefit more than yours. The process, while not as terrible as what you just witnessed, can still be painful to some with lower tolerances for that sort of thing."

Lin pulled his arm away from the junior scholar attempting to strap him in. "Do I look like I have a low tolerance for pain? Hmm. Was it my many scars or still-mending wounds that gave that impression?"

"Fair enough," Yona said.

The jar was opened and one by one, twenty or so squirming, dark leeches were placed on Lin. Mostly near the flesh where he had healed himself.

"And you're sure these leeches this will help?"

Yona laid his forceps down on the tray and shrugged. "Based on what we've seen during tests..." he paused as if weighing how to say the next part. He shook his head and slowly continued. "There is a high likelihood that leeches draw out the essence of madness that inflicts itself on untethered. If you are truly suffering, or beginning to suffer as those addled-minded individuals do, this can likely only help."

"Alright." Lin shifted, easing himself flat. All he needed was a little bit of time. Tylle had wanted him to handle the untethered problem, but he'd needed to rescue Mellyr. Now she was safe. Or more safe than she'd been before the rescue.

"I'll come check on you later. Sit with these until the sun rises and then we will remove them."

Lin nodded as the High Scholar left, taking three of the seven junior scholars with him. The other four attended to Gritt, casting wary glances his way every so often. Eventually, he stopped watching them altogether.

His mind raced as he stared up at the ceiling. It felt like a sort of fog was lifting in painstakingly slow increments. When he glanced around the room, there were no floating remnants of Velkath's Sigil. No insidious whispers. Just him, his pain, and the quietness of a room meant for healing and rest.

Denny would be waiting for him at Townsbridge. Then he'd meet with Erias's forces, help to push back the Ladricans until the time that the council might reconvene, deal with the untethered problem, and spend what time he had left of his life taking care of Mellyr. Sleep eventually took him and images of Tylle flashed through his dreams. Her lips moved as if she were trying to tell him something. Another parable, or tale, or history. But all the tales had been told, and all the histories repeated. He missed her and felt a pang of guilt as his mind drifted to Denny and her crooked smile. She'd come for him and saved him. They'd saved each other, in some ways. The last thing he dreamt of was her gentle kiss, no less hungry for the softness of her lips.

Sunrise came sooner than Lin expected, the light breaking through the small, square windows near the top of the wall. Gritt rested on her table and scholars passing between Lin and the windows broke the rays of the sun.

"She lives... in case you were curious. Though her state is still being determined."

Lin blinked away the sleep and took in a deep breath. Wounds that would have ached at those same motions not a day ago felt calmed. Not gone, but more than eased. As Lin adjusted where he lay, dried bits that looked similar to shriveled grape skins fell away like leaves falling from a tree. The leeches dead from the blood-letting.

As if stepping from the shadows, High Scholar Anya appeared at his side. Her expression was grim, but she appeared as rested as Lin felt.

"Spending your free time lurking in the shadows?" Lin asked. He swung his legs free of the table and made to grab at the clothes he'd shed the night before. Folded neatly beside him.

"Lin. Perhaps going isn't your *best* choice." Her voice shook and something about the way it trembled just slightly rattled Lin.

Shirt half over his head, he froze. "Why?"

"Contact with your blood poisoned the leeches." Anya's hand swung to the dried bits of debris that had fallen from Lin's chest.

"Oh." For some reason, he'd expected something worse. Like Mellyr's safety or… "What does that mean for my concerns?"

"At this point, you've likely noticed a few things. Hallucinations. A lack of scent on occasion. It comes from a variety of things but I do not doubt that your assumption was correct." She hovered like she planned to take a seat beside him. But they weren't on the ship in close quarters, and here, among impressionable junior scholars, she likely wouldn't debase herself.

"I'm untethering," Lin whispered, pulling his shirt the rest of the way on. He'd felt like he was. Claimed that he was. But there had been a hope somewhere down among all that tamped down emotion and pain that he was wrong. There was so much about Wieving and the magic that he didn't understand. Why should untethering be any different?

The table complained as she settled onto it beside him. "I know what you plan to do is important. But if you… if you can get back to us soon and Bind as little as possible, there might be hope." Anya's grip was firm as she grabbed his hand and squeezed. "You're the Hero of Vellia's fucking Fingers. But I worry that what you're setting out to do can't be resolved with words. It won't be bloodless."

Lin enjoyed seeing the junior scholars' looks of surprise at Anya swearing. And he grunted, changing the subject. "Seems the dagger worked on the Bludwieve's hold on her."

"Seems it did."

"Have you tried it on the letter Aemun left?"

"Of course," Anya chuckled.

"And?" Lin asked, pulling his hand away and rising to his feet. While Anya's kindness was unexpected and appreciated, it wasn't what he wanted. He needed to move before flame took light to the kindling of his bruised heart and burned away all his hope with it.

"You few, leave us for a moment." Anya rose and paced over to Gritt as the junior scholars left the room. She looked down at the sleeping Nooseman, expression unreadable. The door clicked shut and after several breaths, she said, "It worked. Instructions for Mellyr's care, should he die. Which, it seems he expected."

"He expected to die?" Lin slipped one leg into his trousers, then the other. From what he knew of Aemun, that didn't make sense. He'd have had to send it from Wellgrove, or perhaps even before that. Lin shuddered as he tightened the trousers around his waist. At least he didn't have to hear the man's ghost whispering into his ear.

"I understand your surprise. It seemed by the time he Sealed and sent that letter, he expected some terrible fate to befall him."

"And there wasn't anything else?" Lin asked.

Anya frowned and shrugged. "If I say there wasn't, would you believe me?"

Lin chuckled. "Trust is a tenuous thing."

"He confirmed what was long speculated. They have the blood of the man known as Cunning Velkath in their blood. Which so far as we can tell, means little as far as Danican prowess. But..." Her voice trailed off as she stared at Lin's face.

"But?"

"But he warned that Danicans would never be free under the heel of any king, horned or fanged."

"What?" Lin said.

Anya shrugged. "A riddle behind a lock. Ladrica's coat of arms is the serpent. But the horns? I'm at a loss."

There was something she wasn't telling him, and the way her lips pursed she likely wouldn't. Lin shuddered, trying to recall the way the Fall happened at the end with Aemun. As clever and manipulative as the man was, there was no way he'd planned for things to work out the way they had.

Seeing his reaction Anya lowered her head a bit. "He wanted eyes on the Accords, but I truly don't think he expected such a fierce reaction from you and Erias's people. Be that for the better or ill of it. I don't know. If you insist on leaving, your pack is outside the door. Let us hope that King Lodram has better sense than Aemun did, there at the end. I'd like you to come back."

Lin forced a smile. "We can't rewrite the tome I lost if I don't."

"Precisely." Anya nodded and hesitantly moved aside. "Please be careful."

"Of course," Lin said.

Definitely Not A Secret

!You Found A Secret!

Okay, clearly this isn't a sword hidden behind a waterfall or a chest stashed on the other side of a hollow wall, but you've made it to the Secret Scribes page! The Secret Scribes are an affiliation of independent fantasy authors who write varying subgenres of fantasy. If you've enjoyed this book, please check out some other great authors and their titles below.

Alex Schueuermann- The Odyllic Stone

Bella Dunn- The Dreams Thief

Bill Adams- The Godsblood Tradgedy, The Tenacious Tale of Tanna the Tendersword

Damien Francis- The Tome of Haren

Dave Lawson- The Envoys of War

E.H. Bradley- The Ranger

L.M. Douglas- Gharantia's Guardian, Gharantia's Fury

L.N. Bayen- The Wingspan of Treason

R. A. Sandpiper- A Pocket of Lies, A Promise of Blood

R. E. Sanders- Demon's Tear, A Path of Blades, Tann's Last Stand

Sean O'Boyle- The Ballad of Sprikit The Bard(And Company)

And more titles to come!

About the author

After a drunken game of D&D Greg DM'd ended rather splendidly, his closest friends told him he needed to write stories. A hobby that had always burned fiercely in his heart but that he set aside to handle the various hurdles of life. Greg took passion to pen (so to speak), and after many trials, errors, and learning spurts, he finally finished his first novel. When he's not writing, he's spending time with his amazingly supportive wife, playing pickleball or video games, and, of course, reading. Joe Abercrombie is one of his largest modern inspirations, and he wouldn't have started writing if not for the many amazing worlds created by so many other talented authors.

Other works:

Stones, Stars and the Storms Between

The Binding Tenets Trilogy:

Bitter Ends- Prequel Novella

Bloodwoven- Book One

Printed in Dunstable, United Kingdom

74957210R00238

QUASI UNA ROMANZA

De Sandwich-reeks
Onder redactie van Gerrit Komrij

Nr. 1 Philip Hoorne
Nr. 2 De drekpoëten
Nr. 3 Bas Belleman
Nr. 4 O.C.F. Hoffham
Nr. 5 Abdelkader Benali
Nr. 6 Eli Scheen
Nr. 7 Erik Solvanger
Nr. 8 Didymus
Nr. 9 Danny Degenaar
Nr. 10 Peter M. Heringa

Peter M. Heringa

Quasi una romanza

Uitgeverij 521 · Amsterdam · 2005

De Sandwich-reeks wordt in opdracht van Uitgeverij 521 gezet uit de
Dolly en gedrukt door Drukkerij Giethoorn Ten Brink te Meppel.
Het bindwerk wordt verricht door Boekbinderij Callenbach te Nijkerk.
De vormgeving is in handen van Steven van der Gaauw.

ISBN 90 76927 38 3 / NUR 306

Voor meer informatie: www.uitgeverij521.nl

INHOUD

Je kunt jezelf liefdevol laten begraven in mooie bundels met tweecijferige oplagen. Of even te voorschijn treden in vluchtig drukwerk. Of uitsluitend onder pseudoniemen schrijven. Peter Leberecht. H.G. Liebentrau. Bibliofilie en literaire tijdschriften, dat zet geen zoden aan de dijk. Peter Heringa (1945-1987) leek gedoemd tot dat gesloten circuit. Toen in 2001 zijn verzamelde gedichten verschenen was dat ook weer in een beeldschone, kostbare, zeldzame editie.

Het gesloten circuit was in zekere zin de wens van Peter Heringa zelf. De agorafobie van een argwanende gelukzoeker.

Peter Heringa gooide zijn netten wijd uit. Zijn werk telt 268 gedichten en vertalingen. Toch bleef het bij intieme stemmen – *Voces Intimae* luidt de titel van zijn door Ernst Braches verzorgde en door Ger Kleis getypografeerde verzamelde gedichten.

Ger Kleis schrijft in zijn begeleidende woorden over Peter Heringa: ‘Hij voelde zich verwant aan Faverey en Ouwens’. Nu valt er van die dichters weinig terug te vinden. Ik zie Kees Ouwens niet snel een vers met enkel e’s schrijven, en aan Faverey doet alleen de precisie in vastpin- en vluchttechnieken denken.

Eerder herinnert het werk van Peter Heringa me aan het torso van Johannes Baargeld – een dada-kunstwerk opgebouwd uit de Venus van Milo (midden), de kop van de dichter met generaalspet (boven) en een soort biljartlaken (onder). Eros en Mars. Oud en nieuw. En het spel. Heterogene elementen, door de kunst bijeen gehouden.

Eerder ook vallen bij Peter Heringa de maniëristische elementen op, vermengd met brokken uit de moderne klassieken. Zijn werk vormt een heelal van verwijzingen en dichtersnamen en plaatsnamen en klankwoorden. Een amalgaam, een kruispunt, een labyrint (drie heel verschillende manieren) van teksten, auteurs, muziek, klassieken, reisdoelen – alles wat Peter Heringa in zijn culturele bagage koesterde. Een vuilniszak met systeem. De associaties wellen op en je ziet de dichter er met de hand naar grijpen. Vlinders op de vlucht, verzonken cultuurgoed.

Twee keren had ik uitgebreider contact met Peter Heringa. De eerste keer was in een louche café in de Halvemaanssteeg in Amsterdam en de tweede keer in het schildersatelier van Wim Schuhmacher, twee werelden die eindeloos van elkaar leken te verschillen. Het is typerend voor de mix.

Deze werelden hoefden niet verzoend te worden, ze vielen al samen. Peter Heringa had behoefte aan frivoliteit en vrijbuiterij. Hij wilde de bagage van het intellect zo licht mogelijk dragen. Tegelijk kreeg je de indruk dat hij die lichtheid en frivoliteit zo ernstig mogelijk opnam, haast of ze al ernst waren.

's Anderendaags – 't is zonde dat je 't zegt
kun je al niet meer zitten van de pret.
Mooi dat je ziel verguld zich herwaarts rept

lezen we in *Vrijstaat*. Ironie is een zaak die je niet serieus genoeg kunt nemen.

De ironie vormt voor Peter Heringa een dwangmatige tegenmaatregel. Het regent als het ware zinnen als *Adieu, ik moet er weer een keer vandoor* als het hem te heet onder voeten dreigt te worden.

Een dichter was hij van de opsluiting en de wanhoop. De man van het ingeperkte, het claustrum. De Vrijstaat van zijn eigen kerker. Het Oranje hoefde er niet eens bij. Het was vanzelf eerder het oranje van het kunstlicht dan van de buitenlucht en de ondergaande zon. Een vrijstaat, kón er wel bevrijding zijn van wanhoop?

Ik ben de draad kwijt in dit labyrint
En als ik de gedroomde uitweg vind,
zouden we eindelijk naar huis toe mogen?

Ook in het Algarve-gedicht *Xadrez* lezen we hoe de dichter zich moed inspreekt –

De zon verzekert je van je bestaan

maar het loopt voor de zoveelste keer uit op falen en gedoemd zijn –

De zon brandde zijn zegel in mijn rug

– ook de vliegen zijn dan niet ver meer. Dood en verderf loeren om de hoek. *De delvers waren vrolijk aan het werk* luidt het in een gedicht verderop.

Een 'gedroomde uitweg', misschien de gedroomde uitweg bij uitstek, moet voor Peter Heringa de poëzie zijn geweest. Meteen is daar als reflex de twijfel van de pootje-hakende dichter weer. Poëzie, schrijft hij,

Wat is me dat nu weer voor kippedrift?
Alsof er iemand op mijn verzen wacht.

Nog even en ik scheur de boel kapot.

De noodkreet van iemand voor wie poëzie grondslag en vangnet vormt.

Een makkelijk leven moet het niet zijn geweest, de aardse dagen van Peter Heringa. Begrijpelijk dat hij Blas de Otero heeft vertaald, en zó heeft vertaald dat het gloednieuw klinkt –

Hij wil graag blijven. Nog maar verder voortgaan,
Het eeuwige tegen de dood behalen.
Hij waagt het niet te zien. Hij sluit de ogen
Om maar de slaap der levenden te slapen.

Terwijl de dood van binnenuit al toekijkt.
Terwijl de dood van binnenuit al afwacht.
Terwijl de dood van binnenuit al toeslaat.

Lamento, orde – de lievelingswoorden van een dichter die er zich enkel bij heeft neergelegd dat hij er zich niet bij heeft neergelegd. Een complex gevoel dat vogelvlucht en gevangenschap in zich verenigt. In de kooi, de ordening, de eenheid die poëzie biedt.

Wonderlijk, de moeheid en hopeloosheid die Peter Heringa telkens moet toegeven en tegelijk dat fijngeslepen werk, waarachter we de grootste aandachtigheid en inspanning kunnen vermoeden. Alles streeft naar vorm. De kop wordt keer op keer tegen de muur gebeukt maar het loopt niet uit op een vormeloze brij; het resultaat is scherpte, precisie van woord en klank, ondubbelzinnigheid van beeld.

Focus.

Ook het onverfijnde eindigt in verfijning.

De poëzie vomt het enige letterlabyrint waarin deze woelgeest een weg kon vinden. De poëzie is zelf het vlindernet dat de dichter vangt of, om het met zijn eigen woorden te zeggen

Sommige woorden liggen toegedekt.
Sommige woorden draaien zich eens om.
Sommige woorden willen niet gewekt.
Sommige woorden zien met spijt het licht.
Sommige woorden spreken in een beeld
waar je geen weet van hebt totdat je merkt
wat in het signatuur zich heeft verheeld.

De verborgenheid wordt gedicht en blijft in het gedicht verborgen. Dat is geen reden om de gedichten weer te verbergen.

HET BESLUIT

Vijf jaar geleden, op een dag als deze,
ging ik een keer uit wandelen met E.
Wat nu. Ik was nog niet verliefd geweest.

We lagen in het gras zonder te praten.
Wat nu. Ik had nog niemand aangeraakt.

Met wat omhelzingen was het bekeken.
E. kreeg de zenuwen. (Afrukken homaar.)

Ik wandelde voortaan wel weer alleen.

Tien jaar alweer. Ik ben er nog niet uit.

Al twintig jaar. Nu is het wel genoeg.

Kerel! (Jou krijg ik nog, mooi stuk verdriet
in je net pak.) Thans gaan wij over tot
de Tweede Annexatie van de Vrijstaat.

Bij oudoom Van de Wereld hing een prent
van Donkerpoort, oker en ros gehoogd.
De zoon van Rust-en-Vrede gaat zijns weegs.

Mooi weer ligt klaar voorbij de Helderberg.
Motor met zijspan voegt zich in het plan.
De eerste ordonnans weet nog van niets.

Springfontein met de dauw. Brandfort geloogd.
Edenville in verharsend middaglicht.
Heilbron, Vereeniging. We komen er.

Voortrekkershemd, smerige kaki shorts.
Je hemd valt verder open, langs je borst
lekt een zout spoor dat ik traag volg omlaag.

DE TOEGANG TOT HOTEL ARCADIA

Hoe kom ik aan de bak?
                                        Wat staat me daar.
Geen sjoege van die knaap. Een vrijer binnen,
of wat? Het is al laat. Kom bij de baas.

Onder z'n leren jek heeft hij niets aan.
Eerst maar in z'n stug borsthaar rondgewoeld.
Niet zo'n gladakker als Sebastiaan.
Hij zucht al heel gedienstig. Stel je voor

hoe, liefdevol vernederd en vertrapt,
hij half gekeeld zwicht tot bekentenis
in een of ander hortend idioom.
De simpelste bewoordingen volstaan.

Ik heb de juiste toon nog niet te pakken.
Daglicht komt aangedreven. Door zijn haar
strijkt ochtendwind.
                                    Zijn ogen staan op ver.

ALLESVERLOREN IN HET LEGE DAL

Van wensen en verwachtingen ontving
Eén ogenblik het oude hemelvuur.

Nu wist ik niet meer waar het over ging.
Onweer van zeven kanten tegelijk.
Natuurlijk was dit het voorziene uur.

Eer we de klaarheid van het eigen rijk
Verlieten, sloeg de regen op ons neer.
Of dat begreep ik even later al.

Een harde wijn moet nog wat open staan.

Eerst nu ken ik mijn desolaat verweer.

Een laatste glas om weer naar Af te gaan.

A PHOENIX TOO INFREQUENT

In de spelonken van een boze dronk
is hij de vogel van zijn laatste drang,
die neerstreek op een hoegenaamd plateau
waar alles weer van jongs af aan begon.

Hij wist niet beter of dat ging maar zó.

De lucht was door een offervuur verpest.
Het werd me een gefladder van belang.

Hij merkte wel dat hij niet vliegen kon.
Purperen sukkel op vergulde stang.

Hij ligt nog steeds te ronken in z'n nest.
Een dienaar van de schitterende zon.

In de gordijnen klauwt een vroege vonk.

XADREZ

Algarve. Een appartement voor één.
Kleur van de zee die in de folder scheen.

De zon verzekert je van je bestaan.
In hemdsmouwen uit wandelen gegaan.

Een heuvel op. Het leek wel de Transvaal.
Rood, blauw en geel in bloei van lichte taal.

Mijn kiemen stonden al een tijdje droog.
De top die ik bereikte was niet hoog.

Ik liep weer naar de grote weg terug.
De zon brandde zijn zegel in mijn rug.

Een stukgereden kat lag aan de kant.
Er waren nog geen vliegen bij de hand.

CAMPA

Ik trachtte jou te bellen, in de cel
die je een uitzicht op het kerkhof biedt.
De zon brak door. De stenen blonken wit.
Cypressen. De verbinding lukte niet.
Het ijzer van het hek ontsloot zich wel.

De kindergrafjes liggen hier apart.
Er waren een paar ééndagsvliegen bij.
Geen omber foto's in een blikken rand.
Ik struikelde over zo'n klein karwei
en maakte rechtsomkeert, obscuur verward.

Bloemen, meest namaak, alle kleuren, zerk
na zerk. Ik las de woorden hier en daar.
A Very Special Man, heb ik zien staan.
Begraven, lijkt me, zonder rouwmisbaar.
De delvers waren vrolijk aan het werk.

SÉJOUR TE RIVA

I

De bordjes volgend kwamen we pardoes
te staan voor het gezochte heldergeel
hotel O Sole Mio aan de rand
van het bijzonder goedgeslaagde meer.
Wat waren we gelukkig aangeland.
Alle gemakken vielen ons ten deel. –
Onder het personeel was veel gesmoes.

II

We hielden rust en werden prachtig bruin
en lazen tot verblindens in het werk
van edele poëten in exil.
Fluisterend vroeg zo af en toe de baas
of ons de kamer en het zicht beviel.
Dat er iets mis kon wezen leek me sterk. –
Was dit een ordinaire kieteltuin?

III

De spijslijst had ons aangenaam verrast.
De bedden waren ruim en niet te zacht.
We kregen steeds vers brood aan het ontbijt.
Maar als je zuiver naar de dienster keek
wist je: de duivel doet het met die meid.
We hoorden krijsen op een goede nacht.
Je hart stond stil. We zijn meteen verkast.

FERMATE – PETERSKLIP

I

Er zit iets mathematisch in mijn hoofd
op deze nadag dat ik niet meer dans.
Het lijkt me, als ik mijn gevoel vertrouw,
aan de gedachtenis van Maarschalk Smuts.
Hij werd daar nog vereerd, zei Boeti Louw
in Lutzville; en er is een kleine kans
dat alles op zijn plaats valt; als beloofd.

II

Deze beroerdheid komt me slecht van pas.
De aderen staan loodblauw op mijn arm.
Ik lig te simmen als een idioot
en wou zo graag nog één̈s naar Vredendal
wanneer de tovenaar een wijsje floot.
Het hoge veld is nu misschien te warm.
Kon ik maar scherper zien wie ik toen was.

III

Wat dacht u van de macht van het getal?
Verstoor de rustplaats van de dichter niet.
Leipoldt is onbarmhartig bijgezet
onder de rotsen, en in eenzaamheid,
maar naar zijn eigen welgeschreven wet.
Ik kwam voorbij in dat verweerd gebied.
Een derde dichter memoreert: Dis al.

UITSPANNING VAN DER AA

Eéns gaan we er vandoor
alsof het was beschikt
en vieren dagje uit.
Ik ben de jonge guit.
Hoe mijn consumptie blinkt
in glas dat licht weerklinkt
nu het wordt aangetikt.
Ik breng het naar je oor.

Zeg maar de Drentsche Aa
die zich met groen vervlecht.
Oeverloos wil de vliet
zich reppen in het niet
voorziene perspectief.
Ik heb je zeker lief.
De bedding wordt verlegd.
Je zei daar meen ik ja.

Ik doezel maar en droom
voor de gelegenheid.
Bezoek De Ferme Slok
(waar ik je prompt verlok).
Bezopen schuinespuit,
je scheurt je rits nog uit.
Nu wordt het onze tijd.
De wijzer draait in chroom.

QUASI UNA ROMANZA

Hoe zal ik je ontmoeten
Mijn liefde en mijn leven

Op aarzelende voeten
Terwijl mijn handen beven

Maar jij vertrouwt het zoete
Gestreel en rilt heel even

*

Hoe zal ik je ontvangen
In minder hoge sferen

Met mijn bezeerd verlangen
Wil ik je toch niet deren

Ik haal je met mijn bange
Vermoedens uit je kleren

*

Hoe zal ik je betasten
Voor ik het heb verkorven

De vrijers van mijn kaste
Zijn enigszins bedorven

De wormen mogen vasten
Mijn lijf is onverworven

STILTE GEBODEN. DAT SUBLIEM GEWELF
is Allerzielen voor een mooie keer.
De weerglans op de overkant verstaat
zich met een licht dat ooit is aangedaan. –
Het is misschien nog altijd niet te laat
voor een gebedje tot de lieve heer.

De inspiratie komt ook niet vanzelf.

MAAR NOOIT MEER VAN EEN SUKKELENDE GOD.
Ik denk aan immanente levenskracht
en regels die in stenen zijn gegrift
opdat ze gelden voor het nageslacht. –
Wat is me dat nu weer voor kippedrift?
Alsof er iemand op mijn verzen wacht.

Nog even en ik scheur de boel kapot.

VAARWEL U HULPELOZE POËZIE.
Vaarwel bitter bevrijdende muziek.
Vaarwel wereld genadeloos verbeeld.

Vaarwel bijna verlaten schemerwoud.

Vaarwel, Étienne, als je nog bestaat;
vaarwel, mio caro, nobel kunstenaar;
vaarwel, jij nooit gesuste babetjie.

SKYE

Dit landschap is geen werk van god.
Ik leef ook niet naar zijn gebod.
Van kinds af was de regelmaat
Gebarsten. Vrijheid is een psalm
Tegen elk beter weten in.
Het wakker worden is een kunst.
Nee, goud uit Ofir is het niet.

In d-mineur

Ik ben de jongen die jou nakeek, toen.
De man die nog geen haartje wijzer is.
De demon van het zwarte notenbeeld.
De dromer zonder reden van bestaan.
De dreumes die z'n grote broertje zocht.
De duvel uit een doosje van fluweel.
De dief van je verleden en je lijf.
De dwaas die onbeschaamd heeft liefgehad.
De dervisj dansend buiten het gareel.
De drinker die een bende heeft gemaakt.
De dutter die de tijd voorbij liet gaan.
De djinn die nog een keer verschijnen wil.
De domoor die geen deficit aanvaardt.
De dichter die er niets meer aan kan doen.

STACCATO OP EEN THEMA VAN MONTALE

Ik merk: het daagt.
Oudzilver licht.
Weerkeer van zon.
Alles is stil.

Waartoe? Ik denk
Aan de magie
Die zich vertoont.
Ik zal. Ik zal –

Sneeuw, ongerept.
Weefsel van licht
Onzichtbaar in
Een blij gedicht.

Tekens in zwart:
Nieuw alfabet.
Verleden tijd
Weer ingeprent.

Niet één gerucht. –
Een maartse haan
Danst op de lucht,
Strijkt ergens neer.

ALS IK MIJN STEENTJES OVER WATER KEIL
rimpelt er iets en waaiert het weer uit.
Dan wordt mij dat een afgemeten spel.
Ze scheren lichtjes langs het oppervlak,
halen de oever niet, ik weet het wel,
plonzen en zinken met een zwak geluid.
Wat gaf ik voor een lied in grote stijl.

IK HEB GESCHREVEN ALS EEN RAZENDE
om toch vooral niet dood te hoeven gaan.
Dan viste ik maar weer een envelop
waarin godweetwat voor offerte stak
uit de misère van de scheurmand op
en krabbelde weer voort in mijn bestaan.
De regels vormen het verbazende.

NAAR ALBUFEIRA

Als alles meezit eindig ik verstild
en dof als een mesjokke Portegies
en kijk mijn laatste mooie dagen uit
op de banaal aankabbelende zee.
Wat hoor ik daar nu voor een ijl gefluit?
Is het de luchtmacht of gehoorverlies?
Of ben ik door het reisbureau getild?

Laat me vandaag nog eventjes met rust
na het gejammer en gesakker, en
het allesoverstemmende gekreun.
Dit Benedictus uit een requiem
is hedenochtend een geslaagde deun.
Het resoneert als ik vertrokken ben;
neerliggend aan een onbewolkte kust.

Mooie meneren laten me steenkoud.
Ongure plaatjes winden me niet op.
De vriend van al die tijd is aan z’n end.
Rouwranden aan mijn vingers. – Geen gezeur.
Ik ben wel ziek en murw maar ook verwend.
Hoog tijd dat ik met dit geklungel stop
en tot een beter wezen mij verstout.

SOMMIGE WOORDEN LIGGEN TOEGEDEKT.
Sommige woorden draaien zich eens om.
Sommige woorden willen niet gewekt.
Sommige woorden zien met spijt het licht.
Sommige woorden spreken in een beeld
waar je geen weet van hebt totdat je merkt
wat in het signatuur zich heeft verheeld.

EN TOEN BESPEURDE IK DIE LIGATUUR
waar een idee opstijgt en transformeert.
Iedere boosheid was nu afgewend.

LAST ROSE

Veel te vroeg wakker, en in 's hemelsnaam
maar opgestaan. Het eerste licht breekt door.
Zes uur. Dit is het absoluut moment.

Een waas van nevel zweeft over de gracht.
Twee zwanen drijven binnen, op de wijs
van een verdwaald rondeau... Haet ende Nijt...

Hoe wou je dat ik in een vers herrees?
De buitenwerkelijke herfst verstikt
de gensters van het eindigende vuur.

Dat bolwerk pro memorie doet me deugd.
Een vorig leven ben ik weer op school.
Een stad komt vrij. – Daar las ik af en toe

een uurtje in het Faliezusterspark.
The Catcher in the Rye; maar half begrepen.
Nog altijd beter dan de godsdienstles

waarin ik me onttrok. – Realiteit
klonk je aaneen, drong langzaam tot me door.
Een dergelijk traject werd mijn bestaan.

Absentie. Midden winter. Eerste uur.
«schoon rood, schoon groots rood komt over Maastricht.»
Hevig bedacht en schokkend geritmeerd.

Ik heb de hoogste klas niet afgemaakt.
Wij zijn gestorven, en de cijferlijst
van mijn examen is niet meer van kracht.

Iedere orde die je onderkent
gaat in de wereld buiten je teloor.
Het daagt aan gene zijde van het raam.

ÉBAUCHE

Hoor hoe de echo met ons meegaat, hoor!

Onder de loden lucht schrijf ik mijn spoor
in sneeuw naar niets of niemand in het zicht,
en vier het feest van deze harmonie –
met een hoogst onbetrouwbare tenor
vind ik de inzet van de melodie
die toevalt aan mijn sprakeloos gedicht.
Een alleluia voor geen mensenoor.

Adieu, ik moet er weer een keer vandoor.

IK HEB ME IN MIJN LEVEN VAAK VERGIST.
Ik heb ook veel te grenzeloos verlangd.
Ik heb me heel de wereld maar verbeeld.

Amechtig zwalkend naar het paradijs.

De tuin waar een tak groen je spelend streelt.
De tuin die in een schaduwrijk ontvangt.
De tuin waar eigenheid wordt uitgewist.

POSTHUUM

Ik heb het jullie vrienden wel gemeld:
het gaat niet goed, het gaat beslist niet goed.
Maar niettemin hou ik de moed er in.
Het sterven hopelijk een snelle zaak.
Dan ben ik weer terug bij het begin
en glijd er onderuit; met goede moed. –
Mijn dagen zijn nu werkelijk geteld.

FERNANDO, HET KOMT EERDER DAN JE DACHT,
de ziekte van het menselijk bestaan.
Nóg klinken stalen snaren zijlings mee
en raakt een overblijver aangedaan,
want niets had hij gehoopt, en niets verwacht.

HET IS VERWONDERLIJK, NU AAN HET END,
hoe ik geluk met mensen heb gehad.
Mijn dankbaarheid is hoop ik uitgedrukt
in wat gedichten toch niet misverstaan.
Ik wil dat ik nog even overleef
in woorden die ik zelf niet eens begrijp,
al staat er niets van in een testament.

VERZWIJGEN? SPREKEN? ERNST, IK WEET HET NIET
rond middernacht. Zonodig, ook Der Welt
abhanden. Maar dat houd je wel tegoed.

Ik heb het nog niet af, het doodsbericht.
Het wordt ook nooit geschreven want ik denk
dat niemand lezen mag wat ik geloof.

Verwarring dat je nergens thuis kon zijn.
Een tweede keer naar Schotland ging niet meer.
Nu spreek ik met een levende, verstrikt

in machinaties van een zuiderlicht.
Hoe krijg ik dit bijeen met vlijt en ernst,
rond middernacht? Alweer de kleine terts

van deze drie aan Kaap De Goede Hoop.

SANS TITRE

De camera moet worden ingesteld
want anders komen er geen foto's van.
Ik ben afhankelijk van anderen.

Was ik nog maar afhankelijk van jou.

De laatste zomer dat ik foto's kon
maken waren de dagen al geteld.
Je naakte lichaam is nog vastgesteld.

CROÛTE

Veel doodgaan is een bloederige zaak
of eindigt in gekreun en in gehijg.
Jij lag in eigen huis, kalm, naakt en zat.

Of had je een vuil onderbroekje aan?

Dacht je nog in dat laatste ogenblik?
Aan vliegenier zijn? Aan op aarde zijn?
Aan bloei van afrikaantjes op het plat?

HET ONUITWISBARE

I

De Denen zijn het meest beschaafde volk.
Bevrijdingsdag en ik herinner me
dat Christiaan uitreed met een gele ster.
Het kan een fabel wezen, als zoveel.
Maar ik geloof, vandaag, in Denen die
hebben gedaan wat hier niet is gebeurd.
Vandaag hangt over Amsterdam een wolk.

II

Een Joodse burgemeester redt de schijn
dat we zo goed geweest zijn. Nee, ik pis erop.
Hoeveel zijn er verdwenen? Tel eens op?
De sinaasappeljoden zijn vergast.
Die hadden immers maar een schijntje geld.
Ze zijn door Nederlanders afgevoerd.
Vertel me niet dat we zo keurig zijn.

III

Die honderdduizend komen niet terug.
Ze waren niet voor Barneveld bestemd.
Die venters waren er niet thuis geweest.
Hoe werd je ook een erejood gemaakt?
Door geld, met geld, door geld, zo deed je dat.
Nu weet je dat er op bevrijdingsdag
niets valt te vieren. Vreugde keert de rug.

BEEKBERGEN IS BEPAALD EEN IRONIE.
Ik kwam uit Beek, en bergen zijn daar niet.
De tijd die ik er doorbracht was de geur
van natgeregend hout, en ook de kaart
van Nederland waarmee ik speelde want
onzegbare verveling was mijn deel.
Rotzomer lijkt me ook aansprakelijk.

HERDENKING VAN PK

Herfst van getrouwe bomen, in de zon
minutieus verguld, kalligrafeert
een arabesque van het stralenrijk.

Hij wordt beambte van het gulden licht.
Zijn knopen zijn ordeversierselen.
De inspiratie lijkt wel officieel.

Zijn wezen vlucht, in curven van muziek,
bloemenverdeling, schemerkleurig feest.
De kansen gaan verloren in de nacht.

DERNIER MORCEAU

Een sluitstuk in de ware zin des woords
brengt in verlegenheid... Ik wou zoveel
en kon zo weinig en ik deed geen barst.
Maar alles komt in orde want ik schrijf
de regels van dit laatst gedicht zonder een rijm
al is het met één enkel voorbehoud:
de voces intimae geven me koorts.

VERANTWOORDING

De gedichten zijn ontleend aan: Leberecht / Liebentrau: *Voces Intimae*. Verzamelde gedichten van Peter M. Heringa. Sub Signo Libelli, Geesburg, 2001.